GONE LIKE YESTERDAY

A Novel

JANELLE M. WILLIAMS

Tiny
Reparations
Books

An imprint of Penguin Random House LLC
penguinrandomhouse.com

Previously published as a Tiny Reparations Books hardcover in February 2023

First Tiny Reparations Books trade paperback printing: February 2024

THE LIBRARY OF CONGRESS HAS CATALOGED THE HARDCOVER EDITION OF THIS BOOK AS FOLLOWS:
Names: Williams, Janelle M., author.
Title: Gone like yesterday : a novel / Janelle M. Williams.
Description: [New York] : Tiny Reparations Books, [2023]
Identifiers: LCCN 2022038179 (print) | LCCN 2022038180 (ebook) |
ISBN 9780593471630 (hardcover) | ISBN 9780593471647 (ebook)
Subjects: LCGFT: Magic realist fiction. | Novels.
Classification: LCC PS3623.I556783 G66 2023 (print) |
LCC PS3623.I556783 (ebook) | DDC 813/.6—dc23/eng/20220819
LC record available at https://lccn.loc.gov/2022038179
LC ebook record available at https://lccn.loc.gov/2022038180

Trade paperback ISBN: 9780593471654

Printed in the United States of America
1st Printing

BOOK DESIGN BY DANIEL BROUNT

GONE LIKE YESTERDAY

*For Black Women
holding it down and keeping it together
as a means to love on us*

"*Paul Robeson*"

GWENDOLYN BROOKS

1917–2000

That time
we all heard it,
cool and clear,
cutting across the hot grit of the day.
The major Voice.
The adult Voice
forgoing Rolling River,
forgoing tearful tale of bale and barge
and other symptoms of an old despond.
Warning, in music-words
devout and large,
that we are each other's
harvest:
we are each other's
business:
we are each other's
magnitude and bond.

PROLOGUE

Tree hugging, earth loving, nature praising—that shit is for white people. Not for people who are made of bark themselves, who are the air you breathe. So, of course, Zahra being as black as she is, in skin color and attitude, does not feel she can afford to pay attention to the trees until one goes missing and it swallows her breath like a plague of locusts. Derrick Lewis Robinson is his name, and he's her older brother, barely, by a year, and he's gone like yesterday. Just yesterday, they were shooting the shit in their small backyard on the Eastside, making bets at the Battle of the Bands, running late for school and blaming it on 285 traffic. Just yesterday, he was louder than the snap music they leaned and rocked to, more rooted than Gram's ever-revolving love life and Mom's dedication to the cause. Seems like just fucking yesterday Derrick asked Zahra, "You think people can step outside of themselves? Feel two skins at once? Your own and someone else's?" Zahra had looked at him confused, and when he didn't laugh or say *That's wild* or wave his statement away like he was really on one and knew it, she felt a wave of panic that came and went like a late-summer breeze. Now, it is all a wonder. Among everyone. Where did he go? Why isn't he happy? When will he pull through, but then again, it's not cancer or diabetes or any strict science awaiting a cure. So the wondering is prolific and pervasive. Nobody asked Derrick to make like a moth and fly away, just like nobody asked Billie Holiday to sing the blues or the Temptations to masquerade *Cloud Nine*'s despondency with an upbeat. Nobody asked Marvin Gaye's dad to shoot him only for his brother to reveal that Marvin had wished for it but hadn't had the courage to do it himself. Makes a sister wonder, *"What's going on?"*

ONE

One month ago—September 2019,
Harlem, a Saturday night

Buzzed from her third glass of Roscato, Zahra slouches low in the back seat of an Uber headed east down 125th. She knows it's impossible to hide from shame but doesn't forsake the attempt. There are people who make a life of this, aren't there? She's people. A disaster headed to Kahlil's apartment like an MLM victim selling knives or a door-to-door Bible-thumper. Her expectations are low. She'll most likely find Kahlil reading one of his medical books or rolling a blunt. He'll open the door and look at her like he's nearly forgotten she was coming over. It's not that he doesn't like her; he's just that kind of a player, mind games, a one-upper. Even though the back-and-forth has always been their dysfunctional dynamic, she was surprised when he texted. Lately, she never wants his type of intimate fun. A finger maybe, but nothing more.

She was practically in love with him when they were at Stanford together. He was always shooting her smiles across parties or probing her with nonstop questions, stuff like, "You always been this shy?" or "You think you'll get everything you want out of life?" or "What was growing up in ATL like?" He'd follow that last question with something absurd like, "I bet all the girls were poppin' on a head-stand, no? You were different though? You barely dance now." Then he'd grab her waist, and the shock of his hands would send electric-ity up her spine, and she'd imagine a different version of herself, a looser version, someone who slow whines to Sean Paul, and maybe that's what love was, being someone else for a short time. Kahlil was somewhat of the same, a nerd in class, his fuckboy alter ego part of a larger facade.

Now, in the middle seat of a Nissan, Zahra smooths her hands along the nylon upholstery, then curls them into tight fists. She's looking to be unwound. It's not about sex, but she mouths the words to Rihanna's "Same Ol' Mistakes" anyway. She almost doesn't hear the driver ask, "Going out tonight?"

She hates Uber small talk. "I'm already out, aren't I?" Then feel-ing like a jerk, she adds, "Just to a friend's house."

"A friend?" he says incredulously, laughing, then, "Sorry, I didn't mean it like that."

However he meant it, it's enough to shut her up. It's not like she really wanted to talk anyway. She studies him now through the rear-view mirror. Skin the color of cedarwood. Scruffy beard that prob-ably hasn't been brushed in days. A backward baseball cap, similar to the way her brother, Derrick, used to wear his, but this guy's has *Stay Black* on it. He's cute, in a 1990s D'Angelo sort of way, sans straight-backs.

She can't help but think about Derrick and who he used to be. How he sang church hymns in absolute pitch while she leaned against his bedroom door writing sentences that sat comfortably one by one but never added up as a conglomerate, dreaming Black love stories,

The Wood or *Poetic Justice*, come true. He was her only savior then, no matter how distant his eyes were, black pearls swarming in discontentment. She misses him now. It's not the same, though she hasn't stopped trying to convince herself that he'll get back to where he was, that time hasn't weighed on him, hasn't removed the dimple in his left cheek so she sometimes thinks it was never there to begin with.

"Sorry," the driver says again. "I'm in my head about some other stuff, and I guess my manners just went out the window."

"Consider it forgotten."

He nods.

She takes out her phone, sends Kahlil a text. *Hungry. Should we order food?* Food helps with this eerie feeling she's been getting lately, of something gnawing at her, something trying to get in. She's doing everything in her power to keep shit out. If she thinks too hard about things, they'll eat her alive. A brother who's forgotten himself. A mother she can't stand. It's hard to measure over the phone, but she's sure Gram's voice has gotten . . . heavier. Cheeseburgers, medium skirt steaks, french fries dipped in a garlic aioli, help her forget it all.

"What's your name?" The driver again.

"Zahra." It's in the app. He must have already seen it. "It's in the app, you know. You're" she pauses to look "Trey."

"Right. Yeah," he says. He laughs a little. "My niece says, 'So you know what you didn't know you knew.' You ever heard anyone say that before?"

"No, but I work with kids, so I've heard a lot of other stuff." They say Gen Z's got more answers than millennials, but she's not so sure about that.

"You're a teacher?"

"Not quite."

"Counselor."

"Not really."

"Oh."

The pause is so awkward that she just tells him. "I'm a college prep coach. I help seniors with their college applications, mainly their essays."

"Wow."

"It's no biggie."

"My niece is a senior."

She sees him eyeing her through the rearview mirror. He looks a beat too long and has to swerve around a car with its hazards on when he sees the road again.

"Oh, really?" she asks. "Senior year, huh?"

"Yeah, she could probably use you."

"Yeah," she says, thinking he couldn't afford her. The thought in itself makes her feel like shit, and she unbuckles her seat belt and lies down. No need to look out the window when she already knows what's there. Right about now, they're headed under the Metro-North rail. This far uptown, Park Avenue always smells like piss and stale Wendy's, and Lexington is sure to be poppin' with teens and loud talk and blue-collar workers. When they turn on Third, they'll pass Goodwill, and the projects. Kahlil's isn't too far off from there, a building that screams gentrification in one of the least gentrified parts of Manhattan, East Harlem. Zahra was in for a rude awakening when she moved to this city, and the shock still hasn't worn off; melting pot, her ass.

New York *is* a place of numbers though. She leans up for a second, thinking of how many butts have been where her head rests now: Black butts, Latinx butts, white butts, Asian butts. Eventually, she convinces herself that her week-old twist-out is a buffer and resumes comfort. She thinks about how many Black women are in cars headed to see unequally yoked men, not knowing whether it's better to be a solitary fuckup or part of the masses. Her mother calls this a form of selling out. Go figure the woman probably hasn't been laid since the divorce in '95.

When the car gets there, Zahra wrestles herself up, then goes for the door in one smooth motion. It locks, and she jumps back surprised. She turns to Trey, accusatory.

"You locked it!" she says.

"No," he says, playing with the buttons on his door. The back windows go down, then up again. A series of clicks, but when she goes for the handle, it's still locked.

"No, I didn't. I don't know what happened," he tries to convince her.

"If you don't unlock the door right now, I'm calling the cops," she says, more distressed than demanding.

Either way, it's an eclipse of moths that do the job. She's never been able to understand how they appear out of thin air. But here they are inside the car, on the door handle like spotted mold. They're fucking with her again. They've been at it since she was a kid, always fluttering around like picnic flies, always singing their damned ditties—in moments of distress but in moments of calm too. While watching some shitty reality TV show. The night before she left for Stanford. Once, on the dance floor of a nightclub—she was so drunk that it must have been minutes before she realized that she was singing "Dancing in the Streets" by Martha and the Vandellas while everyone else was mantra-ing, "*Slob on my knob, like corn on the cob.*" Sometimes the songs made sense, like a survival spiritual or a nursey rhyme. Other times, they were more confusing than Deuteronomy or Revelations, like trying to decipher a mumbling man with an Atlanta accent, something she'd completely lost the ear for. Somewhere along the way she stopped listening. Because maybe the words, the songs, weren't really for her. Because wasn't she entitled to a sense of normalcy? Because who the fuck was listening *to her*? For two years in high school the moths convinced her that she was schizo-phrenic. Now it's her brother who's lost because of them, out of his skin and into someone's she doesn't even recognize. Now, she sighs and spots Trey coming around the back side of the car.

He opens the door from the outside. "I guess I should get that looked at," he says.

"Don't worry about it." She slings her purse across her body. "It's me, not you."

Trey brings his eyebrows together in a way that almost makes her laugh. The sincerity opens something inside of her, and she sees him now, in a different way than before. Notices that he can't be much older than her, sees that he's been doing the best he can with her poor back seat bedside. She feels the worst for threatening to call the cops on him, a Black man. She knows better. Never good at apologizing, she takes off for Kahlil's walk-up.

But at the same moment that he offers a "Good night," she turns around. Ignoring his salutation, she says, "I could help your niece."

He doesn't say anything back, but his look of uncertainty deep-ens, so she adds, "Here, let me give you my number."

|||||||||||||||||||||||||||||||||||||||||||||||

A WEEK LATER, THE GOONS ARE ALREADY AT WORK, EVEN though it's cold as shit out here. They rock from heel to heel, trying to stay warm, looking for their next sale, greeting passersby like polite doormen. Zahra smiles, knowing the type, blowing into her hands. She notices a schoolgirl wearing practically nothing, a plaid skirt, ripped tights, just a jean jacket for warmth. The girl is a pine tree in a forest with no needles, surrounded by gypsy moths that she doesn't seem to notice. The moths are too far away for Zahra to hear, but the girl brings back memories, fond memories, eternities in the cold waiting to get into Club Love, bodycon dresses exposing skin and insecurity, shame and power, shots of Jose Cuervo, hours later scarfing down a Filet-O-Fish or french fries drenched in mambo sauce, hoping to not puke. It's colder now than it was then, and Zahra is wearing a leather jacket with a Stanford sweatshirt underneath, the hood's strings pulled so tight it smushes her Afro.

She looks around and easily spots Trey's Nissan. This is the intersection he texted her, 120th and First Avenue, all the way on the other side of town, near the zombies of 125th Street, where you can taste the sweetness of K2, crack, methadone, whatever.

She looks up across the street and spots the girl again, digging through her backpack, pulling out thick textbooks and overnight supplies, deodorant and a makeup bag, what looks like lotion or body wash, shampoo or conditioner. She wonders if that's Sammie. Trey didn't mention what she looks like. The girl finds her keys, and stuffs everything back inside her backpack, letting it hang open as she unlocks the door. Zahra runs over, enchanted by the girl and the moths that flock her like a concentrated congregation. Zahra checks the address and barely catches the second door of the double entry.

The clunk of the girl's Doc Martens aren't far away, and Zahra tries to catch up, ignoring the pungent smell of marijuana and Axe body spray. She sniffs at her own clothes, thinking maybe it's residual from last week, the same Stanford sweatshirt, unwashed. She didn't smoke, but Kahlil did, and his high made her feel so low, like what the fuck was she doing with him again? She isn't that kind of woman, like her grandmother, flitty, needy. Or at least she never intended to be. The old pictures Gram stores in neatly lined shoeboxes under the bed keep her stories ripe for the picking. *Oh, that was taken on the day that Lionel almost banged down the door crying, "I done wrong, Billy. Take me back." You never take 'em back when they're that low, or they'll resent you for it.* Never mind that Gram kept opening doors she worked so hard to keep closed. There are a lot of love stories about Lionel, but when Gram gets to Mom's dad, she sighs from pity more than shame and certainly not from admiration.

Zahra remembers that she's her own person, unshackled and free. Honestly, she just wants to help Sammie with her essay and get the hell out of here. She doesn't want to know why the moths are so thick in this place, and she shuts off their stories, their songs. No *Woke up this morning with my mind on freedom*. No *Whisper, listen, whisper, listen*, or *Are you gonna be, say you're going to be*. No *Ready or not, here I come*, the Delfonics nor the Fugees. Instead, Zahra works with the immediate present. She got only three hours of sleep last night and has to be at her restaurant job in a little over four. Sometimes she lies in bed thinking, and other times, her right side aches so bad that she flips over to feel the same low throb on her left. No side quiet enough for her to get any decent shut-eye. Still, she can't be late; it doesn't wear well with her skin color.

By the third floor, she's caught up to the girl, so close she can see up her pleated skirt, but Zahra keeps her head down, focusing on the stone steps. She should be scared, headed to some stranger's apartment like this, a man's no less. She isn't naive to the possibilities, but maybe the girl who she assumes is Sammie at this point, allows her some comfort, the way her box braids are carelessly scooped into a side ponytail. She's sure-footed, just like Zahra was at that age, when socializing and AP scores were all that mattered, when she thought she could compartmentalize her parents and that the "good work" her mother did was a form of mothering in itself.

When the girl gets to the fifth floor and looks for the keys that she's already misplaced again, Zahra realizes that this is the apartment: 5B. She panics, preparing to explain herself to the girl, but the girl doesn't look over her shoulder, and Zahra feels like a ghost, light and translucent, when she steps into the warm apartment right after her. Zahra pauses inside the doorway, a narrow hall, walls littered with family photos. She listens for voices other than the bebops and ballads of the moths.

"So ya finally come home? Not long before your college papers are due, yea?" The voice is motherly, taunting and stern but kind.

The apartment smells like baking bread, coconut, and cinnamon; Zahra imagines her senses will explode once passing through the kitchen doorframe, where the voices, now faint murmurs she stills herself to hear, will settle themselves.

"You sent me to that school. You thought it would be good for me, remember?" The slamming of something on a table, the girl's backpack maybe. Zahra holds her breath.

"Ya smart, aren't ya?" The motherly voice sounds West Indian.

"That's relative." And the girl's doesn't. American, New York.

"Smarter than your uncle, that for sure. Don't tell him I say it."

"I have ears, thank you." A man's voice. Trey, her former driver?

"I'm not smarter than Uncle. He's just insecure." The lilt in *insecure* makes the girl's statement sound like a question, and Zahra smiles at her wit. How very white female comedian of her.

"Not sure why my manhood is being tested here," the man says. He doesn't really seem to mind the girl's snarkiness.

So the girl laughs. "And that's just it. I didn't say anything about your manhood."

"Ya too smart. Watch yaself. Ya still young, yea?"

Zahra recognizes that tone from her childhood when she backtalked her mother or accused Gram of mismanaging the money. She revisited the tone in her own voice when she was a substitute teacher.

"Sorry, Uncle. I didn't mean it like that."

Trey snorts, and Zahra hears the unzipping of the girl's bag.

The pause in conversation pushes Zahra forward, and she wishes she would've just knocked but goes on anyway, past what seems to be a bedroom to her right and into the kitchen, where everyone is in sight, the motherly voice a six-foot figure at the stove, hair cropped close to her head, wearing an oversize T-shirt of Michelle Obama. The girl is at a round table, a four-seater, situated in the middle of the kitchen, and a handsome woman, maybe ten years older than Zahra, is next to her, shirtless, a matronly bra supporting E or F tits—she's sewing a button onto a blouse. Far back, where the kitchen fades into a living room, Zahra thinks she sees Trey but can't be sure. He looks younger now, his face shaven, eyes less transfixed as they dart between her and a muted TV.

Their indecision seems to notify the motherly woman at the stove, so she turns to Zahra and squints her eyes as if trying to place her. "Can I help ya?" she asks. "Ya forget to lock the door again, Sammie?"

The last question is absorbed by Zahra's presence. They all bore into her with beautiful, dark brown eyes. She's grateful that their reaction is more muted than she thought it would be. It's clear they don't consider her a threat. Still . . .

"I'm here to meet with Sammie," she says, shaking. "Trey texted me."

"Oh?" the shirtless woman says without looking up from her sewing.

"Um. Yeah." Zahra points to the girl. "You're Sammie, right?"

Sammie blinks as if she's confused, doesn't know her own name. A moment of silence.

"Ya awfully skinny," the sewing woman says, as if Zahra has offended her in some way.

"Jesus, Aunty. She already looks scary," the girl says coolly. She reminds Zahra of Derrick. The girl's got something akin to him. The confident way she speaks, how she counters her aunt's judgment with candor and a hand—half-raised, palm up. She squelches the tension.

"Just saying," the aunt says.

"It's OK," Zahra says. "I get that a lot."

"You from around here?" the girl asks. "You don't look it."

"I'm from Atlanta."

"And ya people?" says the mother at the stove, who Zahra now guesses might actually be Sammie's grandmother.

"Atlanta and Mississippi, mostly."

The family is simultaneously welcoming and unwelcoming. She's a little annoyed that Trey hasn't intervened yet, and she considers walking out, but the minute she does, she'll be back in her own reality, and it's a shitty feeling, to want to step out of your own skin. She didn't realize she wanted that until now; maybe it's because this family reminds her of her own, just more functional, more together. Derrick used to say their family was completely normal and that crazy shit happened to everyone. Maybe he was right.

"Well, are you ready to get started with your essay?" Zahra asks the girl, who still hasn't confirmed that she is in fact Sammie.

The girl looks sorry for Zahra now. She's confused when she says, "Yes, but I don't need any help with it. Uncle didn't even tell me he'd hired someone."

Zahra laughs. He didn't actually *hire* her. This isn't a paid gig. "I just thought, well, if you need help with it. That's what I do. I mean, I'm here to help."

"Why ya want to help a complete stranger?" The sewing woman puts down her needle and thread.

"I don't know."

"You don't know?"

"He asked me to," Zahra says, pointing to Trey, passing on the unsaid accusation like a child.

"Thank you, but I think I've got it all figured out. I have a counselor," Sammie says.

"Well, I tried," Zahra mumbles, turning to the door, but not before catching sight of a hidden mound of CDs stuffed under the TV console in a far corner of the room. She's reminded of growing up, scouring stores for music. She walks out quickly, with the eerie feeling of having met the family before. She hears Trey running after her, calling her name, but she's out the door and down the steps before he finally catches up.

"She needs your help," he says.

"Doesn't seem like it."

"She's a morally just kid, that's all. When I got her into her prep school, P and P, she didn't want to go, said she didn't want to encourage America's economic divide. Get that." He laughs in reverie. "She was only thirteen then. She's always been like this, stubborn, fair. Almost like someone's in her ear about it all. But really, she doesn't understand that people need a leg up, and that's all I'm trying to give her, right?" He looks to Zahra for confirmation, but she doesn't have any to give him. "I'm really sorry about today, but maybe she just needs some time. A day or two? I'll call you."

The last three words are more thrilling than they ought to be. The idea of Trey calling her, of hearing his voice over the phone, unfastens Zahra. He's different from what she's used to—men bragging about what they do and what they know. Khalil reciting passport stamps like a book of poetry. Trey, on the other hand, has said nothing of himself, so the mystery of who he is beyond Sammie's uncle is tantalizing. She goes soft in response.

"Yeah, sure," she says, fluffing her 'fro, suddenly self-conscious of how Trey sees her.

TWO

Zahra works for a family that has old money, Park Avenue–penthouse kind of money, but running into Mrs. Jacobs, wife and mother, you would never guess it with her saying things like, *Do you know how expensive avocados are?* And it's like, *Shit, yeah, but do you?* Of course Zahra never says anything as Mrs. Jacobs comes in from the grocery store with just three avocados in a bag, like who goes to the store for nothing but avocados? Who has the time? Still, Zahra imagines Mrs. Jacobs bitching to her friends, *I have so much to do. I have to run to the store for those expensive avocados.*

Zahra's official title is collegiate preparatory coach. She works with Sophia, seventeen-year-old daughter and arbiter of all things timely. *God, that's so 2019,* Sophia says about almost everything, especially things that have no obvious relation to time. And she says it with no regard for the fact that it is, actually, 2019. Cool Ranch Doritos, blue fingernail polish, keeping your phone on ring—all antiquated.

God, where have you been? Sophia accuses.

It's not to say Sophia isn't a smart girl. She is.

She's writing her college essay about a tree, which doesn't appeal to Mrs. Jacobs's taste at all. She thinks Sophia should be writing about her ninth-grade service project or volunteering at a soup kitchen every third Wednesday. It's actually not a bad essay, and it has Zahra thinking about the oak tree that used to grow in their backyard until the gypsy moths moved in and Uncle Richard cut it down, though the moths populated anyway, as Gram said they would. A few years ago, when Zahra was in between living in DC and New York, Derrick said he could relate to that oak tree, how it must have felt, rotting from within like that. The way he said it, his face all scrunched up and tight, his eyes pointing like a laser beam, made Zahra wonder if he saw them, their family, as feeding meta-morphosed moths, as the moths who'd begun following them, singing ditties and cantatas, lyrics and lays against their ears. "I didn't realize we were that bad," she'd said, and he'd looked away, flicked a caterpillar off the picnic table.

Their mom's side of the family, maybe. Willful and ornery, sometimes reckless. But Mom had chosen a solid, dependable man to mate with. Dad's family rented out a church recreation room every Thanksgiving, first giving thanks to Jesus for allowing them to share the space, for health and familial wealth, for enlightenment, and then denouncing the pilgrims for anyone under the age of twelve who had yet to hear or comprehend the travesty of English entitle-ment. Dad's family never chose their Blackness—futile attempts to save the community as a whole—over each other or cheap praise over dignity. They were light-skinned and privileged enough to take hold of opportunities, as few and far between as they came, so Dad's sisters and brothers, uncles and aunts, cousins and cousins-once-removed became doctors and lawyers, teachers and engineers, raised cute little families in the Southlands or Brook Glen. Dad would've raised her and Derrick if he could have, if mom hadn't felt the need to own everything she touched.

"Maybe we're not the moths. Maybe we're the tree," Derrick said.

In light of the voices she and Derrick discovered in childhood and their growing disconnect from each other because of them, Zahra knew what it meant to be cobwebbed across branches, so she said, "Definitely. We have holes, big gaping ones that we try to cover up with glitter and gold."

"Macaroni and cheese and collard greens," Derrick added.

"Dogged, dismissive prayer," Zahra agreed.

"Music. Lord, the music. Works sometimes though," Derrick said, laughing, calling out his own introverted behavior.

"Marches and sit-ins," Zahra said, and just as quickly, Derrick stopped laughing.

He straightened his back, shook his head to the ground as he said, "Black folks needed the marches."

"But still . . ."

One of those quiet moments that Derrick did so well, and Zahra bit her lip, wishing she hadn't said anything at all, but now that they were already here . . .

"You can't deny it. She missed everything," Zahra argued against Derrick's silence.

"I'm not denying it. You're just so mad at her."

"She wasn't there."

"Neither are you now. You don't pay attention to shit around you, and you know it."

"Fucking gypsy moths," Zahra said under her breath, but Derrick heard her anyway. He was good at that, at hearing everything, things said out loud and things that weren't said too.

"You're not supposed to call them that. Gypsy—it's derogatory." Even-tempered. Not accusatory at all. His usual tone.

"I didn't mean it like that." Defensive.

"You didn't have to."

"You're so much smarter than me," Zahra said, and looked immediately for his rebuttal, because honestly, everyone knew she was the smart one, that he was all ideals and superego. Zahra was the one who aced tests without even trying, who got a 1450 on her SAT, who used her yearbook committee pass to cut school and eat ice cream cones from Chick-fil-A while reading the latest John Grisham novel or something more worldly like Chinua Achebe. Derrick was an empath, said Zahra's intelligence was beautiful but also seemed somewhat skeptical of it. He didn't refute Zahra's comment, didn't say anything in that loud way of his, so Zahra only huffed, went back inside the house under the pretense of not having to look at that damned stub of a tree any longer, slammed the patio door, and then turned around to see if Derrick would scold her, but he hadn't moved at all, hadn't even turned to watch her go. Maybe she should've known then, that going away would make her lose him.

Now, Zahra scratches at the oak table in Mrs. Jacobs's kitchen across from Sophia, who is biting her nails to the stub, trying to find a better word for *persistent*.

"*Tenacious*?" Sophia looks up with desperation. Back straight, Sophia is tall, and Mr. Jacobs never fails to point it out, and though Zahra usually rolls her eyes at him, she understands how the revelation of Sophia's height can come and go.

"Maybe. Put it in the sentence," Zahra says.

"'It isn't that the tree is *tenacious*, or even any different from any other Manhattan tree, but it's been in my yard for the last sixteen years, so to me it has a voice, a testament to perspective.'"

"Sounds pretty good to me."

"Wasn't really going for *pretty* good."

"I don't know. Sometimes it feels like you're making a lot of small statements with this essay but that you don't really have anything big to say."

"Tell me how you really feel."

"Yeah, you wanna get into Stanford, don't you?"

"Well, yeah, if I'm operating through the limitations of my society."

Zahra rolls her eyes, hates petulant Sophia, woe-is-me, rich white girl. Zahra reminds herself that Sophia is just a teenager, new to life. Zahra has fifteen or so years on her. Still, comments like that are hard to stomach.

Zahra's phone rings. She looks at it, only because Mrs. Jacobs isn't in the room, so there isn't anyone to question what could be more important than Soph's college essay. It's Trey, and she wants to answer, but not in front of Sophia, who will no doubt listen to every beat of the conversation. Zahra ignores the call but rests the phone on the table, face down, just looking at it, disregarding Sophia's college essay completely.

Sophia crosses her arms, uncrosses them, and redoes her messy bun. Zahra yawns. They're silent for a while, each pensive in her own way until the phone rings again. Trey's persistence is annoying, albeit impressive.

"Are you going to get that?"

"It's telemarketers, probably," Zahra lies.

Sophia picks up the phone. "Zahra's line," she says, smiling, loosening up from harping on every syllable of her 671-word essay. At first it looks as if Sophia knows what she wants to say to whoever's on the other end of the line, but then she's reconsidering it, resorting to the same facial expression she wore when looking for a synonym for *persistent.*

"Wait, how do you know her?" Sophia asks, and Zahra sits up, holds her hand out for the phone, but Sophia's not returning it so easily. "You were her Uber driver?"

Annoyed by Sophia's possibly innocent but profound emphasis on *Uber driver*, Zahra snatches the phone. "Hey, Trey," she says.

He's quiet for a second, maybe wondering who he was just on the phone with. He doesn't ask her about it but goes straight into scheduling instead. "Sammie's free tomorrow. Would that work for you?" he asks.

She pulls up her calendar, checks the next day's plans. A minute later, wondering if he's still on the line, she says, "Hello?"

"I'm here. Just waiting to see if you can help her or not."

"Of course I can help her." Zahra has a reputation, a good one, of helping kids get into Stanford and Penn and Princeton. Overrated schools, she thinks to herself, but she never says it, even though she has firsthand experience, having gone to one of them, against her mother's wishes, which was part of its appeal. Thinking back, she wishes she hadn't given her mother that much power. She knew as much right after graduating from Stanford, so she moved to DC and blended in with the alumni of Howard, and people could never tell if she'd graduated with honors from an HBCU or lost herself in the violent breeze of Silicon Valley. After all, she was a woman who wore her hair in box braids and passion twists and faux locs, often a little overgrown, kinky edges that she let remain natural or slicked down with edge control. She was a color that her first white friend, made in college, called Honey Nut Cheerio. She was stylish in the way of someone not trying too hard, neutral-tone tops, well-fit jeans, a face with just a hint of makeup. She'd wanted to have chosen Howard, but then maybe she was a little scared of it, a little scared that it wouldn't challenge her, a fear she blamed on society but still couldn't refute, no matter if her mother was an activist who marched with Jesse Jackson and Hosea Williams and John Lewis.

"What schools is she applying to?" Zahra asks.

"The big ones. I can't remember all of them. Early decision to Stanford, I think. Maybe Yale too? Penn and Tufts. Spelman . . ."

"There's hope for her yet."

"Well, you haven't heard the whole story. I found out yesterday that she hasn't started. Not one word. It's like she doesn't care sometimes. It's that school, I think. They're all fake. Making her smart in all the wrong ways."

"She only has a little over a month if she's applying early decision. Deadline is on the first." This is what parents don't get: Zahra's not a magician. You gotta have a good kid, and your kid's got to be willing to put in the work.

"I know."

"So tomorrow?"

"Could you?"

Sure she could, but she also hates last-minute appointments, off principle. She wants to help the girl though. Maybe she can point her in the right direction, which is Spelman, most likely, at least if Sammie is anything like Zahra was at her age—seeking, easily distracted. Spelman seems like the kind of college a Black girl can grow deeper roots, become more like herself. Maybe Sammie wouldn't grow up to be a chagrined fledgling in the wind. And Atlanta's a great city, just not big enough for all the Robinsons, with her mother's ego taking up all the breathing room.

"What time?"

"Five o'clock could work."

"Great. I'll see her then. I'll text you an address."

"What's your fee?"

"What can you afford?" Zahra asks, and Sophia rejoins the conversation with her eyes, but when Zahra meets them, she defers to the computer again.

"That doesn't feel like a good way to do business."

"I'll text you." Zahra hangs up quickly and gives Sophia an apologetic smile. "I told you not to answer."

"You just said you thought it was telemarketers."

Zahra nods.

"She's applying to Stanford too?"

Zahra nods again.

"You're cheating on me," Sophia jokes, or maybe it's not exactly a joke. "What if you help her steal my spot?" It's not a statement Sophia would make knowing Zahra's new student is Black. She's too sophisticated for that sort of thing, at least too sophisticated to say it out loud.

Zahra smiles, laughs a little. "Then it was never really yours to begin with, was it?" She pauses. "Your essay is better than you think it is. Not quite *A Tree Grows in Brooklyn*, but damn good."

||||||||||||||||||||||||||||||||||||||||||||||||||

141ST STREET IS AN ABERRATION. A LITTLE FARTHER NORTH, and the neighborhood grows more international, more commercial. A little farther south, and there's the silence of senior housing, right up against the park, card tables, shirtless men doing pull-ups, free-flowing alcohol, children running amok, but the blocks themselves are quiet, cast in shadows. 141st has a mouth to it, a body that bounces off brick walls, the punch of a heavyweight boxer. Zahra's friend Janie always makes a note of it when she comes to visit, "Damn, your block is hot," she says. "It's like all the niggas come to 141st Street. It's a fucking parade one day and a party the next. You live on a block of rats."

Zahra doesn't mind the commotion. She likes opening her window and hearing a BMW blast Dipset, soprano voices singing cusses, watching a man bust a car window open and then slink his whole body through the window when he could've just popped the lock. But the trees are barely here, little scraggly things, naked women in winter, and Zahra never thought she'd care either way, and maybe she really doesn't because trees are something that unbothered people notice, people nothing like her. Zahra has bigger things on her mind—a grandmother who floats among men like creek debris, a brother who drifts like butter sliding off a hot roll, but she's begun to admit pausing every now and then to consider the London plane trees or pin oaks, whatever they are. Maybe she moved here to get away from trees. Maybe she doesn't want to breathe.

Now, Janie is waiting outside her apartment. She's bundled efficiently, a chunky scarf wrapped three or four times around her neck, loose jeans rolled to the ankle. She makes everything she wears look fashionable. Even those utility hiking boots in which Zahra is sure she's stuffed two pairs of socks for fifty-degree weather. Janie is from the South too and always talks about moving back, says New York is colder than a motherfucker and that niggas are scared of commitment here. It's not not true.

"I thought you would be home sooner," Janie huffs. "It's cold as balls out here."

"You could've just pressed all the numbers. Someone would've buzzed you in."

"I'm sure that makes you feel safe."

"It doesn't really make me feel any way. Whoever keeps stealing my packages is probably not getting buzzed in." They take the rundown, sometimesy elevator to the fourth floor.

"True. But still, what took you so long? You're like twenty minutes late."

Inside Zahra's apartment, the heat meets them eagerly, as if it's trying to leave through the front door. They take off their coats and drop them carelessly on Zahra's old futon, something she bought off Craigslist and, with Janie's begrudging help, carried six blocks to her building.

"I'm sorry. I didn't mean to leave you hanging. You know how iffy the trains are."

"True."

"Plus, I got a call from an old Uber driver," Zahra says, even though he's not the reason she was late. Maybe it just feels good to mention him.

"An old Uber driver?"

"Yeah, it's a long story, but he wants me to help his niece with her college essay."

Janie laughs. "Can an Uber driver afford you?"

"I'm going to do it for free."

You really don't have to, he'd texted after she'd sent a simple *No charge*. And of course she doesn't *have* to. But for some acute reason, maybe because Trey is an enigma and Sammie is just the opposite— a distorted image of Zahra's teenage self, like looking into one of those fun house mirrors—she *wants* to. And as for payment, well, it's just not the same when she knows it's from a half-dry well— considering their apartment in East Harlem, that family doesn't really have the money to give.

"Uber driver must have something you want. Is he cute?"

"He's . . . well, it's not about him."

Janie throws her head back, scoffs. She plops down on Zahra's bed. "Um-hmm," she says. "If you say so. . . ."

Zahra rolls her eyes. "Don't you have anything going on? Let's dissect your life, give mine a second to breathe." She tidies up her room. She was in a rush this morning, and it shows.

"Well, I'm still waiting for that promotion that I was promised months ago. *New York Times* pretends to be all progressive, but my department is just a bunch of white gay"—she pauses, uses air quotes to modify—"'liberal' men. They think they know what's what because they're a part of a marginalized group. Marginalized my ass."

Zahra met Janie in DC, deejaying a party near U Street, a time before its current severe state of gentrification. A friend of a friend introduced them, said DJ Jane Dough had gone to Howard and made a name for herself there on the turntables. Zahra remembers feeling somewhat envious of Janie's Caesar fade, neon green headphones, bright orange lipstick, mustardy-brown skin, and a dimple that reminded Zahra of Derrick's. Most impressive, Janie was famous for knowing almost every Lil Wayne and Jay-Z and Biggie verse ever spit, regular singles *and* remixes, nondiscriminatory.

But they didn't really get to know each other until New York, when Zahra spotted Janie at Mist and was emboldened enough to approach her, ask if she was deejaying in New York now, and Janie said no, that she'd gotten bored, and Zahra was even more impressed than before. She knew it wasn't easy to walk away from popularity, from doing something you'd learned to do well.

"You've been waiting for that promotion for a really long time now," Zahra says, sorting clean clothes from dirty. Lining her shoes along the wall in a neat row.

"Longer than most."

"You thinking of leaving?"

"Hell yeah, I'm thinking of leaving, but then it's like, leave and go where? To the next fucked-up company?" Janie rolls onto her back, hugs her face so only her forehead and mouth are left of it.

"True." Zahra is satisfied with her work and sits on the bed next to Janie, cross-legged.

"Shit is driving me crazy." Janie uncovers her face and looks at

Zahra pleadingly, as if there's something she can do to help. When Zahra comes up empty-handed, she changes the subject.

"Well, how's Isaiah?"

"Isaiah?"

"Isaiah. The flavor of the month."

Janie never keeps them for much longer than that.

"God, the flavor of last month," she says, shaking her head, which puts her hoop earrings in motion. "He was super clingy."

"Just what I'm looking for."

"You say that now."

"Yeah, I actually want men to respond to my text messages. To call me just to say good morning and all that lovey shit." Zahra stretches out her legs, picks up her phone, knowing she's missed nothing—no new texts, no missed calls, her Instagram barely refreshes.

"You don't act like it sometimes."

"You're just trying to make me feel better. It would be nice if I was self-sabotaging, but I'm really not."

"What do you call Kahlil?"

"An idiot."

It's hard for Zahra to admit that she's never really been in an adult relationship, so she doesn't admit it often. Never to Janie, who seems to open her palms to the world and watch sunshine rain down. Even the job Janie is bitching about pays more than Zahra's seventy-dollar-an-hour college prep sessions, and much more than her part-time gig at Common House, a restaurant on the Upper East Side. And men love Janie, no matter what she's wearing, no matter if she falls asleep on their shoulder and drools on one of their most expensive shirts, a real-life example. Men like Zahra too; she's never denied this, but it's not in a way of maturation. They like that she's smart until they begin to hate her for it. They like that she's eloquent until they grow tired of hearing her talk and begin to cut her off mid-sentence. *But when it comes to Black women*, she'll say, and they'll sigh exaggeratedly, roll their eyes, tune her out, back out of the conversation with discontent or discursion. There's some method to dating that she hasn't been able to figure out. Gram says it's about deference; and her mother, Mary, says she just has to stop caring about that sort of thing; and, of course, there's Janie, who doesn't rely on a rubric at all but sheer intuition.

||||||||||||||||||||||||||||||||||||||||||||||||||

WHEN JANIE LEAVES, ZAHRA IS LEFT WITH THE SOUNDS OF rats gnawing, scratching, and scurrying; they're inside her fucking walls, maybe on the roof, or no, in the neighbor's apartment above her. She imagines that one day they'll break free, that one day they'll eat right through the Sheetrock and come claim her apartment, her bedroom, as their own. She hates it here, in New York, but then it's like what Janie said about switching companies, leave and go where? She has nowhere to be, is on no set schedule, has no one true dream. And as much as she hates New York, she also loves it—the hustle and bustle, the intersections, the demand.

Zahra sprawls out on her comforter, arms and legs extended, looking up at the ceiling, imagining it as Atlanta's inky-black night, in reverie with her brother. But there, in the corner, half-concealed by her steam pipe, is a web. She stands on top of her bed to get a closer look at it, and shit, yeah, it's just what she thought. The web is crawling with little caterpillars that she knows will eventually turn into moths that sing to her, an endless looping lullaby. Zahra runs to the kitchen for a broom, comes back to her room, and smashes the web apart like Gram used to take down the spiderwebs that formed when she and Derrick were away from home for long periods of time—at their other granny's house or the one year they went away to summer camp. And now, having gotten rid of the single most annoying insects of her life, she feels accomplished and nauseous all at once. She lies back down. She closes her eyes but opens them again when she can't fall asleep.

"What the fuck?" she screams, nearly breathless. There must be twenty or thirty moths, fluttering, floating, forcing voices from small, impossible bodies. Their voices are as beautiful, as powerful as ever, but they're also in discord. Rhythm and blues, funk and Afrofuturism, jazz and house, trap and snap all at once. They haven't learned how to harmonize, are trying to sing too many songs at once. She doesn't swat them away like normal, doesn't scream so loud that her voice drowns them out but concedes that listening to their melodies might be better than hearing the rats shave down their teeth.

THREE

Sammie is being watched. She's sure of it. It is a similar yet different feeling from roaming the halls of Principles & Progress with all eyes on her. *There she is*, they seem to say, *the girl who started the sit-in, the Black girl, the angry one*. The eyes are timid but persistent. Now, she slams her locker shut and distinguishes the difference—this new feeling of being watched is here in her most intimate moments, while sitting alone in front of school waiting for Uncle Trey to pick her up, while using the bathroom, all neighboring stalls empty, while in her bedroom at night, fully awake, thinking about what's ahead of her, wondering who she'll be in this life, imagining herself with a guy like Noah, mouths wide open when people hear the news. Throughout it all, she feels like someone or something is there, here now, and she shivers.

Sammie is happy the school day is over, and when Uncle Trey pulls up, she slides in the front seat eagerly, tossing her backpack behind her. Loose change and writing utensils clang as it clashes down. Uncle Trey gives her the look he always does, one where he pulls his head back and raises his eyebrows, and it seems as if he's spotted something new about her, but he only says, "What's up?"

"Nothing much," she says, shrugging. She won't tell Uncle Trey about the feeling. He worries too much, is too much of a fixer. He'd probably blame it on all the crime TV she watches and try to limit her content, or he'd jump to an even more random conclusion, like that she's not getting enough sleep or is dehydrated, and buy her a Fitbit.

"Want some pizza? I'm in the mood for Patsy's." He turns on the radio, and Sammie knows she'll have to throw her voice to be heard over it.

"Tempting, but I told Leila I would meet her at her house. Can you drop me off?"

She is excited to see her best friend. They have a lot to discuss. Sammie's mind has been reeling lately, and Leila's the only person who can slow it down. Uncle Trey looks a little sad that that person is not him. Recently, Uncle Trey has grown into the likes of a TV parent, hovering, trying too hard. It's obvious that he's completely miffed by her adolescence and missing the old, easy connection they had when she was younger. Sometimes he's annoying, and Sammie doesn't even try to hear what he has to say. She doesn't mean to be this way. It's not like she doesn't want to hang out with him, but she does wish he had a different prop in his life, something other than her to hold him up.

"Maybe we can do something this weekend," she offers.

"But it's only Monday. That's five whole days away." He's joking. Somewhat.

"You'll be fine," she assures him.

Uncle Trey nods, smiling. "Does Leila's family know you're coming over? You know we don't do that whole showing-up-to-people's-houses-unannounced thing."

"She asked. It's fine." Sammie feels just a little bad about lying, but she's getting used to it. Recently, she has begun telling small lies, ones that don't really matter, the sort of lies that barely shift the world at all. Harmless. It's easier this way, and it's not like Leila's parents ever care. They'll set Sammie a plate, like any other day. Uncle is being old-fashioned, and she knows he's not above lying either. His lies are like bubbling bacon grease when they discuss her mother; they pop and burn her when she gets too close to them. Those are the sort of lies she'll stay away from, those are the sort of lies that change everything.

‖‖‖‖‖‖‖‖‖‖‖‖‖‖‖‖‖‖‖‖‖‖‖‖‖‖‖‖‖‖‖‖‖‖‖‖‖‖

SAMMIE AND LEILA SIT ON THE CARPET AT THE FOOT OF LEI-la's bed, backs against it, staring at a blank wall; the one behind them is littered with pictures—Leila graduating from kindergarten, Leila in her middle school lacrosse uniform, the stick behind her neck, arms thrown over it. There is a photo of Leila and Sammie together, taken at one of Sammie's high school dances where Leila had been her makeshift date, and Sammie had spent the night apologizing for everything that suddenly felt wrong about P & P. *Sorry there are so many white people. Sorry the music isn't that great. Sorry no guys are asking us to dance.* Still, they'd had fun with each other, dancing recklessly to songs that didn't belong to their culture, jumping up and down alongside Sammie's white friends. The wall Sammie and Leila stare at now tells none of this. It is just the color Leila's mom painted it when they were in sixth grade, a shade of purple, lavender maybe.

It's chilly outside, but Leila's room is scorching, almost suffocat-ing. The privacy is worth it. If they go into the living room, Leila's mom will ask them a million questions about nothing or Leila's little sister will beg them to play Uno. They stare at the wall in silence for a little while, Sammie trying not to move, lest she drive up her body temperature even further.

Leila is moody. She doesn't want to practice TikTok dances or stalk cute boys—sometimes girls, in Leila's case—on Instagram. She doesn't want to switch outfits—Sammie in Leila's crop top and skin-tight jeans and Leila in Sammie's school uniform, rolling up the pleated skirt so it's shorter than intended and lying stomach down on her bed, kicking her legs—*Take a picture of me*, she'll say. But today, Leila is sulky, and Sammie is following her lead in just sitting here, knowing it's her job to get out whatever's bothering Leila, to cheer her up.

"What's up? Just tell me," Sammie pleads. "You didn't sound like this earlier. So what happened between now and then?"

Leila sucks her teeth, and Sammie knows that she's deciding whether to tell her the truth. It doesn't matter. Sammie always knows when Leila is lying and will easily call her out on it.

"You're going to think it's silly," Leila says. "You're annoyingly confident about these kinds of things."

"Try me." Sammie is already onto where this is going. "We tell each other everything, remember?" A pact made when they were in elementary school and Sammie had kept what felt like the biggest secret there ever could be—Mother Ma was not her mother. Leila had gasped, had said *grandmother* as if she were piecing together the word for the first time.

Now Leila rolls her eyes, acquiescing to the mantra. "These stupid college applications," she says.

Sammie sighs, shakes her head. "What's the big deal?"

Sammie can't help but be just what Leila assumed. She thinks everyone is stressed out for no reason. She thinks it's not as hard as they say to get into college. She has always been smart, has always won awards and been a fraction of the best. She doesn't recognize that things are different for Leila, that she works and works, and though she is an all-A student, it isn't easy. Leila does extra credit to make up for bad test scores, but her SAT and ACT scores have no extra credit to cover them, and she doesn't go to a fancy prep school with a national reputation. Things don't come easy for her.

"What's the big deal?" Leila asks incredulously.

"Yeah. You're going to get in."

"Of course I'm going to get in. It's the *where* that I'm worried about."

"You're going to get in somewhere good," Sammie relents.

"Somewhere as good as you? Because if we're halfway across the world from each other, does that still make us best friends?"

And Sammie realizes what this is really about. It's a competition between them, and has always been to some degree. When it comes to academics, Sammie comes out on top, but Leila's not stupid. Not at all. Not even close. She's good at a lot of things that don't require a textbook, things like making people laugh; and making spontaneous, random new friends; and dancing in a way that looks more sexy than silly. Sammie considers these gifts equivalent to, if not better than, her own. She looks at Leila now—not so different from her in size or complexion but with sharper, narrower features, thinner eyebrows, smaller nose, lips just as plump but half as wide. She wears her hair in braids too, but hers are Fulani and Sammie's are box. Twin, they call each other. And Sammie understands how a gulf between them would feel impossible. It's already bad enough now that Sammie goes to a white private school in the Bronx, one that looks more like a college campus than the beat, prison-inspired high schools around their way, like Leila's school. And Sammie can feel how ashamed of it Leila is sometimes, so Sammie downplays P & P—*It's not that big*, she says. *The kids aren't that smart. The classes sound like college courses but not really. Not so different from your school at all.* Leila doesn't buy it.

Sammie never wants to say the one obvious truth—that they are jealous of each other, Sammie of Leila's perfect family, a mom and a dad and a cute little sister, a family of four, perfect size, perfect pictures.

Maybe it's not about the distance between colleges at all but who will go to the better school. Similar but different has always been their way. When it comes to colleges, if they're not of similar status, it will shake their equilibrium. It will throw them off-balance. Sammie tries not to think of it. She wants to discuss more important things instead, more pressing.

"We'll always be best friends," Sammie says. Then she falls back on Leila's bed, in love.

"We spoke again," she says, knowing she doesn't have to explain the *we*. Leila will know.

"Who spoke first?" Leila asks.

"He did."

"Good sign. What did he say?"

"He asked me how my weekend was."

Leila squeals. "Perfect. That's perfect. That means he wants to get to know you. He wants to know what you do outside of school and stuff. What did you say?"

"I told him I didn't do much, that I met up with you for ice cream and that I played a game of HORSE with my uncle. That I helped Mother Ma cook stew chicken. Well, I said dinner, since he might not know what stew chicken is."

"Who doesn't know what stew chicken is?"

Sammie has been holding back the obvious, and she bites her cheek for giving it away now. "He doesn't live in Harlem. Not everyone knows what stew chicken is," she says defensively.

"All right. All right. I guess. He's missing out though. OK, so then what did he say?"

"That my weekend sounded like fun."

"And you said?"

"And I said it was. And I asked him about his weekend."

"And?"

"And he said it was good. That he played video games with his little brother."

"So cute."

"Totally cute." And Sammie catches the word after it's already too late, after Leila has already hiccupped a laugh. *Totally*. Totally white. Her white friends at school say it all the time, words that end in *ly*—*totally*, *definitely*, *obviously*, *literally*. It's hard to turn the words off and on.

"OK. *Totally*," Leila mocks her. "Then what happened?"

"The bell rang."

"Damn, OK. Well, how do you rate the encounter?"

"Seven?"

"Did you touch him? Did you touch his arm or anything while you were talking? Did you flirt?" Leila has always been better at this than Sammie, which is why she has a boyfriend and Sammie doesn't. These surface, staccato conversations between Sammie and Noah should seem childish to Leila, and Sammie knows it, but Leila never acts any less interested. She doesn't trivialize the things that aren't trivial to Sammie, and Sammie knows she has done good in choosing a best friend.

"I was too shy to really flirt," Sammie says. She pulls the pillow from under her and covers her face with it.

"Next time," Leila assures her.

"Next time," Sammie agrees, her voice muffled by down feathers and a floral pillowcase that smells of berries and coconut oil.

"You have his number," Leila says. "You could always call him, like a nineties TV drama."

Sammie jerks up, tosses the pillow across the room. "I can't do that."

"Well, you *can*."

"No, he didn't give me his number to use in that way." The number exchange was just another one of their awkward conversations, but this one stemmed from a class they were taking—Introduction to Middle Eastern History—and the teacher was a complete hardass, and she and Noah knew they were better as one thinking unit than apart, so they'd agreed to study together, had exchanged numbers. But one never called the other, and so the numbers sat in their phones, tempting but unused.

Sammie wasn't this shy about boys before she started attending P & P, and still, talking to boys around the way comes much more naturally to her. Facing, talking to, flirting with Noah seems an altogether new concept, and she has somewhat reverted to elementary school in social maturity.

"He didn't really give you his number to study together," Leila says. "He gave you his number for"—Leila twerks against the bed, hands on her knees—"you know what." She laughs so hard that she can barely catch her breath. Sammie laughs with her, and yes, she will miss this. It will be hard to be away from Leila next fall. But for now, Sammie joins Leila in laughing so hard that they cry.

When they come down from this episode, Sammie thinks it's a good time to discuss what else has been on her mind, the eerie feeling of being watched, the cutting sense of a shift, in temperature and mood and something else she can't quite pinpoint. "Does the world seem like it's changing to you?" Sammie asks Leila.

"What do you mean?"

"I don't know. I've just been getting this weird feeling. Like something's coming."

"Shit, that's creepy. Something like what? Like duplicates of us, who've come to untether themselves?"

Sammie laughs, shakes away the thought of the most recent movie they've watched together. "No, no. Nothing that dramatic. I don't know. Just . . . sometimes I feel like I'm being watched."

Leila's eyes widen, and it's obvious she's grown serious in a matter of seconds. "You think you have a stalker?"

Sammie realizes that Leila doesn't get it, that her worries, her understanding of the world is too literal, too on the nose. Sammie, on the other hand, is aware of the things that move just beyond the surface of her comprehension. "Forget it. I was just being weird."

"Well, don't do that anymore." Leila shakes her head.

Sammie laughs to lighten the mood. "I won't. Promise. I'm totally normal from now on."

||||||||||||||||||||||||||||||||||||||||||||||

WHEN SAMMIE GETS HOME, IT IS JUST PAST SEVEN O'CLOCK, and she has a shitload of homework to do. Her plan is to get right to it, but as she's heading to her bedroom, she overhears Mother Ma and Uncle Trey talking. Their voices come from Mother Ma's bedroom, and though they're not yelling, their deliveries are sharp enough to demand Sammie's attention. She pauses, trying to make out what they're saying, kneading the worn, brown carpet under her Vans.

"Ya not she father. I understand, ya love that girl like ya own. But what about ya sister? What about she mother?"

Sammie realizes they're talking about her, and she holds her breath.

"How does this end up being my fault? I was there for Rochelle. I still can be."

Sammie's mother's name is like a pinprick. It feels good but also hurts to hear it said aloud.

"Sammie goin' off to school soon. Then what?"

"Then it's as it should be. Sammie becoming the woman she *should* become. With or without she stupid parents."

"Ya not being fair."

"I'm doing what's best for Sammie."

"Ya doin' what's best for you."

"How?"

"Ya know how."

"I can't win with you."

A violent silence. Sammie wonders what's happening, if there's something she's missing, something she's too far away to hear.

"I'm out," Uncle Trey says, the sound of his voice startling her. "Be back later."

Sammie runs from the door on the tips of her toes. She's in the kitchen when Uncle Trey stalks out of the house, the door slamming behind him. She jumps, and Mother Ma comes out of her room, wobbling like she does on abnormally cold or damp days. Sammie waits a beat or two, knowing that Mother Ma's feelings take time to even out. She will bark at you if you do not give her time to digest her anger. She's too old and Sammie is too grown for her to take out the thick, leather firefighter's belt she used to wield to win arguments, but still, Sammie is afraid of her wrath. Mother Ma is the safest, softest, most sacred place and, simultaneously, the most reprimanding.

"What happened?" Sammie asks, almost a whisper.

And Sammie can see that Mother Ma isn't angry at all. She's disappointed. Sammie knows this face well, Mother Ma's brows low on her face, her eyes sunken and half-shut, lips in a slit so straight Sammie does not know which is nearer, a smile or a frown. It is the face from when Sammie brought home her first report card from

P & P, all A's and one C, the face from when a jay fell out of her backpack, right onto the kitchen table while Mother Ma was stringing beans. But there is something else in her face too. Something that makes Sammie stand back, away from her, lest the feeling jump from one body to the next.

"Nothing ya should be concerned with," Mother Ma says.

Sammie tries to gulp down the lie, but her throat is dry and scratchy. She goes to pour herself a glass of water and leaves the conversation, knowing that Mother Ma is a boulder that cannot be moved.

SAMMIE'S ROOM IS SMALL, CLOSET-SIZE, BUT IT'S HERS, AND she loves it. Sometimes she can hear Uncle Trey snoring through the thin walls, a nighttime lullaby. He's breathing; he, unlike her parents, hasn't neglected her. And sometimes she can hear Mother Ma's TV set to Lifetime, the sappy family dramas or Black romances she loves so much, the characters' voices like faraway friends. But now, Sammie's room is as silent as the sky before a storm. She doesn't turn on her music like usual but lies on the bed, staring up at the ceiling, the cracked crown molding. She sighs and closes her eyes. She opens them to look at her phone. It's been almost an hour since she's checked it, and who knows who might've called. Maybe Noah.

Not Noah. It's never Noah. She rolls her eyes. One text message from Leila.

Wat about Spelman? R u going to apply there? I sorta want to but idk. Pretty sure my counselor thinks I can only get into the Black schools. She's always pushing them.

Spelman. Sure, Sammie's thought about it. She can see herself there, sort of. And it would be nice to be around Black people again.

But it doesn't sound the same as Stanford. She whispers the name aloud. *Stanford, Stanford, Stanford.* She practices telling everyone the good news. *I'm going to Stanford. I got into Stanford.* She'll downplay her excitement, of course, but still, it feels good to say it now, and it will feel even better when it's actually true. Stanford sounds like money, like the freshest pair of new sneakers, and everyone will know she's super smart. She won't have to prove herself like she had to at P & P.

She lies back down, connects her phone to the charger that she keeps plugged in behind her nightstand, promises herself she'll text Leila back in the morning.

She hears something soft, a voice, a song, something familiar. She thinks it must be coming from Mother Ma's room. It sounds like the gospel music Mother Ma sings on Saturday mornings or the low family radio that she plays while she is cooking or ironing or cleaning. She is constantly finding things to do, seeing things that need improvement. She is constantly humming, singing along to her movements.

Now Sammie wishes Mother Ma would turn down the music, but she knows Mother Ma is already mad, and there's no sense in making things worse. Sammie doesn't know that asking Mother Ma to turn down the music wouldn't make any difference anyway; the music isn't coming from Mother Ma's room at all. Sammie doesn't see the cobwebs, does not watch the moths hatch from their hairy brown cocoons. She does not look underneath her bed or along the books stacked in no certain order on the shelf by it. She does not see the moths burrow themselves anywhere they can find room, claiming cracks and creases as their own, singing their hearts out in new terrain.

Instead, Sammie goes to sleep confused, about her family and college and a boy who she wishes would just call her already. She is almost dreaming now, almost in stage three of NREM, almost out like a light, but then she shoots up in bed, beads of sweat along her pressure points, panicked, but about what? She opens her eyes wide, glaring through the darkness, sure that someone or something is there, here now with curled wings, watching her, twenty or thirty pairs of eyes, coal black and piercing.

FOUR

"Ever heard of a tree cemetery?" Derrick asked her a couple of months ago, dead serious. It sounded like some white-people shit, but also, Zahra never completely dismissed her brother's musings. He was older than her, and always, to this day, more intuitive. Math, language, statistics were Zahra's jam, but Derrick's were less definable. As a kid he wanted to be an anthropologist until he realized that the profession was more about digging than resurrecting. *What's the point?* he asked. Ten years later, he studied philosophy and African American studies at Clark only to graduate asking the same thing. *What's the point, Zahra? If no one wants to listen, what's the fucking point?*

Derrick was good at nearly everything—basketball, baseball, swimming, drawing, writing, acting. He never stuck anything out. Dad called him a chameleon, said he could fit in anywhere. To Zahra, it was just the opposite, he couldn't help but stand out. But whether classmates called him the next Mekhi Phifer or coaches said he could really go places didn't matter shit to Derrick. He wanted something just beyond reach, something he could never properly articulate but Zahra bit her cheek trying to figure out. He was spiritual, in touch with things outside of himself in a way that made Zahra uncomfortable, as if he chose to never wear clothes around her, as if he allowed any old energy to swallow him whole, more and more so as they got older. By the time she turned twenty-five, he wasn't holding anything back, would hurt your feelings with blunt honesty. But it was never about you, never about Zahra at least, maybe he just wanted people to see what was right in front of them.

So that summer night, sticky from her broken AC unit, Zahra googled the tree cemetery, a real thing in some German town where she guesses the people are paler than shaded snow. What she learned was the ongoing debate about the intelligence of trees. Some say that they communicate, that the mother trees help their saplings with the nutrients they miss for being so short and losing out on the sun, that they form a mycorrhizal network and send distress signals. It's a crock of something, a reason for white tears, temporary avocation, but then one thought does stick with her—the idea that trees are dependent on one another, that they find it hard to part with the dead, that one dying can trip a line of dominoes, another dropping after the next, an epidemic. So if a tree falls and there's no one around to hear it, well, the trees still give a shit, don't they?

She's thinking about magnolias and dogwoods and redbuds and evergreens when the caller ID says it's Derrick, but the line sounds dead. He doesn't call her often, so she wonders if this is a butt-dial but hopes it's not. They haven't spoken in a while, and she's been getting this antsy feeling, as if their world is on the precipice of something. She bites her nails on the edge of her bed, teetering between screaming out for her brother and hanging up.

She remains calm. "Derrick?" She waits a beat. "Derrick, you there?"

Zahra's worry for Derrick is extensive—from the irrational fear of him being kidnapped and eventually possessed by aliens to the very real fear of him not being able to handle his emotions and resorting to outside resources, drugs, or a religious cult. In the movies, it's always people like him, intrinsic and searching, who fall prey to predators. And there are a myriad of threats against Black men, everything from the judicial system to hip-hop white Barbie wannabes. She hates admitting the ways in which their mother, Mary, has been right, but there's no denying the power of racism, systemic or interpersonal.

"Yeah, I'm here," he says at last, and she exhales.

"Where have you been? I've been calling you. Did you get my messages?" She hopes her frankness won't push him away. It hasn't worked well in the past. Simple observations were enough to silence him for days.

"Yeah. Yeah." He clears his throat. "Shit, Zahra. I'm fucking up, aren't I?"

She doesn't know what to say.

He sighs loudly, and she can almost feel his defeat through the phone.

"Where are you?" she asks.

"I'm everywhere and nowhere," he says, laughing. She's quiet, and maybe that's what urges him to add, "It was just a joke. I'm at Terrence's house."

Terrence. The name reassures her. He's Derrick's friend from Clark. He's levelheaded, calm, not so different from Derrick's demeanor in high school. But for the first time in maybe forever, she's not sure she believes Derrick. His first response was too quick, everywhere and nowhere. That's exactly where it sounds like he is. There's something in his background that she can't make out. It's a loud crackling, like he's by a major highway and what she's hearing is the sound of wind, of cars shooting by him.

"Can I speak to him?" she asks.

"To who?"

"Terrence."

Derrick starts to laugh but then asks, "Do you still hear the moths?"

She doesn't answer, because of course she does, because she doesn't want to talk about them. For once, she just wants to have a normal conversation.

Almost as if Derrick agrees with her, he says, "Remember the first time we got drunk? Senior year of high school. Well, it was junior year for you. But I remember feeling so outside of myself. I remember feeling like, like fuck all the bullshit. I could conquer anything. I had so much power, and I knew it. And then the next morning, when I woke up on Julian's couch, I looked down at my hands, my arms, my feet, and it was like they weren't mine. It was like I was seventy-five years old, with all of these memories that weren't even mine, but I was still me, you know."

"Like a medium or something?" Zahra is only half joking when she says it. Really, she is terrified of his response.

"Nah, nothing like that." He laughs.

She doesn't. "Then?"

"I just wanna be me, you know? But then sometimes, it's like, how can I be me when there are so many people who've made me, me? Ancestors and family and shit. For a second, I get a glimpse of who they are, who they *really* are, or were, and it makes me feel more connected and disconnected from myself all at once. That time at Julian's house was just the start."

"Yeah," she says, not knowing where he's going with this. She's not sure she's ever felt that way, but she does remember that night, how a crew of them raided drinks at a white classmate's party and then stole off to Julian's basement, where they ate take-out Waffle House and played Never Have I Ever.

"Those were the good days, weren't they?"

"Yeah, but today's not so bad either, is it?" She's trying to convince him. Of what, she's not sure. Like talking someone off a ledge when they're already sitting down.

"Shit." He draws out the word. "Life is a motherfucker."

She wants to contest but can't really. Derrick will know better, so she doesn't say anything at all.

"Look, I gotta go. Don't be a stranger."

But before she can tell him that he's been the strange one, the absent one, the estranged, there's the click, and he's gone. She hangs up the phone. She'll call Gram later, reassure her of something she's not so sure of herself—Derrick's all right. Don't worry, she'll say, but the words will be as thin as loose thread.

It's an eerie night, a disquiet created by the wind howling outside of her window, the rats scratching like crazy, and a largely present moon casting light on her wall of photos, the eyes of her family staring back at her. Her skin feels hot. She looks at her hands, her arms, her feet as if they don't belong to her. But if not her, then who?

FIVE 🦋

The next day, Sammie looks different, trendier in her black leggings and oversize sweatshirt with gold chains of varying lengths decorating it. When she peels off her coat and sits down across from Zahra in the Au Bon Pain on Seventy-Second Street, Sammie looks relaxed but indignant. Zahra can relate, but she forces a smile anyway. The espresso machine sings from the barista station to Zahra's right, and there's heavy chatter between tables, the smell of cinnamon hanging just above them.

"Hi," Zahra says. She doesn't get up to greet the girl but waves, more spirited than her usual collegiate preparatory coach persona. She's determined to make a better, more compelling second impression.

"Hey," Sammie says, sitting on the edge of her seat. "This is really nice of you and all, but I don't think I need help. Plus, I have a college counselor, and she's always blah blah blah in my ear. I mean, I'm sure you're great at what you do, but I want my essay to be mine. Not something that some college coach wrote for me. No offense."

"None taken," Zahra says, thinking they were past this argument, but clearly, this is going to be harder than she thought. Her excitement wanes, and maybe it shows.

Sammie rolls her eyes, exasperated-like. "Look, it's not your fault. It's my uncle's. I just have other things to do. Senior year is really busy."

Damn. It's not like Zahra is some groupie or something. If the girl doesn't want her help, she doesn't have to get it. "Your family is worried that you won't finish the essay in time, but to be honest, I have a ton of shit to do myself. So why don't you do what you have to do, and I'll do what I have to do, and we'll leave in an hour." Zahra sighs. "And everyone's happy." She raises her hands, extending the offer.

Sammie takes it silently. She sits back. She looks relieved but also shaken.

"It's not like your family is paying me anyway," Zahra adds. She opens her bag and pulls out her MacBook, pushes her iced latte to the side. She ordered one for Sammie too and, remembering it now, points. "That's for you."

"I don't drink caffeine," Sammie says quietly.

"Of course you don't."

"But thank you."

"Yeah, no problem." Zahra is already deep in her Gmail inbox. She looks up and can tell that Sammie wants to say something. Her mouth is half-open, and her eyebrows are raised, but when Zahra says, "That's cool with you, right? That we just sit here?"

Sammie shakes her head, an accidental no, then nods. Following Zahra's lead, Sammie takes out her computer.

Zahra doesn't really have that much to do, at least not much she wants to do. She could be looking for a job, a full-time job, something that will allow her to save money, to take vacation days like a real grown-up. But she checks Facebook instead, and when she's done reading rants about Donald Trump and melting ice caps and the New York City Transit system, she takes out her phone and opens Instagram. A lot of her friends from DC have posted, and it looks like they're having fun, some of them at a housewarming, some traveling—to Ghana and Iceland and Japan—some showcasing their crystal-clear skin accentuated by a well-chosen filter. Eventually, she opens a Google Document and begins writing a monologue.

"Do you think it's OK to reference Kendrick Lamar? In my essay?" Sammie asks.

Zahra has almost forgotten that the girl is across from her, but the question is easy enough to answer. "Sure, I like Kendrick Lamar. The essay is still about you though?" she says without looking up from her computer, considering both Sammie's essay and her own monologue, which is currently a rant about dating—the common combination of low-quality conversation and bad sex.

"Yeah, I think it is," Sammie says, then hesitates. "I know I said I didn't want your help, but you can read it if you want."

Ha. She can read it if she wants? "Thanks, but I'm OK."

"You're just going to sit there?"

"Sure. I'm doing a little writing myself."

Zahra is still looking at her computer but can see Sammie's perplexed face just beyond it. Sammie bites her lip, considering something. She moves to speak, then stops herself. She moves to speak again, and Zahra considers asking her what she has to say, but chooses to wait instead.

"Can I read what you're writing?" Sammie finally gets it out, and Zahra finally looks up. She initially thought the girl was a reflection of herself, but the more she sits across from her now, the more she sees someone far away. Sammie is the girl Zahra wanted to be in high school. Smart but not obsessed about it. Thoughtful but outspoken. And it doesn't hurt that she's physically striking, seems to hide a smile with everything she says, skin like slow-moving molasses, young and dewy. Three holes in each ear, hoops on hoops on hoops. Unarched eyebrows, bushy and straight, slightly overwhelming if not for her eyes, round pennies that keep your attention. She really likes Sammie, something about her, a straight shooter.

"No," Zahra says. "No to reading my writing, but let me see what you've got."

"You didn't want to read it two minutes ago."

"I changed my mind. I'm allowed that, aren't I?"

Sammie starts to laugh, but only a smile comes out. She passes Zahra her computer. Zahra sets it on her lap and backs away from the table.

Sammie has only written three paragraphs, but so far, the essay is profound, and Zahra takes a deep breath thinking about everything going on in the brain across from her. In the essay, Sammie questions what it means to be all right, using Kendrick Lamar's lyrics for reference, a song Zahra loves, knows from its start—discordant, interrupted beat, persistent jazz horn—to its spoken-word finale. The song is meant to be uplifting, and maybe it is, but Sammie knows *all right* is a plea, is doubtful of itself, is convincing and convincing and convincing the more Kendrick Lamar says it, and still, it's not convincing enough. Sammie questions if helmeted Black bodies on performance for 103 million viewers, many of whom don't care about the Black community, is all right; if the prison-industrial complex, disproportionately locking up Black fathers, mothers, sisters, cousins, is all right; if it's all right how her grandfather Daday disappears and then reappears, in her memories, her dreams, hallucinations. He's a ghost, like mist, an *ectoplasm*, and Sammie wonders if she's defective, says there are days when she can't pull herself from bed, feels small and swollen at the same time, feels like her physicality changes with the weather. She recalls the night after two white boys at school said Black girls would always be jealous of white girls, and she was there to hear it but didn't say anything, and it was in her head, stuck like a fat, wet leech. Was that all right? *I just sat there like any other plaid skirt and navy blazer.*

Zahra looks up, sees Sammie for more than she imagined, realizes that Sammie is a well, an endless pit.

"Don't be mad at yourself," Zahra says. "About not saying anything. Don't be too hard on yourself. Trust me when I say that there will be plenty of opportunities to say the right thing, the hard thing."

"Well, I didn't get to finish the essay, but I did do something. I organized a sit-in."

"At school?"

"For three days."

"Wow." Zahra grips her latte but is too taken aback by Sammie to sip it.

"That's where I was coming from on Sunday."

Zahra shakes her head, still in disbelief. "What were your demands? That white boys stop being white boys?"

"That the administration do something about it. It wasn't just about the comment. There was video footage that surfaced, of those same boys screaming the N-word."

"Whoa. And how did the administration react to that?"

"Every year some white student gets caught saying the N-word, in a derogatory way, not that it's OK otherwise. Or a teacher overhears someone making a racist joke, calling Black women ugly—something like that. Sometimes, there's even video footage, but the administration doesn't want to ruin the so-called futures of the wealthy white heirs of P & P. So they do nothing. Brush it under the rug, you know what I mean. But the sit-in worked. The boys got suspended this time, which is a start."

"Right." Zahra tries to convince herself that this girl is nothing like her mother. Doesn't talk or dress or look like Mary Simone Robinson. Doesn't sound like her either. Plus Sammie listens, doesn't she?

"So what do you think of the essay?"

God, what does Zahra think of the essay? This changes things. Or no, it shouldn't. The essay is still good. The essay is damned good. She fucking loves this fucking essay. So far. "Yeah, it's good. I would take out the part that hints at depression or mental illness."

"Oh?"

"Yeah, not exactly what schools want to hear. That you could be fucked up in the head."

Zahra bites her tongue, knowing she's said the wrong thing. Sammie looks more taken aback than hurt. She's judging Zahra now, probably.

"I didn't mean," Zahra tries to clear things up. "Sorry, that sounded really bad. I didn't mean for it to come out like that. I just . . . Colleges don't want to accept someone who might, er, go through things and drop out."

"No worries," Sammie says. She takes the smallest possible sip of the latte, holds it in the air, a mock cheers. "Thanks again."

<hr>

ZAHRA CURSES HERSELF ON HER TRAIN RIDE HOME. SHE doesn't know how she's going to work with Sammie again, taking out her mom issues on the poor girl like that. So much for being a professional. They're meeting again in a couple of days, and she has to get her act together. She took on this pro bono job for a reason; she wants to help out someone Black for a change. She's sick of working with white and East Asian American teenagers and wants to help someone who looks like her, wants to help someone whose essay doesn't reek of privilege. She's sick of that being her job, to dismantle the privilege, to tweak and tweak and tweak until these kids whose parents can afford seventy-dollar-an-hour sessions like it's nothing, who compare her rates to some of the most notable companies and call it a steal, have an essay that presents them as grounded, understanding, and not at all who they were raised to be.

She's too wound up for this. She needs an outlet and stops by Janie's place, but she's not home. Zahra calls Gram, no answer. She's in such a shitty place that she calls Khalil, thinking his attraction to her will make her feel alive, more of who she thought she was, but his phone just rings until she hears the beginning of his professional voice mail and hangs up. She goes to a bar in Harlem, the basement of a row house, a place that has exceptional jalapeño macaroni and cheese and overrated oxtails. She's been here so much that a few of the bartenders know her but not by name. She orders a grapefruit and tonic, then pulls out her computer and hides behind it, like usual. She orders another and another and just one more.

SIX

Like High Point, North Carolina, in the sixties, Principles & Progress is considered a progressive place, right down to its name. In some ways, maybe it is. Its nonwhite population, at 20 percent of the student body, is fairly high in comparison to other private institutions where the tuition is well over half the national median income. The classes are rigorous but diverse—AP almost a thing of the past, the focus is now on college-level courses—humanities instead of language arts, societies of the world and ethical reasoning instead of social studies. The teachers are mostly white but liberal—they've all read the latest books by Zadie Smith, Chimamanda Ngozi Adichie, Colson Whitehead, Ta-Nehisi Coates, and they encourage their students to do the same. They use language like *empathy* and *equity* and *egalitarian*. Of course they subscribe to basic individualism and meritocracy—work hard and the sky is the limit, your future is up to you, the world is your oyster—but who doesn't?

The impetus behind the sit-in was fairly simple—stop mislabeling us, stop allowing others to demean us. At first the idea of starting a sit-in seemed unconquerable, but then Sammie ran across the name

Mary Lou Andrews, who was only fifteen years old when she decided to replica the famous Greensboro sit-in in High Point. Now, it was more than fifty years later and Sammie had two whole years on Mary Lou, and how hard could it be? It just sort of happened. Once the idea was out of her mouth and onto the cafeteria table—where nearly all the Black girls ate—the words flat in front of them like a side dish, right next to P & P's infamous zucchini noodles, there was no going back. But as Sammie roams the halls every day, she looks for the impact: Do her Black peers look any happier? Do they take up the space they deserve? It's the seemingly little things, the things people with privilege tell you not to sweat—white girls walking three people wide, so there's no room for the sixteen-inch span of Sammie's shoulders, resulting in a shoulder charge so willful that it throws her off-balance, literally and emotionally.

Now a tap on Sammie's shoulder turns her around wildly, caught off guard. "Damn. Jumpy much?" Broderick asks.

"Your face is a little scary sometimes," Sammie jokes, knowing how on edge she's been lately.

"Oh, ha ha ha." Sarcasm serves him well. Broderick is just a junior, but he has a good sense of humor, and he's kind of cute. He's got a following too, of cultlike swooning sophomores. Sammie cocks her head to the side, considering what they see in him, and it's sort of obvious. Tall. Dark with creamy, blacker than brown skin. And handsome in the way of YG or A$AP Rocky, guys who don't bother with overt masculinity but don neat cornrows or flamboyant fits instead.

In a way, she and Broderick are one and the same, both Black, from low-income neighborhoods in the city, and sort of stumbled their way into P & P, Sammie by way of someone her uncle dropped off at a Yankees game one day. But she and Broderick never acknowledge their similarities out loud, opting for side-eyes and sneers, nothing more.

"You partying this weekend?" Broderick asks. "I don't want to be the only . . ." He rubs his hand, the black side. He doesn't want to be the only Black person there.

"I don't know. High school parties are getting kind of old. Some of us are headed to college soon."

Broderick throws an arm around her, and it feels nice, not in the way of romance but comfortable all the same. "You know you still like to party with your boy," he says.

"You know what happened the last time I hung out with everyone. . . ." Sammie rolls her eyes.

"They were just kidding."

"I didn't find it funny."

She looks over to Broderick to make sure he's on her side, and he wipes the smile from his face nonchalantly. "You act like I said it." He pauses when she doesn't respond. "No cap," he says. "I didn't."

"Right." She shakes her head.

He tries to lead her toward the cafeteria, but she veers the other way, slinking from underneath his arm. "I have to go see my counselor, but we'll talk later. Maybe after school."

"Bet," he says. "You have Ms. Kennedy, don't you? Good looks. Praying I have her next year too. If nothing else, she's hot."

Sammie rolls her eyes as Broderick walks away. She can hear him call out to someone else, his Yeezys squish-squashing on the tiled floor.

||||||||||||||||||||||||||||||||||||||||||||||||||

THERE'S A LINE AT MS. KENNEDY'S DOOR, ALL SENIORS SAM-mie recognizes, almost all white but for an Asian girl who Ms. Kennedy welcomes in now. Though there are other counselors, she's the favorite, so even students who haven't been assigned to her wait for her advice. Sammie falls in line behind a girl named Elizabeth. She and Sammie know each other, but they're not cool enough for Sammie to spark a conversation. Once at a party, a drunken Elizabeth laid her head on Sammie's lap and said, "Can we be friends? I want to be your friend. You seem really . . . cool!" Now, Elizabeth smiles over her shoulder, and Sammie smiles back. Everything's different when the lights are low and alcohol is flowing; people are freer to say what they want, race more of a motivator than a barrier.

"I'm not going to have time to eat lunch," Elizabeth says, though she's no longer facing Sammie, and the boy in front of Elizabeth is leaning against the wall, his head resting in a way that makes Sammie think he could be asleep. Sammie doesn't know what to say, so she purses her lips and scrambles in her bag for headphones. She puts on Chloe x Halle as she waits, and for all she knows, Elizabeth doesn't say anything else.

"Sammie," Ms. Kennedy says. "Sammie?"

Sammie jolts out of a musical daydream, realizing she's reached the front of the line, not knowing when Elizabeth and the sleeper had their turn or gave up on waiting.

"Hi, Ms. Kennedy," Sammie says, walking into her office. It's nice-size, almost all the offices at P & P are. Ms. Kennedy's desk is practically bare, but behind her is a shrine to her two-person family. Ms. Kennedy and her Indian American husband getting married; he and Ms. Kennedy on top of a mountain, faces bright and sweaty; he and Ms. Kennedy in running gear, with 5K tags pinned to pink T-shirts; he and Ms. Kennedy holding newborn babies, not their babies—Ms. Kennedy doesn't have kids.

Today, Ms. Kennedy is wearing a pink mod dress with a mock collar and lion-head earrings, and Sammie thinks she's the best-dressed faculty member at P & P, maybe the youngest too. She's a white woman with straight blond hair and rose-gold-trimmed eyeglasses. She puts them on top of her head like sunglasses, then shuffles papers around.

"Aha," she says, presumably finding Sammie's transcripts and essay. Her eyes scan them like a nervous mouse.

"You're doing well, Sammie. Really well. I think you could get into any school you want. Maybe."

Sammie nods. "And what about my essay?"

Ms. Kennedy raises her eyebrows. "Would be nice if you completed it. And maybe part from the lyrics a little."

"Too much?" Sammie asks. "It's just . . . the lyrics explain how I feel perfectly, and I think they were a part of my realization of what it means to be . . . you know, Black."

Ms. Kennedy nods. "Right. Well, then, that's lovely, Sammie."

But that wasn't what she just said, so now Sammie isn't sure what to believe. The day before, Zahra seemed impressed with her writing. A little whiny, a little bitchy, sure, but impressed no less.

"What schools are you considering again? Remind me," Ms. Kennedy says.

"Stanford is my top choice, but I'm also applying to Yale, Harvard, Penn, Tufts, and Spelman."

Ms. Kennedy looks up at Sammie's last choice, then says, "Good schools. All good schools."

"Even Spelman?" Sammie asks, pushing for what Ms. Kennedy hasn't said.

"Of course. Spelman is a great school. It just surprised me, that's all. Wasn't quite in alignment with the other schools you mentioned."

Sammie is confused by this. If they're all great schools, why wouldn't Spelman be in alignment? She nudges Ms. Kennedy further. "I don't know what you mean by alignment."

Ms. Kennedy takes her glasses off her head and puts down Sammie's printed, half-finished essay. "I didn't mean anything by it. Just an offhanded remark, I guess."

Sammie nods, smiles, feels as if she has pushed enough. Her last session with Ms. Kennedy was similarly confounding, so now her expectations are low. Maybe it's why she eventually said yes to Zahra. Maybe she's looking for someone who can discuss her Blackness without blushing.

"It's not a secret that you're the one who started the sit-in, Sammie. I'm proud of you for that, and I think Spelman might be a great fit for you," Ms. Kennedy says.

It is a compliment, Sammie guesses. It doesn't quite feel like one though.

"So you think that's where I should go? To Spelman?"

"No, I didn't say that."

"Then Stanford? You think I should go to Stanford?"

Ms. Kennedy scoots back from her desk and crosses her arms. Sammie wants to know her thoughts but waits patiently for Ms. Kennedy to say more.

"I can't tell you where you should go for college," Ms. Kennedy says eventually, putting her eyeglasses back on and bringing Sammie's college essay close to her face, as if she has practically gone blind all of a sudden.

"What can you tell me?" Sammie asks sincerely.

"That I think you're headed in the right direction and you should follow your gut. Spelman is an amazing school. I didn't mean to insinuate anything less, but if you want to go to Stanford, to California, don't sell yourself short."

"Right," Sammie says. "Thank you, Ms. Kennedy." Though she's not sure what she's gotten from the meeting.

Ms. Kennedy smiles hard and deep, and Sammie wonders if it's because she likes Sammie or is relieved to see her go.

‖‖‖‖‖‖‖‖‖‖‖‖‖‖‖‖‖‖‖‖‖‖‖‖‖‖‖‖‖‖‖‖‖‖‖‖‖

AFTER SCHOOL, SAMMIE SITS ON HER FAVORITE BENCH, HALF-cast in sunlight, half-shaded by an old oak tree. By now, she knows this campus well, and the Riverdale neighborhood in which it's located. It's weird to her sometimes, how at home she can feel here. How one moment she belongs, and the next she doesn't. Sometimes she imagines her classmates kicking her out of their well-planned bubble to, for someone like her, a more appropriate place, where the unemployment rate is higher and way fewer families own their homes, where she'll blend in with the Black and Latinx population of the South Bronx. Sammie knows about her school's privately owned enclave with mandated single-family homes. And outside of it, the stately mansions and synagogues of Riverdale. And farther still, the urban decay that comes with exploitation and red lining and welfare hotels and slumlords. She learned all about it in her urban-planning class. Mr. Rivers was a great teacher, one of her favorites.

She spots Noah across the way, on the other side of the courtyard, and butterflies go crazy in her stomach. When he looks her way, she looks down and busies herself with her backpack, pulling out her sketch pad and a graphite pencil, drawing the tree leaning over her. When she sees his Off-White x Jordan 1s coming nearer, she wills herself to look up and catches the glint in his eye. He smiles deeply, and she looks down again, smiling into the intricate stump she's drawn, with exaggerated roots like tremors from an old-timey movie she watched with Uncle. Now, she hears Noah's voice.

"Hey," he says. He stands in front of her, and she sees his dirty Jordans more closely.

"Hey," she says, looking up, shielding her eyes from a nonexistent sun when, really, it's Noah she has to squint to look at.

"You're drawing?" he says, pointing to her sketch pad.

She closes it quickly. "It's nothing. Just doodling, I guess."

"Looked like a tree."

"No, no," she says, then considers what she's saying. "Well, yes, it was a tree but not a very good one." Truth is, she's gotten better at drawing trees. She used to draw them because they were easy, the stump one long leg and the branches gangly, wrinkled arms. But it was Leila who flipped through Sammie's sketchbook one day and said, "You know, trees never die of old age. They could live on forever." Makes Sammie wonder—if not of old age, then how? What's it like to live forever? What's it like to have a thousand rings, more than any pawnshop in the South Bronx? What's it like to keep stories inside of you like holding your breath? She wants to ask Noah these questions but can't seem to get anything out.

Noah nods, says, "OK. I like it though."

Sammie nods with him, at a loss for words. Nervous, she tucks an imaginary strand of hair behind her ear. Really, there is nothing to tuck. Really, her braids are too thick to be tamed by anything short of a ponytail holder with extra elasticity.

"Well, I should get going," Noah says.

"Yeah, see you around," she says.

She watches him walk off, toward the parking lot, where he'll get in his new, shiny blue BMW and drive home or to hang out with friends or somewhere to grab a bite to eat. She wishes she were going with him. Even at P & P, a lot of kids don't have cars, a lot of her New York City classmates don't even know how to drive one, but Noah is an anomaly in many ways.

Sammie exhales dramatically, catching her breath. *He's just a boy, he's just a boy, he's just a boy*, she says to herself. Then she looks around, opens her sketch pad, and focuses on the tree she's been drawing. She eyes a tiny caterpillar, Crayola green. It looks persistent as it edges up the trunk. Sammie feels like she can relate to the little guy, so it has to be out of sheer impulse that she flicks it, and it's off the tree, in the air, and on the concrete slab of sidewalk that cuts through the courtyard at seventy-five-degree angles. She feels like a monster. "What the fuck, Sammie?" she says under her breath. "What did he do to you?"

She begins to pack her things, gets up, smooths down her skirt, and readjusts her tights. She picks up the caterpillar, disgusted by touching it but dedicated to its survival, and places it back on the tree, as it were. Then she hears it, music, what she thinks might be coming from the headphones buried in her bag until she finds them, tangled, a knot of wire. They are not even attached to her phone. She looks around to find where the music is coming from but can't spot anything or anyone who might be playing it. She wants the music to stop, but she's allured by it too—the sound a big-boned mama makes when she sings from the gut and opens her mouth so wide that you'd think a freight train was coming through it. She has no idea that it's the moths singing, *There are times when I look back, and I am haunted by my youth.*

SEVEN

Mary used to say that there were spirits in the basement. There was a time when the basement was habitable, before the leaks, before the spiders as big as sewing needles, right after Big Al, a family friend trying to get on his feet, moved out of it. Zahra and Derrick were new to being teenagers, new to attitudes that nipped like snapping turtles, a time when all they wanted was to be left alone and yet, they didn't have a thing to do in their alone time. But talk about sex. A crass conversation that adults would've gawked at, especially seeing that Zahra's and Derrick's reproductive organs are different, but it was never like *that* between them, never *We're different and shouldn't discuss this*, always *But didn't you hear*, always *But I don't think it works like that*, always *But what if* . . . Sex talk made Zahra feel icky and sticky, and still, she couldn't help herself. Derrick was more mature about things, which even he understood was atypical for a boy.

So there they were, asking each other questions that neither of them knew the answer to when they heard a calling out, something different from the singsong voices of the moths, something more similar to their own voices; the eerie but distinct way one's own voice might sound coming from afar.

They ran upstairs as if fire were at their feet, Zahra leading the way, skipping steps, using the rickety rail for leverage. They hadn't sought out Mary. No, she was there, at the top of the steps, waiting for them like magic, like she knew they'd be coming up quick and had to be there to greet them, so they huffed out what had happened.

"It was . . . ," Zahra began.

"Loud." Derrick finished her sentence.

"It sounded like . . ."

"Someone was there."

"Like, like . . ."

"A person. A real person."

"There but not there."

"Here but not here."

Mary looked at them funny, as if they were speaking another language, tongues. Then she laughed; she barreled, holding her stomach and the rail for support. "I forget you two are from the city." As if she were different, as if she wasn't their mother.

"What is that supposed to mean?" Zahra asked.

"That things are always more than they seem, and you can't be surprised when something jumps out at you. From the dark, I mean."

Zahra reached behind her, for Derrick. He was still there. Safe.

"'Cause you know I think there are spirits down there anyway," Mary said. Then she laughed a little more, and Zahra had nightmares night after night, even after Gram had clarified that *Yes, there are spirits, but no, they're not all out to get you, and guess what, they have business of their own. Mind yours, and they won't have to.*

MARY MIGHT SAY THE SAME THING ABOUT SAMMIE'S APART-
ment. Though it is snug, the home has a living energy, maybe an
excrescence of all the pictures. People made small by the mountains
in Trinidad; a weary house with a thatched roof; baby Sammie gur-
gling on Trey's lap; Trey smiling next to a beautiful woman, teenagers together, maybe Sammie's mom. Some of the pictures are in
frames, lopsided, others proudly upright. They're tucked into any
nooks and crannies that will allow them a place to sit. Wedged in
between a fifty-inch mirror and its plasticky wood frame, pinned to
the refrigerator door with seashell magnet souvenirs from the Baha-
mas and Costa Rica, smashed between the colorful tchotchkes that
decorate the kitchen's windowsill. It's as if the family has something
to prove, their existence. It's a lot like home but different, more ag-
gressive. Gram's pictures are mostly tucked away, where these are
on full display.

It seems like she and Sammie are the only ones here. The house
is so quiet, which feels off, so many loud photos but no voices to back
them up. Zahra squints at a picture of Trey. He is young; well,
younger. In his twenties maybe, wearing a backward fitted and a
loose baggy white tee. He's smiling through his gap with an Ari-
Zona iced tea in one hand, both arms loosely extended as if he's saying, *What? Don't hate the player, hate the game*, and gosh, he is
charming.

"He's always been like that," Sammie says, sitting down at their
kitchen table. No dining room, just this four-top.

"Oh, I . . . ," Zahra starts but realizes she has nothing to say.
She's embarrassed to have been looking at his picture for so long.

"A ladies' man," Sammie adds. "My friends can't get enough of
him, but it's like God, he's old. You know?"

Zahra laughs, draws comfort from Sammie's candidness. "Yeah, he's so old," she says sarcastically.

"How old are you?" Sammie asks.

"Add five years to your best guess." People always think she's younger than she is.

Sammie nods as if she's figured it out. "Welp"—she takes out her computer—"guess we should write this thing."

"You," Zahra clarifies. "You should write it." She takes out her computer as well.

Her computer's wallpaper is old, a photo from high school. Senior skip day—Derrick's—Zahra was still a junior, newly single, Chase having recently broken up with her. They're at Julian's house, and she and Derrick are holding Smirnoff wine coolers from his basement fridge. Julian's house was on the good side of town, no break-ins, no beat-downs, manicured treeless lawns, BMWs in two-car garages. His parents had moved out of the Eastside to a house five minutes from Perimeter Mall, so here they all are on the come up, growing up. Drinking and leaning to snap music on Julian's brown leather sofa, cold, a house where the AC was always blasting. Zahra is smiling, looking beyond the camera, and Derrick is dreamily looking directly into it, daring the picture taker to ask him a question. *Why you always got that look on your face?* the picture taker might ask, and Derrick might say, *'Cause I'm neither here nor there.* And Zahra gets that, understands it.

Derrick is always in two places at once, sometimes more. He used to cohabitate between places well. One moment he was imitating school staff—Mr. Green's LL Cool J limp, the principal's lisp, the teacher whose name Zahra has since forgotten but used to tell them to *stop flubbing the dub's* country twang—one moment Derrick was hand beating "Grindin'" on classroom desks, and the next he was buried in his room with a book, ignoring whatever girl he was dating so she sent Zahra text messages like, *Is your brother mad at me?* or *Something wrong with Derrick's phone?*, and Zahra beat down Derrick's door until Whitney or Keyauna or Brittni was his own problem again. One day he was Ms. Seller's favorite student, and the next he was the Marshawn Lynch of AP Lit, just there to graduate, he need not explain why he wouldn't read another book from the white male canon. Maybe it was what people liked about him, that he wasn't there for the taking, that there was always more to look forward to. He was like walking into an old Circuit City, racks on racks on racks, a YC music video, sub CDs for bankrolls. When MP3s and LimeWire, and even iPods if your stock was up, came into play, music became ubiquitous, and you didn't have to go anywhere particular to hear it. Kind of odd that Derrick started drifting just as music grew legs, in everyone's ear, a playlist for each personality.

The first time Derrick heard voices that Zahra didn't, they were riding in Uncle Richard's old Chevy, listening to "People Get Ready" by the Impressions with the windows rolled down because the air-conditioning hadn't worked in years. Derrick had started listening to oldies on repeat, and Zahra liked this vibe on him, so she always nodded along. But it was those same songs that made him hear what she couldn't, so he leaned closer to the speakers, and said, "This song is about more than you think it's about. They're asking for something. Of me and you." But all she heard was, *People get ready, there's a train a comin'*, and Derrick's face was too serious, his eyebrows too furrowed, his mouth too tight for her to ask him what he meant, what the song was asking for. Zahra was too scared to find out.

It was the same year Uncle Richard cut down that tree, the one she and Derrick used to climb together, wrapping their thin arms and hairless legs, prepubertal, around its trunk and then inching up like caterpillars. The flaking bark, dry and brittle, used to nick their legs then fall to the ground, slow and steady, an airplane landing. "You're so slow," Derrick teased her from high above, sitting in the fork of the tree where the trunk split into two. She made it to him, always, eventually. Then he went left, and she went right, always, shared secrets from opposing branches, never their own but things they'd overhead, some about people they knew and others about names that didn't have a corresponding face.

One day, climbing was for losers. And the next day, they were in high school, where Zahra caught feelings and Derrick interpreted them. He watched and watched, everyone and everything until the sound of Uncle Richard and his chain saw cut into the tree's soft pulp, and Grandma said, "Damn gypsy moths. Call the tree removers before you kill yourself."

"You OK?" Sammie asks, and Zahra is jolted into her present reality. Sammie cocks her head to the side thoughtfully. "I mean, you weren't exactly *nice* the other day, but at least you were present."

"I'm sitting right across from you."

"You know what I mean."

The girl is too perceptive. Zahra relents. "Sorry, I just have a lot on my mind."

"Like what?"

"Like your college essay." Of course this lie isn't meant to be convincing.

"Right. I'm working on that." Sammie refocuses, brings her face down so it's only inches away from her computer as if seeing the words more clearly will fuel her inspiration. She squints hard. She sighs, shakes her head, sits back in her chair, and bites her lip.

"I like a white guy," she says without looking up at Zahra, her voice small but casual.

Zahra doesn't know why Sammie is telling her this. "OK," she says. "So what? It's 2019, isn't it?" Zahra hears Sophia in her words and laughs to herself. But Sophia has never shared personal things, crushes or concerns outside of school, outside of impersonal politics, ideologies that are almost neutralities in New York—gun control and the disuse of plastic straws—but never more, never anything that might actually reveal who she is at the heart of things, so this is new territory for Zahra, and she's a little squeamish about it. "Black men like white women every day, don't they?"

"Yeah, but kids are brutal. You have no idea."

Try the lunch table in seventh grade, Molly Guyer calling her ghetto and uncouth. "No, I get it."

"And maybe it's not even just us kids. Issa Rae got complete shit for even suggesting that Black women date Asian men."

Sammie is right. This is one of the few controversies that made Zahra into a Twitter warrior. She couldn't allow men and pick-me's to come at Issa in that way; it wasn't right. Issa was down for the brown, and loud about it too. So why did people have their panties in such a bunch?

"Yeah, I heard about that," is all Zahra says now.

They are silent for a while, until Zahra tries to get them back on track. "So, about your . . ."

But Sammie is smiling to herself. A hiccup, a smirk and then she's laughing, laughing, laughing louder. Holding her stomach, she can't seem to stop herself. Laughing so hard she can't breathe. It's impressive—Sammie's ability to loosen up in such a defenseless way around someone she's just met—Sammie holds out her hand, a stop sign. Then a finger, one minute. Finally, Sammie says, "God, I'm such a loser. Can I tell you what he's like? You wouldn't believe it. He's so . . ." She begins laughing again, hysterically, and Zahra thinks about how far they've come, from radio static to this.

"He's so what?" Zahra asks.

"So . . ."

"Jeez, Sammie. Get it out."

"So freaking white. Like I had to pick the whitest boy at school, like pasty, like I'm repulsed by melanin. It's just so ridiculous. I'm ridiculous."

"Is he cute?"

Sammie seems taken aback by the question, as if she'd already answered it when she called him pasty. "He's aight."

"Then what is it you like about him?"

A moth has landed on Sammie's collar, and Zahra eyes it precariously. If it starts singing, she won't be able to hear Sammie across from her.

Zahra reaches across the table to flick it away. Her fingers graze Sammie's collarbone, but the moth doesn't move, and Sammie is alert now, to the threat.

"Ahhh," Sammie squelches. "Get it off."

The moth is white, with small brown specks, as if its wings have been sullied by ground coffee beans. Sammie is holding deathly still, and Zahra is perplexed by her caution. It's not like the thing has a stinger. It's a freaking moth, blindly attracted to light.

"Stay still," Zahra says anyway. She reaches across the table again and flicks it, once, twice, three times.

"Son of a bitch," Zahra mutters under her breath, lifting the moth by its wings. She looks for its eyes but can't find them. She carries it to the kitchen, where the window is slightly open to curb the uneven heat distribution of New York apartments. She's always preferred apartments that were too hot over apartments that were ice-cold. She places the moth outside, on the sill, erasing her quiet worry, her quiet wonder about why the moths are so attracted to Sammie.

When Zahra sits back down, Sammie looks pensive again, but in a different way than before. "I've told you something, something really personal. So, it's probably a good time for you to tell me what's going on with you."

"You're a kid."

"I'm mature, and you know it."

It's not a lie. Sammie seems awfully mature for her age, even taking into account her schoolgirl giggles. Zahra recognizes that Sammie is not her peer, but that doesn't mean she has to be detached with her either.

"I've just been getting this feeling. Like I'm on edge."

Sammie's eyes light up like she knows something. She piles her braids on the side of her shoulder and then flings them behind her again. She bites her thumbnail. "I think I know what you mean," she says.

Pfft. Zahra shouldn't have said anything. Now Sammie actually thinks she can relate.

"Do you ever feel like someone is watching you?" Sammie asks.

The question is shocking, uncomfortable. Zahra shakes her head, no, it's not quite like that, but it's something so similar that she can't ignore it. She turns to Sammie, innocent-looking, the smooth round face of a Black cherub, something she might have seen on one of Gram's old Christmas decorations. Behind Sammie, she spots a cobweb in the corner of the kitchen, connecting an upper cabinet to the ceiling. It doesn't need to be spelled out any further. There's no mistaking the likeness of Sammie's world and her own. Whatever is haunting her and Derrick is haunting Sammie, too.

EIGHT

October 2019, Harlem, a Wednesday morning

Zahra's phone is vibrating, and she's disoriented by the lack of sunlight. It's really early, too early for Gram to be calling, but here she is. Zahra can't say how late it was when she stumbled into her apartment the night before. She went out with Janie, and though they didn't get white-girl wasted, they were washed enough for the gin to dizzy her head and wreck her stomach. She needs fried chicken and bread, something to suck up the stupidity, never mind the alcohol. She grabs a bottle of water from its place on her nightstand, props a pillow against the headboard she spent way too much money on, and answers the phone.

"Gram?"

"Been calling you and calling you. You don't answer your phone." This is what she always says.

"I'm here now. What's going on?"

"Derrick's . . ." She pauses.

"Yeah, I know. He hasn't been doing well for some time now."

It's hard to define "not doing well," but it generally means that he's holed himself up somewhere, listening to the same songs on repeat, sleeping, saying very little to anyone who tries to engage him. Gram thinks he needs more Jesus, and Mary thinks he needs therapy, and Zahra wonders if maybe he just needs their family to not be so fucked up. They are a quadrant opposite the it-takes-a-village constitution of Gram's rhetoric, but on the flip side, they also fail to meet the basic requirements of the American nuclear family. To be honest, their upbringing should've gone against everything Mary stood for — family beyond just mothers and fathers but a network of relatives including aunties and cousins from a different gene pool. It was odd that even the people in their family, under one roof, were isolated from one another, Derrick's and Zahra's everyday lives ignored by their father and too small for their mother. They were Mary's county court, while her eyes were on the Supreme.

"What is it this time?" Zahra asks Gram now.

"He's gone."

"Gone? Gone how? Gone where?" Zahra sits up in bed, nauseated. "Did you call Terrence?"

"Terrence says he hasn't seen him in months."

The timeline doesn't add up. Derrick said he was with Terrence just a few weeks ago. Zahra huffs. Is she surprised that he lied? She knew something was up, and it's happened before, hasn't it? Derrick's disappearing. But he always comes back, however mangled and fractured, with no answers for his absences. He's never left for longer than twenty-four hours.

"Maybe he's just gone driving. He does that sometimes."

Derrick has always loved driving. It's when he's most at ease with the voices, his "Swing Low, Sweet Chariot" ring shout, a call-and-response—the voices to the moths and then back to Derrick, like the Golden Gate Quartet sampled by Parliament Funkadelic sampled by Dr. Dre. *Swing down, sweet chariot stop, and let me ride.* The car, windows down, vibing, is his mothership to outer space, entrapment and freedom all the same; it's where he feels most connected to the voices, to himself. That's probably what it is. He's around the city somewhere driving, daydreaming.

"His car is still here, Zahra. Keys too."

"Shit." Zahra's stomach lurches, and she runs to the bathroom to rid herself of whatever's trying to come up, day-old alcohol or the ground that has just fallen from underneath her. She puts Gram, who's muttering incessantly, on mute, then dry heaves until the good stuff finally comes out. The previous day's huevos rancheros and later, a salmon burger with bacon, but also, all the memories— climbing trees, skipping rocks over the creek, driving, gliding, vibing, the excuses—*I missed your call, my bad, Zahr, you know how it is*, the songs—"I Want You" and "Trouble Man."

Now someone or *something* sings from outside her half-open bathroom window, *What does he care if the land ain't free? Old man river, that old man river, he must know something.* Maybe she's finally over the edge. Memories flash through her mind like a family reunion slideshow, her life in one-second clips, her brother the star, the favorite, now missing, gone like a snap of the finger, always on beat.

Zahra wipes her mouth, unmutes the phone, breathlessly asks, "How long has he been gone?"

"Saw him at lunchtime yesterday. He looked normal as can be." Zahra can hear Gram's shallow breathing. "Police say there's nothing they can do. He's over eighteen. He doesn't *have* to come home, they said. We tried to tell them—he's different, emotional, spiritual, but none of that matters, I guess. I couldn't convince them to understand."

Zahra processes the information, trying to find the loophole, the reason why it's not as serious as Gram thinks it is. She wraps her arms around the toilet bowl, feels the cold porcelain against her cheek. She is cool now, like the other side of the pillow, like her brother. "Derrick is missing, but his car isn't. Where is he? Where is he?" she mumbles, trying to intuit his whereabouts.

"Missing? Oh, don't say it like that, Zahra." But what other way is there to say it? *Gone* and *missing* are synonyms. One does not mean any more than the other. But Zahra knows that to Gram, *missing* conjures up past stories of boys disappearing in Atlanta's stale streets, newspaper articles growing by day, the summer of 1980 as hot as a light bulb left on too long.

"Fine. Gone, whatever." Zahra is agitated with Gram, as if it is Gram who has not kept a close enough eye on things, on her brother, who needs constant attention, if not care. "Where have you been looking? What do you want me to do? I'm all the way in New York."

Zahra tries to stand up, but the weight of the world seems to push her down. She lies on the bathroom floor, looking up at the ceiling, moths everywhere, the phone on her chest, rising and falling as she breathes in and out.

Gram is silent. Probably because they both already know the answer to these questions. Gram does not know where to start looking for Derrick. She has never been able to read him in this way. To love him and even smother him? Yes, she is good for that. But to know where he is? To know how his interiors work? Only Zahra knows this. And it's about time she goes home. She has to. There's a pinch in her chest, and she holds her breath until it goes away.

"You used to be so close," Gram says, and her use of past tense makes Zahra feel so small. She wants to be a bigger person but doesn't know how.

"You think I haven't tried to stay close to him?" she asks.

"You gave up."

God, Gram doesn't get it. She never has. How can you grow with something rotting attached to you? Derrick is too big for her to carry. "I have a life to live too. You call that giving up?"

"Now don't go putting words into my mouth," Gram says in a tone that demands quiet.

Zahra practically whispers, "I can't save him."

"Come home." Gram sounds relieved to finally say it.

"The flight is going to be outrageous. I'm barely able to save as it is."

"Well, you decide what's worth it."

Zahra has to go. She's known since the beginning of this phone call. Maybe she wanted to be wanted, needed Gram to beg her. "Of course Derrick is worth it. He's worth everything," she says.

She tries calling him, back to back, alternates between praying and begging him to pick up, holds her breath through all the ringing, which nauseates her with repetition. She switches to text messages, which are nice enough at first—*Derrick, where are you? Derrick, we miss you*—but then become hostile and accusatory—*It's not OK for you to put us through this. Just answer the damn phone already.* Eventually, she gives up on the messages too and pries herself from the bathroom floor. She puts down her phone for a second and lies in bed, but then, left alone with her thoughts, she looks at her phone again.

Gram isn't the only one who's been trying to reach her. There are a ton of Tinder notifications too. She screams silently, punches her pillows. Some of the conversations were carried over from before she started drinking the previous night. Others are new. Faces she hasn't seen before. Bios she never would've approved of sober—men with bare, oiled chests who "want a girl who can carry a conversation" or think well-traveled is a personality trait.

There are white men. Never gone there before. Asian men. Would spite her mother, and she's found them sexy ever since Michael

Xu in seventh grade. She thinks about men hard. She thinks about men so she doesn't have to think about Derrick or the good times.

She sees Kenny and Calvin and Christopher. Men with fades, men with blowouts, Afros, free-form, men whose neat locs grace their shoulders like a knight's helmet. Men in front of the Eiffel Tower and men pointing to the pyramids, men with all sky behind them like they're levitating or the wind will capture them at any moment and carry them away like a memory.

Her own memory takes her to the backyard that was on a slope in a neighborhood named for hills, and all it did was hike up and dip back down, small mountains that ran along a creek where Zahra and Derrick would meet their friends on the other side of the neighborhood. Mary told them not to take the shortcut to school, which involved cutting over the creek, jumping from one big rock to the other, but they did it anyway, while singing "Weak" by SWV or later, practicing the poetry they had to memorize for Ms. Strickfield's class. Derrick and Zahra were always doing things they weren't supposed to. Stealing pocket change from Mary's wallet to buy lemon pepper wings from the trailer by the corner store, licking their fingers while watching 106 & Park on BET or listening to Greg Street on V103.

When Derrick got his license, they stopped asking permission to go anywhere, do anything. They got jobs at Target and Foot Locker to pay for their nasty fast-food habits, for the CDs they bought at Wax 'N' Fax, for the books Derrick stacked along his walls like overgrown vines, nonfiction mostly, history books—*The Marrow of Tradition* or *Genghis Khan and the Making of the Modern World*—and Zahra rolled her eyes, preferring mysteries and romances.

When Derrick got his license, they drove to Publix for subway sandwiches, to Rita's for gelato, Little Five Points for shirts with Bob Marley smoking a spliff on the front of them. Blasting the latest hits all the way there. Clipse or TI or Outkast. Derrick knowing all the words and Zahra faking it, never knowing anything past the chorus. It was always just the two of them until Zahra got a boyfriend. But in those days, pre boyfriend, pre whatever coma Derrick is in now, Zahra felt so free. Those days, worth nothing, meant everything.

Zahra pushes the memories down deep, but one peeks out like a dandelion in Uncle Richard's freshly trimmed grass. A time before they got central AC, when she and Derrick were both in grade school, and they lay next to Gram's bed, on a pallet on the floor because it was damningly hot, and Gram's room was the only one with an AC unit. Zahra rolled on her side and told Derrick that she hated fourth grade, that the kids were mean and called her pint-size, and he said, "Well, I do love a pint of butter pecan," and she was sadder than she was before she'd confided in him. But then, the next day, there he was with a bowl of it, butter pecan, Breyers, said it would keep them cool, said she was the coolest kid in fourth grade, that only an idiot wouldn't know it. And she was cool, cool, cool, from that point on, just like Derrick, crystal cool, cucumber cool, Coolio cool until she became a woman and didn't feel the need to be.

Zahra thinks about the men, men who do not share her bloodline, these men whom she has no memories with, whom she doesn't want to have sex with. What good are they? They don't make her tingle down there. They don't make her tingle anywhere. Still, she looks at pictures and reads bios and swipes and swipes and swipes until she has to get out of her apartment and decides that if she walks it, she'll be right on time for her serving shift.

Zahra gets ready quickly, even though there's still a hour and a half before her shift at Common House starts. And from there, her back-to-back sessions with Sophia and Sammie. They'll each be coming from whatever extracurricular activities they've joined to better themselves or to better the world or, more accurately, to add to their college applications. She knows Sophia is on her school's debate team, part of the LGBTQ+ alliance, and plays volleyball. Sammie's the vice president of the Black Student Union or whatever her school's equivalent of it is. White progressive private schools always have affinity groups. Firstly, there's the need, and secondly, there's the white guilt, insurmountable and paradoxical when there's a shit ton of money involved. The need to do anything but give up the throne that they sit on.

Zahra moisturizes her twist-out and brushes her teeth and applies a light layer of concealer, and when she walks outside, she relishes in the feel of the day on her neck, her shoulders, her arms. By now, she's convinced herself that Derrick isn't actually gone, that Gram worries too much, that she'll get back to Atlanta and find Derrick somewhere obvious, like in the Decatur library or the freshman quad at Clark. Derrick is not someone who runs away, she knows this. He is the opposite, he is someone who plants himself firmly and watches other people run away—Zahra herself being the prime example.

||||||||||||||||||||||||||||||||||||||||||||||||||

THE CHILL OF MID-FALL IN HARLEM WHIPS AROUND HER, AND she pulls her leather jacket tighter, thinking she should have worn her coat. It's almost ten o'clock, early for her, but the streets are busy. There's already the usual crowd around the bodega at Lenox, dealers, kids who've just turned into grown-ups. They laugh loudly and sometimes offer to help Zahra with her grocery bags. She always declines.

There is a long line that snakes from the bus stop in front of the bodega down the block. Elderly women and men with shopping carts, a downtrodden but dignified-looking bunch. They are not waiting for the bus but something or someone else. Zahra doesn't know what or whom. She walks in the opposite direction, south. A woman who always seems to be outside of the liquor store waves, and Zahra waves back.

She walks past the Schomburg and the busy intersection of Lenox and 125th. She hits 116th Street, then goes east, through Spanish Harlem, the sounds of salsa and bachata near and far, like walking through fog. She makes a right on Park, and the area feels grungy but determined. There is some sort of small farmers market. She hits 110th, 100th, 96th, 95th, 94th. She walks until the people outside turn from brown and Black to white. The houses and buildings from run-over to polished and ornate, in less than a mile, poverty knocking on privilege's door. The change is impressive. When she hits the Eighties she remembers that Sophia's school is around here. It's a public school but ranked as the number two high school in New York City, with a startling lack of diversity. Not even 1 percent Black. The nine-story building seemingly for Asian and white students only. You have to score really high on the SHSAT to get in, something Zahra helped Sophia achieve more than four years ago now, when Sophia could barely string two profound sentences together, when Mrs. Jacobs was attending a PTA meeting at Sophia's school and found Zahra's ad taped to the school's entrance, though not for long, as soon an administrator would come and take it down. Just enough time for Mrs. Jacobs to pocket the boosted résumé that said Zahra had helped kids get into the best public schools in New York City at a time when she had just heard about the SHSAT and New York's uncanny ability to sustain one of the nation's most segregated and unequal school systems in the country, de facto. It worked. Zahra got a job, and Sophia got in, and all is well. She guesses.

||||||||||||||||||||||||||||||||||||||||||||||||||

WHEN ZAHRA GETS TO THE BIG HOUSE ON PARK AVENUE, THE nanny, Pam, a Jamaican woman, opens the door while holding Sophia's youngest sibling. He is three years old and an awkward sight in Pam's arms. Too big, too pale. There is a lollipop dangling from his mouth. He takes it out and holds it close to Pam's face as she shows Zahra into the kitchen, where Mrs. Jacobs is at an island the size of Guam cutting apples, and Sophia hovers over, talking animatedly. When Sophia sees Zahra, she falls silent, smiles widely, and Zahra feels her admiration.

"Hi, Zahra," she says.

"Hi." Zahra waves to both mother and daughter.

Mrs. Jacobs takes a break from slicing and looks up at Zahra. "I'm making apple pie," she says. "Do you eat apple pie?"

They are always offering to feed Zahra, and she is always hesitant to accept anything more than their money lest she be deemed a charity case. But yes, she does love apple pie. "I do."

"Well, then, I'll have to send you home with a slice. Or you could eat it here, but you never want to eat here."

Sophia gives her mom the eye, as if she's the parent. In this scenario, Mrs. Jacobs is on thin ice. "How are your other sessions?" Sophia changes the subject.

Zahra looks from Sophia to Mrs. Jacobs, a little uncomfortable.

"Other sessions?" Mrs. Jacobs asks.

"I usually take on four or five clients in the fall." Not this fall. Things have been slow.

"Of course you do. We wouldn't dream of having you all to ourselves."

Zahra smiles awkwardly. Mrs. Jacobs's praise is always awkward, forced and sometimes patronizing.

"They're OK," Zahra says to answer Sophia's initial question.

"Is her application stronger than mine?" Sophia asks, and Mrs. Jacobs scoffs at the question but looks up anyway. *Well?* She wants to know.

"No, not better. Just different."

"It's OK if it's better," Sophia says. "Just means I need to work on mine. And I am. Working on mine."

"Good," Mrs. Jacobs says.

"What's her essay about?" Sophia grabs a sliced apple from Mrs. Jacobs's pile and looks at it carefully before eating.

Zahra considers if she should say. Shrugs. It's not like Sophia could steal the idea. It's not like it would work for her. "I guess it's about being Black and what she can live with and what she can't. It's about coping, about what it means to be 'all right.'" Zahra uses air quotes.

Sophia nods. "Sounds good. Sounds really good."

Mrs. Jacobs holds her knife in the air like she has something to add to the conversation but then goes back to cutting. The room is now stiflingly silent, and Zahra shifts in her seat, looks at her phone, smiles at Sophia. Sophia smiles back, but she looks sad.

"What school does she go to?" Mrs. Jacobs asks.

"Progress and Principles, I think," Zahra says.

Mrs. Jacobs laughs a little. "Well, OK."

"What?" Zahra asks.

"Just not sure I would send my Black daughter—if I had one—to that school."

"Jesus, Mom!" Sophia's disgust is on full display. "Your Black daughter? Do you think before you speak?"

Poor Sophia. Always the benefactor. She's too young and guileless to consider that her false protection is more uncomfortable to Zahra than her mother's remark. Sure, Mrs. Jacobs is patronizing and dismissive and a little obtuse, but at least she's a real person. At least she's standing here in front of Zahra cutting apples and reckoning with whatever she's thinking instead of hiding herself from the Black woman in her kitchen. At least Zahra knows who she's dealing with.

"What's wrong with Progress and Principles?" Zahra asks.

"It's always in the news."

"The news?"

"Yeah, the news, though that might be somewhat of an exaggeration. It was in the news recently, with the sit-in and all, but normally I guess it's just the talk of the . . . the private school parent circuit, not that I'm fully in it. One leg in and one leg out with Sophia here. But Phillip just started three-year-old class at Saint Anne's." Mrs. Jacobs laughs a little to herself, seems to escape the humor of her newly coined term to find Sophia shaking her head and Zahra staring at her.

Zahra is confused. "The sit-in made the news?"

"The *New York Times*. Of course it did."

"Of course . . . it did," Zahra repeats slowly, not knowing what to think.

Eventually, she turns to Sophia. "Well, maybe we should get started?"

<hr />

ZAHRA HAS HAD ENOUGH OF TREES. SOPHIA'S ESSAY EX-
hausts them, not to mention how they conjure up old memories of climbing, scattering up the old oak tree in the backyard with a nimbleness she knows her knees will no longer allow her. After the session ends, she puts on her headphones to try to tune out the past, but she's made the mistake of leaving her Tidal account on old 2000s music, not the R & B or hip-hop stuff that she recounts with Janie, but the white-girl anthems she learned well having gone to a school with so many of them.

Back when Derrick took to poetry and became increasingly contemplative, Zahra was caught between Janet Jackson and the Goo Goo Dolls, music turned down low so no one else had to know, not even Derrick, who almost strictly listened to A Tribe Called Quest at the time. It was around the same time that Zahra started dating Chase, who stuck to her hip like Michael Jackson's chimpanzee. Mary called it then, said the relationship was short-sighted and that Chase would end up breaking her heart, so when it happened, Zahra seethed at her, said she spoke it into existence with her hellish hoodoo, remembering that time in the basement, "'Cause you know I think there are spirits down there anyway."

A call interrupts her music, and Zahra pauses in front of the train's steps, feeling around for her phone and eventually finding it at the bottom of her bag under an old Terry McMillan paperback. She sees it's Mary calling and is hesitant to entertain the woman who has always chosen other things, people, places over her own children. Mary was all court cases and political networking, saving the disenfranchised and the folks who cold-called mad about some random injustice. She was all trips to DC, Selma, Birmingham, and, of course, the mystery places she told Zahra and Derrick they didn't need to know about. Mary missed all but one of Zahra's dance recitals. What was the point in rond de jambe–ing onstage if your own mother didn't care to watch? So Zahra quit when she turned twelve. Mary only asked her about school on the way home from church on Sundays, and even then, she wouldn't listen. Painful how long it took Zahra to realize that her mother didn't actually care. When Zahra walked across the stage at both graduations, high school and college, it was Gram who met her after with open arms.

Zahra answers the phone anyway. "Mary? Did you dial the right number?"

"Oh, Zahra, please. Not today." Her voice sounds weary, nothing like the proud and assertive voice Zahra is used to, no trace of a woman who's used to making speeches, who's used to hurtling her voice over crowds of leering men. Zahra doesn't know how to feel about this new voice.

"Well?" Zahra says.

"Did you book your flight already?"

"No, not yet."

People push her from behind, and Zahra takes the steps down quickly, then finds a corner out of the way, to the left of the teller's booth where a woman complains about her subway card.

She is barely listening when her mother says, "Well, you should do that soon."

"Right."

"At the end of the day, I know Derrick will be fine." Mary pauses, seems to wait for Zahra to say something, but in a sincere effort to stifle the conversation, Zahra keeps her mouth shut, lips pursed, and eventually, Mary goes on, "I'm not as worried as Gram, but . . ."

"Of course you're not." Zahra cannot help herself here.

"It's not that I love him any less."

"Mhmm."

"I don't know why I'm explaining myself to you."

"Me neither." Zahra presses her headphones in tighter.

"Maybe it's because I love you, and one of my children out in the wind makes me want to hold on to the other." This is unlike Mary, to be so sentimental.

Zahra pulls the phone out of her bag and checks the caller ID to confirm that, yes, this is the woman who birthed her. More caring than she's ever been.

Zahra almost falls for it. She comes to her senses and says, "I doubt that's it."

"You need some money?" Not that Mary has any.

"I'm straight."

"I think Uncle Richard's friend Jessa might have a buddy pass."

"No, thank you."

Her mother is silent now, all out of polite offerings, the sort of loose change you hand a homeless person, the empty condolences you proffer a coworker who has a funeral to attend. Zahra will not break the silence first.

"This isn't my fault," Mary says.

"Never said it was."

"You're acting like it."

Zahra knows that whatever she says next will only drag the conversation on, and more than anything else, she wants it to end. She is sick and tired of being angry with her mother, but each new day, phone call, or text message sprouts a new strain on their relationship. The tension is almost unbearable.

"Well, I'll see you soon," Mary says.

"Yep," Zahra says. It is the most of a goodbye that she can muster.

Now, as if her opinion has to vary from her mother's, Zahra is more worried than before. *I know Derrick will be fine*, Mary said. But what if he's not? What does she know?

||||||||||||||||||||||||||||||||||||||||||||||||||||

WHEN ZAHRA GETS TO SAMMIE'S HOUSE, THE STEAM-HEATED apartment feels tropical, like entering the rain forest, the ceiling New York's concrete canopy. Zahra breathes in deep to keep from suffocating, but the world feels like an airtight bubble, her brother locked out, floating soundlessly in outer space. Sammie notices her exhaustion right away and sends her to a chair like a worried parent.

"Have a seat," she says. "Let me get you something cold to drink."

Zahra fans herself, counting pictures on the wall. Ten, eleven, twelve. She's cooling down, at least on the outside. On the inside, she's one big knot, one of those detective corkboards where notes and photos are strung together with colorful thread.

"How's your essay?" Zahra manages to get out.

"Nope," Sammie says. "We're not talking about *me* when *you* look like . . . that."

Zahra takes a moment to collect herself, downing the glass of water that Sammie gave her in one long swallow. "It's just been a long day. Third job," she says, pointing down, here, Sammie the third and final stop.

Sammie nods, cracks open a Coke. "So what's up?" she says.

"Nothing."

"So we're just going to sit here in silence, then?"

It's a third-grade teacher tactic but not a bad one. Zahra doesn't know what to say, is all out of lies, having said enough of them to herself over the years. She knows there's a real issue, something that's not going to go away until she faces it head-on. It wouldn't kill her to tell Sammie, would it? Zahra thinks Sammie knows what she doesn't know she knows anyhow.

"My brother is missing, and I probably need to get back to Atlanta soon."

"I'm sorry to hear that."

Zahra nods. "It's nothing new. He's been this way for a while now."

"I'm sure it still hurts."

Zahra wonders where Sammie learned this, to be so gentle, so nurturing, motherly almost. How can a girl so young, barely past puberty, be so compassionate, so coddling? Nothing like Zahra's own mother, and just as self-assured as Gram.

"It does hurt," Zahra says, small tears collecting. She looks at the ceiling, where she finds a moth, lazy and still by the light.

"I'll go to Atlanta with you," Sammie says, beaming, impressed with herself for the idea.

"You have better things to do with your time." Like school. And college applications. And her own family. Plus, the moths are here too, doesn't she know?

"Like what?" Sammie asks. Jesus, she doesn't.

"Like finishing your college essay."

"That's why I should go with you. I need your help. Plus, I've barely been anywhere. It could be my senior-year trip," Sammie says, then mumbles, "All the white kids do it."

"Too expensive. And where would you stay?"

"With you. At Gram's house, couldn't I?"

She could, yes, in Zahra's old bedroom, still stuck in 2005, still peppered with her high school aesthetic and antics, the celebrities she crushed on, gingerly folded notes to friends and boyfriends inside the desk where she used to write them. Still . . .

"Too expensive," Zahra repeats.

"I could help find the flights. I'm really good at finding cheap ones. Mother Ma asked me to find the flights for when we go back to Trinidad for Christmas."

"I'm not sure I could even afford the cheapest flight right now."

Sammie clucks, looks down at her phone, starts typing furiously until Uncle Trey walks in.

"Hey," he says, warm, but it's clear that he's forgotten about Sammie's session.

"I have french fries," he says, holding up a paper bag nearly transparent with grease. "To help you study. I know you have that big science test coming up." He sets the bag in front of Sammie, and she rubs her hands together anticipatorily.

"Thanks, Uncle," she says.

"I would've brought you some, Zahra, but I forgot that you'd be here tonight. I'm sorry about that. I could run back out though. Grab you a bag?"

He raises his eyebrows like it's a good offer and Zahra should consider taking it. It's very sweet of him, but her stomach isn't as young as Sammie's, and she's been trying to eat better, and she's already nauseous with bad news.

"Thanks, but I'm OK. French fries as a study aid . . ." Zahra considers this, impressed with Uncle Trey's uncle skills. "If it works, it works."

"It works," Sammie says, covering her mouth stuffed with fries. "But I'm not studying or working on my college essay right now. I'm looking for flights. Cheap ones. We're going to Atlanta."

Zahra is taken aback by Sammie's confidence, in how she's wiggled her way in Zahra's world without a second thought. Sammie actually believes she's flying to Atlanta with her, and it occurs to Zahra that Sammie is not used to hearing *no*, is not on Sophia's level but privileged in her own right, in her youth. She started a sit-in, and it worked, and she does not know a time when it hasn't. If Zahra were to suggest probable failure, sure, Sammie would nod and act like she got it, but she still wouldn't. It takes life to become jaded by injustices, by barriers, by a savings account that doesn't have four zeroes.

"*We're* not going anywhere," Zahra says. "You should get back to your college essay."

Zahra expects Uncle Trey to ask what in the world they're talking about, but he doesn't. He only nods as if he agrees with her and leaves the room. She is a little sad to see him go.

She turns her attention to Sammie and sees an easy likeness to her brother, both beautiful bright-faced people, something urgent in their mannerisms. Sammie looks up from her phone and smiles when she catches Zahra staring at her. Zahra wants to smile back, but then she spots the moth, there again, on Sammie's shoulder, flapping its wings softly but going nowhere. She puts her head down on the table, capitulating.

"What?" Sammie says. "What's wrong?"

NINE 🦋

The next day, after school, Zahra's apartment feels false. Like walking through a movie set, Sammie gets the feeling that nothing in here actually belongs to Zahra. Not that there's all that much to go by—a futon, a mock-gilded mirror, a small TV on top of an old wooden trunk. It's an open plan, one where you walk into the living room and the kitchen at the same time.

"It's interesting," Sammie says, "seeing where you live."

Sammie's thirsty, but mostly, she's curious about what's in Zahra's fridge. Zahra can't possibly eat all that much, skinny as she is. Sammie knows she's skinny too, but Mother Ma says she'll round out with age, and Sammie can't imagine herself thirty years old and the same size she is now.

Just as she expected there are a few prepackaged salads and some old sushi. There's nothing good to drink either—no shandy, no sorrel, no soda.

"No wonder you look like that," Sammie says.

"Like what?"

"Like you're still waiting to grow hips." It's not something

Sammie would say to most adults, but Zahra is different, something like an older sister. And now that they've known each other for weeks, the relationship worn instead of tried on, Sammie has begun testing the waters. She wants to know her limits with Zahra. Can she talk to her like Leila? Can she ask her about sex? Can she tell her how tipsy she got at the senior lock-in? If a jay falls out of her backpack, will Zahra say something perverse like, *Sorry, but I can't keep this from your grandmother?* And most important, can Sammie ask Zahra about her brother's disappearance? She gave it a lot of thought the night before. Found it odd that the strange feeling of being watched, of her life on the brink of something, started right around the time she met Zahra.

"There's no point in grocery shopping when I'm heading out of town tomorrow night," Zahra says.

"True," Sammie relents. "How much was your flight?"

Zahra shakes her head. She must not want to talk about it, and Sammie doesn't blame her.

<hr />

ZAHRA HEADS TO THE BACK OF THE APARTMENT, AND SAMMIE follows her, running a finger along the white hallway that Mother Ma would've splayed with family photos, old plaques that displayed things like *Mother of the Year*, and kitschy wall decorations found on sale at Marshalls. In true Zahra fashion, her walls are bare.

"Not much of a decorator, huh?" Sammie asks.

"Apartments are temporary."

Sammie's not sure what Zahra means by that. She's lived in the same apartment with Mother Ma and Uncle Trey practically her whole life. Daday too, when he was still alive. Nothing temporary about that, but she guesses things are different for Zahra. She guesses temporary is what Zahra likes. No wonder they don't usually come here.

Zahra's room is as expected. A plush bed with a clean white comforter. Her computer atop a wooden nightstand, which, aside from her bed, is the only piece of real furniture. The walls are white and mostly blank, save for a textured painting of a Black woman dancing. The woman's head is down, showcasing wild hair made of black thread. The smallest wall, interrupted by her closet, is the only one with pinned photos, as if all of her memories need to be contained to this one sliver of space, as if letting them spill over might mean her completely losing herself in them. Sammie moves to check out the things that seem to haunt Zahra more than whatever it is she's constantly fighting the urge to say. One picture stands out.

"Who's he?" Sammie asks, pointing to a man with a short silver-speckled 'fro and warm crinkly eyes. He wraps an arm around a much younger Zahra, close to the age Sammie is now.

Zahra comes over to take a closer look. "Oh," she says. "That's my dad."

Sammie is surprised. Zahra makes special effort to complain about her mother. She hints at her brother's instability, and talks mountains of Gram. But a dad? She's never mentioned him, and Sammie sort of assumed that Zahra was like her. Dadless. She feels a sense of betrayal in their difference. Zahra with a corny-looking photo with her father and Sammie with very little proof that hers actually exists.

Sammie tries to correct this inconsistency. "But he's not still in your life? Did he die?"

Zahra looks confused. She sits on the bed. "No, he's still alive. What makes you think he'd be dead?"

"I don't know. You don't talk about him." Sammie feels stupid for saying it, for jumping to conclusions at all. Knowing someone takes more than a month or two. Sometimes it takes years. Sometimes you'll never know, like with her own parents. Sammie looks back at the photo of Zahra and her dad. She wonders how much they really know each other.

Eventually Sammie moves on to the next photo. Two boys. Cute boys. The boy on the right is unfamiliar, somewhat of a Broderick type, the smirk across his face a telltale sign that he's used to getting his way. The other boy could be Zahra's brother, Derrick. He looks pensive, almost worried. It's the first photo she's seen of him, and she's drawn to it.

Sammie grabs her stomach. That feeling of being watched comes and goes so quickly that she can barely separate her normal reality from the one that seems to be on display. Still, she feels it now, heavier than just seconds ago. Like a fist tightened in her belly; someone is closer than before. Since the conversation in Mother Ma's kitchen, Sammie hasn't talked about being watched. And now with Zahra's brother missing and all, Sammie chooses to keep it this way. She sits on the bed next to Zahra and leans back, looking up at the ceiling.

"You OK?" Zahra asks.

"Yeah. . . My stomach feels a little weird."

"Want something to eat?"

"Like you have anything." Sammie rolls over on her side, looking at Zahra. "Who are the boys in the photo, the one next to the picture of you and your dad?"

"Hmpf," Zahra says, looking around Sammie, past her, to the collage of photos. "That's Chase, my ex-boyfriend from high school, and my brother, Derrick. They were sixteen, seventeen at the time?"

"You barely decorate and your high school ex-boyfriend somehow makes the cut?" Sammie can tell that Zahra loves hard. She's seen the way Zahra and Uncle Trey look at each other too, but she's kept quiet about it. So far. Chase could be a good segue though.

"It's not him, but the times, maybe," Zahra says. "That's when my brother was different. He was more himself. Now it's like he's a million different people."

Sammie realizes she was mistaken. Maybe Zahra never loved Chase at all, because even back then, she was too invested in her brother. Sammie wonders what's up with him. If he's got some sort of illness like a rare case of cancer or something more common like sickle cell. Could be something psychological like bipolar disorder. She knows the Black male suicide statistics, and everyone's got a drunk cousin who sways when they speak, someone the ground could come out from at any moment but they teeter along, tipsy tightrope walkers. Maybe Derrick is *that* guy, hanging on by a toe.

"Hmmm," Sammie says, weighing the options.

"It's hard to explain." Zahra reaches for her bag, takes out her laptop. It's obvious she's done with the conversation. "Are we going to write today?" she asks.

Sammie's nausea has dissipated, but she's still not in the mood to work. She doesn't want to self-reflect, and it's been like this for some time now. She hasn't written more than three sentences since her first meeting with Zahra. It's much more fun to process Zahra's world. "I don't know. Do we have to?"

"That's kind of what I'm here for."

Sammie is hurt. "I thought we were friends."

"You're like fifteen years younger than me."

"So?" Sammie kicks off her shoes and throws her feet up, on her back again. She puts her hands behind her head, relaxed, staring at the white ceiling. "Did you always know you wanted to be a collegiate preparatory coach?" she asks. It's an odd profession, not the sort of life career most would envision for themselves.

"I didn't even know there was money in it."

"Is there?"

"Not much."

"So what do you want to do?"

Zahra shrugs. "Guess I should ask you the same thing."

"I'm too young to know yet." The sit-in felt good, but she doesn't necessarily see herself on the front lines of protests, as an around-the-clock activist. She was so mad, at the administration, at all the teachers who never took a stand, at the boys who thought they could say anything and get away with it. But also, she admits thinking of Noah just as much as the plight. Three days in a row with him. Students left in waves, some after the first day and others mid second, but a group of them, thirty or forty, weren't budging. And it was something special seeing Noah's Jordans across from her. Now she wonders if what Uncle calls puppy love might distract her from what Mother Ma calls her higher purpose.

Zahra laughs. "Well, so am I. Too young to know what I want."

"I think you want something completely different. I think you want everything and nothing at all," Sammie says.

"You know what you didn't know you knew," Zahra says, and this tickles Sammie. Her own expression used in her own regard. She thinks about what she knows she knows, and the list is not long but particular. She knows how to make fried bake and super-spicy chow, how to fold clothes into perfect squares just like Mother Ma taught her. She knows how to change a word problem into a mathematical equation, and that it's estimated that 99 percent of all species on Earth are extinct. She knows what it's like to kiss a boy she didn't really like in the first place, ninth grade, Tylik from around the way, slimy lips that slid from between hers like lukewarm Jell-O. She and Leila laughed about it afterward.

But so much of Sammie's knowledge has come from P & P, numerous classes with titles she can only half remember, lessons on quantum physics or college-level calculus or the humanities from regions she'd barely been able to match with language. But then there are the more important lessons, in the form of memories, like her first P & P party, where Jared Henderson lifted his shirt and his chest was burned red from summertime Santorini, his nipples as pink as a Paper Mate eraser. He'd said, "I bet Jerome doesn't have tits like these." Jerome was one of the few Black guys at the party. He'd barely said two words to Sammie and Sammie even less back. He'd seemed antsy around her, unsure of himself, so now that Jared was intermixing them in this way, Sammie was confused.

For a while now, Sammie has been hatching a plan, or at least on the precipice of one, like a girl with one foot off the roof of a high-rise. She feels the urge to do something bold, wild, careless. Not only because it is the white boy rite of passage, but because her time at P & P has been frustratingly translucent, and she'd like to put her seal on something more than the yearbook. She looks at the photos on Zahra's wall again, and feels the way in which time can be cemented. Snap—time interrupts 1965 and Malcolm X is still alive. Snap—her mother has just become a mother, without time to shirk the title. Snap—the moment is there forever, and there's nothing anyone can do about it. If she free-falls, she could land on her face, but of course, there's also the off chance that she'll end up flying.

Zahra's stomach growls, and the thought of food comes to Sammie like a revelation. "We should order pizza."

Sammie wants to add that they should have a slumber party but knows Zahra will only say she's too old for that sort of thing, and in reality, maybe Sammie is too. But when the pizza arrives, and they eat it straight from the box, scooping fallen cheese and missed pepperoni with their fingers while laughing at TikTok videos and listening to Sza, it kind of feels like a slumber party. It's warm and cozy here, no matter if Sammie keeps looking at that teenage photo of Derrick on the wall as if his eyes are following her, or hiding something like Mona Lisa's smile. This room is one of her favorite places. Maybe Zahra is one of her favorite people. Maybe this is what it's like to have a mom, so it's ironic when Zahra says, "I have a question for you."

"OK."

"Where are your parents?" Zahra asks.

"Oh." Sammie tries not to be flustered. It's not like she exactly minds talking about her parents; there's just not that much to say. "Well, they're in Trinidad."

"And you're here. Why is that?"

"America is the land of the free, isn't it?" Sammie doesn't really believe this and knows Zahra doesn't either, but it does explain a not so simple story fairly simply. "I'm here for the 'opportunities.'"

She's here because her mom, Mother Ma's oldest child, was nineteen when Mother Ma and Daday moved to New York. Mom was the only one who didn't get a visa. By the time Mom's came through, she was engaged and settled to a man who had a good job at the quarry. Then pop, wow, surprise, they had Sammie, and sent her to America four years later when her dad was laid off by the ministry of works, the town of Sangre Grande. It was the only thing to do, they said. It was the *right* thing to do.

"And they didn't . . ."

"Get their own visas, no, but I'm not sure they tried that hard. My mother is an artist, and the ocean is her muse." Sammie rolls her eyes even though their artistry is their strongest mother-daughter bond. It's all Sammie knows about her. Their conversations are stiff, stiffer as she's gotten older. Sammie has wanted to tell her about Noah, to ask for advice, to show her mom her drawings of Mother Ma dog-earing her Bible and Uncle Trey brushing his teeth and her great-aunt Deanne in one of her yoga poses, but to Sammie it seems that her mother is always anxious to get off the phone, and ultimately, it is easier to act like they have a relationship than to actually formulate one.

"I understand mothers who don't try that hard," Zahra says, and Sammie sees her in a new light. It's obvious now; the two of them, her and Zahra, they're of the same cloth. "What about your dad? What's he like?"

"Worse. He's mad, all of the time. I can hear it in his voice, even though he tries to cover it up. I can't mention Mother Ma or Uncle Trey or Aunty Deanne around him. He's got something against them; I just don't know what it is."

"Maybe he's just mad that they get to see you and he doesn't."

"Maybe," Sammie says, but she doesn't buy it. It's not like he couldn't come visit. The few times her mom has come, it's been alone with some sad excuse about him. He had to work or he hasn't been feeling well enough to travel. On the phone, her dad asks her how she's doing and if she's getting good grades, and hasn't she had enough of that New York pollution, but it's clear he doesn't want to get to know her, not really. And to be honest, she doesn't really care. To be honest, she doesn't want to get to know him either. Kitchen whispers and closeted voices have swayed her; he's manipulative, ignorant, *abusive*—the word that stands out in her mind like a cactus, one she never touches. Plus she has a mother in Mother Ma, and she practically has a dad in Uncle Trey, though he sometimes feels more like a brother. So, so what about biology? It doesn't matter at all.

Like any ordinary (almost) slumber party, Uncle is here too soon to pick her up, and she sulks when she sees his text message, a simple *I'm here.*

"He's here," she repeats to Zahra.

"Who?"

"Uncle Trey."

Zahra nods, raises her eyebrows.

"Walk me out?" Sammie asks.

"I'm so lazy," Zahra says. "And full."

"Oh c'mon, Zahra. Walk me out," Sammie repeats. "You know you want to see him."

For a split second, Zahra reminds Sammie of Leila. It's as if Sammie has taken a picture of Zahra's teenage self and implanted it into this moment. She throws her head back laughing. It's all so wild, what's here and what's just been here. What's to come. Her hands, her arms, her feet tingle all over, and she's laughing so hard she damn near spits out the last sip of her water when Zahra says, "Knock yourself out, why don't you?"

TEN

Trey blends in well with the neighborhood, which is still in full throttle. Pockets of conversation everywhere. Men circled around a game of cee-lo, the smell of sour a persistent player. He sits on top of his car; he looks comfortable waiting for Sammie, like it's something he does often.

Trey's beard is as full as the night he dropped her off at Kahlil's house, but his lineup is crisp, sharp. He wears a puffer coat on top, zipped all the way. Nike sweats on bottom, scrunched up so you can see his black-and-white tie-dye socks with prayer hands on them. His white Air Forces are just as fresh, sparkly clean. It is hard to push down her attraction when he calls Zahra's name, and she faces him dead-on.

The feeling reminds her of when she used to meet Derrick on his lunch breaks at Foot Locker, eating Chick-fil-A or slices of pizza from Sbarro, and his coworker JJ would stop by their table at the food court and grab one of her waffle fries. JJ would smile that eighteen-year-old, two years older than her, smile of his. And in his black-and-white-striped referee's uniform, his light-skin curls cut

short, just a centimeter or so of hair, he always made Zahra feel like
a child. He'd pull the lobe of her ear or ask her, "What's going on in
the world, Zahra?" He'd say, "You look like someone with answers."
She never knew what to do with his flirting, which felt very real on
some days and flippant, almost robotic on others. So when Derrick
quit Foot Locker to work at Taco Mac, where he didn't have to buy
his lunch but could sneak hot wings or nachos from the kitchen,
Zahra never saw JJ again.

Now, the feeling returns. Of liking someone for no reason at all,
for something she can't quite put her finger on. Of being messed
with, of being looked at in a way that makes her feel more womanly
than Khalil ever could, so she is hyper aware of her body, breasts
squashed under her leather jacket, a shadow of her mother's hips, the
punch line of Sammie's jokes, smaller than the average but large
enough to curve her denim. Zahra licks her lips, aware that the cold
has dried them, and she hasn't reapplied lip gloss since before Sammie came over. Trey hops off the car and opens the passenger door
for Sammie. She gets in, and he shuts the door behind her, turns to
Zahra.

"Hi, Uncle Trey," Zahra says, then regrets prefacing his name
with *uncle*. She sounds like a child. "Sorry, I meant Trey. Just . . .
Trey. How are you?"

He looks at his cuticles as if he'll find a response there. He leans
against the car, hides Sammie's silhouette in the window. "OK. But
I should really be asking you. Heard about your brother and all."

Zahra puts two and two together. "Sammie told you."

He nods.

"There's not much to say about it," she says. "I'm flying down
tomorrow night."

"About that," he says. "I can help."

"With what?"

He blows on his hands before using the right one to knock on the car. "Let me take you to Atlanta. It's the least I could do."

"Are you crazy?" He must be. He wants to drive all the way from New York to Atlanta? That's got to be a bajillion hours or something. The thought of being in the car with him for that long, just the two of them . . . She remembers the smell of his car from riding in it nearly a month ago. Cinnamon apple. It's warming up outside, and she unzips her jacket.

"It'll be better, easier, to go down with people who care about you."

The word *care* feels odd coming from him. Maybe she just didn't realize that he did—care. "Right," is all she says.

"And Sammie wants to visit Spelman. It makes sense to go down there now."

She remembers Sammie, a buffer. Of course it wouldn't be just the two of them. Of course Sammie would be there. "Right," Zahra says again, pushing off her hood and fluffing her Afro self-consciously.

"And you could probably get your money back for the plane ticket, assuming it's been less than twenty-four hours since you booked."

"Right," Zahra says for a third time, wishing for more words but coming up short.

"So?"

She considers it. "No." She shakes her head, and the night quiets around them.

They stand at an impasse until Trey crosses his arms and says, "Look, I don't like handouts. Wasn't raised that way. You scratch my back; I scratch yours. It's a little fucked up to think you're too good for my help."

He says it so calmly, so politely, that she almost doesn't catch that it's an insult. Still, she's stuck—it's not his job to take her all the way to Atlanta.

"Sorry about cursing," he adds, an afterthought.

When she's still silent, biting the side of her cheek like mad, he says, "You should take the ride."

Zahra doesn't like men telling her what to do, but Trey has said it with so much compassion that she wants to cave. She would pay him, of course. Gas money, tolls. They could all stay with Gram. Things would be tight, but they could make it work. "Thinking we should leave early tomorrow morning," he says.

She nods. "But Sammie has school, doesn't she?"

"She can miss it. This is important." Yeah, it is, and she doesn't need Uncle Trey reminding her. She hates all the pushing. She doesn't need help understanding the seriousness of the situation, but it's not like she's a detective, and as close as she is, or at least *was*, to her brother, it's not like they've got telepathy or even the intuition of twins. Still, she doesn't scold Trey for his word choice, not considering all he's doing for her.

"Four thirty?" he asks.

She rubs her eyes slowly, lands in the crease with them closed. When she looks at Trey again, her fingers are still pinching her nose, and the way they interrupt his face makes it much easier for her to focus.

"I'll be ready," she says.

October 2019, on the way to Atlanta,
early Friday morning

Zahra couldn't have imagined heading to Atlanta with someone who was just a nosy Uber driver to her a month ago, but here she is, more comfortable with this family than her own, the smell of cinnamon apple a new favorite. She's present in this moment, but also nostalgic, reflective, thinking of how the boxes Gram keeps under her bed are always dusty, the lids half ripped apart so Zahra questions their function. The pictures inside the boxes are endless, many of them of Gram herself, in a crop top or a bathing suit, short shorts and heels, one hand behind her head and the other at her hip. Not much has changed there, Gram still a Betty Boop but older.

Last time Zahra went home, she pulled some of the pictures apart, sticky from someone's fingers a long time ago, or maybe that's just what happens with photos after a while, they morph together like memories. She put the photos that caught her eye to the side, and when she was all done going through the countless boxes, different rectangular shapes, different sizes, she used her phone to take pictures of the pictures, angling the camera just right so it minimized the glare.

Now, Zahra, Trey, and Sammie are leaving New York, and it is dark out, and Zahra is scrolling through those photos, remembering the people she's been inactively missing. First, there's Gram and her five siblings, still young, Zahra's age maybe, all healthy and standing in someone's manicured yard in the sixties, trends of the time, a rare photo, Gram having lost all of her siblings like dominoes thereafter. Then there's a shot of Gram holding a two-year-old Derrick on Uncle Richard's porch swing, and a shot of Zahra and Derrick in their favorite tree, waving to the camera, Zahra sporting braided pigtails and Derrick in an And One T-shirt. There's a photo of Dad and Uncle Richard playing cards, beers on the table in front of them, Dad leaning far back in his chair laughing wildly. And now she almost scrolls past Mary holding her hand at the AIDS Walk. They went every year for five years after Mary's best friend, Aunty Charisse, died of it, but this photo gives Zahra pause. Her hand looks so comfortable in her mother's. She grips it tightly, as if the crowd will consume her if she lets go. She doesn't remember ever holding

Mary's hand in this way. Zahra closes her phone, and, eventually, her eyes.

Somehow Zahra has lost her favorite person in the entire world. Of the most cool variety, Derrick has always been easy like Sunday morning. A good boy, she remembers them calling him, first Mrs. Sellers, their first-grade teacher, then Mr. Nichols and Ms. Peterson, second and third. And, of course, it was true, he was good, he was a boy, but something about the two words strung together was unfitting. Like it wasn't Derrick at all. It was around that time Derrick started doing "bad" things, cursing under his breath and stealing shit he didn't even want in the first place. He outgrew the act but only after Gram spanked him enough, with thin branches she'd pulled from a tree in their front yard and then, loosening up over time, a leather belt one of her beaus left behind. And though Derrick taught Zahra how to be cool, he also taught her how to fight—*Square up*, he'd say, and *If they hit you, hit them harder*, Dad's words flowing from Derrick's mouth like a leaky pipe.

Zahra opens her eyes, looks out the window, and far off, in the distance, she can see the city fall away, piece by piece, the Manhattan skyline. The Hudson, the bridges, the buildings like a force field. All behind her now. The earth widens, and she exhales. She's on her way home, and she is small again. She is not a collegiate preparatory coach or a disgruntled server at Common House, not a Stanford graduate or a DC transplant. Not even a woman yet. She is a sister. Derrick's little sister. That's what people call her at school. Teachers lean down low as if to smell her but only smile, taking her in, sizing her up.

"Your brother is such a sweet boy," they say. "His favorite subject was social studies. What's yours?"

English, she might think. *English*, she might say. And they would squint to figure out how this difference distinguished her from

Derrick. Better or worse, smarter or less so? It occurs to Zahra now how similar she and Derrick were then. In personality, yeah, sure, there was some variance, but she and him were of the same species, inseparable unless they were on that tree in the backyard, legs dangling in the wind like loose ivy, in which case, their separation only brought them closer.

ELEVEN 🦋

Sammie can imagine being like Zahra when she grows up but not so bony, so fragile. The women in her family are made of meat and movement. They don't sit down often but sashay hips made for dancing between people who need them and people who don't deserve them. Their lives are on loan, but they're not unhappy. They're Mother Ma and Aunty Deanne and Aunt Liz back in Trinidad, and she can imagine being like them but then not at all.

Zahra is asleep in the back seat; her neck cranes in a way that allows her head to rest against the window, and her knees are curled into the fetal position. She looks uncomfortable, but she's definitely knocked out, so Sammie jumps at the opportunity to talk to Uncle Trey. He has one hand on the wheel, top center, and the other drums his knee. He's listening to Leon Bridges. *They're* listening to Leon Bridges, and Sammie doesn't mind it, but then, she also has something to say.

"You like her, don't you?" Sammie asks.

Uncle Trey's eyes dart to Sammie, then back on the road, quick, like window wipers. He doesn't answer, and Sammie thinks to drop it but then remembers eighth grade, Shawn Tucker, how Uncle Trey drilled it out of her, she was different, yes, she'd kissed a boy, yes. Even let him touch her tit, the left one, she didn't tell Uncle Trey that part. It was enough that she'd admitted liking Shawn, really liking him, so much, so embarrassingly much that she'd cried when she told Uncle Trey, had felt so outside of herself, outside of control, giddy but uncomfortable. All the emotions had rolled together and watered her eyes.

"I tell you everything." Sammie nudges Uncle Trey.

"Everything?" He cuts his eyes at her.

"A lot of things. I would tell you something like this. You're thirty-five years old, Uncle. You shouldn't be shy about liking a woman. And she's beautiful." Sammie turns around in her seat to look at Zahra, sees her 'fro, a twist-out, Sammie guesses. It's wild and distorted, parted by the window. Zahra's brown skin is so perfect, so dimple- and pimple-free. Beautifully plain. Her eyes are closed, but Sammie knows them by now, deep set and piercing. Not the eyes that boys at her school call pretty, not green or hazel, but the darkest brown Sammie can imagine, a labyrinth to lose yourself in. Sammie faces Uncle Trey instead of staring down the interstate, puts her hand on his shoulder, and grips it tightly.

"It's OK to like a woman, and it's especially OK to like a smart, funny, beautiful woman."

Uncle Trey laughs. "Well, if you already know the answer, why do you keep asking the question?"

Sammie takes this as confirmation and claps her hands. "OK. I have a plan."

"Whoa, whoa, whoa." Uncle Trey cuts her off. He looks through the rearview window and whispers, "I'm not a high schooler. I don't need . . . a plan."

"So you're just going to . . ."

"Let it flow."

"Let it flow?"

"Yep. I've got this under control. You just focus on things that seventeen-year-olds should be focused on. School and . . . school and the future, society and the environment. Shit like that. The bigger picture. When you get older, you start to see smaller, so look at all the big shit while you still can."

"You're treating me like a kid."

"Because you are one."

Sammie scoffs.

"And I love you. Just don't grow up too fast. You have all the time in the world."

Sammie hates it when people say that. As if they weren't her age once and old as shit now, not that Uncle Trey is *old* old, but Jesus, she wouldn't call him young either. She wonders what he was like when he was her age. When he was seventeen, he'd just moved from Trinidad three years before. He doesn't talk about it often, but when he does, he says American kids made fun of him at first. He didn't have the right name brands, the right Nike sneakers, didn't wear his jeans the right way. He had to get used to the smell, the unearthed scent of New York, of everything but land and water. Sammie wonders how long it took her uncle to lose his accent, something he puts on and takes off like costume jewelry now, on with Mother Ma and off with her. On with Aunty Deanne but off with the women he sneaks in and out of the apartment at odd hours. She never hears them do anything more than talk but knows that can't be it. She's seen these women do their lazy, leisure walks of shame. She wants to know them but then doesn't want to know them at all. Uncle Trey is like a father to her, but these women are nothing like the little she knows of her mother.

Still, there are all sorts of them—Black women, white women,

Asian, East and West. She knows, from an overheard phone call, he likes women like Rashida Jones, the actress. She cringes thinking of Rashida's J.Crew appeal, not at all like the Trini women she's grown up admiring. Women who wear bright colors, peacock feathers, who aren't afraid to show stomachs that are rich with love handles and whine shea butter–smooth asses at carnival. Aunty Deanne took her to carnival a year ago, and Sammie yearned to grow into one of those women, sensual and divine. She would be one of those women soon, in college maybe, sometimes she feels herself tingling into one of those women now. Maybe if she wishes hard enough she will be more Trini than American, though it doesn't feel like that most days. Most days she feels largely disconnected from the islands, but Leila, who has two African American parents once said, *Trust me, you couldn't be Black like me if you lived here for a million years, wouldn't matter if you were born here either.* She said that Sammie had a connection to a place outside of Harlem, outside of New York, outside of the United States, and that made her *different*.

But going to P & P that first year, her freshman year, she didn't feel any different. The Black jokes didn't land any lighter on her, she didn't have a cool Trini accent to use, and people didn't call her exotic, not that she'd wanted them to. But maybe she did. Want them to call her exotic. Now that she's a senior, she's become well-liked, popular even. Fashionable to the white girls, and down to earth to the Black. She's heard some of the white boys say that if they dated a Black girl, it would be her. And the Black boys—they respect if not love her, though it doesn't always feel that way. It doesn't always feel that way when they don't have your back, when they hear something racist or rude and fall silent, when they date the exotic girls first and flirt with the white girls second and call you their sister last. It isn't all of them though. Kenny Sampson likes her, admitted it in front of everyone in their class. She doesn't like him back, though she feels like she's supposed to. Because what kind of person does it make her when she feels some sort of way about who the Black boys date but then when one of them finally likes her, she doesn't like him back? She wouldn't date Kenny if someone paid her to.

The truth is, Sammie usually likes Black boys, neighborhood boys, not the ones who go to P & P with her. She likes the boys who go to public school, who hoop and hang on the weekends, who call her *Prep School* whenever they catch sight of her, buying a slice from Patsy's or down 125th, window-shopping at American Eagle or Victoria's Secret with Leila. She likes the boys whose sentences are lyrical, whose laughter is loud and raucous and demanding of everyone around them. She likes Trini boys and Senegalese boys and *Harlem* boys. Boys who can equally talk politics and Swae Lee poetry. *Usually*, they're her type. *Usually*, they're the ones she daydreams about.

Sammie bites her lip, not daring to think about Noah, pasty, polite Noah. He is somewhat similar to the boys around the way in his self-confidence, in how he doesn't try too hard to be what he is. He is not like some of the white boys at P & P who attempt to shirk their own skin and wear hip-hop instead. He is just himself, and he is just . . . so easy to talk to whenever they finally get to talking. Sammie shuts herself up. She's not sure if Noah would like a girl . . . like her. Still, he is an anomaly, and she's drawn to that.

It's not often she thinks of Mother Ma as a much younger woman, a girl even, but every now and then she finds herself thinking about what made Daday love her so much. Sure, Sammie's seen younger pictures of Mother Ma smiling in that infectious way of hers, the small gap between her two front teeth gleaming but not overshadowing her full lips and long lashes. Her hair plaited down the middle, so two braids just reached the peak of her shoulders. Daday was so gentle with Mother Ma; Sammie would watch him unbraid her hair or massage her feet or grab her elbow to take the easiest flight of stairs, though he himself was knock-kneed and less easy on his feet.

Daday wasn't a soft man by nature, not if you let Uncle explain it. To Uncle, his daddy was an ass-whooping man with conversation that mostly amounted to delegated work. *Take out the trash*; *grab that lug wrench—we gotta change out the tires*; *clean the bathroom—make sure to get the grout in between them tiles, and get it good*. Even to Daday's sister, Aunty Deanne, he wasn't a man of words, but Sammie realized early that he didn't need them to say a whole lot. Like when she drew a picture of him in first grade and wrapped it for his Christmas present. He'd opened it, then looked up at her with searching, intense eyes and said, "Hmmpf." Or when she used to play basketball for the Harlem Jets and Daday would sit in the stands stoic, almost sad-faced until she would go running up to him after a win, and he would laugh and laugh at her excitement.

"Well, all right," he'd say.

Daday's been dead for six years now, and it seems cruel that she should be mother- and fatherless, and then lose one of her surrogates. Sammie sighs, leaning all of her thoughts into the headrest.

⸻⸻⸻⸻⸻⸻

KENDRICK LAMAR COMES ON, AND SAMMIE TURNS UP THE music, then curses underneath her breath. "Oh shit, I forgot Zahra is sleeping back there. She's so quiet."

Sammie turns down the music, lower than it was before. Whenever Uncle Trey used to drive her around the city he would say that the stereo was his. His car, his rules, his tunes. She was just along for the ride. She would reach out to touch the dial, and he would playfully pop her hand, saying, "Don't lose a finger." Eventually, he would cave and she'd get to put on Ed Sheeran or Ariana Grande or whatever junk she was listening to at the time, stuff she is too cool to play now that her and Uncle Trey are on the same vibe and agree on more conscious artists like Kendrick and Chance, Noname and Smino.

"I guess you're the one who inspired my essay, Uncle Trey?" Sammie says while Uncle Trey nods, reciting every other word to "Money Trees."

"Oh, really?" he asks.

"Yeah. Remember when I used to ride Uber with you, shotgun? All you played was that Kendrick album, the one with 'King Kunta' and 'Alright' on it? I'd look out the window and see the addicts on Lexington or the projects on First, and I didn't really get it then, but maybe I did in a way I just couldn't fully comprehend. Because we'd get back home, after seeing and thinking about all that, back home to Mother Ma, and I'd smell stew chicken and rice and peas cooking, and I knew what Kendrick meant."

"Well, look at you. It didn't have anything to do with me after all. Just you being you, all smart and shit."

Sammie takes the compliment. "Thanks, Unc." She's silent for a while before adding, "But I had to get it from somewhere, and it sure wasn't your sister."

"Don't talk about your mom like that."

"I didn't—"

"There are things you're still too young to understand." This is what they always say when there is no real reason, when they don't have any way of backing up what they've said. Uncle, Aunty Deanne, Mother Ma. It's infuriating, but Sammie knows better than to argue it. She crosses her arms and pulls away from Uncle when he playfully throws a peppermint her way.

It seems like Uncle is about to say something, when Zahra starts mumbling, and Sammie turns around to see who she's talking to, what she's talking about, but Zahra's eyes are still closed, and she's in the same ungraceful sleeping position she was in thirty minutes ago.

"Is she talking in her sleep?" Sammie asks.

"Probably. There have been stranger things."

"Sounded like she was saying something about . . ."

"It's not polite to listen to someone when they're talking—"

"Shh," Sammie says, her finger to her lips, straining to hear what Zahra is saying again, even though she can see Uncle Trey shaking his head in the corner of her eye.

"I think she's talking to, or maybe about, her brother. I think she's really sad, Uncle."

"Well," Uncle Trey says, sipping his coffee. "She wouldn't be the first person to feel that way." And there it is. Another moment where Uncle Trey says something that makes Sammie see outside of who he's always been to her, outside of the uncle who picks her up from school blasting Bunji or leaves peppermint surprises in her backpack, the uncle who's lost to her in every game of HORSE they've played over the last two years. There is something beneath the man she knows, and it's as if she's holding her hands over her eyes not to see it.

‖‖‖‖‖‖‖‖‖‖‖‖‖‖‖‖‖‖‖‖‖‖‖‖‖‖‖‖‖‖‖‖‖

SAMMIE GOOGLES HOW FAR AWAY THEY ARE. STILL NINE hours, but she likes it here in Uncle Trey's car riding the breeze. She likes thinking on the road, far away from the world. They are a traveling microcosm, and Sammie is warm and complacent, not at all down on herself, not at all questioning. She is anxious, but in a good way. She has never been to Atlanta before and is looking forward to seeing the southern city, to seeing any southern city, as she's never been farther south (in the States) than Washington, DC. She doesn't know much about Atlanta other than its hub for rap music and what she's seen on *Real Housewives of Atlanta*, but she imagines that everyone has a country accent and knows how to twerk. Zahra doesn't seem like she's from Atlanta at all. She doesn't seem, well, gritty enough, though Sammie's sure there's plenty to hide. Sammie remembers that first day at the coffee shop, when Zahra pretty much called her fucked up in the head. It stung, sure, but Zahra was sorry after she said it, and the words had seemed lazy and projective. Still, Sammie wonders why this sleeping, sad woman is in the back seat of Uncle Trey's car right now. She remembers Zahra saying, *It's not like your family is paying me anyway.* So what's she getting in working on Sammie's college essay with her?

〰〰〰〰〰〰〰〰〰〰〰〰〰〰〰

WHEN THEY STOP FOR MCDONALD'S, THEY ARE STILL SEVEN hours out, and getting back in the car, Uncle Trey asks Zahra if she wants to sit in the front seat. Sammie sees the glint in his eye and knows that this is his sad attempt at flirting. She opens the back door before these two have the time to make things awkward.

"Or I could drive. You have to be tired," Zahra says.

He holds up a large iced coffee. "My second wind," he says, then, "just need some company, that's all." He opens the door, getting comfortable behind the wheel quickly before Zahra can protest, and she is the last in the car.

They eat like a family, in fairly quiet but efficient unison. *Pass this, was there any more of that? Is there a trash bag? Let's use this one.* Sammie watches Zahra salt her cheeseburger, something she's never seen before. Then she watches Zahra dump her fries into a bag and shake them with salt. She wonders about Zahra's blood pressure. God, is this what people do in the South? On the other side of the console, Uncle Trey, not much better, is wolfing down a Big Mac with one hand, special sauce dripping from both ends, onto his fingers, which he eventually licks clean. The two are made for each other. Sammie finishes her chicken nuggets and stretches out for a nap, turning away from the front seat and curling into the back, her forehead pressed into the crease. She is almost asleep when she hears Zahra say, "Thanks for doing this. For driving me. It's so . . . selfless of you. Are you always so selfless?"

Sammie listens intently, wondering if Uncle Trey will lie. He is not a selfless man, not in the least bit, though she's constantly impressed by his random acts of kindness. Coming home to a fresh set of graphite sketch pencils, watching him help Mother Ma shuck corn or iron her church clothes unprompted. Uncle Trey drove Sammie all over the city to look for a dress for the school dance, something cheap that would hold up against the rich girls' outfits.

"No, I'm not," Uncle Trey admits. "But, then, is anyone really?"

"Guess not."

"It's nice to get away. I've never been to Atlanta. Sammie's never been to Atlanta, and it's good for her to go check Spelman out."

"Of course."

Shit, Uncle Trey. What a bubble buster. Sammie wishes that he would be honest for five minutes and tell Zahra that he's doing this for her. Sammie overheard him talking to one of his friends about Zahra; she believes the words he used were *pretty* and *magnetic*. It's all for Zahra; Sammie knows her uncle well enough. He's a hardcore romantic, disgustingly so. Sure he's "dated" (for the lack of a more crass word) lots of women, but when he really likes one, it's discomforting and nauseating. And it's only then that he says stupid stuff like—*Sammie's never been to Atlanta, and it's good for her to go check Spelman out.*

Like, WTF is he thinking? Sammie thinks.

"You also said you needed some company. Have things changed

in the last five minutes?" Zahra asks, and Sammie thinks she's good. If anyone is going to get Uncle to open up, it will be her.

Uncle Trey laughs his awkward laugh, not the one he uses at home, deep and throaty, but a laugh that comes from his chest instead of his gut. "Nothing's changed," he says. "So umm . . . How do you feel about going back home? Are you looking forward to it?"

"I'm looking forward to seeing Gram and finding my brother. But with the good, comes the . . ."

"Bad?"

Sammie listens for Zahra's answer.

"No, not the bad. It's not that simple."

"The questionable?"

"Yeah, maybe."

"The forgotten?"

"Yeah, some of that."

"The impenetrable?"

Zahra sucks in, and Sammie knows Uncle Trey has hit the nail on the head.

"What are you?" Zahra asks. "A mind reader?"

Sammie can tell Zahra is smiling.

"No, but I like words. Words and colors. Two of my favorite things."

"I've never heard anyone say anything like that before, but I think you would get along well with my brother. He's weird like that."

"Ouch."

"No, I meant it as a compliment."

Of course she did, Sammie thinks.

"Of course you did," Uncle Trey says.

Sammie starts to laugh out loud, and it's too late to hold it in. She can tell she's been caught eavesdropping. They're both silent now. She can feel Uncle Trey looking through the rearview mirror and hear Zahra's slight twist to look at her in the back seat, and she knows she's ruining everything. She has a solution though, to their privacy concern. Without turning around to face Uncle and Zahra, Sammie reaches for her headphones and puts on some Marvin Gaye. She's grown to love oldies. Uncle Trey plays them on Sunday mornings, a bacon ritual.

When a love song comes on, she will not allow herself to day-dream about Noah, not while listening to R & B. It doesn't feel right, but eventually her brain, or is it her loins, has its way with her, and she goes to sleep with "Sexual Healing" on repeat and Noah's pasty perfect face saying, *Look, we listen to the same music. Look, we eat the same snacks. Look, we like the same books. You watch* Stranger Things *too? Of course you do. Of course you do.* Of course she does.

In a lucid dream something lands on Sammie's face. A moth maybe? It feels good at first but then quickly becomes an itch, an annoyance, a bother. She flicks it away and wills herself to wake up, but the sleep is too deep.

|||||||||||||||||||||||||||||||||||||||||||||||

WHEN SAMMIE FINALLY OPENS HER EYES, IT IS FROM THE car's abrupt stop and not of her own volition.

"Sorry," Zahra says. "Haven't driven in a while, but it's coming back. Trust me. It's pretty much all we do in Atlanta."

Sammie is more confused by the seat change. When did they stop? Why didn't they wake her? Does she have to pee?

"How far away are we?" Sammie asks.

"Four, five hours. Passing through Charlotte."

Sammie looks out of the window to see that the sky has opened up and even though it's fall, the earth is all green grass and trees with exploding foliage. Sammie thinks this is a place where you can stretch yourself, where you can lie down and not be afraid of getting hit by a car, where you can spread your arms out and reach and reach and still not touch anything or anybody, nothing but nature. The earth is flat here, and she likes it.

"What was growing up in Atlanta like?" she asks Zahra.

"Probably not so different than growing up in New York." Zahra pauses, shakes her head. "Well, that's a lie. The way of life is just different in Atlanta. I mean, it's spread out, stretched out like taffy, but New York is a whole 'nother flavor, compact. Know what I mean? General Sherman burned down a good portion of Atlanta during the Civil War, so it's a fairly 'new' city."

Sammie nods.

"There are hills everywhere; Atlanta is known for them. 'The hundred hills of Atlanta are not all crowned with factories. On one, toward the west, the setting sun throws three buildings in bold relief against the sky.'" Sammie thinks Zahra is a poet until she says, "Du Bois wrote that about Clark Atlanta, which is a part of the AUC, Atlanta University Center, with Morehouse and Spelman. You'll get to know that area well if you decide to go there in the fall."

Columbia and City College are the universities on hills in Harlem, the only hilltop schools Sammie is familiar with. They sit practically on top of the neighborhood, opposite home, west, farther uptown, so when Sammie considers them, they are looking down on her, with their neighborhood's farm-to-table or French-inspired or far-too-expensive restaurants. But a college on a hill for Black people? Never heard of it.

"Yeah, maybe I will," Sammie says, really thinking about it, picturing herself growing similar to Zahra, swapping places with her, Zahra in New York, and Sammie in the hills of a new city.

"Atlanta is big for Black people, you know. The center of Black politics and Black churches, and I guess they're somewhat one and the same, religion and politics. MLK was a preacher, so was Andrew Young and William Holmes Borders, preachers and politicians. My gram was big in the church, raised my mother, and then Derrick and me, there. My mother went the way of politics, but she still prays. It's important to. Or at least I think so. Can't leave everything behind."

"Mm-hmm." Sammie prays, well, sometimes. Mother Ma prays, and Sammie listens at her door, unsure if she should join in, but sometimes she closes her eyes for solidarity, so God knows that she wants what Mother Ma wants, that they are a team. But on her own, Sammie is confused. Her classmates have such harsh things to say about Christians; it is hard to admit being one, even if only somewhat, even if only on the periphery. Sammie wants to ask Zahra how to pray, but Zahra has already moved on.

"Atlanta is a city, and I wouldn't have said this when I was still living there, but we did some country shit growing up. I mean fun was riding on the back of my uncle Richard's pickup truck, holding on to its body while bouncing over speed bumps. Going to the candy lady's house for all sorts of stuff. Bubble gum, sour straws, rock candy, you name it. There was a creek where we would dip our toes in and then wonder if the water would make them fall off. We would find honeysuckle and inhale the nectar like addicts. My gram's boyfriends, which were plentiful and transitional, used to come over and fry food. Seems like she didn't like healthy men or something because we were always eating chicken wings, and pork chops, and country-fried steak, and catfish or whiting, and fresh-cut french fries. God, Garry made the best french fries. And Gram's men— they were always bearing gifts, candies or candles or televisions that had conveniently fallen off the backs of trucks."

"Wow," Sammie says.

"No lie," Zahra assures her.

"The schools are bigger in Atlanta, and two schools in one

building is basically unheard of. My school had a swimming pool in it. Pretty rare for a public school, but still, that's Atlanta for you. Sports in general. School life is built around them. Football games. Homecoming. Pep rallies."

"Pep rallies?"

"Yeah."

"What's . . . ?"

"You've never heard of a pep rally?"

"Well . . ."

"You're not missing much, but then you're sort of missing everything. You literally get to skip class to see the cheerleaders cheer, and the dancers dance, and the athletes wave." Zahra imitates them, and she looks intentionally goofy. "And then there's just music and chants and stuff. It's one of the epicenters of a high school's social network. Pep rallies and games and after-parties. At the games, cheerleaders make these big banners for the football team to run through. And it's like school spirit on steroids. Face paint, matching shirts, all of that!"

"You liked high school, didn't you?"

"I liked driving. I gained a sense of freedom in high school."

"Me too," Sammie says, even though she doesn't drive. Not yet. She wants to learn though. Uncle says he'll teach her over the summer. She's a little scared but doesn't want to be the typical New Yorker who goes to college without that basic life skill.

"So . . . yeah, that's it. That was growing up."

"Um-hmm . . ." Sammie thought Zahra would mention her brother. Instinctively. That she wouldn't have to ask the impolite question, that one thing would lead to another, and he would just come up, but Zahra seems simultaneously open and closed, so Sammie decides not to ask anything more for now. She tucks her lips in, as if anything is bound to come spilling out of them.

Zahra sees her in the rearview. "What? Why are you looking at me like that?"

"Will you tell me about your brother?" Damn. She said she wouldn't ask. She can't help herself. She can never help herself.

"What about him?"

"I don't know. What's he like?" Sammie clarifies, "What *was* he like?" She leans into the console, seat belt straining against her, and Zahra corrects Sammie's self-edit.

"He *is* the most understanding and raw person I've ever met. He's fun but not in the usual way of the word, you know? He's one of those people who makes you feel like you're getting to know yourself better when you're around him. Those are the best type of people, I think."

Sammie does know what she means, though she can't pinpoint anyone like that herself.

"You're kind of like that," Zahra says, looking over at her and smiling a beat too long, so Sammie is a little uncomfortable with the compliment and watches the road instead of relishing in it.

Zahra straightens her back, redirects her attention to what's ahead of them. "He loves music. He feels it in a deeper way than most of us."

Sammie nods.

"We used to do this thing, where we would only speak in lyrics. Drove Gram and my mother crazy. They'd ask us what happened at school, and Derrick would say, '*When I went to school I carried lunch in a bag. With an apple for my teacher 'cause I knew I'd get a kiss.*'"

Sammie's impressed with Zahra's flow. Didn't know she had it in her. A little grittier than expected.

"You know the song?" Zahra asks, having fun with this memory, and Sammie is glad she's opened her up to it. Sammie shakes her head though. No, she doesn't think she's ever heard it before.

"OK, I'll give you another one," Zahra says. "Derrick used to play basketball, and Gram would ask him about practice or a game, and he'd say something like, '*It seems we lose the game before we even start to play. Who made these rules?*'"

Sammie shakes her head again, embarrassed. Should she know these songs? Zahra's like, what, ten to fifteen years older than her?

"Lauryn Hill. 'Everything Is Everything.' You'd know it if you heard it."

"Yeah, I think I do know that song."

"Derrick and I used to climb trees or play basketball for hours. We were outside a lot. At least when we were younger. Gram used to kick us out so she could clean. And, of course, Derrick and I both had our own friends, but more than anything else, we had each other, and he is only a year older, but I looked up to him. He was a quiet leader."

"What does that mean?" Sammie cuts in, and Zahra looks taken aback by the question, but Sammie only wants to know if she's one of those too, a quiet leader.

Zahra clears her throat before saying, "Everyone always thought he was cool. Everyone liked him, wanted his laid-back swag to rub off on them, but it didn't work that way. Hanging out with Derrick just made the difference between you and him more grave, more pronounced. There were days when he was a gossip, a joker, a rapper, and then there were days when he was as quiet as a mouse, and that's when people wanted to impress him the most. It was as if they'd do anything to get him to talk, but he'd give you two or three words and a thoughtful expression and set you on your way from there. Except he wasn't like that with me. I could always get more from him."

"You think that's what it is now?" Sammie asks. "He's waiting for you to pull something out of him? Maybe he wanted you to come looking for him?"

"I don't know what it is. Things have been different for a long time now. It started hurting too much to keep trying."

Sammie nods, wishing she had something insightful, something helpful to say, but she's coming up empty. Still, she hopes to meet Derrick, to see him and compare him to Zahra, to compare him to herself, hoping she'll gain some better understanding of who she is, hoping she'll breathe easier, and Uncle Trey will stop giving her those worried looks.

It's not enough that Sammie swiped the photo of him, that it currently rests in the front pocket of her book bag. She couldn't help herself; his eyes kept looking at her, and she considered that eyes like those could be the ones watching her. She convinced herself that it wasn't stealing. But borrowing, not as weird as it seems. Zahra doesn't even like looking at that photo wall, and Sammie promised herself to eventually put it back in its rightful place.

|||||||||||||||||||||||||||||||||||||||||||||||||

THEY'RE ALL AWAKE NOW, AND THE CAR IS HOT WITH THE midday sun. They're less than an hour out, and they can feel the city approaching, quiet but intense. Sammie has grown fidgety with anticipation and draws invisible pictures on the window. A butterfly, a house with a galvanized roof, a hand with long, absurd fingernails.

Zahra's phone rings, and she stumbles to answer it. When she finally does, her hello sounds more irritated than it ought to. Zahra has been nothing but nice to her and Uncle Trey, so why the attitude all of a sudden? Whoever is on the other end of the line must be a real bother.

"Mary, I just told you, we're less than an hour away," Zahra says, and that solves it. Sammie remembers that Mary is Zahra's mother's name. She wonders just how similar their relationships with their mothers are, but no, Sammie doesn't talk to her mom like that, not with that tone. Mother Ma wouldn't have it if she did.

"I'm doing the speed limit. This isn't my car, you know."

"Don't let me hold you back, speed racer," Uncle Trey says jokingly, but even that doesn't loosen Zahra up.

"I'm not doing this with you. I'm just . . . not right now," Zahra says before hanging up abruptly, and now, she's back to the breathing exercises.

"Can I ask what happened?" Uncle Trey asks, and Sammie is glad for it.

"It's . . . My mom doesn't know anything. She's never been . . . involved, you know? She always has a shit ton else to do, so, yeah, she doesn't know anything. We'll get there, we'll fix everything, we'll go to the AUC, including Spelman of course, and we'll be out. I'm already tired of being *home*, and we're not even there yet."

"Ha. Try living there," Uncle Trey says.

Zahra laughs a little. "Right. But that seems to be your choice."

Uncle Trey turns to face Sammie, and he raises his eyebrows, and she knows exactly what he means. His choice? No, Mother Ma needs the help, has needed it ever since Daday died. Uncle Trey is their refrigerator; he's the most important appliance. Sammie has seen the burden wear on him, how his smile creases his eyes sometimes, he's wishing so hard for something *else*.

"My choice?" he says now. "Depends on how you define the word."

"Well, I could tell you about my mom, but how long do you have? I mean, I should have started this story when we were coming out of the Lincoln Tunnel. She's so self-righteous, so self-righteous, so self-involved but claims that it's for the good of everyone. Really, she just wanted to be the next Rosa Parks, the next Angela Davis, but it was never *really* about the movement. It's all ego with people like her."

Uncle Trey is listening intently, and he has that look on his face, the same sly smirk he used to give Sammie when she said she was scared of the dark or when she had to ride the train alone for the first time—sixth grade; she was eleven. It was like he knew something that she didn't.

"I think . . . ," he says now, but then stops himself from finishing.

"What?" Zahra asks.

"No, no, you go on," he says.

"No, please."

"I didn't mean to be rude."

"Not rude at all. I want to hear what you have to say."

"Not until you've finished."

"This is getting ridiculous," Sammie chimes in. "Someone please just talk."

"Well, then, let's talk about something different. Let's talk about . . . documentaries," Trey says.

"Documentaries?" Zahra asks.

"Jesus, Uncle," Sammie says. "Way to squelch the fire." And it is true. Uncle Trey is always changing the subject at inopportune times, right when you are getting to the thick of something, right when he is about to say more than he ever wanted to, more than he deems fair or necessary or safe.

||||||||||||||||||||||||||||||||||||||||||||||||||||||

CLOUDS MOVE SLOWLY, LIKE A TIRED MOTHER AFTER HER toddler. They eventually get the upper hand on the sun, and the car is no longer burdened by bright rays. Sammie can see the effect of the weather, sky and circumstance, on Zahra. She drives straight-faced, pensive, and Sammie wonders what she's thinking about. Derrick. Of course she's thinking about Derrick. Sammie wonders what it's like to lose a brother in such a mystical way, to lose him without losing him at all. She wonders what it's like to have a brother. Or a sister. Her mom said she wanted more children, but it never happened, and Sammie didn't ask why not, because what if it had happened? Would her sibling get to stay in Trinidad? Would her parents want them in a way that they don't want Sammie now? Would this new kid know what it was like to have a normal family? Mom and dad together like an eighties sitcom dream, like the American dream? Sammie would hate them. She even hated the idea of them. So she didn't ask what happened; she just quietly thanked God.

A fog is up ahead. It seems the closer they get to Atlanta, the thicker it becomes, like a blanket slowly coming down from the sky. Zahra turns on the headlights.

"No worries. I just have to slow down, that's all. Atlanta gets like this sometimes. One day when Derrick and I were in high school, we were on our way home from a party, a white party. At our school there were parties thrown by white kids and parties thrown by Black kids, and they were distinctly different—the white kids' parties were unsupervised, with beer games instead of dancing, the dress code ripped right out of an Abercrombie & Fitch ad, no Ecko red, no Baby Phat, sub Birkenstocks for Jordans—but never mind that, on our way back from the party, the fog was so thick that we could barely see the road in front of us. I was driving and damn near hyperventilating, but Derrick was cool like always and just told me to slow down, that I only needed to see a meter ahead of me, and that we knew our way home, that we would get there eventually. And we did. It makes me wonder though. Like how is he so cool, so cool, and so fucked up too? What kind of shit is that, you know?"

Zahra slows down, so slow that it almost feels like they aren't going anywhere. Sammie doesn't know what to say, and Uncle Trey is looking at Zahra with compassion but doesn't seem to have any words either, so the fog is the only one left to answer. They're approaching the center of it, aren't they?

"Is that fog or . . ." Uncle Trey's voice trails off.

"It looks like it's moving. Does fog move like that?" Sammie asks.

"Well, I don't know. I guess it does look a little weird," Zahra says.

Then they are in the middle of it, and it is not fog at all, and yes, it was moving. Just not all together. A million moths at once, a million beautiful and frightening wings flapping gracefully like the Trini flag in the wind, the one Uncle Trey used to keep in one of the car's back windows before the clumsy and chatter of too many drunk passengers made him take it down. The moths are bespeckled white; they almost look like butterflies, and Uncle Trey is late at rolling up his window, so they are inside the car now, landing everywhere. On the peaks of Zahra's Afro, all over the windshield, on Uncle Trey's arms like white freckles, and here one is on Sammie's fingertip, balancing with wings unfurled and proud.

Sammie wonders where they've come from, where they're going as Uncle Trey says, "God, I think one went into my mouth." He swats aimlessly, while Zahra looks unworried but determined.

"Do you hear them?" Sammie asks.

"Yes, they're in my ears," Uncle Trey says, but Sammie meant the rhythm.

Did he hear the moths in song, like a gospel choir, voices reaching so high for so long that they're almost one solid yell? Did he hear them praising and promising? The voices, so together but so distinct, voices she's heard before—Mother Ma and Aunty Deanne, Calypso Rose and Mary J. Blige. In one moment they're all—*Give me all your love and don't stop. My love's waiting when you reach the top*—and the next they're—*Don't got de money to take me back to Trinidad, fine Calypso woman.* The voices are as loud and menacing, as intriguing and inviting as the insects swarming, swarming, swarming. And then suddenly gone. A passing tornado.

"What was that?" Sammie screams, and her confusion is not surprising because here's what she knows—that they're attracted to light. Not much else. About moths, that is. She certainly doesn't know that they like the saccharine smell of her, baking sweet bread or a trumpet tree in bloom, and thereby find themselves perched atop her bare knee, on the peak of her nose, scurrying for her armpits. Sammie has never even heard of gypsy moths or invasive species, and is only mildly and commercially acquainted with the word *gypsy* itself. She's heard of gypsy cabs, and gypsy pants, and associates anything "gypsy" with a free-spirited lifestyle, but she has no idea where the word actually comes from. Sammie is smart, but she's nothing outside of a seventeen-year-old young woman. She's never heard of a lot of things, like jojoba oil or endometriosis or floppy disks. She is seventeen, lyrics to a Spinners song, "Ghetto Child." But most fittingly, she is a song by the Crystals, because seventeen is a sweet and innocent ballad, or at least it should be. *Whoa, what a nice way to turn seventeen* sang in a nostalgic voice, almost sad, but charged like a parked car with lovers burning hot inside of it.

"Shit if I know what that was," Uncle Trey says.

"Clearly, it wasn't just fog," Zahra says, but it seems like she knows more. What isn't she telling them? What does she know that they don't?

|||||||||||||||||||||||||||||||||||||||||||||||||

THE HOUSE IS HERE NOW. ZAHRA WAS RIGHT. SHE DID KNOW the way home. Slow enough, and they made it to the brick ranch, the carport mottled with grease stains; even against the slow start of rain, Sammie can see them. A boy in the yard next door watches them pull up. He stands in the rain like it's nothing. He doesn't wave but smiles like he can see Sammie through the fogged-up windows. She looks down at her hands, which were in the middle of texting Leila something that seems altogether inconsequential now.

Everyone in the car is silent, and has been silent for almost the full half hour since the moth debacle. Ahead of them squats the place Zahra calls *home, home*. The house looks like something Sammie has seen or read about in a book somewhere, one-story and small with ivy growing up one side of it and large front windows opaque with white blinds. Sammie eyes Zahra in the rearview mirror, and she looks at the house like it's a lover, an ex who's gotten away, teary-eyed and pouty. Sammie's scared as hell of going inside that thing, eerie as it is. And something travels with Zahra, something loud, something Sammie worries she's gotten herself knee-deep in the thick of. She wants to go back to New York, to crush on Noah and hold his pasty-white hand, to hug Mother Ma, her hanging breast the only barrier between them, the Victoria's Secret perfume she bought Mother Ma for her birthday transferring from her body to Sammie's own. Sammie unbuckles her seat belt but makes no move to leave the car, looking at the forbidding house and thinking, *What in the world is going on in there?*

TWELVE

October 2019, Metro Atlanta, Gram's place, a Friday

The rain is coming down hard now, and to Zahra, it is a sole comfort, thunderstorm tranquility Derrick used to call it, a similar effect to the serenity Gram's old afghan would bring Zahra on lonely nights, pulling the blanket tight under her toes, forcing her fingers in and out of the well-knit holes. The car ride was long but mostly easy until that swarm of moths—she's been ruminating on them ever since. It's evident they've got something say, but damn if she knows what it is. Two options are lumps in her stomach—that this trip is predestined, that she'll find Derrick here and all will be well with the world. Or just the opposite—they're warning her, screaming at her to stop, a fruitless plea that there's no one here to save but herself, and maybe Sammie. Normally, Zahra would offer to help Trey with the bags, but now she's too anxious to get inside. When Zahra lets herself into the only place that's ever truly felt like home, she can feel Sammie on her neck, breathing heavily.

The house is just as she remembers it, though whenever she

comes home, she expects some significant change. But no. The smell of fresh pound cake. The scratched pine floors, the living room's wall-to-wall windows, so the space feels big and small all at once. The scalloped curtain valance over the kitchen sink, the double-door turquoise oven, the crumbling brick wall that leads to the basement, which is probably flooding, so Gram will need to wear her rainboots when she goes downstairs to do the laundry. The three bedrooms are in the farthest part of the house, on the opposite side of the carport, smushed and lined up like little Monopoly properties. The rooms will haunt her, she is sure. With Derrick missing, the rooms are tainted. When he was here, they were overburdened.

The house has always been full of sounds, creaking floors and squeaky doors, and the hum of heat or air-conditioning, a house that puts effort into standing, a house that doesn't take things for granted. Haunted, they used to say. Teasing at first but then with the moths and the spirits and the endless, looping sounds, it became clear that the house really was screaming. There was something there, is here now, so it is hard to distinguish between the real sound of someone entering the house and the phantom people who live within its walls. Gram and Mary are in the kitchen, both in house shoes, but Mary's are still and Gram's tap at the linoleum impatiently, and neither of them notice the car pull up or the front door open.

Zahra approaches them from behind, but even so, they look alike, mother and daughter. Two thick heads of hair, kinky and combed out and you can see that their Afros are airy and well moisturized. Gram's is full gray now.

Zahra is so deep in the constitution of the women who created her that she almost doesn't notice her dad, smiling like usual. He sits away from the table, enough space to allow him to prop his ankle on his knee. He leans back, arms crossed like he's posing for a magazine or something.

Gram turns around. "Zahra," she says. "You're here."

Mary turns around now too, but it's her dad who rushes around the table first, wrapping her in his arms. She feels small, like she's in elementary school again. To the women, Zahra gives less significant hugs, loose with Gram and even looser with Mary.

"Want a slice of cake?" Gram asks, knowing she does. This is how so many problems have been solved, with a slice of Gram's pound cake. She and Mary wouldn't have made it through Zahra's teenage years without it, one of them would have overpowered the other. Strangulation or suffocation for sure. Now Zahra imagines putting the pound cake out the front door like a mouse trap, Derrick taking the bait and returning home doe-eyed like Shadow in *Homeward Bound*.

"Yes, please," Zahra says. "Thanks, Gram."

"And your friend?" Gram asks.

"Sammie, would you like a slice of pound cake?"

"Well, I . . ." Sammie seems to be at a loss for words.

"She would, yes," Zahra answers for her.

The door shuts loudly, and everyone pauses as Trey comes into view. He is wet, soaking actually, and Zahra feels bad for not telling anyone she was bringing home a man, not her man, but a man all the same.

"Another friend?" Gram asks. "Zahra, you didn't tell us you were bringing company. For a man of that size"—she looks over Trey and seems impressed—"I should've baked a second cake."

"Oh, Gram, I told you," Zahra lies. She didn't want to make it a thing, but obviously, it's going to be a thing.

"Yeah, well, the dementia."

"What?" Zahra says. "Dementia?"

"It's a joke, Zahra. Calm down. I'm looking younger than you are these days."

"We have a lot to talk about," Mary says. Her voice is disorient-
ing, calmer than usual. She clears her throat. "And it doesn't matter
who's here to hear it." There she is. Authoritative. In control. The
woman Zahra has grown up loathing.

||||||||||||||||||||||||||||||||||||||||||||||||||||||||||

THEY ARE ALL AT THE TABLE. GRAM, MARY, DAD, SAMMIE,
Trey, and Zahra. It's a small table, and they are well acquainted with
one another, elbows bumping if their arms come above the tabletop
to eat their cake or reach for a drink of water. Zahra sits in between
Sammie and Gram, across from Trey, and does everything in her
power not to look at him. What made her think this was a good idea?
Bringing a man home? Home, home! At a time like this. She is more
vulnerable than she ever was with Kahlil. More vulnerable than she
was with any of her ex-boyfriends. Trey is going to think she's crazy.
When he really gets to know her family, he's going to think she's
batshit, but if they find Derrick, and he's one whole piece again, then
it will all be worth it. Then anything is worth it. She should've come
back sooner, she knows. *This* is her fault.

"I think it's spirits," Mary says, and Jesus, it's like the woman
doesn't know any better. It's like she thinks everyone's family goes
around blaming family dysfunction, family *disappearances* on spirits.

"We have to pray he has discernment," Gram says. "Then he
will come back to us."

"Any idea *where* he is?" Zahra asks. "I mean, you've thought he
was overcome with spirits for years now, Mary, so why is he all of a
sudden gone? What's different? Please. Enlighten me."

"It's hard to enlighten someone with a closed mind." Here she
goes again. "When you're in touch with your ancestors, it can be
overwhelming, to say the least. And Derrick is someone who listens,
in the way that you don't. So of course he *hears* people."

"People or spirits?"

"Both."

"So how do we find him?"

She shrugs. "Maybe they want him to know something."

"They?"

"Ancestors, Zahra. You know this."

Sammie's eyes light up, confused and incredulous, and Zahra thinks about when she and Derrick were children. Mary emphasized their obligations to their ancestors like a list of chores. Wash the dishes, *listen to your calling*, shake the rugs, *settle the score*, mop the floor, *learn the stories*, water the plants, *reclaim the land*, take out the trash, *reclaim your mind*. The obligations weren't specific; they were obvious.

"What sort of things do they want us— I mean Derrick. What sort of things do they, the ancestors, want Derrick to know?"

"Probably what everyone wants someone to know." Dad's voice is jarring, deep. He strokes his salt-and-pepper beard.

"And that is—?" Zahra begins to ask but is interrupted by a persistent buzzing. Her phone. She reaches in her purse, which dangles from the back of her chair. She holds up a finger for the group to hang on, just a second. She pauses when she sees who it is. Sophia. Did she forget to reschedule their session today? Whatever. She'll call her back. She thinks back to the spirits, to the ancestors, to the people Mary says Derrick listens to, wondering if they're the same. "What is it that everyone wants someone to know?"

"That they exist," Dad says, like he's got all the answers.

"OK, I really don't understand what we're getting at here," Zahra says with discomfort.

Gram shrugs. "It's not always for us to understand."

"Most things aren't," Trey says, and Sammie looks at him like he's conspiring against her.

Zahra wants to reach out to Sammie and tell her that this world gets easier, or maybe it doesn't, maybe it gets harder, but she won't say that. She can't decide what to say to Sammie when her phone rings again. Sophia. Slide to answer. She can wait; Zahra silences it.

"What are we going to do?" Mary asks. "What's our plan?"

"I'm going to all the places that made Derrick who he was, who he still is. If I have to revisit every memory, I'll do it."

"He's not just hanging out on some random corner, Zahra."

"You don't know that. You weren't even there. You barely know him."

"Zahra . . . ," Gram starts, but Mary stops her.

"I've always been here when you needed me," Mary says, as if she even knows what that means. *Needed*. How conveniently oblivious of her. Zahra gears up to tell her everything she's never said, when Sophia calls again. The persistence of the privileged. It's impressive.

Zahra answers this time, stepping away from the table, plugging a finger into her left ear, even though no one in the kitchen is talking.

"Hey," she means to say in her usual warm but reticent Zahra voice, but it comes out clipped, irked. "Did we have a session scheduled? I'm in Atlanta. I thought I told you, but it's completely ——"

"Sorry, I don't mean to bother you. I wouldn't have called more than once, but my mom thought I should. She said you would want to know how I'm feeling . . . about my essay. And it's not that I don't think you care, but I also know you have your own life, and I'm very sorry to disrupt it. Is this a good time?"

No, it's not a good time. It's an awful time. "Sure," Zahra says. "I have ten minutes or so. . . ."

"Oh, well, I guess I just feel like it's not good enough. I don't know how to make it better. It feels like *my story* will never be good enough."

She called to fish for compliments. Now Zahra is more than a little annoyed with Sophia. They've already discussed what she needs to fix. Her essay is trying to say too much. With 650 words, what can be conveyed *well* is limited. And she has to make sure that it's applicable to the world around her, because no one gives a shit about thoughts. It's actions that matter.

"It is. It is," Zahra breezes over her reassurance. "You're just trying to say too much. What's the one thing that really matters? What's the one thing the tree and its ever presence in your life has taught you? There aren't a whole lot of trees in New York, you know, so why does this one matter so much? Why does it matter *to you*, and how will it help you understand the many people you'll encounter in this world?" Zahra feels weird talking this way, in her college prep voice at *home* home. Like her high school self is hovering over her, shaking her head, asking, *Who the fuck are you? Whose voice is that?*

"Who is that?" It's not the ghost of her sixteen-year-old self but Gram.

Zahra pulls the phone away from her ear, covering the microphone with her free hand. "A kid I work with. You know how I help seniors get into colleges?"

Gram nods thoughtfully. "You can't tell her it's not a good time?"

"Yep, doing that now." But sometimes it is hard to tell Sophia the obvious, to tell her anything she doesn't want to hear because she's not used to it. She's not used to *no*. She's not used to hearing that her essay isn't good enough because she doesn't know how to self-reflect, and hasn't felt the need for self-reflection in all of her seventeen years of life. She doesn't know how to step outside of herself because she's never had to. And simply, her essay is about a fucking tree. Sophia is a prodigy for almost having pulled it off. Her writing is beautiful, fluid—the language in itself moving. But her essay won't get any better if she's unwilling to see the people outside of her bubble. Sophia has been across the country, across the world five times over but has she ever really left the Upper East Side? Zahra bets Sophia will break through eventually. But until then, she shouldn't expect Zahra to think for her. And sometimes it feels like *that* is what she wants more than anything else.

"Look, you've got a good essay. A really good essay. But is it as good as it *could* be? Do I think you should *push* yourself? You mention this tree as a witness of sorts, right? You mention the things it has seen you through, and you mention how its ability to witness is different from your mom's or dad's because a tree is static where they are dynamic. That's great. But what about Pam, your nanny? She's a Black woman; she's walked by that same tree too. How is it different for her? How is it different for the man who drops off your mail, for the man who collects your garbage? *That* is what I mean by the world around you."

Zahra doesn't begin to say how self-centered the essay is. The tree as a witness? How egocentric, to believe a living thing as your voyeur and not of its own business, its own volition. She thinks of how much Gram and Mary and Dad and Uncle Richard used to say, *Mind your business*, a Black proverb, for the people who know that everyone has business to mind, that even the air around you has got a job to do.

When Zahra hangs up, she feels like she's written the end of the essay for Sophia. And it irks her for Derrick more than anything else. Because the day was supposed to be about him, because the Sophias of the world shouldn't always get to interrupt. Not when it comes to her family. Not when it comes to her brother. She excuses herself from the think tank at the table; she runs a bath.

||||||||||||||||||||||||||||||||||||||||||||||||||

SHE PUTS ONE FOOT IN AT A TIME, THE WATER SO HOT THAT it draws her breath in, makes her bite down until her body is acclimated to the heat. She sits down tentatively, then slips under the water, so it's up to her neck, only reaching out of the tub to slide the frosted glass shower door shut. She has no idea how old this house is, but shower doors over a tub are odd, aren't they? Growing up, they were her normal, having never needed a curtain, but now she sees the many ways in which this house deviates from standard. Still, she feels safe here, shut in like a pet fish.

She leans her head back and closes her eyes, trying not to imagine the world without her big brother, making completely reasonable but highly unlikely excuses for his disappearance. He's checked himself into some sort of rehab. He's traveled to a remote village without working Wi-Fi or cell phone reception. He's gotten so frustrated with their mother that he's taken a vow of familial silence.

She rubs water on her face and opens her eyes to see moths perched on the showerhead above her. Annoyed, she screams without opening her mouth. The fucking moths are part of the problem, and she knows it. Just wants them to leave her the hell alone already. She tries to relax again, but her body is rigid. Amid the moths hitting their high notes, she resigns to just soaping up instead.

Please pardon me, but I'm longing to speak. . . .

THIRTEEN

Zahra puts her ear against Derrick's door and imagines him behind it. She can hear the songs he used to listen to—DeBarge and Dru Hill and Donny Hathaway—and if she closes her eyes tight enough, he won't even be missing. She'll open the door and find him lying on his old navy-blue bean bag staring up at the ceiling or reading a book in bed or drawing pictures of people she's never seen before at his makeshift desk, an old slab of wood with cinder blocks for a foundation. But when she turns the old rusty knob and the door creaks so loudly that it sounds like it hasn't been opened in ages, the air is muggy and the room is uninhabited, save for whatever creatures—spiders, caterpillars, moths—have spun their webs. This room seems dustier than the others but not particularly less cared for. The bed is made neatly, with military corners passed down from Dad's dad's time in the service. There are mountains and mountains of CDs, lined along the walls like military trenches, some in racks that spin like lazy Susans and others zipped away in travel cases stuffed into a single row of a bookshelf. The room wants to say something but has been sealed away, snapped shut, and Zahra wonders how long Derrick's really been missing.

The CDs remind her of Dad's house and how their time there was accompanied by a nonstop soundtrack, sounds by Cameo and Funkadelic and the Gap Band. Always songs that made you want to dance and sing along. Even on Dad's worst days he carries joy, an effervescence that reminds Zahra of the first sip of a cold Sprite. Dad would impersonate Barry White's low tenor, Al Green's snap and wobble, or the Temptations' two-step. The musical joy was all good until they skipped him over for a promotion at the law firm he worked for when she was in high school. She wasn't supposed to know all the details but overheard him talking to Mary on the phone. This was the third time. They gave the job to a white guy fresh out of college. They said Dad was next in line. He hung up with Mary abruptly, came out of his room, and put on Con Funk Shun, and it was like nothing happened. It was like every other night with the singing and the dancing and the impersonations, and for the first time, Zahra understood that she didn't know her dad at all. The man she knew was Michael Cooper, and George Clinton, and Charlie Wilson, but who was Montgomery Mackenzie?

Now Zahra can only stand to be around Dad, and his disingenuousness, in small increments. Her most recent trip home she'd asked him if this is what he'd imagined as a kid. If he thought he'd work for the same bullshit company for almost thirty years. If he thought the proverbial ladder would just give way after a while. If his life went according to plan. He'd said, "So you learn to live with what you got. My generation was prepared for it. I don't know that yours is."

Zahra knows it wasn't just Mary who messed up Derrick, but she never blames Dad. It's impossible to point the finger at a smiling caricature.

It doesn't really matter whose fault it is. She looks around the room for clues. Anything that might point to Derrick's whereabouts. Anything that might help her see his mental state.

When Zahra was closer to Derrick, when they were younger, they were almost telepathic. She'd think something, and then he'd look at her as if he knew exactly what she meant. Or they'd laugh at the exact same time, no outside influence, just their own memories of a moment, of something funny that had just come back to them.

She looks around the room again, and everything seems in order, but the trash can tucked in between Derrick's desk and closet stands out. It's full, and as she approaches it, she sees the crumpled paper. Perfect round balls and nothing else, no gum wrappers, no clothing tags, no used tissues. She takes one of the balls out of the basket and begins to pull it apart gently, the crinkled paper like an accordion. She's scared to see what it is, scared the paper will yell or sing at her. It will disappear her just as it's done Derrick. So when she feels a cold hand on her shoulder, pressing down, she jumps, startled.

"Oh, I didn't mean to scare you," he says. Trey. It's just Trey.

She sighs, relieved. Not sure what she was so scared of to begin with.

"You didn't scare me," she lies.

Trey's eyebrows curl together, and he laughs. "Well, something did. What's that?" He points to the paper in her hand, only half unraveled.

"Trash," she says, reshaping the ball. "Just emptying it." She reaches for the can, but Trey stops her.

"Let me," he says. "Just point me to the trash bags."

Zahra gulps, not wanting to admit that the trash means something to her, that she'd planned to rummage it. "This way," she says, hiding the crumpled paper behind her back so he won't remember it's there.

She shows Trey to the kitchen, where instead of dumping the

smaller trash into the larger one, he pulls out the big bag, deciding to take them both out.

"This way," she says again, walking him to the carport, where they're safe from the rain, but the water is loud around them. She's grown so unaccustomed to the sound of the rain on the thin carport ceiling that it almost sounds fake to her, a pitter-patter of tiny children's footsteps, a noise-canceling sleep track.

"I love the rain," she says, hesitant to go back inside, where everything is so still and layered.

"Doesn't sound like this in New York," Trey says. "Reminds me of Trinidad. Rain on a galvanized roof."

Zahra imagines picking up and going to Trinidad with him and can't see it. So far away from home with someone she barely knows. "Why did you come?" she asks.

"What?"

"Why did you come? It's a big commitment, driving from New York to Atlanta, staying out here for what? A week on a whim? Helping me look for my brother?" She bites her jaw, contemplative. She knows she sounds like an asshole but can't help herself. There's something simultaneously honest and dishonest about Trey.

"I told you. Sammie—"

"It's bullshit," she cuts him off.

Trey nods, accepting defeat. "Maybe I just wanted to know what knowing you would be like."

"Why?"

He takes a moment, cocks his head to the side, and looks at her funny, like he's trying to find the words to explain himself. He takes a step toward her, crosses his arm. They're unnaturally close now, as if what he has to say is a secret. She blames the rain. Maybe he doesn't want to shout over it.

"Something you said when you were in the Uber that night," he says. "You probably don't remember it."

"Try me."

"I said I would take a look at the locks on the back doors, and you said, no, that it was you. So it made me think . . . I don't know. Maybe there's something you need from me?"

"I need?"

"Or it could be the other way around. Something I need from you?"

"Like?"

"Like," he says. "Like, you know." He looks sincere, serious behind his shadow of a beard. His face is so young, all pulled taut, with only the crinkles growing in the corners of his eyes. He looks simultaneously young and old, like there are conjumbled memories, secrets behind those eyes, and in just one blink, one happenstance, he might give them away.

"You think your car doors locking is a sign that we're meant to be together?"

He shrugs. "Maybe I wouldn't think that if you weren't beautiful."

It's one of those cheeky, cliché compliments that she shouldn't give two shits about but does. It's so bad, it stings, leaves her nerves on edge. She tries to ignore the feeling. "So that's the real reason you offered to drive here all the way from New York?"

"It's not the only reason," he says. "I really do want Sammie to visit Spelman. I think it would be good for her, to be around a bunch of Black girls who love school as much as she does." He looks away. "I hated school. Didn't go to college."

"You regret it?"

"I don't know. Not sure I'd be doing what I want to be doing even if I did, probably just making more money."

"Not if you're anything like me." She bites her nails. "So what do you want to do?"

"Well, when I was in high school I wanted to be a rapper."

"You're kidding."

"Rapping was what got you out. Rapping got you money, girls. Is it so wrong to want that?"

"I guess not, but . . ."

"Then when I was in my early twenties, I wanted to be a chef. Had this idea for Trini Asian fusion." He hesitates, then adds, "I could still chef you up something." It's the first time he's looked at her in a while. His eyelashes flutter.

"I may take you up on that," she says, her cheeks burning. They're still so close. She can practically feel his breath against the humidity.

"You should." He smiles before growing contemplative again. "But now I don't know. My dad died. Sammie started getting older, my mom too. Their lives felt more important than mine. Lost track of time. But Sammie's still got it, plenty of time. And I want her to get it right. So when you came along, it was like—win, win. Win for me, win for Sammie. You're all smart and shit, like a fucking walking almanac."

"An encyclopedia?"

"You know what I mean."

But she's not sure she does. *Win-win* sounds like some opportunist-type shit, and at the moment she only sees his opportunity (not hers or that she politely handed him the opportunity the night he picked her up in his Uber). It doesn't occur to Zahra that what Trey likes about her is what the other men she's dated have so clearly resented, so she rolls her eyes, steps back from him.

"Look, I'm trying to find my brother. He's really missing."

He nods. "Sammie's really invested in helping you find him."

"It's not her job."

"Do you push everyone away like this?"

"Are you always so sensitive?"

"I didn't mean your brother. Sorry, I didn't mean that at all. It's just . . . There's something around you, something that makes it hard to get close, and . . ." He reorients himself. "It's not what's on your mind right now. I get it. But I'll be here, if you need any help"—he clears his throat—"looking."

||||||||||||||||||||||||||||||||||||||||||||||||||||

ZAHRA WAITS FOR A MOMENT TO HERSELF, ALONE IN HER teenage room, sitting crisscross applesauce on her bed, to unravel the paper a second time. She gets the same feeling as before, a disquiet, a feeling of unrest, as if she's opening Pandora's box and knows it. So she does it all in one swift motion, like ripping off a Band-Aid. In one abrupt second, there is a hand-drawn image of her brother but not quite. He reminds her of the one photo she's seen of Gram's father. He died young, in his thirties or forties, when Gram was still a young girl. What Gram remembers of the story is not much: something about the world, the Marks, Mississippi, earth like dried-up clay, the smell of a slop jar in the parlor, the droning of a night's rainstorm, something about the buzzing of a country you knew too well during the day but feared at night, something that made people die or go crazy, something about smoke thicker than bad breath. Gram's father died in a fire. Who set it and why remains a mystery to Zahra, and maybe to Gram as well because she clams up at the mention of it.

Zahra looks down at the image of Derrick and remembers that one photo of Gram's father in a fedora. A thin, toffee-colored man whose eyelids hung low like lazy dog ears. Gram says her father made moonshine and that he was always in the mix of something he shouldn't have been. Gram's mother used to say her father wanted more. Maybe more money, maybe more life. Zahra looks around her as if the answers are here in this room, this house, this city, but the answers are impossible when the questions themselves lay murky, underwater.

Then Zahra remembers Derrick saying that he felt like a seventy-five-year-old man, and she throws the drawing like it's burned her. The thought is so ridiculous. There's no way in hell . . . She leaves the paper there, eventually kicked under her bed with storage boxes full of old clothes and the many, many cobwebs that flank them.

THROUGH THE REST OF THE NIGHT, THE COMING AND GOING of dinner and the silent second serving of dessert, Zahra racks her brain thinking about where Derrick could be. It's a long list, and she knows she'll have to leave early in the morning if she wants to make it to all these places before dark. She's always been scared of the dark. It's not a disabling fear but one that arrived in childhood and never went away. Now that Derrick is missing, and she's back in this house, her fears have grown rich with history. Only Derrick is not in the room one over, there for her to shake awake and ask, *Did you hear that?* Or, *Do you believe in ghosts?* Or, *Is it easy to pick a lock?* His answers were always simple—*yes, yes, yes.* But then one more *Yes, all right, you can sleep here*, and he'd throw a pillow at his feet for her.

ZAHRA AND SAMMIE GET SETTLED IN. THEY'RE IN ZAHRA'S old room, the one she shared with Derrick, then Mary, then Gram. A revolving door of roommates, a continuous attempt at rearranging the three-bedroom house so that it accommodated everyone who lived within it. Now, Gram has moved out of this room and back into the room next door, Mary's old haunt. And Mary lives in Stone Mountain, a few miles away, with Uncle Richard.

"We should work on your essay," Zahra says.

Sammie sighs, and Zahra wonders why such a good writer is so reluctant to tell her story.

"Can we have a moment to, like, chill?" Sammie asks. She walks around the bedroom, stopping at decorations or trinkets that pique her interest—a tattered paperback copy of *Their Eyes Were Watching God*; a monkey Beanie Baby named Bongo; Zahra's high school senior portrait, where she is draped in black velvet and wears Gram's old plastic pearls. Her hair is straight and long, curled under an inch or so below her shoulders. She felt beautiful that day.

"You're pretty," Sammie says. She turns to Zahra and then back to the portrait. Zahra, the portrait. Zahra, the portrait. "I like the Afro better, but still."

Zahra wonders how Sammie will be different fifteen years from now, if she'll look at her own senior portrait and consider how far she's come from box braids or those hoops she always wears. But then, Zahra thinks Sammie is more ahead of the game and might respect her old decisions in a way that Zahra doesn't.

The room is as Zahra left it however many years ago. The full size bed has the same cranberry-and-gold Morocco-inspired duvet. It took a lot of convincing to get Gram to buy it. "It's expensive," she said. "A blanket within a blanket, what's the point?" She wanted to know. "You always gotta be so fancy." And it was true. Zahra knew it then, knows it now, that she is the kind of person who likes things to feel inspired, who wants the finer things in life but doesn't want to step on any small people to get there, so here she is, lost. And ultimately, she stepped on people anyway, or at least over and around them. What else would you call her relationship with Derrick?

The poster of Missy Elliott seems to mock her. One of her and

Derrick's first concerts on their own, without Dad or Uncle Richard as chaperones. It was well past Missy's *Supa Dupa Fly* days, but that was the time when Zahra was most intrigued with her, when Missy was blown up in a black trash bag with black lipstick or not far from Mars in a red-and-white robot suit. When Zahra and Derrick listened to her music, they made stank faces, like walking through rotten eggs, because Missy was mean as hell. She was something impossible, and Zahra eyed Aaliyah in those spaces too, becoming sick with envy. The poster hangs neat, nearly untouched, over a desk so old that the drawers scream when you open them. There she is in a pink puff coat with fur trim, and from looking at Missy sitting so cool by that old-school boombox, Zahra has always felt that there must be a million women inside of her.

"Mind if I play some music?" Zahra asks, taking an old mix CD from its designated place on the rack, between TLC and *Now That's What I Call Music! 11*, and putting it in the throwback stereo, a nod to the late '90s or early 2000s, when trips to Circuit City and Best Buy excited her. She would flip through the rows and rows of CDs, sometimes putting on the display headphones to hear a sample, sometimes holding a CD high in the air, like found treasure, calling out to Derrick, who would be doing his own thing not too far off, and saying, "Did you know this was already out?" Or "Love them, right?"

Now Sammie plops on the bed, and it's the most childish thing she's done all day. Zahra smiles, imagining the feeling, coming home from school after a long day, lying in bed, listening to music.

"Who is this?" Sammie asks.

"You make me feel so old sometimes," Zahra says. "This is Arrested Development."

Sammie nods, at first to Zahra's response and then to the music.

"You have your computer?" Zahra asks.

Sammie reaches across the bed, to the foot of it, where her Fjall-raven backpack hangs open. She takes out her MacBook. "Got it," she says.

Zahra sits down, scooching back until her feet can no longer touch the floor, farther until her back's against the wall. "So, where are we?" she says. "How do you feel about the essay so far?"

"I like it. But I guess I wonder if it's not personal enough, you know? Is it more about Kendrick Lamar than me?"

Of course, this question. The one teachers and parents every-where seem to have implanted in every high school senior across New York City. Zahra rolls her eyes. Honesty is always personal. Honesty is always about the person whom it belongs to, no?

"It doesn't really matter what you write about, as long as you're coming from a place of authenticity, as long as you've let your guard down. Think you've done that?"

Sammie flips her long braids so that they no longer fall in her eyes but are out of the way, graceful, behind her shoulders. She makes a concerted effort to show that she's thinking. "But I can't talk about my depression, right?"

"You're depressed?"

"To be honest, I'm not really sure, but sometimes it feels like I'm in a hole that I don't know how to get out of. And when good things happen to me, say I get an A on a test or I win a debate match, some-times they don't make me feel good at all. But shouldn't they?"

"I don't know that you should ever feel any particular way." Though the debate team? That's impressive.

Sammie nods. "It's hard to explain."

"And that's exactly why you can't write about it," Zahra says. "You can't write a personal essay about something that you haven't figured out yet. So what *do* you know? What *have* you figured out about yourself, about this world, about the people around you?"

"I'm not sure."

"Well, take some time to think about it."

"But I don't have a lot of time."

"Sure you do."

"Not if I'm applying early decision to Stanford."

"You are?"

"Maybe . . ."

"You shouldn't." Zahra doesn't like telling her students what to do. It's not her style, and frankly, it's not her business. But Sammie is different from the others. The stakes are higher here, with a girl who's Black like Zahra, who will have to figure out how to navigate the moths, who will have to figure out how to navigate the white girls, the white boys, the white faculty. She will have to figure out where to get her hair braided, where to buy her hair products, where the Black people party and pray, partake of soul food and well-seasoned poultry. She will be desperate to find a Black roommate, someone who wraps their hair at night and lotions their whole body after every shower.

"What's wrong with Stanford?" Sammie asks.

Zahra sighs. She hates talking about her alma mater and doesn't really want to pull that trump card, but Sammie's leaving her no other option. "I went to Stanford," she says.

Sammie huffs. "So then you should get why I want to go."

"Never said I didn't."

"Well, then?"

"Well, it won't make you feel better about yourself. In fact, it might make you feel worse. In fact, Stanford, although a great school, doesn't give a shit about you. All they do is uphold the status quo. They're elitist."

"So I've heard a lot of HBCUs are too."

"It's different."

"How?"

"It's different when the people look like you, when they don't have years and years of racism and brainwashing to back up their prejudice, trust me."

Zahra knows it's a big request, asking Sammie to trust her with such a difficult decision. She remembers her own senior year of high school, how choosing college felt like cherry-picking her future, how her classmates decorated their lockers with college acceptance letters, some people with as many as fifteen letters taped one on top of another, paper peeking from underneath more paper, just enough room to see the school's name and *Congratulations*. An Ivy League trumped everything else—HBCUs, state schools, scholarships. Going to your locker every morning was a measure in self-assurance, *I'm going places*. Now Sammie wanted that same feeling, a little bit of pride, a little bit of *fuck you*.

"I'll think about it," Sammie says. "It's not like I have anything against Spelman."

Zahra nods, closing the conversation. The music seems louder, and Zahra dismisses the endless needs and navigational skills Sammie will have to tend to at a white school, the vindication she's sure not to receive there. "God I used to listen to music all the time. Derrick and I both. Music was such a core part of who we were." She changes the subject.

"Were? You don't listen anymore?"

"I forget to. Isn't that crazy? There are whole days when I just forget to listen to music." And she doesn't feel like herself anymore. But now, here, in this moment, she does. She is high school Zahra again. The one with all the feels, who hadn't distanced herself to any one emotion because lying in her bed, listening to music, she would feel them all. Songs on the radio, all day, new music, old music. "God, when did I lose the capacity?"

Sammie looks like she wants to offer an answer but only shrugs. "Do you want to be young again?" she asks.

"God, no. I wouldn't go that far."

Sammie smiles like she understands. She tilts her head, looking at Zahra, scrutinizing her. It's a little uncomfortable to be looked at so intensely. Zahra covers her face with her hands until Sammie says, "You're so much like Uncle."

"Am I?" Zahra shifts her hands to the side of her face, so that they frame it now.

Sammie nods excitedly. "Yeah. You're both so shy. On high alert, like you're looking for all the ways someone will make you mad, or sad. He likes you, you know."

Sammie's confidence changes the way Zahra sees her last interaction with Trey. Sammie's right—Zahra's been on high alert in the worst way. She'll push him away if she keeps up the attitude. But now she tries to hide a smile. She likes him; she feels like more of a high schooler than she ever was in the 2000s, though this tickly feeling is definitely familiar. She tries to keep it together in front of Sammie, who's dramatically covering her mouth with both hands, as if she needs the physical barrier to keep from saying any more than she's already divulged.

"He told you that?" Zahra needs clarity.

Sammie nods, still refusing to speak.

Zahra tries to downplay it. "Well, it's not such a big deal, is it? I mean, we're both adults. Single adults. It was nice of him to drive me here."

"That's what I said," Sammie says, quickly giving up the charade of silence.

"You know," Zahra says, thinking about Sammie's boldness. "This is how you should tell Noah. I mean, just throw it out there. What's the worst that could happen?"

"He could say he's never thought of me like that, which would be the worst."

"The absolute worst, but it won't happen." There is something about Sammie. A twinkle then a thud. Both soft- and sure-footed. How could a boy not like that? Not to mention, she is commercially pretty, the sort of Black beauty that people deem an exception. Zahra knows that this is how people see her too. It is what she loves and hates most about herself.

Zahra looks up and sees the little scaly-winged creatures she knew would be there. The moths, three or four of them, are swarming the ceiling fan that Gram replaced when Zahra was in tenth grade. The fan's walnut-colored blades move slowly and the moths navigate it like an obstacle course, over, under, through.

One day the moths are tiny caterpillars, ones you let inch along your knee while you marvel at their accordion-like abdomens, and the next day there is a single, lonely moth that you think nothing of, that you can barely remember. Then there are hundreds of them, they have taken over your backyard like dandelions or crabgrass, and they begin to fall in love with you, so they follow you, singing as they go. And you think you're the only one who can hear them, you and Derrick, of course, but now, here's Sammie. Sharp, sensical Sammie, and she can hear them too.

Now is the time to ask Sammie what she's really been dying to know, but if Sammie meant something different in the car or if Zahra misheard what she thinks Sammie said . . . Well, Zahra just has to be very delicate with how she asks the question. Sammie doesn't seem to notice the moths overhead, but Zahra pushes the question out anyway.

"Sammie, I want to ask you something, and I don't want you to get weirded out or worried, but it's something you said in the car, when we drove through all those moths. I thought I heard you say that you could hear them. . . ."

Sammie's face says it all.

"You did hear them. Didn't you?"

"Well, what do you mean by *hear*?" Sammie's face is all contorted. She leans away from Zahra, as if the conversation is contagious.

"The music. The voices."

"I thought . . ." Sammie pauses. "Are you crazy?"

Zahra shakes her head, surprised by Sammie's bluntness but not thrown. "I hear them. All the time, but I've never met anyone, other than Derrick, who can hear them too. And I sort of think . . . Well, it's far-fetched but there's something your uncle said earlier that makes me think maybe, *maybe*, they brought me to you." Zahra looks away from Sammie, realizing it's a lot to dump on her.

"You think moths did what?"

"It's just . . . they were all over you that day, the first day I met you. They were everywhere. How could you not notice them?" Zahra points to the ceiling. One, two, three, at least ten of them. Doesn't Sammie see them? She looks at Sammie for confirmation, holding her arms out, palms up, *Well?* . . .

Sammie shakes her head again. "This is a lot. This is *crazy*."

"This is the way it's been my whole life. You'll get used to it."

Sammie backs away farther. Now she's on the edge of the bed. "But I'm not like you. I'm really different from you."

Zahra is hurt, and her face must show it, because Sammie says, "It's not a bad thing that we're different. It's just . . . I don't really believe in voodoo, you know? And I'm not interested in practicing . . . witchcraft."

"I'm not a witch, at least not the dramatic televised definition," Zahra says. "I don't have any powers. I don't know anything about magic."

"But moths sing to you?"

"But moths sing to me."

Sammie seems to consider this. She rubs her forehead hard. She shakes her head in what Zahra guesses is an attempt to free her thoughts.

Sammie says, "I don't know, but I'm really exhausted. It's been a long day."

"It has." Zahra nods, not wanting to talk about it anymore either. "Tell me more about Noah."

They lay on the bed, facing each other, propped up on opposite elbows. Zahra has worked with students for years now, but she has never felt the simultaneous need to teach and protect or the constant worry that she's saying all the wrong things or, for the lack of a better, more appropriate term, *motherly*. She and Sammie fall asleep with the lights on, music turned up, on top of the covers, comfortable.

||||||||||||||||||||||||||||||||||||||||||||||||

ZAHRA WAKES UP AT AROUND ONE IN THE MORNING. SHE turns off the music, which has come back around to "Tennessee," and throws an afghan on Sammie. She stops and stares at her for a second, wondering if it could be true that an invasive species she used to think nothing of brought them together. That it wasn't Sammie's college essay but something less fortuitous, something of God's design.

The wooden floors creak loudly. A haunting? No, just the house settling itself, Gram would say, but Zahra always imagined differently. Footsteps, growing up they were definitely footsteps, because she could not imagine a house settling itself in the way that Uncle Richard sat in the big armchair after work, rocking slightly from side to side, digging each buttock into the chair until he was at maximum comfort. No, a house would not settle in such an extreme way. Unlike Uncle Richard, it didn't clock a nine-to-seven Monday through Friday or push a lawn mower that's cord needed yanking every few yards to restart on the weekends. So she worried that someone was there, someone coming to get her. She would run to Derrick's bed and sleep at his feet—the only polite way for sisters to sleep with their brothers.

Now Zahra is not so scared as much as curious, having already rebutted the rules of science years ago. She leaves the bedroom and walks to the living room, the one with the good couch, which Gram will not let you sit on without throwing down a sheet first. If you spilled food or drink, your butt was on the line, and if you didn't, your butt was still on the line because that couch was for special occasions, and your skin was dirty. Now, in the dark, the couch's green viny design is almost imperceptible, though she can see the moon waxing crescent in the floor-to-ceiling windows behind it. There, in the center of the three windows, is where the tree used to stand like the house's witness, a bailiff but not a judge. She looks for it now, and though she knows Uncle Richard cut it down a long time ago, she can almost see it. Thriving, tall, wide, and leafy.

She can feel a moth, like an itch, on the tip of her nose. She doesn't swat it away but allows it to look with her, at what used to be, at a time when she and Derrick used to laugh together, when laughing came so easy, too easy. They laughed the first time they heard the moths, like marionette Marvin Gayes and Tammi Terrells.

"No way," Zahra had told Derrick. "You're making things up." But then she had heard them too, while on the tree singing, *Jig-a-low, jig, jig-a-low*, dancing on opposing branches, friends and cousins echoing from below. She'd looked at Derrick wide-eyed, and then they'd laughed so hard, holding their stomachs, almost falling to unpropitious fates, which Mom and Gram continuously warned of.

One day they heard Gram and Uncle Richard talking about the gypsy moths and snuck off to the library to read about them. What Zahra remembers is now in snippets, shaken up and mixed together with her more recent Google searches—*can completely defoliate trees*; *hundreds of eggs*; *flying long distance*; *spreading*; *but at some point, doesn't an invasive species become native?*

Zahra walks up to the window. She cups her hands around her eyes and peers outside. At the space where the tree used to live. She gasps, thinking something's there. But just as quickly, it is gone. Her eyes readjust to the darkness, and she backs away from the window.

FOURTEEN 🦋

It feels good to be behind the wheel. She'd forgotten this feeling of freedom having been sucked into the public transportation of New York. Where could Derrick have possibly gone without taking his Honda? She moves the seat up, compensating for Derrick's long legs, and feels as if she's interrupted the equilibrium. A creature of habit, how long has it been since he's changed anything in here? It's like this car has been on pause since he got it in 2010.

She sniffs the car's confined air, the steering wheel, Derrick's Clark Atlanta sweatshirt in the passenger seat. Trey offered to come with her, and Sammie begged and pleaded, but she needed this, didn't she? This alone time in Derrick's car, with Derrick's things, and Derrick's smell. She takes off her jean jacket and replaces it with Derrick's sweatshirt. She rubs her elbows, feels the worn-down fabric against her fingertips. She leans toward the windshield and breathes in the smell of Black Ice, three air fresheners hanging from the rearview mirror along with an African wood necklace, something he might have gotten from South DeKalb Mall or the Underground. She slides her hands along the dashboard, the console, picking up dust. This car is almost a part of him. She feels closer to him here. This is what Derrick has always been attached to—driving, riding, listening.

She takes out a map that she bought on the way here, at a gas station somewhere between Auburn and Atlanta. It feels good to have paper in hand, something that doesn't reduce Atlanta to a few left and right turns but shows the wide expanse of it. The map unfolds so far out that it tickles the passenger's door. She looks for home, or at least for Panola Road or Covington Highway, but as she follows 285 down the left edge of the map, she finds that the Eastside has been cut off, the map's key in its place. Annoyed, she tosses it in the back seat, realizing that it wouldn't be helpful anyway. She knows the places, has the route sketched in her head like a connect-the-dots game.

She turns on the car, and the radio rattles to life. The Supremes are singing "Come See About Me," and a memory of the song startles her. She and Derrick headed to Clark to move him in freshman year, the back seat of the car packed to the brim, and Uncle Richard tailing them in his pickup truck. This song coming on in the mix of other old R & B and Derrick pausing their conversation about what dorm life would be like to say, "Must be something crazy in this world to make Florence Ballard just stop singing. You know she wouldn't for a while, right? Wouldn't sing at all? Not a note, not a riff."

He looked so pensive when he said it, like he wasn't watching the road at all but revisiting something or someone somewhere else. The thought frightened Zahra, so she said, "I bet you'll have a girlfriend by the end of the semester, bet you'll be sneaking her into your dorm room." But even then, she'd known better. That Derrick was the solo type, not that there'd never be romance, but that he wasn't someone a person could attach themselves to. He might shake them free like a wet dog.

When Zahra takes off, she can barely steer the wheel, she's so drunk on the memories of Derrick, on the thought and smell of him. There are so many places he could be, so many places that are special to him, a true ATLien, a true Eastside stomper.

Atlanta is nothing like Gram's, not a domain unnaturally trapped in history but a locale very different from how she remembers it. Boarded up or torn down where there used to be buildings, cranes and halfway-there construction where the land used to be low and grazing. The place feels foreign, and Zahra quickly realizes that she doesn't remember the intricate twists and turns of the backroads that used to take her through thickets of forests and suburbs to the northside by North DeKalb Mall or farther up by Perimeter. *Memorial Drive to South Indian Creek, then Brocket Road to Lavista, was it?* How could she forget?

She goes to the other side of their neighborhood creek; the hot wings trailer; Golden Glide; Memorial Drive, where Yasin's used to slang the best whiting sandwiches in the area; Stone Mountain Park; the Dekalb Farmers Market; the Decatur library, or *the big library* as they called it as children; Wax 'N' Facts; the Omni; the Tabernacle; the Underground; the Shrine of the Black Madonna. But these places are just shells of the past, and they offer no trace of Derrick other than the memories they evoke. Of breezing along Covington Highway with the windows down, of panicking when they left J. R. Crickets after a N.E.R.D. concert at the Tabernacle to find that someone had stolen Dad's Jeep Grand Cherokee and they had no way home. Going to parties where they cranked music and the batman, but Derrick was the same old Derrick no matter where he went—the farmers market or the library or the Underground, white parties or Black parties—which meant he was too cool for school let alone to be caught dancing outside of his routine head nod, which got faster and stronger as the beat dropped. It was a staple dance move, and Derrick rocked it the best while driving—one hand on the wheel and leaned back like Terror Squad.

She goes by Julian's new house, the one he bought a few years ago near up-and-coming Bankhead, a revamped road D4L used to rap about. She knocks on the door restlessly for at least five minutes before acknowledging that he's not home, and she should've called first. When she does call, he says that he's at work, and no, he hasn't seen Derrick in like over a year or something. She hangs up quickly when he asks what's going on.

She goes by Terrence's midtown town house. He is Derrick's closest friend from college, one who seems to understand him almost as well as she does. He answers the door, shirtless and sweating, asks how she's doing, asks if she wants to come in for a glass of water or lemonade or sweet tea. She remembers why she liked him so much. His boyfriend comes to the door now too, and they are beautiful together, a chiseled and cheery couple. Their happiness confuses her; it is so opposite her own feelings of despair.

"Is Derrick here?" she blurts out. "Have you seen him?"

Terrence invites her in again, but she shakes her head. She just needs to know. "Have you seen him?"

"No," Terrence says. "It's been over a month. Maybe two. He seemed sad the last time I saw him, and not in his usual melancholy way but really lost, Zahra. I'm sorry. I should have been more—"

"No," Zahra says. "It's not your fault."

She races back to the car, where she just sits for a while. She tries to think like Derrick. She listens for the voices, but none come to her, not even the moths. Eventually, she realizes she's forgotten to check Fellini's, Derrick's favorite pizza spot, where they used to go on weekend afternoons when there was nothing better to do. Sometimes they weren't even hungry.

When she gets there, she cannot force herself to leave the car but breaks down crying, wiping tears and snot on Derrick's sweatshirt. She's exhausted, and she's losing steam, hope.

She hears her phone vibrating, and when she finally moves to answer it, she sees that it is Mrs. Jacobs. She knows she shouldn't answer, but she needs the money. Maybe Sophia wants to do a session over Skype.

"Hi." Zahra tries to gather her voice so that it doesn't sound like she's been crying.

"Zahra, I'm so happy we've finally gotten in touch." Odd. Zahra doesn't think she's missed any calls or text messages, but completely inadvertent statements like this aren't unlike Mrs. Jacobs's usual refrains.

"Me too," Zahra says. "How is Sophia? Is she feeling confident about her essay?"

"About that," Mrs. Jacobs says, as if they'd have anything else to discuss. "I know it's your *job* to coach, Zahra. And you've done that amazingly. You really have. But Sophia has been feeling a little *down* about her essay."

Mrs. Jacobs's emphases are making Zahra's stomach curl, and she wants nothing more than to end this phone call, but Mrs. Jacobs goes on.

"Sophia doesn't think it's *good* enough, and frankly, I'm not sure it is either. And maybe you've done all you can. Maybe she's not *meant* to go to Stanford. I mean, she's her *mother's* child." Mrs. Jacobs laughs a little, and Zahra cringes. "Anyhow, *two* things. Let's schedule another session to see if it can't get a little *better*? And I just don't want Sophia to lose her fighter spirit, so if you could be a little *softer* with her, that would be nice. She's a great girl, and I don't want her thinking anything *less* of herself. She seems to think she's too *myopic*, her word." Mrs. Jacobs pauses, as if the word needs an applause. "But you know Sophia. Always talking about some injustice; she's such an *empath*. So what she's feeling, what she's thinking about herself can't be true. We both know that's not true. Right? Wouldn't you say, *Zahra?*"

Zahra would say that *myopic* is a good word for Sophia, but Mrs. Jacobs is not really asking for Zahra's opinion here, and she recognizes that. No, Mrs. Jacobs wants reassurance, wants to know that Zahra will not break her little girl, will not ask her to reflect in any way other than one in which she comes up with a solid 650-word essay. Stanford and the preservation of Sophia as she knows it, that is what matters to Mrs. Jacobs, so Zahra says, "Sophia is a deep thinker. I'll make sure she knows that. How about six tonight?"

"You couldn't do any earlier?"

"No, I'm in Atlanta, and I'm actually looking . . ."

"Right. The family emergency. I hope everything is OK."

Zahra sighs. "It's OK," she says.

"Then maybe three or four?"

"That's in an hour, and I'm not even home right now."

"Right. OK. Five? It's just Sophia has plans with her friends at six, and she would kill me if . . ."

"I'll see her at five."

"You're the best. Thank you so much, Zahra."

Zahra hears a tap on her window, then a full palm banging on it. *Oh my god. Is that Zee?*

"Zahra!" Zee screams. "Zahra! Open up, girl."

Zahra opens the door and rushes into the arms of her oldest, best friend. It feels good to hug her tightly, like things could go back to the way they used to be, when she and Zee used to make up dance routines to Mariah Carey songs.

"I knew that was you, girl. What are you doing back home, and in Derrick's old Honda no less? It's been forever. You weren't even gonna call?"

"I'm sorry," Zahra says, a simple apology but not for just this one slip-up. It's also an apology for losing touch, for going off to Stanford and then DC and then New York with barely a goodbye, with a million I'll-call-you-backs that she never followed up on, and a relationship that grew colder until it became something that only exists over social media and Zee's persistent offhanded text messages that Zahra only sometimes responds to.

Zee pushes Zahra to arm's length and takes a good look at her. Zahra tries to smile, but it's not fooling Zee, and she asks, "You all right, girl?"

Zahra's eyes water, and she looks up to the baby-blue sky using all the muscles in her face not to cry.

"C'mon," Zee says. "Let me buy you a slice. We'll get your favorite. Sausage and mushrooms, OK?"

Zee's memory is stronger than Zahra's eye muscles, and she starts full-blown sobbing. She follows Zee into the restaurant, to the front counter where they order food and then through the tables, all round four-seaters, most at full capacity and haphazardly placed. They zigzag their way to a corner table under a retro tin sign of a pair of prayer hands and the invocation *Pray for Atlanta*. Zee places the stand with their order number on the center of it. Quietly sobbing, Zahra keeps her head down as she sits. It is a relief, not only to cry but to have someone here as she does it.

When there are half-eaten slices of pizza and fizzy soft drinks in front of them, and Zahra has collected herself, her tears buried in a mountain of napkins on the table, Zee says nonchalantly, "So what's up?"

Zahra can't help but laugh. "God, you were always so good at this, at making everything seem light and fleeting."

"Well, you learn to be that way when you lose a parent at a young age." Zee leans back in her chair, resigned to the past.

"Right." How had Zahra forgotten watching Zee's dad grow ill, thinking he'd recover like everyone else Zahra knew, and then one day, he just didn't. It was weird how he never got better. It was the first time Zahra felt close to death, and yet, she wasn't close at all. To this day, she doesn't even know what Zee's dad died of. Back then she thought it might have been cancer, but now, the hush-hush of it all makes her think it was AIDS.

Zee didn't exactly become different after her dad died, but she wasn't the same either. Sometimes Zahra felt like Zee was role-playing the old version of herself, or like a new clone had come to replace her. Zahra couldn't pinpoint the difference between the old and the new, the real and the fake, but it was there.

Zahra looks up at her old friend. Just as she remembers her, Zee's curly more than kinky hair frames her light brown heart-shaped face. She wears round eyeglasses, and there's a tiny stud in her nose. Zahra decides that this is the real thing, the real Zee, the one who used to slide her notes folded in perfect little triangles in between classes. This is the Zee who she went to senior prom with when neither of them could find dates, the one who became a Girl Scout with her only to quit two badges—cooking and woodworking—later, the Zee who would regularly burst out in song or in full-flowing tears but still maintained that Zahra was the emotional one.

"Derrick is missing," Zahra says, thinking Zee will understand if no one else.

Zee's eyes go wide and then back to normal. If Zahra blinked, she would've missed the reaction.

"I saw him," Zee says. "It wasn't that long ago. Maybe a week? Week and a half?"

"Really?" Zahra is surprised. Derrick had become such a recluse. "How did he look? Did he look like himself?" A table of three sits down next to them, two white men and a small child, three or four maybe.

Zee shrugs. "It's hard to say. I thought about speaking to him. I really did, but he seemed . . ."

"Yeah?" Zahra asks, but it doesn't seem like Zee can find the right word, and the white kid is hovering over their table, too close for comfort.

"He seemed . . . preoccupied."

"With something or someone?"

"I don't know."

"Well, where was he? Where did you see him?"

Zee's about to speak but pauses. The kid is an unwanted third party. He calls his dad but is still looking at her and Zee, all droopy-eyed. The dad reaches out a hand but seems too preoccupied with his spouse or friend to pay the kid any real attention.

Zee leans forward to barricade her words. "Downtown. At an art show, something really kitschy and lame."

"Were there people from high school there? People Derrick might know?"

Zee takes a second. "Yeah, some, but it's not like Derrick really hangs out with the old crowd like that."

Well, no, Derrick doesn't really hang out at all anymore. He might sit and talk to you but not in a large group and not for a long time. It's like people began to tire him out, like they drained the life out of him.

"Excuse me," Zee says loudly to the men at the table, and they finally see the problem. Still, Zee says for extra effect, "Your kid."

"Jerry," the dad says, and the boy follows but he's still looking at them. The dad doesn't apologize, doesn't seem to care that his kid has made them uncomfortable, but then their pizza arrives and the boy's attention finally averts.

Zahra shakes her head and brings the conversation back to Derrick. "That's not really much to go by."

"I know. I wish I had more for you." Zee bites her lip, considering something. "Well, I don't know what this means or if it matters, but he had a stack of papers with him, a thick stack, in both hands, papers the size of church programs, you know . . ." She formulates a rectangle with her hands.

Zahra nods as if she understands, but really she doesn't get it at all. She doesn't understand what Derrick was thinking, why he's disappeared, or why he had a mountain of papers not long before he just poofed and was gone.

But then she thinks back on the crumpled paper, the image of Derrick but not Derrick. "And you didn't see what was on the papers?"

"He was too far away." Zee seems to think back. She takes a sip of her Pibb Xtra, brings the straw to her mouth without looking down at her cup. "When my dad died, for a while, I thought he was leaving me signs," she says.

"What sort of signs?"

"You know, if a door closed on its own, I thought he was in the room with me. If lightning struck or thunder sounded as I was contemplating something deep, I thought he was answering. Stuff like that. But then . . ." Zee stops, as if this next thought will be more profound than the others.

"But then . . ." Zahra urges, and Zee continues, but she seems more reluctant about it.

"My dad wasn't much of a singer. He would hum around the house, that was his thing mostly. Sometimes he would whistle. But one day, one day I could have sworn." She takes a deep breath. "I was listening to the Temptations, 'Just My Imagination,' you know that song? And I could have sworn it was my dad's voice in place of Eddie Kendricks. It sounded just like my dad. And at the time, well, I was at the point in my life where I needed him more than anything else."

Zahra doesn't know what time Zee's referring to, but she can bet money that she wasn't around, more likely at one of her Stanford meetings, the Black Student Union or the Caribbean Students Association, SEESA or NAIJA, trying out any and all Black organizations, never finding the ease she was looking for with just one. Or maybe she was out fountain hopping during freshman week or shooting shots in Palo Alto as a senior. Wherever she was, Zee didn't reach out or maybe she did, and Zahra just didn't care enough to answer her phone.

Now, Zee leans back in her chair. "Huh, I've never told anyone that before, that I heard him, you know."

The ease with which Zee has restored trust in Zahra makes her cringe. She feels the need to share something as equally discomforting with Zee, but there's only one thing that comes to mind, and she's not ready to talk about the moths with anyone who can't hear them, so she says, "I think people hear what they need to hear sometimes. You needed your father, so he came to you. No shame in that." Shame or not, Zahra won't apply this logic to her own life.

"I could help you look for him," Zee says. "You know I used to have the smallest, almost nothing, barely anything little crush on him, right?"

Zahra smiles, surprised. "You didn't!"

"I'm so ashamed."

"Bitch! You were never going to tell me, were you?" Zahra crosses her arms.

Zee looks away, covers her face with her hands, but Zahra can tell that she's laughing. "I mean, he was fine."

"Please stop."

Zee grows serious again. "My offer stands. Anything for the Robinsons."

"No, no. I can handle it. He's my brother."

"You always were possessive." Zee throws her hands on the table as if that wraps everything up. "Should we get out of here?"

They should, but then Zahra has grown so comfortable here, with one of her old best friends, that she nearly grabs Zee's hand across the table and begs her to stay. Instead, she checks her phone and is blown by the time. She's going to be late for her appointment with Sophia. Zahra imagines Sophia's face when she pops on the link at five fifteen, a mixture of disappointment and disbelief, rosy round cheeks that will look more innocent than Zahra could ever dream them, that couldn't be more different from Zee's features across from her now, having grown softer with age but for a crease in her forehead that seems to suggest she is always thinking. Zahra wonders if that crease has been there since they were seventeen years old, like Sophia is now. What has she missed, with Zee, with Derrick, with the moths? How is it possible she's just now seeing?

FIFTEEN 🦋

Sammie was right about everything. She sees things here, lurking in the shadows, Zahra's people or old pieces of furniture. She blinks, and they're gone, everything back to normal. There are sounds that everyone says is just the way an old home groans, but she knows better because she feels an energy too, like the feeling you get on the dip of a roller coaster, her stomach lifting outside of itself. Sometimes a hand creeps down her back and she jumps as if a bug is inside of her shirt, but then nothing's there.

Sammie's on edge being alone here, but Zahra is still out looking for Derrick, and Gram went to run errands, and Uncle Trey is in the back, sleeping after their long three-hour college tour. Realizing that she left her swag bag with brochures and clicky pens and a Spelman sweatshirt she begged Uncle to buy in the car, Sammie goes outside, through the side door, to get it. She walks along the fence separating this house from the next until she gets to the front curb, then the passenger door of Uncle's Nissan when she hears a whistle, not a catcall but something more melodic, the sort of whistling someone does while they work. Sammie jumps at the sound, then looks over her shoulder and sees a boy, shining like a clean quarter on the street, as beautiful as the day. Could have plucked him right from the freshman quad at Clark, but he's her age or not far from it and wearing old cutoff shorts and a vintage Michael Jackson T-shirt. She remembers him watching them pull up the day before. Was he watching her just now? Well, boys are always watching Sammie.

"Hey," he says. "You moving in?"

She considers this. Obviously, she's not moving to Gram's, but to Atlanta? "Maybe," she says. "You live there?" She points to the house behind him, a mismatched brick house with overgrown grass that looks like it's tickling the boy's ankles.

He eyes her intensely, as if the answer is a secret, and he's determining whether she can keep it. "Maybe," he says.

She smiles. "How old are you?"

He closes the gap between them, throwing his fingers through the chain-link fence and grabbing a hold of it. He leans forward so the fence bends a little under his weight. "How old do I look?" he says.

"I don't know. Seventeen? Eighteen? Does everything have to be a question with you?"

He shrugs. "Sixteen."

"Younger than me," she says.

He raises his eyebrows. "You in college?"

"I will be."

"A senior?"

Sammie nods.

"How's it feel? To be a senior?" he asks. "You ready to leave high school?"

Sammie hasn't considered things in this way—if she's *ready* to leave. Well, why shouldn't she be? She's worked hard enough. She's smart enough. She'll miss Uncle Trey and Mother Ma and Aunty Deanne no matter where she goes, but she'll broach those feelings when she gets there. "I'm ready to be my own person," she says.

She can tell by the way he pulls back from the fence that he likes her answer, maybe that he's a little blown away by her. He shakes his head. "Well, excuse me."

"Aren't you ready?" she asks him. "You can only stay in high school but for so long."

"No lie there," he says.

Then, so randomly that she almost turns away from him, he says, "You're pretty. Very, very pretty."

Her stomach turns, and she doesn't know what to say back. She could say he is cute or handsome, and it won't be a lie, but she isn't sure she wants to up the level of flirting. She doesn't know this guy, doesn't know this neighborhood, doesn't even know this city.

"Thank you," she says. "But I have to get going. So much work senior year. You'll see."

He shrugs, and she dips into the car for her bag, then heads back inside, thinking they didn't even exchange names.

||||||||||||||||||||||||||||||||||||||||||||||

SAMMIE SITS DOWN AT THE KITCHEN TABLE TO WORK ON HER college essay. The house feels empty, silent, eerie. She works on her computer but holds a blue-and-white Spelman pen in her right hand, clicking it absentmindedly, the sound welcome over the house's hunger pains.

Sammie enjoyed the tour of the AUC. She could see herself on Spelman's or Clark's campus next fall, rushing to class in a college-branded crewneck, making friends like her Spelman tour guide, a girl with perfectly arched eyebrows and contoured makeup and a black, silky weave that she flung across her shoulders as she spoke.

Sammie sees them laughing on the quad, going to house parties, flirting with cute boys like the ones she saw huddled together at Morehouse. She sees herself taking all sorts of art and history classes, English and literature. Maybe she'll join a sorority. Maybe she'll run for student body president, something she could never see herself winning at P & P.

Sammie wonders what would happen if she and Noah started dating now and remained an item through college. What would visiting her be like? Would he be uncomfortable around so many Black people? She'd *had* to grow comfortable around the white people at P & P, so maybe it would be only fair for him to have a similar turn.

It would be much easier to be with a boy like Gram's neighbor, who is Black like her and does the same knotty mess to her stomach as Noah. She wouldn't have to explain things to him, wouldn't have to hide whole parts of herself. She sees herself touring Atlanta with Noah, then with the neighbor, then without a boy flanking her side at all, all alone or with a group of girlfriends, taking in long green landscapes and the sounds of birds, then classmates, then crickets. But just like New York, she could never imagine Atlanta quiet. There's always something happening, something moving—things she can see, and things she can't, too.

Sammie thought she saw Derrick today. Derrick hitchhiking on the side of the highway, Derrick flirting with a woman in the AUC library by the Tupac archives, Derrick using one of the vending machines near the coed dorms at Clark, and finally Derrick sitting right across from them at the Busy Bee cafe, where they stopped to eat lunch. She has memorized his face from Gram's pictures, so she sees Derrick at all ages. Sometimes he's just a young boy, ten or eleven. Then he's close to the age he is now, only now he's never smiling but pensive in a way that makes her want to save him from himself.

She takes out her stolen photo of Derrick, now kept in her

sketchbook, a bookmark between blank pages and her doodles and drawings. She stares at him intently, his eyes a maze and a magnet. A feeling washes over her, and she looks over her shoulder to see what's crept into her space, the kitchen, Gram's house. The feeling of being watched has only grown stronger since she's been in Atlanta, no longer just a pair of eyes, but a hand too, on her shoulder, pressing down on her. She tries to slink away from the hand, but her shoulder remains just so, and the feeling of being watched grows more tangible day by day. She shakes her head, puts the picture away.

She rereads the paragraphs she's already written. She's proud of herself. The essay is good so far; she's confident in it. She just has to wrap things up. She has to show that she *knows herself and that she can apply this knowledge to better understand the people around her.* Zahra's words. Got it. She can do this. She picks up where she left off—

She types—*I am a Black girl.*

She erases it and types—*I am a Trini American girl who is alright. I have a mother who I don't really know, and a father who doesn't love me, and on most days, I feel like I'm in two places at once, but like Kendrick Lamar says . . .*

She erases it and types—*I am a Trini American girl who is alright. I hear voices, moths in song, and there is someone watching me, creeping up like a caterpillar.*

She erases it and types—*I am a Trini American girl, and sometimes I think I am beautiful and sometimes not. I like a white boy who I am scared will never like me back.*

She erases it and types—*I am a Trini American girl, an artist, a writer, a fighter, and most important, a perpetual asker of questions.*

She erases it and types—*I am a Trini American girl who is alright. I know how to cook stew chicken, and I know all the lyrics to "Blank Space." I listen to everything around me, and I know it's not all alright, and I'm working on how to fix things. Not only for me, but for Mother*

Ma, and the biological mother I know very little of, and my uncle Trey, who I know better than the shape of my hands. I am in a Kendrick Lamar song, but also, here I am coming out of it. Alright, alright, alright.

She erases it and text messages Leila.

This college shit is hard.

"Here." The voice startles her. She turns around to see that it is Gram in a bedazzled white shirt that isn't wholly fancy or casual. She holds out a slice of cake.

Sammie smiles. "Thank you," she says, taking the offer and placing it gently on the table.

Gram sits down beside her, and she smells warm and woody, distinctly different from Mother Ma but the feeling she provides is similar. Sammie wants to lay her head on Gram's shoulder, but she smiles again instead. This time wider.

"You working?" Gram asks.

Sammie nods. "On my college essay. It's supposed to reflect who I am."

"Mm-hmm," Gram says, then points to the cake. "Eat."

Sammie does as she's told, and it's so good. But it's not like she's never had pound cake before Gram's. Uncle Trey likes to buy the store-bought kind, the one in the blue-and-white box with a clear plastic window showing off the yellow cake inside. But this is something altogether different. Lighter and sweeter. She savors it, and Gram nods as if she knows it was the right thing to give her.

"Thought I could help you out with that," Gram says, and Sammie thinks she's talking about the cake, but then she adds, "Let me tell you a story." She takes Sammie's hand and squeezes it softly, an assurance. *This is going to be a good one. Trust me.*

"I'd like that," Sammie says, squeezing back.

"Bet Zahra didn't tell you much about her mom, did she? Like that she went to Spelman?"

Sammie shakes her head. Seems like something Zahra would've, should've mentioned.

"Graduated top of her class. Went on to law school. Did very, very well. Smart."

Zahra's mom hasn't seemed so bad, not how Zahra describes her at all. "Did something happen to her?" Sammie asks Gram.

Gram shrugs. "Well, she ran for the House of Representatives. She was still young then, midthirties maybe, hot little thing too. Had all the men swarming; she got that from me." Gram pauses, straightens her back. "And it seemed like things were going well. She was always speaking out somewhere, marching with someone, protesting, a right little Shirley Chisholm I had on my hands." Gram looks like she's gone back in time, like she won't say much more, but then she seems to remember. "Zahra tells me you're an organizer too."

"It was just a school sit-in, and it wasn't all that hard to organize. I didn't have to convince a lot of people to get on board."

Gram laughs a little. "Be careful with that. Be careful with not giving yourself credit. That's honey for men."

Sammie's not sure what Gram means by that but nods anyway.

"Oh, right, the year she ran for House . . . Zahra and Derrick were still young, six and seven. 'Ninety-three, no, 'ninety-four, I believe. Montgomery, their dad, and Mary never married, but they were still together at the time. Off and on, but together most of the time, you know how that goes."

Sammie doesn't, but she listens anyway.

"Mary comes home one day, and she's all dressed, a red two-piece, tight skirt set. And I didn't think nothing of what she was going through back then. Always seemed like a hot mama to me, always seemed like she had it together, two kids and all. You may not believe it now, but at one point in time, Yvonne Burke was her idol. First congresswoman to take maternity leave, a Black woman. Mary thought if she could have a baby at the nip and sign legislation, she could have it all. Went full steam ahead. Rode a platform that pioneered three things: education, equal housing, and rethinking crime. If you ask me, the last one is what got her. She went against Bill Clinton and his saxophone-playing, jive-talking, ain't-never-met-a-Blackman-he-don't-think-he-know self. You'd think we didn't know no better, but, Sammie, the answers have always been here."

Sammie is unsure of which *here* Gram is referring to, if she means here in the figurative sense or if she's being more literal, here in this house, in this city, in Georgia, in the United States of America.

As if Sammie has asked the question out loud, Gram says, "You know I've lived in this house for almost twenty-five years now? Longer than you've been born."

"That's a long time," Sammie says, thinking her family hasn't even been in the States for quite that long.

"Mm-hmm," Gram says. "Long time. Time enough I thought this house was my home. Silly, huh?"

Isn't this Gram's house? If not hers, then whose? Not knowing what to say, Sammie gulps down the lemonade she poured before Gram distracted her with cake. The glass is sweating with so much condensation that she almost drops it.

"Careful, there," Gram says, then revisits her reverie. "You know houses have personalities?"

Sammie shakes her head. No, she doesn't. Or at least didn't. Not until recently. Not until visiting this house, with its electric currents that run like a pulse, so she feels its breath and its wild, beating heart. Sammie shakes her head, but she knows enough now, that this house is not just a house, that this house has something in between the walls, under the floorboards, something lurking and uneasy. She looks around the kitchen and finds nothing amiss, the white cabinets wiped clean with Clorox, the linoleum slick and shiny, the faucet with a rag thrown over it but no dirty dishes in the sink waiting to be washed. Impeccable. Cleaner than even Mother Ma's haunts.

Now, the house croaks so loudly that she thinks it's heard her thoughts, but Gram stands up and without looking behind her to see who it is, says, "Montgomery and Richard. Nothing and nobody to be afraid of." She smiles a smile of recognition, and Sammie stares into her empty glass, the wooden table underneath it distorted by half-melted ice cubes, trickles of liquid between them. Did Gram finish her story? Sammie's not sure, though she doesn't think Ms. Mary made it into the House of Representatives, did she?

SAMMIE'S PHONE BUZZES, AND SHE LOOKS DOWN AT IT. IT'S from Noah, and her heart thumps. She opens the message.

Yeah, tell me about it. Still working on my essay. Due soon.
You done?

Wtf is he talking about? Then she scrolls up and sees that she accidentally messaged him instead of Leila. She nearly shrieks, but then, considering his response, she smiles. She sits on her response. Maybe Zahra can help her with it.

WHEN ZAHRA GETS BACK HOME, SHE RUSHES OFF TO HER room and shuts the door. Sammie goes to check on her. She presses her ear to the wall and can hear Zahra talking Sophia off a ledge. "No, no, it's good," Zahra says. "You're going to get in. Trust me."

Sammie goes back to the kitchen and eats dinner with Uncle Trey and Zahra's family, as they wait for the police to call.

"Any day now," Gram says on loop. "Bet they're not even looking. Bet they're out arresting Black boys for stealing bags of sunflower seeds." Everyone around the table nods, but no one else has anything to say about the matter, and Sammie feels like Gram is a different Gram from whom she spoke with earlier. This Gram is on edge, her confidence suffocated, her voice crackling with more than age, with a fierce generator that Sammie feels cannot easily be undone or turned off.

"We should have something for this, you know. Our way of finding people who've up and gone," Gram says.

Sammie wonders what that thing might be. You can't just put a grown man on house arrest. You can't GPS your cousins or metal detect your parents. When a person wants to go missing, they have every right to make like mist, don't they? And when they want to be found? Well, maybe it's not that easy to find your way back.

They eat a box of fried chicken that Ms. Mary bought from Publix then leave the table one by one, in five- or ten- or twenty-minute increments. Ms. Mary says she should be getting home, then Uncle Trey excuses himself to take a shower. Sammie looks over, and it's just her and Gram again, Zahra still in the back of the house somewhere, having never made it out to dinner. Sammie gets up to go, but rushes to Gram first and wraps her arms around her. Sammie makes no promises, can't think of any profound well-wishes, but Gram says, "Mm-hmm," and Sammie feels a little better about things.

SIXTEEN 🦋

Zahra can't sleep through the night anymore—she's got too much going on, too much on her mind. This night, at random, she shoots up, out of her sleep like a new mother. She's parched, fell asleep unexpectedly, without a glass of water next to her bed like usual. She convinces herself she's not afraid of this house or the dark that fills it and plops one leg off the bed then the other like someone just learning to walk. She rises ungracefully and heads to the front of the house, eyes still caked with sleep. She was dreaming about something weird—Mary stepping in the middle of a street fight and Zahra screaming *Mom* after her.

Mary is Zahra's mother, but she isn't *Mom*. It took Zahra crying about stolen Halloween candy and Mary saying *There are bigger fish to fry* with the care of a bored teenager for Zahra to distinguish the small but pertinent difference. Moms braid your hair and tell you bedtime stories and scream *That's my baby* at games and recitals. At the very least, moms show up, for pivotal life events like weddings and graduations, but also, when you're really happy or really sad. When they see their son grow more and more introverted, when they see the change, a metachrosis right before their eyes, moms ask questions, don't they? A simple *What's going on?* Well, not Mary. Mary just speaks of politics and justice, so Zahra knew words like *recidivism* and *adjudication* at the rightful age of twelve, and years later, this jargon still wouldn't find its place in her long list of SAT words.

It's not to say that Mary is all bad. The woman is mesmerizing; there's no denying the look of her in a thrift shop pantsuit or the clapbacks she delivers on camera, in court, to crass men who put their lives on the line by catcalling her. Zahra loves that Mary can laugh in one second and then gather you up like a suction cup in the next, saying things like *But you just don't know any better*, or *Child, please, go read a book*. And her passion, you can almost see it slobbering down her mouth. She has a goal, a want, a need, something that keeps her up at night; she's an untamable pit bull.

Zahra knows she is more like her mother than she ever wished for or thought possible. She is emotional when it comes to injustice, ignorance, impervious systems that keep innocent people in poverty and prison. She makes fists while watching YouTube clips of police brutality and thinks for hours about microaggressions that have gone unaddressed.

Zahra cannot only blame the men she dates on her loneliness. She has the same demanding immaturity as Mary. A cross-her-arms-and-pout-loudly way that makes men want to shut her off with a remote. Her fury is not uncalled for. It's expected even, but that doesn't make it any less tolerable. Men want to claw their eyes out with all of her droning, on and on, the things she can't let go of. It does not occur to her that she has to act in order to shake free the scars or that the flocking moths are not only their own species but also symptoms of her madness, like goose bumps when it's cold out or that tingling sensation that comes with a new cavity.

When Zahra heads through the living room and into the kitchen, she's forgotten exactly where the lights are. She feels against the wall wildly, scared to hear or see something in the resounding darkness. She finds the light but just as quickly hears a chair scratching the floor. She knows something or someone is here. She jumps before she can process Gram's muumuu tucked between her knees, her blue bonnet high off her head like Marge Simpson.

"What are you doing up so late?" Zahra asks. "And sitting in the dark?"

Gram does not look at her but takes a sip of her tea as if she might not respond. After a while, she says, "Thinking about you and your brother."

"You miss him?"

"Of course I do. I've missed him for years now."

"Me too," Zahra says. She goes to the cupboard for a glass and then runs the tap. She comes back to the table and sits next to Gram, scooting her chair closer, disrupting the table's even spacing that Gram works hard to maintain throughout the day.

"It's not all him, you know, that worries me. It's you too."

"Oh, Gram. You don't have to worry about me. I'm doing fine, good even."

"I always knew Derrick would struggle. He was too heady as a child. He was stressed, even when he was young, three or four."

Zahra smirks. It seems absurd that a three-year-old would be stressed out. How would Gram know if he was?

Gram looks at her with pity. "He used to grind his teeth at night. He'd pick at open scabs, at hangnails, at any little bump or bruise. Sometimes he wouldn't eat. He would ask all of these questions, and I never had the answers, and I felt so bad. Questions like, *Why do good people do bad things?* Imagine, a three-year-old. You realize early on that life will be hard for him. But *you*, I didn't worry about as much. You were thoughtful without being destructive. Bothered but unbothered. I thought you were a good balance, a smart kid but not so emotionally stunted. I'm worried I was wrong now. I'm worried you might be worse than your brother."

"Gram, what are you talking about? I'm doing fine. I'm the one sitting next to you right now."

"I dated a guy like you once, Willie McDonald, going nowhere but up the street and around the corner. Always coming back the same, nothing changed. Couldn't seem to put one foot in front of the other in the way of the rest of the world. He was the worst of them, you know. A hamster in one of those things that turns. What's it called?"

"A running wheel."

"Mm-hmm," Gram says. "You think you're grown."

"I am, Gram. I'm thirty-one years—"

"You're not grown."

Zahra will be thirty-two this December, and she's not sure where Gram is going with this. It's not like she's some kid living off her grandmother's dime or in her grandmother's house. So what constitutes *grown* in Gram's eyes?

"You want kids?"

Well, not until recently. Now she thinks she could be a mother. "Maybe." But what does it have to do with anything?

"Mm-hmm, that's what I thought. Forethought, Zahra. Maybe your mom was thinking ahead of you. To your children and your children's children. Ever consider that? It would take you stepping outside of yourself. It would take you learning how to be someone different for a day." The house rumbles, and Gram seems to listen to it. She waits a while to speak again. "Go on and say it. Say what's on your mind."

But she's not sure what to say. She doesn't know what any of this has to do with Derrick. She just wants to find her brother. For things to go back to how they used to be. She's not looking for the future. Just the opposite. She's looking for the past. And what's so wrong with that? "I just want to find Derrick," she says. "I can't think about anything else until I do."

"It's like you and Derrick don't know the straight and narrow. Haven't I taught you at least that much? He went this way, and you went that way, but you were supposed to go straight, and you were supposed to go together. And now look where we are."

"You're blaming me?"

"I'm not blaming you."

"You're blaming me." Zahra cannot look at the disappointment wedged like wrinkles between Gram's brows, so she looks at the wooden floorboards, her unkempt fingernails, the same dinner table that she ate at as a kid, almost blemish-free. She looks toward the back of the house, watches shadows play tag along the living room wall. She closes her eyes and listens for what the house might have to say about this, but it is more silent than ever. She pinches her nose and takes a second before saying, "Maybe you're right."

"I don't mean to be," Gram says.

Zahra gets up from the table, full of grief and contemplation. She's never felt particularly successful, but in this moment, she feels like an absolute failure. She gulps down her last swig of water and places the cup in the kitchen sink. She heads back to bed and hears Gram call after her. "There's church in the morning," she says, and that's just like Gram, to think she can just pray Derrick back.

|||||||||||||||||||||||||||||||||||||||||||||||||

WHEN ZAHRA WAKES UP THE NEXT MORNING, SHE THINKS IT is Derrick playing the music. An old mix. Brandy leading into Monica.

"Derrick," she calls out, drowsily walking over to her stereo and smashing down the off button. But the music doesn't stop. She does. In her tracks, hand still on top of the power button, remembering that she is not in high school and Derrick has gone missing. And it's her fault. She rubs the sleep from her eyes and turns around to see that she's woken Sammie up. Sammie peers at her sadly.

"You OK?" Sammie asks.

"Yeah, I just . . ." Zahra can't explain. The music is too loud for her to think straight. *Just one of them days* . . . She pieces together where it's coming from. Damn gypsy moths. Zahra spots one on her old dresser and without hesitating or thinking it through, she grabs the closest book, a hardback copy of *Shake Loose My Skin* and slams the book on top of it. When she picks the book back up, the moth is gone. She spots it on the back of the book, dead, so cleanly smashed against the glossy cover that it looks like it might be a part of it. She puts the book down and backs away from it slowly, as if she hasn't just killed something but instead, *she* is the body in threat. She feels the urge to get out, out of the house and far away but maybe just outside will do. She heads to the patio.

Zahra doesn't process it at first. But then clear as the day, clear as the song that won't turn off, like the sun hot on her skin, is the tree. This was their tree. The tree they climbed liked swinging monkeys, singing across branches to each other. This was the tree that introduced them to bottomless voices. This was the tree Uncle Richard cut down, the same one that was overrun by gypsy moths. Here it is, neither a phantom nor a figment of her imagination, but rooted, strong as it ever was. Brown and red and yellow leaves the size of her palm. How the hell? How the hell is it here looking back at her?

"Gram," Zahra calls.

Then she is running, racing to Gram's room wondering how it can be, wondering how long it's been there. A second chance, a second chance at living.

"Gram!" Zahra screams.

SEVENTEEN

Deforestation. Sammie passed on that class at P & P and doesn't know what she doesn't know yet, about the old Atlanta Prison Farm, aka Honor Farm, that once housed convicts, many Black, with minimal, questionable offenses. A place of more than four hundred trees and small, graceful streams, deemed a beautiful experiment by some and a place of lynchings and lawlessness by others. Believe what you will, it burned down in 2009, just ten years ago. Then another fire hit in 2017, like kicking someone who's already down. Imagine the fire licking three acres of red soil, the black smoke creating a haze over the city, drifting through the sky so children look out of their airplane windows, point, and ask, "Mom, what's that?" And yet kudzu climbs determinedly, not to be damned by fire or smoke, but a snake with no head, no tail. The forest is like that, you know? Not really, Sammie doesn't know shit. Not yet. But still . . .

You're going to change the world; that's what I like about you. Sammie repeats it to herself over and over again, and it only gets better as she does. *You're going to change the world; that's what I like about you. You're going to change the world; that's what I like about you.*

Today is a good day, one where Sammie believes that she can, and these are all just moments she'll explain in a documentary down the road. And it's true; she *does* have a plan, inspired by the Black women entrepreneurs she's heard about so much lately, watching *She Did That* on Netflix, or closer stories, of their neighbor Ms. Davis selling cakes by word of mouth, then on Facebook, then off the website her son created for her. Of Leila's cousin Marie making skirts and crop tops from African prints and selling them on Etsy. Of the Black woman on the bus handing out cards: eyelashes for sale, get your locs twisted, get your face contoured. Sammie's not sure what business she'll jump into, but whatever it is, she sees herself as an executive, pencil skirt, heels, iPhone in one hand, laptop tucked under her arm.

She can't wait to get there, but then she knows that where she's at is somewhere special too. She's heard enough from Uncle Trey and Mother Ma and Aunty Deanne about how she'll look back and miss what's right here in front of her. She'll ache for it, they say, and she believes them, because she aches for it now, even though she's still in it. Sometimes she just wants to crawl deeper inside of herself, carving space for everything she wants to remember, everything she can't forget. She wants someone to share her memories, her dreams with. Mother Ma is nice, and Uncle Trey and Aunty Deanne and Leila too. But she imagines love, and she thinks she knows the start of it; she wants that just as badly as the business, the money, the success.

Sammie shan't be bothered by Zahra's wicked world. No trees. No moths. No voices. No brothers gone missing, dastardly grown-up magic tricks. Sammie is in love or something like it. She is as most new lovers are, completely self-absorbed, and does as most new lovers do, ignoring everyone around her except for her singular interest of heart. Cute boy, smart boy, funny boy; it pounds. Noah.

She texted him again last night. And this was his response. *You're going to change the world; that's what I like about you.* She practically jumped out of her skin when she read it. A response to her frankness—*You're really cool; that's what I like about you.*

Thanks, she wrote.

Thank you, he wrote back. *So you like me, huh?*

Just a little, as a friend of course. Saving herself from rejection. She waited for him to say more, to say that he felt differently, more than friendly.

. . .

. . .

. . . He was thinking. What was he thinking?

. . . Then nothing. And her heart sank just a little, but she still has this one line to hold on to. *You're going to change the world; that's what I like about you.* It's hard for her to focus on anything else. I mean, Noah is honest without being loud or proud about it. He is the boy who asks the teachers questions before she can get them out herself. In economics, he goes: *But how can capitalism cure capitalism?* And in Colonial History of the Caribbean, he asks: *But wouldn't the maroons constitute as an autonomous nation?* So, she doesn't think of the moths. Or Zahra. Or Spelman. And not of a stupid tree, though she doesn't mean to be dismissive. Instead, pasty, polite Noah situates himself in the center of her mind, and stays there, like an immortal jellyfish. The fact that he believes in her, believes she can do what she knows she's meant to do is exhilarating. She bites her nails, tries to keep from smiling too hard.

THEY'RE ALL AROUND THE TABLE AGAIN, THIS TIME DRESSED for church. Well, everyone is dressed up except for Uncle Trey. She and Uncle didn't bring any church clothes, didn't expect to be going to First United Baptist Church of Greater Atlanta at eight this Sunday morning, but Zahra gave her an old dress from her closet, pretty black and white striped, a perfect fit; Uncle Trey is the only one in jeans and a sweatshirt. Ms. Mary and Gram remind Sammie of what Zahra said of politicians and preachers, her mother and grandmother appearing to be one or the other, together both. Zahra's mother is sharp but simple, Michelle Obama–ish, wearing a black sheath dress with lace panels. Gram has gone to much greater lengths to impress, and yes, Sammie gives her five stars for living up to the southern-Black-church-lady stereotype in her cream skirt suit, wide brim hat, tulle bow. Maybe this is where Gram finds what Zahra refers to as *the men*. In church? Either way, Gram is in stark contrast to Zahra, who sits beside her in high-waisted wide-legged pants. Sammie envies the look, though it doesn't compliment Zahra's nasty attitude. It's like she woke up on the wrong side of bed this morning. It's like she's a whole different person from the night before last, when Sammie and Zahra spoke of everything from noisy moths to potential boyfriends, music to movies to moms who dismiss their children like day-old leftovers. Zahra is different even from the night before, when Sammie found Zahra sleeping so peaceful like a milk-drunk baby, cocooned in blankets. It was hard to be mad at such a sight, but Zahra has torn into Sammie's life like a tornado and left her with the pieces. She's all Sophia, Sophia, Sophia, even though Sammie is the one helping her find her lost brother. Sammie doesn't want to point out the obvious, that Zahra is old-school CREAM: cash rules everything around *her*. And it's obvious that Sophia has a lot of it.

|||||||||||||||||||||||||||||||||||||||||||||

"IT'S A GOOD SIGN." MS. MARY AND GRAM SAY IT AT THE SAME time. Ms. Mary goes on. "You never believed in signs, but here it is. Proof."

"Cut down one day. Back the next," Gram says. Sammie can't see her eyes, the brim is so low over them.

"A tree doesn't just regrow. I didn't so much as see a branch last night. It was that same stump. I'm almost sure of it." Ms. Mary collects the plates, all clean now. The waffles were great though Sammie misses regular syrup, Aunt Jemima or Mrs. Butterworth's, instead of the thick molasses Zahra referred to as Alaga.

"It's impossible," Zahra says now, arms still crossed, and Sammie makes a mental note to ask her what's wrong when they get a second to themselves, maybe whispering on their way to the car or in the church pews. She wonders if it has to do with the tree, which Sammie can't say was there or not yesterday. She hasn't fully bought into this story—that a tree has sprouted overnight, that it was cut down a long time ago and is there today like magic. It's all too much to believe—the moths, the tree. It's one or the other for Sammie, and the moths are somewhat explainable; they are angels or ghosts, not so wild, *not so wild at all*, she tries to convince herself.

"Nothing's impossible," Gram says. "After all, you're going to church with us this morning."

"I go to church, Gram."

"You do?"

"Just not to your church. It's all political there."

"So prayer isn't meant to be political? You think you get a president like Obama out of thin air?"

Zahra rolls her eyes. "We're going to be late. We should head out soon."

"And get there early?"

"Now we can't get there too early?"

"The usherettes always stand outside talking their gossip in their worn-down hats, and I don't want any parts of that. Better to wait for them to go on in. Let church be about what it's meant to be about."

"We'll leave whenever you're ready, Mom," Ms. Mary clarifies, and Zahra rolls her eyes again.

|||||||||||||||||||||||||||||||||||||||||||||||

SAMMIE HAS SEEN MOTHS IN ODD PLACES SINCE THE CAR ride on the way here. Under the covers when she woke up this morning, on her cell phone when she checked for any missed messages from Noah, on the car door's handle so it looked like the little thing might be a gentleman and open it for her. But she hasn't heard the singing much. The moths have fallen so silent that Sammie wonders if she really heard them in the first place. If not for Zahra's own confession, she would have chalked the singing moths up to disorientation or delirium. Now, there is a lone moth peeking out of the pew in front of her, from in between the Bible and the book of hymns. She tries ignoring it and looks up, to the man who is hollering from the front of the room.

The preacher is kind-looking, at least fifty years old with an impressive head of hair, a thin mustache and a thin goatee to match. His suit looks like something Steve Harvey might wear on *Family Feud*, crisp with a perfectly folded pocket square, three sharp points so it looks like a crown is protruding from his chest. He is someone she might see on TV, if not for his handsomeness then his mannerisms; he jumps out at her with arms gesticulating, his whole torso pushed on top of the pulpit before it is altogether too confining, and he leaves it behind, taking the steps down to meet the congregation. Sammie is in his line of fire and does not want to be singled out but it feels that way when he asks, "Are you closed-eyed to your calling? Well, are you?" Then he shakes his head, begins to walk away, throwing his hand back dismissively as he goes. He turns around quickly, and his plea is more urgent than before. "Do y'all hear me, saints? Y'all don't hear me. Is anyone in God's house today?"

There are murmured hallelujahs and amens and a growing
applause.

"Do y'all hear me?" he asks again.

And yes, Sammie does. She closes her eyes and imagines her
calling. *You're going to change the world; that's what I like about you.*
But how, how is she supposed to do that? She is not a superhero, not
a savior, and on some days she holes up in her room dreaming about
love and luxury, everything she hopes to have one day, never mind
who she will be or what she will do. Still, she is proud of the sit-in
she organized at school and can see it as a jumping-off point for her
future. She imagines herself not much different from the preacher in
front of her, calling on people to do their part, calling on people to
end interpersonal and systemic racism. She will be so loud that her
voice scratches, so loud that her voice leaves her body and becomes
its own entity. She won't even be able to control what comes from
her. She will be a vessel.

It is real one minute and impossible the next. It is what she wants,
then nothing she asked for. She sees herself as an executive, then an
activist, then a little of both. She sees herself then nothing at all.

But there is the moth again, this time with wings outstretched. It
flies to her, lands high on her sternum so she feels cross-eyed when
she looks at it. The preacher is silent, and a beautiful voice, something similar to Jazmine Sullivan's or Jennifer Hudson's fills the
space. Sammie looks up for the choir, but they are still sitting in the
front row, nearly fifty bodies in matching purple robes and varying
hairstyles, no two heads the same. The choir is silent except for their
cosigning, raised hands, the throwing of handkerchiefs. The kind
and handsome man is still preaching, but his voice is muted, replaced
with singing, and Sammie looks to the moth on her chest and gasps
with realization.

Well, one of these nights around twelve o'clock, this old town's gonna really rock, the voice goes, and Sammie can't keep denying that the moths are literally singing. And Zahra was right. The moths are what connect them; the moths are why she's in Atlanta right now. She is the one who has to find Derrick. Maybe she knows more than she thinks. She racks her brain, wondering what she's missing. She racks her brain, imagining Derrick a man like Uncle Trey but more inward. She considers something Gram said the day before as well as the persistent feeling she's gotten since arriving in Atlanta, and taps Zahra's knee to tell her that it's been Derrick who's watching her, and she's pretty sure the disappearance has something to do with the house, maybe because it's haunted. But Zahra is reaching for her phone. She pulls it out of her bag, and Sammie sees that it is Sophia again. The girl is always calling. The girl can't write anything on her own; she is needier than a TikTok thirst trap.

Zahra, Zahra, Zahra, Sammie wants to say. She taps Zahra's knee, then her shoulder with urgency.

"Zahra, Zahra," she begins to whisper, but by the time Zahra is ready to listen to her, by the first time Zahra seems to notice Sammie at all, Sammie has lost some of her confidence. It doesn't add up that Derrick's disappearance would have anything to do with an old moaning house, a house that has always been moody. It's nonsensical, impossible.

"I . . . I . . . ," Sammie says. Then: "Never mind."

||||||||||||||||||||||||||||||||||||||||||||||||

THE CHURCH PARKING LOT IS MADE OF GRAVEL, AND SAMMIE kicks rocks around with Uncle Trey as Zahra gives what seems to be a lecture on her phone, and Gram and Ms. Mary circulate between cars, handing out hugs and prayer words. Sammie could hear them at first, when they were closer to the exit doors, and families poured out of them in one big heap. But now, they are far away, having moved in opposite directions of the parking labyrinth.

"Not so different from church back home," Uncle Trey says, and Sammie scoffs. Atlanta has all the differences, from wider, shaded venues set in small pockets of forest to church mothers who traipse in low, cream-colored heels to their cars, singing liturgies as they go.

"Seems different to me."

"Bunch of praying mothers and ogling deacons? Same air of want, of change? Same fatigue. Everyone wobbling, like the world is on their backs."

Sammie laughs at the image. "You have an imagination, Uncle," she says.

"Got to in this place."

Sammie wonders what place he's referring to. Church? The States? The world? She doesn't ask him, for fear he'll say all three. Instead, she spots a woman with the same brown shade of skin as hers. She's a beautiful woman wearing a knee-length floral dress and nude pumps. Her hair is picked out, maybe blown out, in fat, puffy curls. She holds a toddler on her hip and the hand of a five- or six-year-old girl, a miniature version of herself, but the heels are replaced with black Mary Janes and white socks with lace trim. The girl holds a ratty stuffed animal to her chest, and it is the only besmirched thing among the three-person family. Sammie wonders what it's like to hold the hand of a woman like that, all put together, a mother whose hand isn't an ocean away. The woman looks like everything Sammie ever wanted—confident and careful, smiling and assured. She looks like she might be a doctor or a lawyer, a scientist or a professor. She looks like a good mother, one who reads her daughter nighttime stories and slices peanut butter and jelly sandwiches diagonally down the middle. Yes, of course, Sammie has had some of these qualities in Mother Ma, but with Mother Ma being older, she has been tired all of Sammie's life, having trekked to the States at middle age and then losing a husband shortly thereafter. Mother Ma has always given Sammie space and has better held the place of a grandmother than someone more immediate.

"I remember when you were that little girl's age," Uncle Trey says, and Sammie didn't know that he was watching her watch this woman. She doesn't know how to explain the urge she has, to run over to the woman and steal her hand.

"I know," she says.

"You were so smart."

"Still am," Sammie says confidently. The family of three walks to their car, a big white SUV. The six-year-old climbs her way inside while the mother straps the toddler in a car seat.

"Too smart."

"No such thing." Sammie can barely see the mother handing out juice boxes or applesauce before she shuts the back door.

"Which reminds me, we gotta get you back to school. I think we'll head back tomorrow."

"But what if Zahra's brother is still missing?"

The mother gets in the passenger side of the SUV and awaits the driver, and Sammie wonders how whoever that is will fit into this shiny, smiling family.

"We're not detectives, Sammie. It's not our job or our business to find him."

"Haven't you heard of predestination?"

"Don't start with the big words, Sammie."

"What? I just . . ."

The man is tall and handsome, a former football or basketball player, just as Sammie suspected. Beautiful brown, the shade of pecans, the ripe ones that have fallen from nearby trees.

"You belong in school. We'll leave tomorrow."

"Wednesday." She's hopeful they'll find him by then.

"Tomorrow."

"Tuesday." As freaked out as she is, she also kind of likes it here.

"Tomorrow."

"OK, fine. Whatever. You always get your way." Sammie feels a well-worn anxiety creep up on her. She crosses her arms and prays that this is the day they find Derrick.

ON THE CAR RIDE HOME, ZAHRA IS MOSTLY SILENT, AND SAM-mie has a lot on her mind, but Uncle Trey is in the back seat, and what she's got to say requires alone time with Zahra.

"Did you all enjoy service?" Zahra asks.

"Sure. It was great," Uncle says, and Sammie agrees absent-mindedly.

"Yeah, great."

Zahra seems to wait for one of them to say more, but when they don't, she says, "I'm going back to the creek. It's the most likely place I'll find Derrick, and the tree . . . the tree has me thinking, but it's not just the tree." Zahra sighs. "It's . . . well, everything."

"Everything is a lot to do by yourself," Uncle says.

"Welp." Zahra sounds defeated.

"Well, let us help. What can I do for you?"

"I'll go to the creek with you," Sammie interrupts before Uncle Trey can take her spot.

"No, no," Zahra says. "Work on your college essay. Supplements or scholarship applications."

Sammie is bruised, but she doesn't object, not wanting to show Uncle or Zahra how deeply invested she's become in a brother she's never even met.

||||||||||||||||||||||||||||||||||||||||||||||||

BACK AT THE HOUSE, SAMMIE PACES AROUND THE LIVING room, light cascading in from both directions, the blinds open to the front of the house and the uncovered windows to the back, the resurrected tree sharing Sammie's spotlight. She is trying to put together her thoughts but is torn in too many directions. Singing moths. Magical trees. Spelman. Noah. Mom. Zahra. Derrick. She lingers on Derrick, as if solving this one mystery will unfold answers to all the others. Not having much else to go by, images of Derrick flash through her mind, replicas of the pictures she's seen throughout the house, the one still safe in her sketch pad. A younger Derrick, straight-faced, cool, charismatic, a basketball tucked under his arm. Derrick in tenth grade, a school portrait, smiling, one dimple, a thin gold chain around his neck. Derrick in an open navy graduation robe, his arm linked around Zahra's neck, her head on his shoulder. Derrick and Mr. Montgomery shoulder to shoulder, the same height but for Derrick's chin tilted up like he's mid-nod or tipping you off that there's something more important to see in the sky.

Sammie pauses, puts her index finger to her lips. The one thing Zahra hasn't really tried to figure out is what was bothering Derrick. This is the angle she will take. If he's run off, then something was wrong. If he's run off, then what was wrong will point her in the right direction. She looks out the front window and sees him. She blinks hard in disbelief, and it is only the neighbor whose style isn't so different from Derrick's in one of the pictures. Now, the neighbor wears a green, yellow, and blue track jacket, the sleeves pushed up to his elbows. Remembering how short she was with him the day before, Sammie runs outside, through the grass, which she'd politely avoided thus far.

"Hey," she calls out. "Hey." She waves as she runs. He's no

longer in front of the Robinsons' house but the next one over, away from his own. "Where are you going?" she asks.

He smiles, placing her, and Sammie is thrown off-balance by the low fire it ignites inside of her.

"Sup?" he says. "Going to the corner store. Wanna come?"

She's not sure if she should, but what's the worst that could happen? It's broad daylight, a Sunday. She's still in her church dress, and the corner store isn't that far away. Just one right turn and up a steep hill; they pass it when they come and go from the neighborhood.

"OK," she says. "I forgot to ask you your name the other day."

"Rashad. Yours?"

"Sammie."

"Like the singer," he says, but she's not sure which one he's referring to. "You listen to music?"

"I love music," she says.

"Yeah, but do you listen to it? I mean really listen?"

She nods. "You?"

"Same. I like all the feelings that people put into it. Seems like almost every Black mama can sing because they've got so much stored up inside of them. They throw songs out like rotten food. You know Mahalia Jackson?"

Sammie shakes her head.

"Missing out," Rashad says. "I'll lend you a CD."

But Sammie would have no way to play it. Anyhow, who listens to CDs anymore? First Zahra, now Rashad, and it's like Atlanta is stuck in a time warp.

"I'll find her in Tidal," Sammie says.

"Tight."

Sammie considers how differently Rashad speaks. "When you say the corner store, you mean the gas station, don't you?" she asks. "Can't pump gas at the bodegas around where I'm from."

"Bodegas? I could tell you aren't from around here."

She shakes her head.

"Then where?"

"New York."

He looks impressed.

"What are you doing down here? Don't you have school?"

She does, yes. She hates thinking about the quizzes and tests she'll have to make up. The mounds of homework she has to finish. "Yeah, but it was important for me to come visit Spelman, and . . ." She's not sure if she should say about Derrick.

"And what?"

Well, maybe he could help. Maybe he knows something. "Do you know Derrick? He lives in the house I'm staying in now, with Zahra and her gram, but he's missing, and we're here to find him."

"Of course I know Derrick."

She stops in her path, but Rashad goes on walking like he's just said it's a nice day out.

He turns around, realizing that she's no longer with him. "Why wouldn't I know him?"

She shrugs. Maybe it's because Derrick seems like a made-up person, one that only Zahra and her family can know. "Well, do you know where he is? He's missing."

"Wish I could say."

"What do you think of him? What is he like?"

"He keeps it real, and I like that. Always got something smart to say. Always reading and shit. Always listening to what I have to say when other people get mad that I never shut up." He laughs, but Sammie is thrown by this. Rashad hasn't seemed annoyingly talkative.

"Well, what is it you're always talking about?"

"Life." He says it as if it's a simple thing. "What do you like to talk about?"

"I don't know," Sammie says. Or maybe it's just hard to say. With Leila, she likes to talk about boys and school and celebrity gossip. With Mother Ma, TV movies and Mother Ma's past and Sammie's own plans for the future. She talks about music and Harlem and art with Uncle Trey. She's not as close to her great-aunt, who still works long hours—*Because someone has to*, she always says—but when they do talk, it's mostly didactic, about schoolwork or Aunty Deanne's job. And with Noah, she doesn't talk much at all, but she'd like to tell him that she likes his *Stranger Things* blazers, and he has a nice smile, and she was impressed when he corrected Ms. Garcia that time she compared the Holocaust to American slavery. And with this new, cute boy beside her now, talking flows like a river during a hard rain, and she feels more at home than she's felt in a long time. He makes her want to keep on walking, past the corner store, and through the city, sweeping around the AUC, and farther still until it's night and her feet ache so bad that she can't keep on going.

"Maybe I like talking about life too," she says.

"Did you know that Tupac was revived seven times before he died?"

Now Sammie understands that when Rashad said life, he was speaking literally. "No, I didn't even know that was possible, to be revived so many times."

"It can happen," Rashad says. "I've always wanted to be a doctor."

It's nice. Rashad knows what he wants so definitively. Sammie is on the brink of wants, to be an artist or an entrepreneur or a politician or an activist, but no one want is clearer than the others.

"Why a doctor?" she asks.

"Lots of people need saving."

"But there's no one way to save people, is there?"

Rashad looks at her so intensely that she wants to hide her face.

He does not turn around quickly to watch where he's going but strides leaning forward slightly, arms tucked into his pockets, head cocked all the way to the side, as if he's looking for something on or inside of her, and he hasn't quite found it yet. When they get to the left turn for the corner store, he almost passes it, almost walks straight into a highway of cars.

"This way, right?" she says.

"Oh yeah." He laughs. "You got me all worked up."

She beams, can't help but smile, so she hides it under her hand.

"You say Derrick is missing, right?" he asks out of nowhere, pausing right before they've fully turned.

"Yeah," she says, wondering if he knows something. He looks like he might.

"Well, he's a dreamer, so wherever those are, I'm sure you'll find him."

"What do you mean?" she asks, swatting at the mosquitos who've also stopped to bite her exposed arms.

"I don't know. Maybe some place with a lot of people."

That could be anywhere, and Zahra says Derrick's an introvert. A place with a lot of people doesn't make any sense at all.

"Anyway, I hope you find him," Rashad says.

She wants to press him for more, but it looks like he's said all he's had to say. He starts walking again, and she follows. "Me too," she says under her breath.

|||||||||||||||||||||||||||||||||||||||||||||||

THE CORNER STORE OCCUPIES MORE LAND THAN NEEDED, and there's a lot of unused concrete before they pass the wings trailer that Zahra said hasn't been good since one family sold it to another in 2010. Zahra said the old family was white and the type with so many members—sisters upon sisters and brothers identical to cousins—that you could never tell who'd be working, but it was bound to be someone with greasy hair streaked with highlights or dyed dark red, maybe a gold tooth or two, a big smile, a warm greeting. *Order for the Robinsons?* they might say, knowing Zahra and Derrick and Ms. Mary and Gram from years of patronage, one of the brothers having been in second grade with Derrick, and the whole family in a house that stands out with blue vinyl siding on the opposite end of the neighborhood. Zahra said it seemed impossible, even growing up, that white folks would make the best lemon pepper wings on the Eastside but that the family was as rough as the rest of them, and it isn't up to anybody to steal away their strengths.

They approach the corner store, just a few feet from the wings trailer, and Rashad says it's nothing like it used to be. He says it's smaller now, renamed Citgo and that they stopped selling the good stuff. Where are the Bugles and the spicy sunflower seeds and the Munchos? Where are the twenty-five-cent barrels of Kool-Aid and the multiflavored Mambas?

"You have a good memory," Sammie says, thinking she can't recall the snacks around when she was younger. All she's ever remembered are Doritos and Utz and Hi-Chews and AriZonas.

"Memories are important," Rashad says, and he looks like he's stuck in one of them, eyes cast so far away that Sammie waves her hand in front of him, and he doesn't even blink.

EIGHTEEN

It's been a long time since Zahra has made this walk. The creek was more than a place to hop rocks, but even back then, there was something about it that entrapped the magic of her childhood—maybe the way it seemed to sprout from nowhere, like walking through a random backyard to Narnia, or Gram's explicit rule they were breaking in visiting it. Things changed when she and Derrick got into the Evermount Magnet School for High Achievers, and there were no creek shortcuts to get there. Instead, they took the bus, two buses, one to a depot on Memorial Drive and the other all the way north, to Dunwoody, the white part of town. They didn't think much of it then, how exhaustive the two-hour rides were, how polluting, how interesting to watch the brown lot of them shuffle off storybook yellow school buses, joining their white counterparts whose parents had the means to live in the *better* parts of the city. It's 2019, and Zahra knows that the parts haven't changed much, the white people still north of I-20 and the Black people south of it.

Zahra looks around and doesn't see what's so wrong with the south side, what's so wrong with a little noise, what's so wrong with a little energy. Who doesn't love a good cookout? Who doesn't want to feel like they're in an actual community and not some sterile suburb? She laughs remembering wanting to live closer to school, remembering the first time she was invited inside one of those white homes and how she envied the space of them, the polish, the shine, everything just a bit newer, glossier, better than what was waiting for her back at home.

But the bus rides—they were long, and she and Derrick had to wake up damningly early in the morning, and if they missed the first bus, then Gram had to drive them to the Memorial stop and they stood the chance of missing the second one too. But also, the bus rides were where Zahra bonded with her best friends, Zee and Ruqayyah. Where she got her first experience with flirting sitting next to Chase, letting his arm rub hers, letting him rest his head on her shoulder or grip her knee like palming a basketball. And on her days of introversion, she slid into one of those brown cushioned seats, knees up so they pressed into the person's back in front of her, and she listened to music on the CD player Uncle Richard got her for her thirteenth birthday; it skipped on the speed bumps. She closed her eyes, and the ride felt like floating, and the moths were there, but by then she'd grown accustomed to them.

She didn't think of her ride as part of Atlanta's growing pollution problem, didn't see how the segregated neighborhoods created economical, but even *better* ecological despair. Now she breathes in Atlanta's shitty air quality considering its fast and unbalanced growth, leaving northern parts of the city treeless and congested, the southern parts with aging and environmentally damaging infrastructure. Now she thinks of the many college essays she's helped white kids write about saving the planet and recycling and composting and reducing waste and going vegan, and how she's never once told them to add atoning for white flight and white metropolitan suburbs to the list. No, she nods her head to their rants, lets them live happily with seitan and cashew cheese instead. After all, they're only kids. After all, their understanding will grow, dynamic, unlike the tree outside of Sophia's house on Park Avenue. *But will they ever really understand?* she asks herself. *Or is the tree more likely to?*

||||||||||||||||||||||||||||||||||||||||||||||||||||||

THANK YOU, THANK YOU, THANK YOU, THE PARENTS SAY WHEN their children receive Stanford and Tufts and Brown acceptance letters. *I couldn't have done it without you*—her students echo their parents' sentiments like screeching macaws. They give her Starbucks gift certificates and mugs with catchy phrases and terrariums with succulents deemed unkillable until they have browned and dried two weeks later. And she smiles, pleased with herself, genuinely happy for them, but with a lump in her throat that makes it harder and harder to swallow, the next kid's bullshit won't go down, the next kid's silent but dedicated plea, *Write it for me, write it for me, write it for me*. Why should she write their stories, when she's so lost in her own? She gasps for air, in corners, when their sessions are over, and no one else is around.

Now she hears footsteps behind her and turns around to find Trey running to catch up, waving his hands over his head, calling her name,

"Zahra. Zahra," he huffs, and she smiles with her hands on her hips, anticipating the company, full of nerves and fervor, back to her schoolgirl self, to back-to-back bus rides with cute boys.

"Gram said I'd find you this way," he says.

|||||||||||||||||||||||||||||||||||||||||||||||||||

THE CREEK IS STEADY TODAY, THE WATER STILL FRESH FROM the previous night's rain. There are days when there's almost no water at all, and the rocks that line the bed wait dry and crusty for the next downpour, the next storm.

"Gram didn't like us coming down here," Zahra says, remembering how they used to hop rocks; they were so young then and the water was so alluring, so magical.

"Why not?" Trey asks. "Seems safe enough. Weak current and all. Can't you swim?"

Zahra laughs. "It's not deep enough to swim in, though we would have if it were. I'm not a great swimmer, but I can keep my head above the water. I bet you're practically a dolphin, coming from Trinidad."

Trey shrugs. "I like the sand, digging my toes in it. And I guess I like the water too but not as much as the sand."

Zahra nods. "I went to Trinidad once. With some friends. I was fresh out of college, and my new paycheck was burning a hole in my pocket. The water there is beautiful."

"The best."

"Yeah."

"But this is nice too," Trey adds quickly, and Zahra's laugh shakes free the nerves that course through her. Trey smiles, goes on, "It's a very American neighborhood. Like you grew up in a movie or something. The Forbidden Creek."

Zahra sits down on the overgrown grass, grateful she changed into jeans. Trey sits beside her, a little closer than expected, and she has the urge to move away, but she puts her hands on her knees and brings them to her chest. She considers what he's just said, what he's just named this place, *The Forbidden Creek*, an appropriate title.

"I think Gram not wanting us to come out here had something to do with the missing children. A lot of them were found in or near the Chattahoochee. During a storm, this creek rushes, and it can seem bigger and scarier than it actually is."

"Missing children?"

"Yeah. Happened before Derrick or I were born—'seventy-nine, 'eighty, 'eighty-one. In those few years, twenty-eight or twenty-nine Black kids, mostly boys, went missing—turned up behind dumpsters or in the woods, and then eventually, bodies in the Chattahoochee River. Floating. Washed up." She tries not to think of Derrick's body washing ashore, but her mind has been going to the worst places lately, and she sees him bobbing and bloated. She closes her eyes to the image and reminds herself that Derrick is not a child, that he is tall and heavy, that he's aware.

"Derrick was obsessed with the murders for a while; I guess he felt some sort of kindred spirit with the boys, most of them around fourteen when they died. When Derrick got his license, he would drive out to those neighborhoods, across town, to Red Wine Road and Browns Mill Road and the Peachtree City corridor, over by the Omni." Said he could hear them, could hear one boy in particular singing, and it would keep him up at night, and maybe the boy was trying to tell him something. She can't say it all to Trey, but she wants to, wants the story off her soul, to stop it from crushing her. She remembers those days clearer than the rest, when Derrick would just sit out on Henry Thomas Drive and say the boy's *range was sick* or *not everyone can sing like that, not everyone at all*.

"Why those neighborhoods? What would Derrick do there?" Trey asks, and his voice almost sounds like Derrick's.

Zahra shakes the thought from her head.

"Because that's where the boys were, where they lived, where they were found. He'd look around. Think. I'd just sit next to him, and it's not like we'd be there for long, five or ten minutes, and he'd turn back around, come back over here, to the Eastside."

It's warm out, but Trey looks cold. He rubs his arms, and she thinks maybe she's scaring him.

"Just a kid playing detective, that's all," she says, ignoring how dedicated Derrick was, how he named the voice Pat Man's before they'd done any of their week's long research at the library. How when she found Pat Man's face in a newspaper, her eyes had practically popped out of her head, then they'd swelled with tears, and Derrick only said, "See I told you. I knew it."

She'd always been afraid of Wayne Williams, the convicted murderer, though she, like almost everyone else she knew—Mom and Gram and Uncle Richard—weren't sure he'd actually done it, thought maybe it was the KKK, thought they were always behind the evils of Atlanta.

"Let's talk about something else," Trey says.

"Let's talk about something else," she agrees, trying to push the impending memories from swelling.

"There are roads everywhere, and they just get bigger and bigger. Seems like there are a lot of places to go," Trey says. "But then there are trees too, so it doesn't always feel like a city. Nothing like Harlem."

Zahra nods. "It's definitely a city made for driving."

"Yeah, I like it here."

"You do?"

She moves her attention from the calm but steady water flow and looks at Trey. His eyes are beaming, and he's smiling so wide that she notices the hint of a dimple, something she's never seen on him before, left cheek, overwhelmed by full lips and large white teeth. He's cleanly shaved today; she's just now noticing that. On any other day she might push him away, convince him that she's not interested, but something about today or the atmosphere, or the creek like a time capsule makes her different.

"What do you like most about it?" she asks him.

He shrugs, laughs a little. "It's obvious, isn't it?" He pauses, seems to consider what he wants to say. Begins and then stops. Begins again. "I like that you're the one showing it to me."

She nods. "You're good company too."

"When was the last time you went on a date?"

"Ugh." She laughs. "Don't ask me that. That's a horrible question."

"But you look like you need one. You're stressed, I get it. But even before, even before all of this, you just looked . . ."

"That's enough. I get it. Thank you."

"I didn't mean to be . . ."

"I know," she says, and it sounds curt, but she's not mad. She is scared. She sees that she will let Trey get away with things that she would chop other men's heads off for, and it's not a relieving revelation but a terrifying one. "Are you like this with everyone? So prodding?"

"Not everyone. You. And Sammie; she needs it though."

"She's a cool girl. Wouldn't mind being like her when I grow up."

Trey nods, but it sounds like something else is on his mind when he says, "I'm worried about her."

"Why?" Zahra asks.

"Ever know someone who sees too much, feels too much? Like they're in two places at once? Like they can feel everything you're feeling and what they're feeling too? And if you have, ever wonder what that does to a person?"

The notion is so close to her own reality, to Derrick's absence, that it stings. It's so close it's unreal. Her chest tightens, and she reaches for the water bottle she failed to bring. She opens her mouth to speak but doesn't know what to say. She looks at Trey, and his eyes are dead set on her too, piercing, unwavering. He moves in to kiss her, and though she wants to move away, though she wants to run miles and miles away, she follows his lead, the creek's water lapping low in front of them, their only witness.

NINETEEN 🦋

In the backyard, Rashad teaches Sammie how to pick honeysuckle and lick the nectar. He plucks a dandelion and tells her to blow it, *make a wish and make it count.* He says he doesn't *believe in wishes, that that's not how the world works, but they're fun anyway, and what did you wish for?* Sammie won't tell him, but she wished to find Derrick. She'll do her best at praying on it before bed tonight because she doesn't really believe in wishes either.

Rashad sits on the brittle grass, leans back on his elbows and gives her a look to follow suit. She does, even though she thinks the grass will be itchy, and she's already got a handful of mosquito bites. She looks up at the clear blue sky and wonders what's waiting up there. God or just cumulus clouds? God or just rich people in jets? Maybe it's ridiculous to think of God as a man in the sky. He's supposed to be everywhere, isn't he? She looks at Rashad. His eyes are closed, head tilted back.

Sammie is bold. She is not herself at all when she leans over him. She wants to kiss him. She wants to lay on top of him, something she's never done with a boy before. But when he opens his eyes, he startles her, and she backs off quickly. She sits up straight.

"Sorry," she says.

"For what?" he asks, smiling.

"I don't know." She shrugs, picking at the grass at her sides, uprooting full chunks of it and then smashing it back down into the hard, dry soil.

"Sammie! Sammie!" It's Uncle's voice, calling out to her from above. She looks behind her and spots him on the patio. He looks worried. "I've been calling you," he says, holding up his phone as proof. She looks at her phone, and sure enough, two missed calls. She doesn't know how she didn't hear it or at least feel the phone vibrating.

"Sorry," she screams up at Uncle.

"Come inside," he says. "You're gonna get eaten up out there." She thinks Uncle is being dramatic, that he just wants to get her away from Rashad, that he's being overprotective. Still, she obliges.

"I'll see you later?" she asks Rashad.

"Yeah, later," he says. And she leaves him lying there, fully stretched out as if this is his domain, his own backyard, and he has nowhere else to be.

TWENTY

Derrick was nine when he realized he could swing his words, or the lack thereof, like a lasso. He learned when to pause, when to hold back completely, and when to string people along with a story so enthralling that they couldn't help but ask him to repeat it. He began to think of his voice as a thing of harmony, a way of singing without singing, not so different from rapping, some brothas even called it that.

In high school, girls loved his way with words so much they'd use any excuse to touch him. A fallen eyelash. A piece of lint. Nothing but the sun hitting him at the right angle, and there'd be a hand on his back, his elbow, his shoulder. For the bravest, his face. But he liked it—their attention and their touch. It confirmed something—that what he said had value. And admittedly, he recalls being thoughtful and sensitive as a teen but also a subscriber of hip-hop idolatry—money, cars, clothes, with an emphasis on hoes.

But in most cases, he didn't entertain girls for long because he simply didn't like being responsible for their feelings. He began to see how words could be used against him, how they could be mistaken or misconstrued. And what happened when the feelings were mutual? Inevitably, he put too much weight on those girls, and his own thoughts and concerns and the merry-go-round of voices stained them.

To some degree, his inability to commit spread across other facets of his life—in finding a career. In moving to a new city or even signing a lease in the one in which he'd lived his whole life. It's not to say other shit didn't factor into his choices. Of course they did. He felt an obligation to Atlanta—a city that was changing too quickly for the people who rightfully claimed it to keep up. And there was a nagging too, not only from the moths but from the back of his own mind, that he wasn't doing enough. He told this to church elders, to therapists, to life coaches, but none of them were able to get to the meat of it. Maybe they couldn't comprehend anxiety by way of American history or were dealing with the same shit themselves and still trying to find the answers.

His college major, philosophy, with its emphasis on ethics and information management and the reason for reasoning itself, didn't save him but only made his head denser than it already was. He researched answers and found some in Atlanta's deforestation, gentrification, in its urban planning and redlining, in the things it tried to hide but they only found new places to resurface—like an old game of Whac-A-Mole.

Zahra was always mad at Mom, but to be honest, Derrick understands that she tried, was trying, her best. He thought he'd gotten a girl pregnant once, and his reaction to the news startled him. Here it went: *Wow, how did that happen? Of course he remembers the how, but why? Why him? Why now?* There were already enough voices in this world. What business did he have in bringing in another one? And into a suburb, a city, a country that wouldn't do anything but bear down on a child with a million weights, a million unanswered questions.

A couple of days ago, he met a girl he really liked. The way she looked stirred his nostalgia, an easier time, those teen days of pride and power. He met her by the creek. He was there to get his mind off things, to listen to some music, to watch the water rush by, but she was just lying back on the grass, basking in the sun. She wore baggy low jeans and a backward A cap. A jet-black bob and fluttering, thick eyelashes. She waved long neon fingernails as she spoke.

He asked her, "Just taking it all in, huh?"

"I guess you could say that," she said, coming up on her elbows to look at him better, then bringing one hand up to shield her eyes from the sun.

"You from around here?"

She looked like it, but it wasn't like girls from around here to just sunbathe.

"Yep," she said. "Same place as you." Like she knew him. Then she turned her cap around to show him the ballpark Atlanta script.

"Why haven't I seen you around this way?"

"Been busy, I guess."

"Life bes that way," he agreed.

She nodded. "It doesn't stop for anyone, especially with capitalism and shit at play. Communities change with inflation. My parents used to know everyone in the neighborhood, could tell you where their folks were from and what grades their children were in, or if older, where they moved to, what they were doing with their life. Now, no one knows anyone, do they? People can simply disappear." She pursed her lips. "I counted my losses a long time ago."

"So what's left for you, then?" he asked of her, but more for himself.

"Shit, I just like existing, watching. TV. Movies . . ." She shrugged. "People. You're interesting enough."

"You don't even know me."

"You remind me of a guy I dated once. First love. He was so . . ." She pointed to her mind. "He could always tell what I was thinking. He was good at seeing people in that way. A gift and a curse."

"Tell me about it."

"I just did."

They laughed.

"Tell me something else," he begged. She took his mind off things. She quieted it.

They spoke for hours.

They spoke until she fizzled out in front of his eyes, like a hologram, the same way the sun sets. There and then not there, like magic. Sure, he'd heard voices. Sure, he'd seen faces. Sure, the moths were always singing. Sure, he knew what it was to feel two skins at once. But to see a real person, to grow invested in her and then have her disappear right before his eyes—what the fuck was that? He'd created a woman so realistic that he could damn near reach out and touch her.

That night the moths sounded like a bullhorn they were so loud.

Weeks later, when he realized what Gram was hiding, it all made sense. The house, the moths, the spirits. He had no choice but to get out, to disappear.

TWENTY-ONE

Sunday after church, October 2019,
six days since he went missing, or by other definitions, gone

Zahra is alone at the creek now, Trey too accustomed to New York, skin too thin to withstand the thick of mosquitoes. He went back to Gram's, and Zahra sits in peace with the moths she used to pay no heed to. In moving away from Derrick and with no one to share their songs, she resented the moths, being inundated by voices she never asked for, the Whitney Houston riffs, the Patti LaBelle holler, the deep guttural sound of a voice like Anita Baker's or Toni Braxton's.

Now the moths flutter around her like butterflies, and she relishes in their company; they remind her of her brother. She walks closer to the bank, and they follow her. She takes off her shoes and dips her feet in the water, tentatively at first, with just one toe. The cold water is shocking but refreshing, so she plunges both feet in.

There were no fights in seventh grade, Zahra's first year at Evermount, not one single fight, at least not the kind she was used to,

busted blurple lips or braids pulled so hard that you thought someone was bound to limp away bald-headed. Instead, there was a jolly
old white man, not too unlike Santa Claus, the principal, who roamed
the hallways asking multiplication problems, factorials, to define
SAT words like *sagacious* or *detritus*. There was the white girl named
Molly Guyer, who looked at Zahra and said that her parents had already saved $6,000 for her to go to college, and there was Derrick,
a year at the school already and in eighth grade; he wasn't ashamed
of the fried pork chops, the macaroni and cheese Gram packed him
for lunch, all tossed together in a gallon-sized Ziploc bag. Zahra
begged for pizza Lunchables and somehow got Gram to relent.

In their brief but obnoxious year at separate schools, when Zahra
was still in sixth grade and hadn't reached middle school yet, Derrick began hanging out with the loudest kid in the cafeteria. A year
later and back in one building again, Zahra slunk down low in her
chair when that kid, nappy-headed and ballsy, declared that she
looked like a fighter, like she'd *knock a nigga out*. And Derrick nodded his head, ever cool, saying, "That's my sister. They haven't seen
nothing yet." The ballsy kid, whose name she can't remember now,
always had grease all over his mouth, and Zahra wanted to punch him
in it. Would prove him right, she guessed. So she switched tables,
started sitting with her own class, where there was only one seat left,
by the white girls, right next to Molly Guyer with the $6,000 savings
account and an identical pizza Lunchable. The table talked about
summer horseback riding and shaving their legs and playing spin the
bottle and going to see Good Charlotte in concert—all things Zahra
had never done before. However, it was at the Good Charlotte concert, where Molly's and Jessica's moms let them stay out until one
o'clock in the morning, that a fight broke out, which horrified but
also seemed to thrill them.

"But you're not supposed to fight," Molly said. And Zahra

thought of her parents' rules, that if someone hit them, her or Derrick, they should hit back, hard, harder than they were hit. They were never to start the fight, but if it came to them, they'd better be the ones to end it. In other words, Mary and Montgomery weren't raising any suckers; it was one of the few things they agreed on.

It was then, finally, Zahra saw a crack in the conversation, in which to slink her way inside of it. "Yeah, you're not supposed to start one," she said.

"No, you're not supposed to fight at all."

Zahra took a moment to think about this, and it didn't make any sense. Hadn't Molly heard of self-defense?

"So, if I hit you, you wouldn't do anything?" Zahra asked, and the whole table was watching them, quiet and intrigued, some of the other girls shaking their heads. But what were they shaking their heads for? Zahra didn't know.

"I'd tell the teacher," Molly said with pride.

"How are you going to tell the teacher if I'm on top of you?"

Molly used her index finger to scoop some pizza sauce into her mouth and shrugged her shoulders.

"Aren't you afraid of being a snitch?"

"A what?" Wide eyes all around the table. Zahra had used a word they weren't accustomed to, a Black word.

Zahra rolled her eyes. "People at my old school used to call me a teacher's pet sometimes. But I think you're worse. Way worse."

Molly whipped her head away from Zahra, so dramatic that her ponytail landed right in Zahra's pile of pepperoni. The girls laughed.

"Gross," Zahra said. Then she flicked Molly. On the side of her puffy pink cheek, aiming to turn it red. She flicked her as hard as she could, middle finger to thumb style. She flicked her because she wasn't listening, 'cause she was a know-it-all, 'cause her parents had already saved $6,000 for her to go to college and she went around bragging about it like a little bitch. The girls watched in awe, deer in headlights.

Molly flinched and swung back around to face Zahra. "Stop that."

"Make me," Zahra said, flicking her again.

Then again for good measure.

"Stop it."

"Make me."

"Stop it."

"Make me."

"I'm going to tell Ms. Vaughn," Molly said.

"Go ahead. I'm an all-A student. She'll never believe you."

Turns out, Ms. Vaughn did believe Molly, though Zahra had tried giving the vice principal puppy-dog eyes as she recounted what happened. Ms. Vaughn didn't seem to be listening. She was misunderstanding, restating everything Zahra said but in a way that made the "fight" at the lunch table completely different than Zahra remembered it. Ms. Vaughn looked her in the eye, then away, in the eye, then away, as if each time she met Zahra's pleading stare, it was all wrong, and she was looking for a different set of eyes altogether. There were so many around there—brown and dark oak eyes, green, verdant, the principal would say, hazel, baby blue, and there were wide eyes, wired, slanted, sunken, and sneaky. Jamie had one eye half-shut and Jason had eyes with pupils that bounced off each other so you could never tell where he was looking. Kinsey had unusually light eyes for her skin tone that everyone called beautiful, and the ballsy kid had eyes like a magnet, so Zahra always found herself staring him down. This new school was full of different people from different parts of the city, but it was clear that there would be no fighting, no flicking, self-defense or otherwise.

Zahra had gone back to Derrick and the ballsy kid's table the next day, and when they asked her what happened, she said, "Fuck that blue-eyed bitch." It had sounded so unlike herself that she'd dry-heaved after it came out.

Then the ballsy kid said something she wouldn't forget for years, that she still remembers as if it were yesterday. One of those things that you mull over, letting it stew or simmer like a good roux. Something that you swish around in your mouth like Listerine or suck on for days like a jawbreaker. Always in the back of her mind but mostly unreachable unless revisiting that seventh-grade cafeteria table chipping around the edges and with mounds of gum stuck underneath it.

"It's better to just be embarrassed," he said.

And she wondered if he meant what she thought he meant. Had he known she was humiliated by him? That she'd switched tables to get away from the contagious embarrassment? Only to learn a hard lesson that boiled her insides like lava and made Molly Guyer an arch enemy from that day forward.

Years later, she'd heard the ballsy boy had died, but by that time, he'd stopped going to school with her and Derrick, and they barely knew him. So word never made it to them how he died, but it could have been some disease that harps on young bodies like childhood leukemia or something super tragic like suicide. It could have been something rare and exotic like West Nile or something all too commonplace like a car accident. Or maybe it was that at the age of fifteen, after his sole caregiver Aunt Betty died and several nonviolent behavior incidents including but not limited to running away and drug usage, he landed himself in a residential treatment facility, and then by an even more unfortunate turn of events was released from the facility only to be stabbed to death by a former roommate with a vendetta. At only sixteen himself, the roommate's eyes looked wide and pleading because he hadn't bought into the idea of living until this moment of a ballsy boy's blood leaking like an old pipe. But, of course, Zahra's imagination isn't so extensive. She looks around at the tall pine trees whose roots she's heard grow into one another. She imagines them as an underground family so intertwined that they cannot separate limbs, one arm belonging to two trunks, one leg as long as a freight train.

Zahra sees how different she is from her seventh-grade self. How muted, her voice worn down like the smooth stones under her feet. She is not a fighter, self-defense or otherwise. Suddenly, she is so frustrated with this damn creek that she runs away from it, rushing up the hill as if the water is chasing her.

She takes the shortcut home, hits the backyard breathless, places her hands on her knees, staring at the tree. She looks up at the branches she and Derrick used to sit on, irrationally believing that he will be there. He is not. It occurs to her that he hasn't really been there since college, since he went to Clark and a year later she went all the way to Stanford. It was more than the middle states that sat between them, but there was an air of understanding that their lives were headed in separated directions. When she tried to tell him about Ujamaa's program on African American vernacular English, he couldn't understand her excitement; after all, she could've gone to a Black college like him.

"Those conversations are simultaneously ubiquitous and internally irrelevant here," he'd said. And of course, when he tried to discuss the songs, the voices, the moths, it didn't feel right in her new environment, and she tried to convince him that he was put on this earth to live his own life, not a million others, that the voices were a distraction.

"But what do *you* want? But what do *you* want?" she'd asked him over and over again, though she knows now that he was telling her, *I want what they want. I want what they want.* It was like they were at two different tables in the cafeteria, only this time, one could not find their way back to the other.

|||||||||||||||||||||||||||||||||||||||||||||

WHEN SHE GOES BACK INSIDE, TREY AND SAMMIE ARE AROUND the table again, and Parliament's "Flashlight" is playing from the old sound system. Dad and Uncle Richard are here now, and Dad is shuffling a deck of cards.

The flyers sit on the table in front of Dad. He deals the cards around, and Zahra picks up the picture of Derrick casually looking up from a book, not smiling or frowning but merely acknowledging that his photo is being taken. It's a recent shot, one Zahra has never seen before. Dad and Uncle Richard have been posting these flyers around the neighborhood, around Clark, anywhere that adheres to tape and staples, while Gram and Mary have practically dialed straight down their contacts, one number after another, the same spiel, same questions. *He's just gone. Have you see him?* Zahra puts down the flyer, just as Dad is done dealing. She wonders how these two moments can exist at the same time, laughing and talking smack and wishing for Bostons, while Derrick is away, missing, tugging at her heartstrings like a puppet master.

Would things be like this if they lost him for good? Would they just go on about their business, never reneging and always cutting to the right, dealing to the left? How long would it take them? To act like things never happened, to act like Derrick was never a Robinson, hadn't been born first, a perfect order to watch over the equally scared and untamable sister who would come after him only to forget him later.

Dad sees her face—maybe desolate, maybe contorted—and gets up to embrace her, wraps his long arms around her tightly. Uncle Richard is much slower about things; he shows his age, a wobble in his step now, more heavy footed than she remembers him.

"Zahra," they say at the same time.

"Hang in there," Uncle Richard adds.

"It's good to see you, Uncle Richard." And it is. Uncle Richard has always been a steady pulse, a constant to Mom's fluctuations.

"Pull up a chair, honey," Dad says. "I'm teaching these two how to play bid whist." He refers to Sammie, whose head is bent down low studying the cards splayed out uncomfortably in her hand, and Trey, who looks up and gives her a sly smile. She grabs a desk chair from the family room and squeezes in between Dad and Uncle Richard.

"What about Derrick?" she asks the group. "Any news since I've been gone? Did the police call back? It's been a long time now."

"No news," Uncle Richard says.

"I don't know why you all are so worried," Dad says. "I know my son, and I know he's just out there doing some work."

"Some work, Dad? What work?"

"I don't know. His business, not mine. Just says he wants to help people, and Derrick has his ways, you know. He's an intuitive. I wouldn't understand it if I tried, so I don't." He places his cards in a neat stack in front of him and looks at Zahra, searching. "How are *you?*"

"I'm good, considering everything," she says quickly, afraid that Dad will expose something she's not expecting him to.

"Hmm," he says as if he doesn't fully trust her. Everyone goes silent, and the music pervades the space spiritedly. Dad nods along. Begins to sing George Clinton's ad libs. "*Shake your funk, shake your funk. Ha da da dee da hada hada da da.*"

"Just 'cause you're new at this game and you're young doesn't mean this old geezer is going to take it easy on you. Now, what's your bid, youngin'?" Dad looks at Sammie expectantly.

"Four, maybe five," she says.

"No, no, no. You can't bid like that in bid whist. This ain't spades."

"Take it easy, Dad," Zahra says. "She's learning."

"Five," Sammie says confidently. "Uptown."

"Learning my ass," Dad says. "Now that's a bid."

Sammie smiles wide.

"C'mon, partner," Dad says to Trey, who looks more nervous than Sammie. He scratches his forehead, and Zahra gets up to go look over his shoulder, to see what his hand looks like.

"Naw, naw. Don't help him," Uncle Richard says.

"But—" she protests, and Dad cuts her off.

"He's got it, grown man and all."

She looks over Trey's shoulder but doesn't say anything. Keeps the bid to herself, *Five special*, which would beat out Sammie and give him control of the game.

"Pass," he says, and Zahra grimaces at the missed opportunity.

"You better get it, Ms. Robinson," Dad says, and Zahra turns around to find Gram dancing in with a bag of groceries. *This*, this energy is why she has always loved her dad. This feels like a whole different house now. There is a togetherness, a happiness. Gram's dance is directed by her shoulders, bouncing, her right one leading the way. She heads to the kitchen and drops the brown paper bag on the counter, freeing her to do more lively moves. Mary is behind her, less of a dancing machine but feeling the music just so and singing along. Zahra looks around the table, and they are all moving, shimmying, shaking, snapping, singing.

She thinks this is what life without Derrick would be like. It used to be this way when they were kids, teens even. But Derrick's more recent sadness sucks them all dry, except for the rare occasion where he is his old self, introspective and slack but spirited, his smile giving way to your joy over his. In those cases, rare and rarer as time goes on, life is more for the living than it's ever been.

If Derrick never comes back now, Zahra thinks they'd still go to church on Sundays and sizzle bacon while listening to the Spinners on Saturday mornings. They'd still play bid whist and eat collard greens and canned cranberry sauce on Thanksgiving. They'd still use Candler Park for family reunion cookouts, fry fish on Fridays, where they talk shit about the workweek, school days, coworkers and classmates, waiting for the beat to drop, the O'Jays' "Livin' for the Weekend." How could they just go on like normal? But it's not like she wouldn't be with them; it's not like she's not with them right now, even tapping her foot in place, singing absentmindedly.

She imagines them all as one big family; she imagines Trey as her partner and Sammie as her knucklehead teenager, one whose moods she'll nonstop complain about, one who she will be more proud of than anything else in her life. She imagines *home, home* as one she's created on her own. She imagines the moths as beautiful decor, a secret between her and her daughter. She would be a good mother; she would be better than her own. She exhales deeply. One day maybe, if she could find that way, extract the lump in her throat, detach the weight from her back. She is overwhelmed by the thought and sits down at the table again. She bites her lip, a wanting has come over her so strongly. Still, she doesn't know where to go next, and as for her brother, where is he? And what if *his* wanting is reliant on her?

The door opens, and Zee dances right in, as if it's 2008 and she and Zahra are best friends again, friends who know each other's families and feel a shared ownership of home. *Go on back to y'all's room*, Gram used to say as if the space didn't belong any more to Zahra than it did Zee. Now Zee sashays in until she sees that everyone is watching her and breaks out into the running man to really give them a show. Gram comes in with a hug like a hurricane and catches Zee mid run, one leg up and arms already outstretched. Four whole beats and Gram doesn't let go until Zee takes a deep breath, relaxing into the embrace. For the first time, Zahra considers their relationship, how it existed outside of her own with Zee and how impossible it is that she never noticed it. When Gram backs away, there are tears in Zee's eyes, but Dad doesn't mind them.

He's up next and stands back to look at her, saying, "Fifteen years later. Same old knucklehead." He hugs her, muffling her response.

"Hey, Mr. Montgomery. Nice to see you too."

Zahra waves from behind him. She silently calls Zee over, as everyone else nods hellos, Mom's as lukewarm as it's ever been, since she never really got to know the girl, and Sammie's exaggerated but quick wave, excited to grow the party.

"Hey," Zahra says. "I didn't know you were coming over, but thanks. It's good to see you again."

"Of course. Seeing you again made me decide to give your grandmother a call. She invited me over." Zee grabs Zahra's hand and squeezes it tight. "And you need me right now," she says.

Zahra can't look at Zee but wraps her left arm around the one that's holding on to her; she curls sideways into her old friend, and when they're close enough for no one else to hear, Zee whispers, "I remembered something."

Zahra looks down at Zee's gray Converses, wondering what it could be before slowly saying, "Maybe we should talk outside." As they leave, Sammie's eyes trail them over her deck of cards.

"Remember something like what?" Zahra says out in the front yard, watching a blue Charger pass them by.

"That time we went to Evermount at night? Late after an away football game at one of those Catholic high schools?"

"We wanted to hang out but everything was closed except for Waffle House."

"Right. And you can't smoke in Waffle House anyway. I was dating Nico at the time, and all he ever wanted to do was light up."

"So we went to our home stadium."

"Through the side entrance, opposite the bleachers. The one that lets out on one of those shadowy back roads."

"We could barely see through all the trees."

"It was pitch-black."

"God, I was so scared."

"You were dating Chase at the time."

"The good days," Zahra says, remembering her puppy-dog romance. Chase with those wide shoulders, big biceps she grabbed like a life vest that night they snuck into the stadium, the crunch of dry leaves underfoot and the wind biting through the letterman's jacket Chase had draped over her shoulders. Them looking back every five minutes, thinking Mr. Dunlap, the principal, could pop out from anywhere, or worse, it wasn't the wind howling but something more dangerous, a loose Doberman or a stray serial killer. Derrick led the way unfazed, pushing branches aside and steady on his feet, Julian just behind him.

Finally, they were on the field. "We laid down and looked up at the sky." Zahra remembers leaning over Chase and picking a moth from his eyelashes, laughing when he swatted her hand away. She doesn't remember much else, let alone what this has to do with Derrick or why it matters now that he's missing.

"What does it all matter, Zee? That was ten, fifteen years ago."

"You don't remember what Derrick said? You don't remember the question we asked each other?"

"No. Should I?"

"Where would you go if you had nowhere else to be?"

The memory comes back in waves. "You said to heaven to visit your dad."

Zee nods, smiling. "And you said anywhere with sand and water. That you could float all day. God, you're different, Zahra. When was the last time you found yourself floating?"

Zahra shakes her head, disappointed that she hasn't actualized any of her childhood dreams. "It's been a long time," she confesses.

"Remember Chase said he'd be right there beside you?"

"Yeah." Zahra laughs at the ridiculousness. She feels so far away from her teenage self and even further from her ex-boyfriend, a fantasy that they ever dated at all. She's heard that Chase is married with kids now, a real estate agent or an accountant, something so drastically different from the music producer he claimed to be in high school that it nauseates her. "What did your boyfriend say?"

"Strangely, I can't remember. He's lucky I remember his name."

They laugh quietly, not a shared laugh but simultaneous.

"I remember Julian said traveling the motherland. He was ahead of his time, and Derrick . . . How could you forget, Zahra?"

She's ashamed; she has no idea. "I don't know, Zee."

"He said right here. Right there, I mean. The stadium, the football field. He said he had a feeling he'd leave things behind and would need to go back looking for them. He said, all the people, the players, the cheering, the lights, that there was a hope in Evermount's stadium you couldn't find anywhere else. I remember thinking it was such a Derrick thing to say, that he couldn't just be normal like the rest of us."

"He can't be there, Zee. School is in. Kids would see him. Football teams have practice."

"Not at that old stadium. You haven't heard? They rebuilt Evermount a mile away from the old one. Nice and shiny now. No overflow trailers. No gravel pit. No broken lockers that you have to jimmy to open."

"So . . . Derrick could be . . ."

"He could be there," Zee says, smiling.

THE DIRECTIONS COME BACK TO HER LIKE RIDING A BIKE.
Onto 285. Through Spaghetti Junction, which Zahra used to imagine as God's dinner from high in the sky, expressways looping
around and into one another like noodles. Zee tries turning on the
radio, but Zahra says, "Can we not?"

Around the exit's bend and onto Peachtree Industrial. *Be careful
here*, Gram used to say, cars whizzing past as Zahra tried to merge in
with them. Car dealerships and fast-food restaurants up the long
stretch of highway until a right turn on Cole Road brings you to a
clearing, a picture-book high school, nestled in a thicket of trees,
vines climbing up the dull red brick. It's deserted now. Strange that
such an affluent community would leave it here like highway litter.

Zahra's hands pulse on the steering wheel, and she slows the car
more than necessary. They inch like a caterpillar to the gravel pit,
and the crunch of tires on rocks conjures a familiar feeling. Parking, she remembers how they used to blast music and open car doors,
juking ya boy or leaning and rock, cranking the batman or doing the
saditty girl.

"So many memories," Zee says.

Zahra nods. "We used to have so much fun."

"Well . . . ," Zee says, opening the car door, and the rest of her
statement is swept away in a cool breeze. Zahra follows suit, and
soon they stand together, looking at the stadium precariously.

"Should we try to go in this way? Through the front? I really
don't want to go through the woods," Zee says. It's getting dark, the
sky now a shade of purple that will quickly give way. Zahra doesn't
want to have to trudge through trees either.

"It's abandoned, so maybe we can just walk right in." Only Zahra can barely remember how to get through the concrete stadium until she sees the gate to the right of them and points.

"Is it open?" Zee asks.

"Hard to tell."

Not quite open, but not closed either. There's a gap, one part of the gate pushed back, just enough room for a person to sidle her way through it. Zahra does just so, her shirt catching on one of the links. She gently tugs herself free, and Zee follows. They come up the side of the stadium steps and walk onto the track made of red rubber that Zahra remembers pulling up in little small pellets during PE, throwing the pieces of rubber back at her feet or onto the football field.

She looks up to see how expansive it all is. The football field as long as a New York block, the stadiums rising high above her like a stone monster. "Do you remember it being this big?" she asks Zee.

"My nephews play at stadiums like this, the one on Memorial, you know? They go to Southwest."

"Oh," Zahra says. "Nephews?" Zee doesn't have any siblings.

"Yeah. Jasmine's kids."

Ah, Jasmine, who went to high school with them, who was always closer to Zee than her. "Jasmine has kids?"

"Three."

"God."

"Yeah," Zee says.

Zahra looks around, wondering where Derrick might be. The field is so open, it would be hard to miss him. That leaves under the bleachers as the best bet. "Should we check the bathrooms?"

"Guess so. You take the boys', and I'll take the girls'?"

Zahra doesn't necessarily want to split up. She's getting an uncomfortable feeling out here. Like it's abandoned but not. Like there are too many animals and plants and possibly even people that might live here, the bathrooms the best place for shelter, the most likely to be inhabited. "Sure," Zahra says anyway. It's her brother. She has no right to be too scared to look for him.

She and Zee take long strides up the steps, diagonal, until they reach the middle set that offers an extra half step and a direct route to under the stone stadium, where the concession stand used to be, the girls' and boys' bathrooms on either side of it. Zahra goes to the right, remembering the way, and Zee goes to the left.

It smells like piss. Reason to believe that someone has been here. A year after use, a bathroom wouldn't still smell like pee, would it? She looks at the low sinks, no mirrors above them, rusty double handles that look like they'd be impossible to turn. Behind her there are three stalls. One has no door, and she can easily see that no one's there, so she doesn't go any farther. She hears a creaking sound, like someone shifting their weight in one of the closed stalls, and she backs away quickly, keeping a close eye on the gray doors stuck tight in place. She's brave enough to bend down and look under the doors for feet. She doesn't see any but eyes something just behind the first toilet. A piece of clothing? What is it? She inches closer, her feet shuffling along the dirty concrete floor. A cold hand grabs the back of her neck, and she screams before she has time to look up.

"Sorry," Zee says. "I didn't mean to scare you."

"No, no," Zahra says, regaining her composure. "I'm just on edge, that's all. And look, there's something there."

Zee bends down to take a look. She stands back up without a second thought. "Don't see anything."

Zahra was sure . . . she could have sworn . . . She walks up to the door, and with Zee behind her, calm and reassuring, she pushes it open hard. The mound that she thought was an article of clothing— a shirt or a hat—comes to life, transitioning slowly at first, like a sleeping monster just woken up, and then swarming her like a storm. Fast flapping white wings. They are mad she's bothered them. They are vigilant, preservers of their home. She flings her arms, but they don't mind her fight, rushing around her like a tornado. Then, quickly enough, they are gone, out of the bathroom like a lightning bolt.

Zahra looks behind her to find Zee wide-eyed, mouth agape. "What the fuck?"

Zahra shrugs, her heart calming itself. "Just moths," she says, now hearing the remnants of their song "Midnight Train to Georgia."

Zee shakes her head. "They damn near attacked you."

||||||||||||||||||||||||||||||||||||||||||||||||||

AFTER THE MOTH DEBACLE, ZEE WANTS TO LEAVE, BUT ZAHRA convinces her in one last look. Back on the football field, they spin around in circles, looking in every direction their eyes can find from afar, in a near darkness that has come down like a blanket of black. They sit on the brittle brown grass, both facing the forest of trees they'd walked through over fifteen years ago to get in here and stare up at the night sky, young dreamers. Now, it's clear that Derrick isn't here. He didn't come to the one place he said he would, and Zahra worries that he's nowhere at all. She wonders if she's even looking for him in person, or if she's looking for their memories together instead, trying to piecemeal his person through the old times, the best times, her nostalgia. Does she want the brother who cocooned himself away or the one whose easygoing charm made everyone around him lighter, her first and best friend? She looks at the thicket of trees in front of her like a test of her determination.

"I'm going out that way," she tells Zee.

"I don't think . . ."

"You don't have to come with me," Zahra says.

Zee sighs and mumbles, "Yes, I do."

||||||||||||||||||||||||||||||||||||||||||||||||

THEY UNLATCH THE GATE, AND THE TREES ARE DARK, THE IVY dense. It's not too big, Zahra reminds herself. Thirty, forty yards or so, less than a minute of walking, and they'll be out. She just has to see if Derrick is here, if he's been here recently. She would know his smell, even against all the foliage. She'd know. She walks slow, one foot in front of the other, careful to avoid large roots. She wonders if these are all the same trees that were here when they were in high school, or if new trees have sprouted up or old trees have regrown. She reaches her hand out for a piece of bark, and it breaks like a stale cookie under her nails.

Zee screams, and Zahra whips around. "What happened?"

"My foot. Something grabbed hold of it."

"Something?"

"I don't know. Maybe it was just a tree root. They're poking up around here."

Zahra reaches back to grab Zee's hand, and they finish the walk together, until soon they can see the stretch of a road, the blue-black sky peeking through the last few trees. Zahra is so focused on making it to the clearing that she does not see the flyer that she steps on like a dead leaf. It's got brown, nearly lifeless faces on it, but Zahra wouldn't recognize them anyway.

TWENTY-TWO

Sammie looks out the window for Zahra. She doesn't see her, but there is Rashad, walking again. She wonders what he's doing out so late, where he's going at this time of night. Mother Ma doesn't like her leaving the house past dark, not even to go to Leila's house, which isn't but seven or eight blocks away. Rashad's T-shirt catches her eye, a hunter-green short-sleeve with what looks like a torch on the front of it. It's a symbol she recognizes but can't quite place. It says something too, and she squints to make out the letters.

"At-lan-ta," she sounds out. Then knocks her hand against her head it's so obvious. "Atlanta." The torch tower. A little lost, they rode by it on their way to Spelman. Uncle Trey shrugged when she asked him what it was, but later, her Spelman tour guide had an explanation. The Summer Olympics, 1996. Rashad is sporting the city, walking like he's got a destination in mind but nowhere to be, the smooth way boys walk in old movies, holding the crotch of his baggy jeans. She thinks of running after him again but doesn't want to seem thirsty, pressed, fast, loose—all the things they call girls who chase boys.

Rashad is staring straight ahead but then stops and turns his head in her direction, as if he can feel her watching him. Can he see her peeking through the blinds? She makes the hole smaller, so there's almost no gap in the blinds at all. She has to maneuver her body just so, her knees bent and back angled toward the left, so she can still see out of it. Eventually he carries on, the same leisure walk as before, and she lets out a deep breath.

She tries calling Zahra, but her phone goes to voice mail. She tries Leila, and the same thing. She's got loads to do, but her mind is too jumbled to be diligent. She needs a girlfriend to talk things through. Honestly, she thought coming to Atlanta would be like one of those mystery movies, and she'd be smart enough to put together the pieces. Now she knows there are no pieces at all. Just one large mess that has this whole city under a hallucinogenic spell.

Someone knocks on the door, and she gets excited thinking Zahra's back.

"It's me." Not Zahra but Uncle Trey.

"Come in," she says.

Uncle Trey opens the door, but instead of saying anything, he invites himself in and looks around. He goes to the same graduation portrait of Zahra that interested Sammie that first night. He smiles. His eyes shift to a row of candles, something that hasn't really caught Sammie's attention until now. A Virgin Mary candle, a candle in the shape of an elephant, and a smelly Yankee one. Uncle Trey sniffs it.

He turns around and finds Sammie watching him. "What is it you like so much about her?" he asks.

What an odd question. "I could ask you the same thing."

Uncle nods. He pulls the chair out from under Zahra's desk and sits down. Sammie sees he means to stay for a while and lies on her back on the bed. She stares up at the wood-beamed ceiling, the fan making slow circles, no breeze at all.

"She's a little mysterious," Uncle says.

"You have no idea." It takes everything out of her to keep from saying more.

"It's sad about her brother." Uncle clears his throat as if he's got more to say but then nothing.

"We'll find him." Sammie is sure of it. But in what state they'll find him, she has no idea. The way Zahra describes Derrick, when he's not lost out in the world, he's lost inside of himself, and Sammie's not sure if one way is better than the other.

"You think so?"

"I have a feeling."

"Seems like you've been having a lot of those lately."

Sammie turns her neck to face him. Her muscles strain as she asks, "What do you mean?"

"I don't know. You seem more . . . alert, but also dreamier."

"Not a bad way to be."

"Not saying it is."

Sammie stays quiet for a while, trying to decipher what Uncle really means to say. "You're just worried about boys. In New York, you were worried about Noah. And now you're worried about the boy next door, aren't you?" she asks him.

"What boy next door?"

"The one from earlier today. Laying outside with me."

"There was a boy?"

Sammie rolls her eyes. Uncle always starts with the sarcasm when the conversation isn't going his way. "You probably think I'm going to run off to Atlanta next fall just to flirt. You think boys can sweep me away as if I'm some piece of lint on the ground, no mind of my own, don't you?"

Was that what happened to her mother? Did she lose herself to a boy like Uncle Trey seems to fear? Or is she lost inside of herself like

Derrick? When Sammie talks to her on the phone, it's as if both of their words have dried up; there's never anything to say besides pleasantries. Things used to be a little easier before Sammie got mad, at her mom, her dad, the whole situation. Now Sammie gets excited when her mom makes lame excuses to get off the line.

"I think you have a good head on your shoulders," Uncle Trey says.

"Then trust me to use it."

"You sound like your mom."

It pinches, to sound like someone so close, so important, yet someone she barely knows. Uncle Trey is looking at her now like she's foreign to him. She wants to see what he sees, wants to see what she's like outside of herself.

"When we were kids, your mom was much bolder than me. Granted, she was five years older, but still, if she wanted it, she'd go get it. Couldn't match her in a game of net ball, and when we went to the beach, she swam the farthest out; Mother Ma would hate her for it and send her out of the water mad because we weren't beach kids. We didn't live on the water like cousin Michael. And when we went to Tobago, Rochelle was the only one brave enough to stick her hand in a bamboo crab trap with live ones in it. Stupid, but that's just how she was.

"She used to have these bad dreams, nightmares. She'd scream, and Mother Ma would race in the room and hold her for hours, sometimes humming gospel songs. I asked Rochelle about the dreams once, and she said they were always different—different faces in different places, the Pitch Lake, the lighthouse at Toco, Caroni Swamp, Chacachacare island, where the nuns used to keep the lepers isolated."

This gives Sammie pause. "Huh?"

"The leprosy island. Now the ghost of one of those nuns, who fell in love with a Venezuelan sailor and was forced by the convent to leave him, haunts it."

How has Sammie never heard this legend before? It seems so important now that her mother could be haunted too. Like herself? Like Zahra and Derrick? "Where'd you hear that story? About what's it called?"

"Chacachacare?"

"Right. Chacachacare. Where'd you hear that?"

"Everyone in Trinidad knows about Chacachacare."

Of course. Sammie doesn't count as everyone. She was raised here in the States. "Tell me more about the nightmares," she says.

"Rochelle said that the faces—people all sorts of colors, no two features the same, some eyes open and others closed—always wanted something, and eventually, their nibbling ate her away, that's how the dreams ended. Makes me think of how much she wanted to be a doctor, artist on the side, to move to New York or California and cure people of cancer while helping them decorate their houses with her oil paintings. What happened to all of those dreams?"

Sammie doesn't know how to answer the question or even what to do with this new information, but she shudders considering it all. She moves to get under the covers, warmer while waiting for what more Uncle might have to say. He doesn't normally want to talk about her mother, but maybe Zahra looking for her brother is bringing out another side of him.

"Why don't you talk about her more often?" Sammie asks.

Uncle shrugs. "Got nothing to say."

"Doesn't sound like it."

"I thought I could forget about her. Maybe I thought you made up for losing her, that we had each other instead," he says.

"But then Zahra and her brother . . ." Sammie sits up. She wants to see him more clearly, to trace his face for moments of diversion or little white lies. Nothing. But his arms are crossed, and now he's the one looking up at the ceiling.

"It's one thing to lose someone, but it's something else to *lose them*, lose them. And I'm beginning to see her more, in you."

It's the first time Sammie has ever felt connected to her mother in this way. It's absurd, but then she can't quite tuck it away either, this idea that she's like someone she's spent so little time with, someone she's barely gotten to know at all.

Uncle Trey strokes his beard. "It hurts to see people change, Sammie. One day you realize that everything's different, and it hurts like hell. Just look at Zahra. Just look at this whole family."

Sammie sees what he's saying. Everyone around here's got an itch to scratch. Everyone's falling down in their own way. The house moans loudly, like a howler monkey, and Sammie thinks about its old bones, the changes it's endured. She thinks of Gram, Ms. Mary, Zahra, and Derrick changing rooms like musical chairs, scraping the floors with furniture, painting and repainting the walls, tacking up posters like the one of Missy Elliot over Zahra's desk or hanging photos, Zahra's senior-year portrait or the one of her and Derrick in Halloween costumes, a black cat and a pirate. She thinks this house has been yearning, aging, settling for years, its bones too old for new tricks. She thinks a house might get tired and just close shop abruptly, fall to pieces, the roof collapsing, an avalanche of memories.

Something about the house, maybe its history, maybe its creaks and caws, or it could be learning more about her mother—the dreams, the haunting—some current of understanding (or the lack of understanding) inspires Sammie to write. She gets up to grab her computer, and Uncle Trey claps his hands together, as if his job's been done, and leaves the room.

Sammie revisits her document's version history and finds the last paragraph she wrote and deleted.

I am a Trini American girl who is alright. I know how to cook stew chicken, and I know all the lyrics to "Blank Space." I listen to everything around me, and I know it's not alright, and I'm working on how to fix things. Not only for me, but for Mother Ma, and the biological mother I know very little of, and my uncle Trey, who I know better than the shape of my hands. I am in a Kendrick Lamar song, but also, here I am coming out of it. Alright, alright, alright.

She likes this paragraph more now that she understands where to go next. Because initially this essay was about her, and who she wants to be. But how small-minded of her, to only write about what she knows. What about all the things she's still learning? What about all the things that bubble just beneath the surface? So, she writes:

I am the things I know and the things I don't know, too. When I sit in my plain, white bedroom in East Harlem, I know that it, like every other home that's housed generations of families—all with their own love and trauma—is still seeing and settling, and when my uncle tells me about my estranged mother putting her hand in a crab trap or playing net ball or stories about our homeland, Trinidad—stories that he says everyone knows, but I don't—I know that even my own history doesn't belong to me, that I am a part of more than I could ever realize. And just like when Kendrick Lamar says, "We gon' be alright," without knowing every "we" he references, I know the word alright *is just as prolific.*

Sammie is on a roll when Zahra walks in, so she only notices her when Zahra's shadow looms over the blue screen of her laptop.

"Finally finishing it, huh?" Zahra asks.

"Yeah," Sammie says, then mutters, "No thanks to you."

"Can I see it?" Zahra holds out her hand for the computer. She smells like pine, but Sammie doesn't mind it.

Zahra nods, smiles. "Damn, Sammie. You did that."

It's the most proud Sammie has felt in a long time. "I did?"

"Well, almost . . ."

Sammie's shoulders sink. Of course nothing is ever good enough for Zahra. This, perfectionism, Sammie has learned about her. "What now?"

"Well, if *alright* can mean many things, why don't you help us imagine some of them?"

"Hmm . . . Like . . . *Alright* is hearing my uncle finally open up about my mom?"

Zahra throws her hands in the air as if she's caught the holy spirit. "Yes," she says. Then she's quiet, thinking before she adds, "*Alright* is finding Derrick one day."

Sammie nods, thinks about what she's looking for in the near future. "*Alright* is getting into Stanford and Spelman."

Zahra. "*Alright* is hearing Gram say it's not my fault."

Sammie. "*Alright* is going to get Patsy's with Leila."

Zahra. "*Alright* is reconnecting with an old friend."

Sammie. "*Alright* has been getting to know you."

Zahra pauses, and Sammie grows nervous with how mushy she's made the moment, but also, she wants Zahra to know how much she likes and appreciates her.

Zahra doesn't look at her when she says, "Jesus, Sammie. Who made you?" She shakes her head. "Just when I thought everything was shot to hell."

Now Sammie is prouder than she was even minutes before. Now Sammie has finally finished her essay.

TWENTY-THREE

Zahra doesn't rest easy. She tosses and turns. She thinks of Sammie's essay and revisiting high school with Zee. But more than anything else, she thinks of Derrick, old memories cascading, a waterfall after a fresh rain. She looks over at Sammie with envy; she's a soundless, peaceful sleeper. Zahra gets up without knowing where she's going. Maybe to the living room. Maybe to the kitchen. Maybe outside to hear the crickets and feel an unexpected breeze. But no. Her feet take her to Derrick's old room. She doesn't turn the hall lights on, since she knows the steps well, from when she would peek in on him at night, to make sure he was OK, to make sure he was still there. It occurs to her now that she always knew he would take flight, go missing, disappear without a word.

When she turns the door's handle and peers into the darkness, she is almost startled by the shape of him, of Derrick sound asleep, tucked under the covers, curved like a kidney bean. Then she remembers Trey, curses under her breath, fuck; she's being creepy as shit. She turns around, and the old creaking floors give her away loudly. She hears Trey shift in bed, and the lights come on. She holds still with her back to him, caught.

"Zahra?" he says groggily.

She faces him, believes honesty is the best policy here. "I couldn't sleep," she says. "This used to be Derrick's room."

Trey looks around as if it's his first time seeing it. She watches his eyes circumnavigate, from the rack of baseball caps—Clark, the Falcons, the Braves, an embroidery of Malcolm X—to the bookshelf crammed with bestsellers, self-published novels, textbooks, long-form journalism, autobiographies, memoirs, and pamphlets. Finally, he lands on the quote Derrick inscribed above the closet, "My humanity is bound up in yours, for we can only be human together." Desmond Tutu. Zahra remembers Derrick doing a profile of him in high school, inscribing that quote on the wall after he'd rubbed his burgeoning beard and said, "Onto something, wasn't he?"

Trey rubs his eyes and then nods as if he understands Zahra's insomnia. He sits up, moves over, to the edge of the bed, leaving her 75 percent of it, patting the empty space beside him. She slides under the covers and lies down, back straight, looking up at the wood-beamed ceiling. She's warm but shivers with nerves.

"Thinking about your brother?" Trey asks. It's a forthright question but still gentle. His voice alone is comforting.

"Yeah, I guess. It's not like I wasn't thinking about him back in New York, but . . ."

Trey nods, and she knows she doesn't have to finish her sentence. Instead, she sighs, closes her eyes.

"Zee and I went to go look for him, at our old high school. It's abandoned now. It's crazy we thought he would be there. Just from something random he said however many years ago."

"Like?"

"That he'd be there if he didn't have anywhere else to be."

"Sounds fair enough to me."

"Yeah, I guess. It was weird to be there again. Even though no one else was there, it still felt full, like there were people everywhere. A wealth of personalities—football players, coaches, cheerleaders, parents, runners, kids just trying to make it through high school and adults who've lost the capacity to relate."

"And what was Derrick's vibe?"

"A wave of calm." But that's only how he used to feel. Maybe Zahra lost some of her discernment for him when college took them in separate directions.

"My sister . . . ," Trey says, and Zahra is happy to change the subject.

"Sammie's mom?"

"Yep. Sammie's mom."

"What's she like?"

Trey laughs. "She's a pain in the ass." He stops abruptly. "But she was a good sister growing up. Got good grades, better than me at least. She was active and outspoken, not so different from Sammie."

"Then what happened? Why are you all here, and she's not?"

"She didn't get a visa, and we did. That's how it started. Packed Sammie up with us. Who wouldn't have?"

"Is it that random? Who does and doesn't get one?" It seems odd when she really thinks about it, that Black people should wish to come to a place where the Black people born there are locked up or choked out on camera or holed up in dilapidated projects where the landlords couldn't give two shits. She knows it's not as simple as that. But now that Derrick is gone, she blames this place, America; it's this dysfunction that drove him out of his skin, little by little.

"Getting a visa can be that random," Trey says.

"But it's been years, right? Since you and Sammie moved here? Surely by now, your sister could've gotten a visa."

"Yeah, yeah . . . she could have."

"So what's stopping her?"

He doesn't say anything for a while. She wonders if he's fallen asleep. She pulls herself up on her right elbow, then her right hand, and leans over him.

"Oh," he says, startled by her closeness.

"Oh," she says, realizing that he's awake, and she's invaded his space. "I thought you fell asleep, maybe."

"No, I just . . ." He pauses. "I'm what's stopping her. My sister hasn't gotten her visa because of me." He exhales, then smiles the lop-sided and forlorn smile of someone who's just admitted something dastardly they've been holding in for a while. Zahra gets it, but then again, she doesn't. Why wouldn't Trey want Sammie's mom here, in the States with her?

"What's wrong with her?" Zahra asks, moving back into her earlier position, staring up at the wood-beamed ceiling, the moths perching along the splinters like pigeons on a phone line.

"It's not her. It's her husband."

"Well, what about him?"

"I can't be sure. It's just something that's made its way around, that he uses hands, gets physical. And it's a gut feeling too. I don't like the guy."

Zahra can't decide what to say.

Trey goes on before she can make up her mind. "Knowing the things that happened to Rochelle, I'll be damned if it happens to Sammie."

Zahra thinks that all families have these secrets. The Robinsons sure as hell do. Her grandfather has children she'll never know, and they've all heard but don't talk about how her uncle Quincy can't keep his dick in his pants. Over her dead body she'd let Sammie around him.

"But how can you stop your sister from getting a visa?" Zahra asks.

"It's not something you can do on your own. Moving to a country that might as well be a world away. You need money and you need someone on the other side, to catch you when no one will rent you a place or give you a job or even look at you well enough to remind you that you exist."

"I see."

"Think it makes me a bad person? Think I've done the wrong thing all these years? My mom thinks it's about time I give up this stance, that Sammie's old enough to see her parents for whoever they are."

"That's tough. Your sister wants to come for the right reasons? For Sammie? I mean, why isn't their relationship better?"

"Don't know. She asks me about Sammie all the time. Guess she freezes up when Sammie gets on the line. It's got to be hard, to have a daughter raised in a different place from you, who speaks nothing like you but the sort of English that you relate with tourist hotels and missionary workers."

Zahra nods. "Sammie's still lucky."

"What makes you say that?"

"She has you."

This seems to cheer Trey up, and he rolls onto his side, so he's facing her; his attention feels palpable, like he's touching her all over with his eyes. "You like me, don't you?" he says. He sounds like a child, a middle schooler whose feelings are simple, *yes* or *no* as plain as the difference between day and night. Her current feelings for Trey are not so simple; they are jam-packed against the loss of her brother. A guilt and yearning so dense that she cannot get to any other emotions without those standing in the way. She pulls the covers over her head, but seconds later feels Trey peeling them down as easily as he might shuck an ear of corn from its husk.

He's pulled something down inside of her too, and she can't hide from him any better than she could from Derrick when they'd play hide-and-seek in the dark, and she'd be so scared that she wouldn't hide at all but tiptoe only yards away so all he had to do was stick his arms out and circle around, and bam, she'd be there. But he's nowhere now, and it's Trey looking down at her with those pleading eyes.

"Don't look at me like that," she says.

"Like what?"

"All gooey-eyed."

She smiles when his face drops from her ridicule, and like that, she has picked him back up again.

"You should tell Sammie," she says.

"I will."

"She should know about . . ."

"I don't want to talk about Sammie," he says.

She shrugs, not knowing where things will go from here. A little nervous. A little scared, but mostly excited. A teenager again but more in control of herself. It's been so long, too long, but finally, she tingles all over.

Trey throws his arm around her. It's a careless action, as if it's the natural thing to do, as if they've known each other for longer than just a couple of months now. Zahra feels it too, so she leans in, places her hand against his chest, mimics the rhythm of his heart with slow taps. The music is cued, and Zahra looks around for who's playing it, for where it's coming from, and she sees them, nestled together in a corner. The moths, having their *Little Mermaid* moment, except this isn't "Kiss the Girl" but an old R & B song, a smooth joint that makes her want to two-step. *Girl, I want to shake you down. I can give you all the lovin' you need*, they go. Almost better than Gregory Abbott himself. Zahra smiles, laughs. For once, the moths have gotten it right. For once, they're not singing dirges of the dead. She looks to Trey to see if he hears it too, and though she knows he can't, he rocks her to the beat anyway. How does he know? How does he know without knowing her at all?

TWENTY-FOUR

ammie bolts upright, sweating so bad that she wonders if she's peed the bed. She looks at her phone and sees that it is nine in the morning, later than she usually sleeps. Her heart is pounding hard, and she tries to normalize it with deep breaths, in and out. In and out. In and out. She must have had a bad dream but can't remember it. Was it a Chacachacare dream? She doesn't think so. She feels her face and all over her body to make sure things are still intact; no one has been eating away at her.

Flashes of the dream come back to her slowly. Green grass. Families with cameras. The rise and dip of downtown Atlanta. She remembers looking for something. The heavy lump beside her shifts, and she remembers who she's with, Zahra—it's obvious now. In her dream, she was looking for Derrick.

She is close to finding him; she can feel it. She has written her essay and turned it in, but her work is not done here; she knows that. *Dreamers, lots of people*, she remembers Rashad saying. He was hiding something from her.

Sammie finds her cell phone on the floor, half under the bed. She googles *Atlanta dreamers* and finds links to sites supporting the WNBA. She revises her search to *Dreamers Atlanta lots of people*. Blogs ask, *Is Atlanta right for you?* Or lament *The top 11 things all Atlantans could use a serious break from*. One headline stands out particularly—*Nowhere for people to go: Who will survive the gentrification of Atlanta?* She makes mental notes to come back to these articles but revises her search to *popular places in Atlanta*. She sees the Georgia Aquarium, Centennial Olympic Park, World of Coca-Cola, Piedmont Park, Martin Luther King, Jr. National Historical Park. Two places stand out in relation to dreamers, but then Rashad's green torch shirt comes back to her, a revelation, she gasps. He knew more than he was letting on; he's been trying to tell her something. She googles Centennial Park and finds the *Gateway of Dreams* sculpture. She reads the slogan for the 1996 Olympics—*Come Celebrate Our Dream*. She wonders who *our* is? Atlantans? Olympians? Americans? This is it, she thinks. This is where they'll find Derrick. She would swear on it, would cross her heart and hope to die. She shakes Zahra awake, the need to go is so pressing.

"What?" Zahra asks, still half asleep.

"Can we go to Centennial Park today?" Sammie asks. "Can we go soon?"

Zahra rubs the sleep from her eyes and sits up on one elbow. Her bonnet has fallen off throughout the night, and her hair leans to one side of her head, opposite the side she slept on. "Right now? Why?"

Sammie bites her lip, unsure if she should say exactly what she thinks, what she feels. She takes a chance. "I know I said I didn't believe that the moths brought us together, and the verdict is still out on that, but I feel like I know where Derrick is. I just woke up knowing, and Gram and Ms. Mary, they say to listen to those feelings."

"You're always welcome to quote Gram, but my mother—you might want to lay off of that."

Zahra has completely missed the point. Sammie's talking about Derrick. She knows where they can find him. Why isn't Zahra more excited? Why doesn't she believe her?

"Zahra, please, for one second get out of your ass and listen to what I'm saying."

Zahra's up now. She jumps back, looking hurt and incredulous all at once. "Jesus, Sammie. I'm still an adult."

"I know. I'm sorry, but you have to listen to me."

"What makes you think you know where Derrick is?"

"I had this dream. I can't remember it, but I can feel it. In here." Sammie points to her heart, knowing how ridiculous it all seems. "Listen." She pulls down the covers, sits up straight, and faces Zahra square on, serious. "This makes sense. Derrick and I, I think we're alike. I think we're . . . What do you call it? Kindred souls or something. Sometimes when I look around the house, at all the pictures of him, I get goose bumps. Real, live ones. Look, I have them now." Sammie shows Zahra her arms, hairs on end, little bumps all over as if it's freezing cold in here. It's not. It's warm.

"See?" Sammie says.

Zahra exhales and gets up slowly. Sammie watches her take off her pajamas and pull on the same jeans she wore the day before. They're high-rise, and she shakes to get in them. With just her bra on top, she turns around and looks at Sammie, raising her eyebrows expectedly.

"Well, get ready," she says.

<hr />

THEY ARE GOING TO FIND HIM. DERRICK. THE MAN WHO HAS become a mythical being to Sammie, one that has loads of stories but a phantom face. She tugs at her seat belt insecurely. She holds it tightly with nothing to do with her left hand. In her right hand, she holds Zahra's cell phone. She's been tasked with giving directions, since Zahra only vaguely remembers this city she calls home, a city in which Sammie cannot draw a clear distinction between its mysteriousness and Derrick's. Uncle Trey sits in the back seat. Sammie could tell that he wanted to claim shotgun. He opened his mouth to speak but then shut it quickly when he saw Zahra and Sammie deep in conversation when he got to the car. He doesn't know where they are headed or what tipped them off, but he must know that he is only along for the ride, a bystander. On the way to Centennial Park, Sammie absorbs Atlanta in order to stop the nerves that course through her body.

"We're on Twenty, right?" Sammie asks. "Looks like we'll be on this interstate for a few minutes."

"Twenty," Zahra says. "One of the dumbest expressways ever built. Well, not exactly dumb. Well-planned racism. Built to uphold segregation, completely irrational in its layout otherwise." Zahra presses down on the gas, and Sammie grips the door handle, taken off guard. "It's almost always jam-packed. We're hitting it at a good time."

Sammie nods. *Everything here is racist*, she thinks. When Zahra or Ms. Mary or Gram mention anything about this place, there is a fifty-fifty chance of them following it up with how said characteristic or description is racist. Ms. Mary seems to do it intentionally, but Zahra seems absentminded as she spews these qualifiers, like a robot almost, and sometimes if Sammie asks Zahra to elaborate, she says, "Huh?" as if she has no idea she's just said anything at all. Now Sammie wonders if the traffic is so bad why people don't just take the train like they do in normal cities.

Sammie imagines Derrick on MARTA, a quiet passenger, not someone who cozies up all chatty with the person next to him. Instead, maybe he reads the *New York Times* daily email on his phone or pulls out a thin paperback book from his back pocket. She imagines the trains are as loud, as dirty, as fast-moving, and as full of a diverse array of people as they are in New York. She doesn't know any better. She has never heard anyone acronym MARTA as moving Africans rapidly through Atlanta instead of what it really stands for—Metropolitan Atlanta Rapid Transit Authority. She doesn't know its inefficiency, its history, how white suburbs didn't want the rail system to run through them, and so it swerves around full communities in a way that makes it impossible as a regular, efficient means of travel. In Sammie's mind, Derrick is there riding the train like a New Yorker, and she wonders where he's headed.

Sammie remembers her Spelman tour guide saying that Atlanta has more than sixty streets with some variance of Peachtree in the name, and she recites potential monikers in her head—Peachtree Lane, Peachtree Road, West Peachtree Street, East Peachtree Street. She counts ten before she's forced to circle back to the start. She wonders why this city is so obsessed with peaches, and imagines that at one point in time, there were a million of them, peach trees in every neighborhood, taller than the cookie-cutter houses behind them, peach trees rising from skyscrapers like proud flags, peach trees along the sides of the expressway they're traversing now. The peaches would fall from the trees and roll onto the lanes. The lanes would be covered in juice. The juice would give off a sickly sweet smell when you arrived at your destination and opened your car door.

The car ride is stifling, not too hot or muggy, but the air is thick with tangled thoughts and questions and emotions. Sammie can almost feel Zahra's anticipation pulsing off of her. And Sammie's own knees shake with excitement and fear.

"So we just merged onto . . . ?" Sammie asks Zahra, confused by the navigation's system's directions.

"Seventy-Five/Eighty-Five."

"Right." It says that. "But which one?"

"Both."

Sammie likes Atlanta but finds it confusing. Backward. A city that's not quite a city. Expressways with two names, as if they can't choose where they'd like to go. And where are the peaches they boast of? She's hungry just thinking about them. What she wouldn't give to be off this mission, to be out picking peaches somewhere safe, somewhere where men, sons, brothers, don't disappear in the middle of the day and reach out to strangers in the night to find them.

"Where are the peaches?" Sammie asks.

Zahra shrugs.

"Same place you'll find the apples in New York," Uncle Trey says from the back seat. He's got a point, and Sammie nods, accepting it. Thinking maybe New York isn't so different from Atlanta after all.

"I don't know if there ever were any peach trees," Zahra says. "Sure, Georgia has a lot of peaches, best place to find them if you ask me. But Atlanta? The name *peach tree* comes from the Creek Indians. They named their village something that was translated into English as 'standing peach tree,' but should have been 'standing pitch tree' referencing the pine trees and the pitch that comes from them."

Zahra is an encyclopedia of unusual, often unusable knowledge. Sammie loves this about her.

"Ever seen pine pitch before?" Zahra asks.

Sammie shakes her head.

"It's sticky. Looks like honey. Stay in Atlanta long enough, and you'll know it."

"It's hard to imagine living here," Sammie says.

"No, it's not." Zahra doesn't take her eyes off the road. "You'll be here next fall. Maybe."

"Maybe," Sammie says.

"News to me," Uncle Trey says.

Sammie turns to face him. "I'm leaning toward Spelman."

"A tree that changes direction," he says. "Well, what do you know?"

Sammie smiles. Imagines herself a pine tree or an old oak. Better yet, a peach tree with burgeoning fruit, the kind that will eventually turn into the fuzzy, sweet peaches that Gram eats in nearly just one bite. Sammie will be the only peach tree in Atlanta; she'll be impossible. "And if I live here, I'll get to eat Gram's pound cake all the time. And maybe Ms. Mary will tell me more about what it was like when she went to Spelman."

"Ha," Zahra says. "Mary take precious time out of her day? Probably not."

Sammie shrugs. "I like your mom," she mumbles.

Zahra waits a beat to say, "You don't know her."

"But at least you do." Sammie says it without thinking, and just as quickly, she wishes she hadn't. Now she can feel Uncle Trey's hand on her shoulder. He always does these sort of gestures when she mentions her mom, and it's agitating; he thinks he can just smooth over her frustration. She pulls away from him, rolls her eyes.

"You have Mother Ma, and you have me," Uncle says, and here he goes, always trying to fix things, but this is something he has nothing to do with, knows nothing about.

"Whatever," Sammie says. She looks out the window. The peach trees she's imagined are not here, but the lanes are wide and cars pass them by like lightning bolts. The city has grown up around them, not New York tall but reaching the sky still, the space of the Eastside shrunken, steel gray buildings to the left of them and a small bank of trees to their right.

"Your exit is coming up," she tells Zahra, but Zahra has already veered off the interstate, as if she's known the way all along.

"You'll understand one day," Uncle Trey says, and God, he just won't give it a rest. Sammie tries to focus on the digital billboard coming up. It has rotating red Coca-Cola bottles on it, but she finds that her interest in the billboard doesn't outweigh her opinion, and she says, "No, I won't. Mom's a deadbeat."

Zahra merges onto Spring Street. It's clear she doesn't need the directions, and Sammie puts the phone in a cup holder.

"You shouldn't talk about your mom like that."

"You're supposed to be on my side," Sammie says. "She left you too, you know. She left you to do her job and my dad's job, and she's supposed to be here."

"You're too young to understand."

"You're too self-absorbed to explain."

Uncle seethes. "I wish I had the luxury, but what do you know? You're too caught up in school politics and what the prep boys think of you to see straight."

She can't believe he's finally said it, that he judges her for going to the school he sent her to, that he doesn't remember his own speech about opportunities and his insistence that she could hang out with Leila on the weekends. He doesn't know anything about how he's split her into two people, and she doesn't know which is better, and she doesn't always remember to switch on and off so people receive the version they deem most palatable.

"That's not fair," Zahra says.

And it isn't. Because Uncle has no idea what it's like to be a girl, a Black girl at P & P. Even Broderick wouldn't know shit about it, and he's nearly the same age, attends the same school, hangs out with the same crowd. Still, he would never walk into a room and hear his white friends saying his crush would never like him back. Not that he's ugly or anything, but they just couldn't *see it*. And Sammie wanted to run to the one person who might have understood, but she was an ocean away, and the phone was too heavy to lift.

"You'll never understand what it's like to be a Black girl, but most important, you'll never understand what it's like to be a Black girl without a mom."

"But you have a mom."

"No, I don't."

"You do."

Sammie hears but doesn't process Zahra trying to point out the Georgia Aquarium to them. Maybe Zahra is rambling on about it being the largest aquarium in the western hemisphere, or how activists deemed it the "dying pool" after three beluga whales died from 2012 to 2015. Maybe Zahra says, *You can't just displace species from their homes*, because she subconsciously knows gentrification all too well—the Atlanta, American narrative. And the moths—they're a displaced species too. But Sammie is so pissed at Uncle Trey that she can't think straight.

"She doesn't want me," she says. "We both know that."

"Jesus, Sammie," Zahra says, but Uncle Trey is silent, pensive. Sammie watches him in the rearview mirror but won't give him the satisfaction of turning around.

Eventually he says, "Don't be so naive. People can want two things at once."

"Like that even means anything."

"It means—"

"Nothing," Sammie cuts him off, and immediately, she can feel his steam fill the car.

"It means that I told her no! No, she can't come here. No, it won't be good for you. No, I'm not helping her get a visa, and she can't stay with us. And not a penny, not a penny of help from me."

"You're lying," Sammie says, but she knows it's the truth, that her uncle, possibly her favorite person in this world, has betrayed her. She takes off her seat belt, feeling trapped by it.

"Your dad is an asshole, and you're better off without him, and your mom will never leave him. You can't always ask people to choose." He must have asked her to. She must not have chosen Sammie, and though the thought hurts like hell, Sammie needs to know for sure.

"Did you?" she asks.

"Did I what?"

"Did you ask her to choose?"

"Never mind that, Sammie."

"Did you ask her to choose?" Sammie is getting louder now, feeling like she can't control herself and that there are impulses, beats, moths even, inside of her, waiting to burst out.

"Sammie," Uncle says.

But just the way he says her name unleashes something inside of her, and she is full-on screaming. "Did you ask her to choose?"

"Fuck," he says. "Yes, and she didn't choose you."

"But tell her the rest, Trey. That her mom won't stop calling. That she's always asking about her, about you, Sammie."

"You knew?" Sammie says incredulously. "She knew?" She turns to Uncle now, faces him square on, and he looks like he's about to cry. She doesn't care. He didn't give a fuck about her feelings when he lied to her, over and over again.

"She knew?" Sammie asks again. "You told *her* before you told me?!"

"I thought she could help."

"Bullshit," Sammie says under her breath, still too afraid to curse at Uncle outright. "You're such a coward. You can't even tell her you like her, but you tell her our family's business? *My* business? She's going crazy, did you know that?"

Earlier that morning it occurred to Sammie that Zahra might be too much like her own mother. Why grow close to a woman who can't figure herself out? Who will one day up and decide that Sammie is nothing but a speck to her, smaller than the moths they have in common.

Sammie can feel Zahra's head whip around to face her, and Zahra's eyes aren't so different from the ones she's grown accustomed to, the invisible eyes that watch and wait, only Zahra's are real and right next to her. Still, they don't stop Sammie from saying, "She thinks she can hear moths, that they sing to her. God, Uncle. You were supposed to be the good one."

It all happens so fast. Zahra slams on the brakes. Sammie is unbraced, unbelted for the jolt that should've sent her flying forward, against the dashboard, maybe even through the windshield, but a soft force like down feathers forces her into her rightful position, against the passenger seat, and she is shock-eyed and sedated by the intensity of it all.

Of course Sammie doesn't see the moths come out of nowhere like tiny particles of dust revealed in the light. She doesn't feel the moths fluttering around her like little mothers tending to their sick child. She doesn't hear the radio station click on, to a song she would only be vaguely familiar with anyway, *People get ready, there's a train a-comin'*. And nor does she see the man just yards from the car in a ratty Falcons T-shirt, slowly backing away, one foot behind the other, easy as he goes.

TWENTY-FIVE

S hit, what was that? Did she just hit someone? Something? The car has gone quiet now, the people inside it too. Zahra looks over at Sammie, and she is as still as a statue, eyes wide open, watery. She was leaning over the console, screaming at Trey, but now Sammie is back in her seat. Zahra thanks God for it. She checks the rearview mirror, and Trey is looking around frantically. He seems disoriented. He takes off his seat belt, and Zahra follows his lead, the moths all around her like nosy children.

"What the fuck was that?" he asks.

Shit. Shit. Shit. She doesn't know. "There was a man. I don't think I hit him, but then, maybe I did." Her hands are shaking. She looks at them curiously. They seem disconnected from the rest of her body.

Trey gets out of the car, but Zahra is less bold. She doesn't want to see what she's done. She places her hands on the wheel and grips it tightly. Eventually she sees Trey in front of the car, looking around it, under it. He shakes his head, scratches his beard, comes around to Zahra's window. Her hands are still shaking when she rolls it down.

"Nothing's here," he says.

"But . . ."

"Come see for yourself."

She steps outside of the car, and the day is chilly, but the sun, peeking over clouds, is bright, blinding. She squints at her surroundings. She didn't even need the directions to make it here. The stretch of Centennial Olympic Park Drive in front of her. The Ferris wheel in the distance, shrouded in morning fog. To her right, the arched fence and architectural shrubbery of one of the park's entrances.

She sees a man walking backward, slowly. He is looking at her. His face is unshaven, and his hair is matted, as if he hasn't brushed it in weeks. But the shirt, the shirt she recognizes. Of course there are Falcons shirts everywhere, but this one is black with a hole in the bottom of the right sleeve from when Gram's dryer broke and ripped almost every piece of clothing that went in it. Stolen, she thinks. This man stole Derrick's shirt. She steps closer as he steps away. Closer, away. Closer, away. They dance until Zahra stops and squints her eyes so hard that it begins to give her a headache. The shirt isn't stolen. The man who looks like an addict, homeless, mentally unstable, maybe all three, is her brother. She runs toward him.

"Derrick, what happened to you?" she screams.

He runs away, around people and strollers and tourists clicking cameras, past the Quilt of Origins, the Quilt of Remembrance, the Quilt of Dreams, but just like when they were kids, he is faster than her. He is smoking her, and she is gasping for air. Running, then stumbling, then crying as she loses sight of him. She turns around and bumps into Trey's open arms. He pets her like a bird with broken wings.

"It's OK," he says. "It's OK. Everything's going to be all right. Everything's going to be all right." They walk back to the car like this, Zahra devastated, exasperated, hiccupping, and Trey reassuring her that one of the worst possible outcomes is OK. That things are all right, no matter how much they aren't.

Not far from the car, Zahra spots what Zee was talking about at Fellini's, a pile of leaflets that Derrick has left behind. She picks them up and has no idea what to think of these unrecognizable faces. She throws the flyers in the back of the car so they scatter like dandelion seeds, like the moth eggs that have latched on to the car's nylon up-holstery. She thinks of Derrick as one of the Black Israelites in Har-lem or a brother to the Black woman outside the bus stop who isn't waiting for the bus at all, just biding her time, arguing with God knows who, saying things like "Not on my time you won't," or "Must think I'm a fool, that I don't know where I come from." He's lost. He's lost it. And now, she's lost him again.

TWENTY-SIX

Derrick lights a match, throws it in the trash can, and watches the old photos of his family burn; he's trying to lose memories. The basement is dark and dank but for the light of the fire. It's got windows but small ones that he has to stand on his tiptoes to see out of. An old coworker, Bina, owns it. "Got in while the getting was still good," she said. "Vine City's going nowhere but up," and it's not a lie. Derrick doesn't let the boarded-up houses or the smell of highway pollution fool him. Gentrification is underway. Even the notorious Bluff, anachronized "better leave, you fucking fool," popularized by the raw criminal and poorly shot *Snow on Tha Bluff* documentary, and less than a mile from here, will be different in some years, maybe already is now. When Derrick asked Bina for a place to stay for a while, she took his three hundred dollars quick and without questions, only one demand—*You'll have to find someplace to park your car,* so he left it.

The fire licks the sides of the can and then dies quickly. He throws more photos in. Some of him and Zahra doing cartwheels on the lawn, and one of him older, in high school, sitting on top of his car and eating a bag of hot pork rinds. He lights up another match.

Gram's father died in a fire. Folks said he was insatiable, restless, wanting. Sometimes, Derrick wonders if he's his reincarnate. A fire has to leave something behind, doesn't it? That's what he's hoping for by burning these photos—to replace something, to replace memories. He's got too many, and it's easier to deal with the ones that aren't his.

Still, one memory stands out—a time when Mary came home looking like she'd just whooped the mess out of the world. In a skirt suit and pumps, Derrick knew his mother was tougher than his father. She'd say things like, *Over my dead body*, and *I'll be damned* a lot. But this one time he remembers like yesterday. Mary came home talking about how a man, a Black man, had burned his own home down. She said he'd planted a lawn chair at the end of the driveway and watched the fire like it was a late-night show. She said it happened in one of those homes that stands alone, ivy-covered, not far from the projects, a place the police don't seem to care much about, so the house was halfway gone by the time the fire department got there. She said the man wasn't high or drunk or mental, or at least it didn't seem that way. Imagine, an ordinary man, just burning his house to crisps as if it's nothing, as if it's what he's got to do to get ready for work the next day. When Mom said it, Derrick was in middle school and had been sitting at the kitchen table doing his homework, eating a nuked slice of pizza.

Derrick hugs himself tight, arms gripping the curve of his back, nails digging in. He picks up an old photo of Zahra, from a family vacation in Savannah, one of the only trips they made that wasn't to visit family. In the photo Zahra stands next to a street trumpet player, leaning over him, fingers splayed so she might be playing along. She couldn't have been older than ten or eleven. She's changed, hasn't she?

What was she doing in the park today? She looked at him as if she didn't know him, and what she'd said was even worse, *Derrick, what happened to you?* As if he's the one who left. He stayed. He stayed and watched the neighbors come and go, watched the houses sag with weary, swamped-in For Sale signs, weighed down by cardboard boxes packed with worthless shit from the Walmart off Panola and clothes from the Rainbow across the street, shoeboxes stuffed with memories and trash bags heaping with home goods.

Dad's neighborhood is something of the same dedicated evil. Southland was once an affluent Black neighborhood, up against a golf course, prestigious if not pretentious. But now families can't sell their homes for even what they bought them for. Freedom isn't about money, not even about ownership, but people still think they can buy or bully their way out of being Black. In Zahra's case, she thinks she can run from it. He stayed.

He stayed, and Atlanta is a hot city. Derrick knows this better than anybody, knows that the city can press down on you from all sides and the sun can feel like a light bulb down your back. He thought the fall foliage, the breeze of winter beckoning, could cool him off, but no. He is hotter as the days pass, and he tries to shake the sun in the same way he tried to swallow the moths' songs, words he's grown to know all too well, like the Pledge of Allegiance or the first eight bars of "Juicy," but there is no getting out of this fight. The faces that come to him as easy as looking through a class View-Master, started as a conversation, a simple drop in the everyday mix of pleasantries: *Have you ever heard of Warren Samuels? Of course you haven't,* he might say, or *Reminds me of Minnie. Let me tell you about Tall Minnie.*

Beyond Warren and Minnie, he sees Brittney with the blond wig, and then Shay with her soft round cheeks. He sees Marquise with the scar on his face from flying off a bike and hitting the sidewalk chin first. He sees Princess with keloids and fake diamond studs decorating her ears. He sees the mailman with his patchy salt-and-pepper beard and the autistic person up Gram's street who always asks to shake his hand. He sees the young freckle-faced bartender at the wings spot off Redan. With everyone in this world, Derrick sees more. Now, he sees Zahra's face contorted, a face he knows well, pinched thick eyebrows and intense deep-set eyes, but no less than an hour ago, she looked at him in a way that made his skin crawl. No, it was more internal than that. He wanted to claw right out of himself.

But then he might not have the memories of him and Zahra learning Atlanta like the back of their hands, driving everywhere and having nowhere to be, listening to music all day and not feeling any less productive because of it.

Derrick had friends on top of friends on top of friends, but no one any closer than Zahra. So it hurt like hell when things started happening, things he couldn't explain, voices she couldn't hear, faces she didn't remember, and he couldn't talk to her about them. Truth was, he started seeing inside of people when he was still young, and at first it felt like a superpower. He would close his eyes and dream something he'd catch on the news the next day. And like a smell or sound might jog your memory, so would his senses create realities that obviously didn't belong to him. Bobby Womack might conjure up days spent in the US Penitentiary Atlanta, or Nat King Cole might make him remember learning to fly a plane like one of the Tuskegee Airmen. Moths might tell him stories of people whose faces would come to him like a child begging for candy. Eventually, he felt it his responsibility to tell someone else, to tell the stories that wanted to be told.

When he tried to talk to Zahra about all of it, she'd said, "Derrick, worry about yourself." And "Derrick, you're scaring me."

And, "Derrick, let's just forget about the damn moths, why don't we?" But how could he forget the things, the beings that had eaten at his cool like hungry vultures? They left him wanting and worried. So eventually, he stopped caring about who he was, because the world was so much bigger anyway. He wasn't but one small piece of the pie, but there were ways to be more. There were ways to be more than one small person.

He didn't know the faces would become whole people. The day he met that beautiful woman at the creek was the day he realized he might never know what the world wants from him. To tell stories? To be as restless as his great-grandfather? To fall in love? Well, he doesn't see any point in any of it. But since leaving home, the moths have been quieter than they've been in years, and he's been able to use his voice again, in a way he hasn't since high school. He's been taking some alone time to do the work—the storytelling, so why was Zahra choosing to chase after him now? Didn't she read the note he left?

Lately, something's shifted in his family, and in people like Warren and Minnie too. One day they're men, and the next day they're moths. One day their lives are steerable, and the next day, they're crashing into phantom people, running after siblings who've intentionally strayed, lighting matches in someone else's basement and feeling the fire outside so the one inside might die off.

‖‖‖‖‖‖‖‖‖‖‖‖‖‖‖‖‖‖‖‖‖‖‖‖‖‖‖‖‖‖‖‖

HE BEGAN WRITING THEIR STORIES ABOUT A YEAR AGO. IT seems like he knows everything about them except when or how they died. Warren Samuels was the first. He is thirty-seven years old with three kids, all girls, from two baby moms, one of whom he is married to, or would be if Georgia still recognized common-law marriage. Warren calls Regina Hamilton his wife, and Pastor

Watkins, who they see every other Sunday and surely on the holidays, recognizes their implicit vows too. Warren is a maintenance worker for Georgia Tech, a job that felt elite when he applied and lied on his paperwork that he'd never been arrested. In fact, he has been arrested three times. Once on mistaken identity, par the course for a Black man in Atlanta, once for two ounces of marijuana, and once for violating parole on that marijuana charge when he unknowingly waived a court hearing. Like anyone really, Warren has a range of signature phrases, things like *Be easy*; *Make that money, don't let it make you*; and *As long as the light bill's paid*, he says with his friends, or parables of advice he offers his children like *Mess up now and the stink will follow you forever*.

||||||||||||||||||||||||||||||||||||||||||||||||||||

MINNIE, THEY CALL DAIJA, THOUGH IT'S NOT SHORT FOR HER name and she herself is not short either. But she looks just like her mother, Dina, and Minnie, a childhood name that stuck, is five foot nine with a lace front and a nose ring nearly too big for her nostrils. She works retail at a Dots clothing store where women buy bodycon rompers, mesh jumpsuits, matching sweats sets, and no matter how she thinks they look in them, Minnie always nods her head and says, "I'd buy it." It's not that the sale matters to her; Minnie doesn't work off commission but makes $9 an hour. Still, she's the leading sales rep. She tells people to buy it, and they do. Maybe because she looks damn good in her own jumpsuit, or because her smile lifts the room and the air around her makes you feel like you're floating. Maybe because she *mhmm*s you to death, so you feel like you're old girlfriends or for the men who come to buy gifts for their significant others, like they'd stand the chance of jumping ship or switching sails and sidling up to this tall stallion in front of them. Without knowing that Minnie hasn't dated men in years. She used to until they started tasting tart, a little too salty, a little stale like a bag of chips left open. Minnie is not someone who's been "turned out." In fact, you could say she's been turned in, to her most authentic self, to the woman she was always supposed to be, so when she agrees with whatever you say, *mhmm, mhmm, mhmm*, really, she's just unbothered. Maybe considering what she and Sheila will have for dinner, or thinking about what flavor of pie she'll take her dying grandmother for dessert.

||||||||||||||||||||||||||||||||||||||||||||||||

NATASHA REYNOLDS IS THE LATEST STORY, AND THE YOUNG-est as well. She is ten, and she herself also likes to tell stories. Sometimes they work to her benefit. *I have a sister named Rianca*, she might say. *She lives in Florida and sells seashells by the seashore. She is going to come save me from this pathetic place and take me somewhere limitless. She just has a few more seashells to sell.*

    Lies, Mr. Gibson tells Natasha, but she does not see her stories that way. Her stories are no different than the ones Mrs. Kirkpatrick, her former teacher, used to read on the circle rug. When Natasha asked Mrs. Kirkpatrick if a story really happened, she'd shrug and say, "Maybe."

    Maybe any story is possible. Maybe any story can be true. Natasha lives with her parents, DeJuan and Kiana, who are hardworking lower-middle-class folks and have no idea that their daughter is gifted because of course the school does not see Natasha's storytelling as a gift. Frequent notes and calls home have led the Reynolds to whisper behind Natasha's back, *I don't know what we're going to do. She is who she is, isn't she?* They are not mad or defensive but almost relieved when a teacher suggests that Natasha go to a behavioral class. No one questions the why. Why the need for storytelling? No one knows that Natasha would say something like this—*I like stories, and maybe they're true, and if maybe they're true, then maybe you should listen, and if you listen either way, then maybe you'll learn something, because you can always learn, right? That's what Mom says. My real mom, the one right over there,* and Kiana would be standing there, as brown and beautiful as tree bark, as real and alive as the day, the floor under their feet, proof.

||||||||||||||||||||||||||||||||||||||||||||||||||||||||||

DERRICK ORGANIZES HIS PAPERS, NEAT STACKS ON THE small IKEA desk in the corner of the room. He tries to shake the way people look at him when he hands them out, but those faces are stuck in his mind too. Just the other day, "Brother, brother," someone called out to him, and he almost ran away from the title instinctively, but he looked over his shoulder and found a face so warm and familiar that he stopped in his tracks and waited for the tall man in a purple dashiki to catch up with him.

"One of my best students," the man said, and Derrick finally placed him. How could he have forgotten?

"Dr. Milton," Derrick said, clearing his throat. "How are you?"

"Good, good. And you?" Dr. Milton acted like he didn't notice the change in Derrick, but Derrick knew he did. Whenever Derrick runs into someone he knows, they look at him like he's a pariah and ask if he's all right. *Well, are you?* he wants to ask them but smirks instead.

"I'm just . . ." Derrick doesn't want to give his usual spiel. "Just . . ."

"What do you have there?" Dr. Milton asked.

Derrick handed him the leaflet, and Dr. Milton laughed heartily. Derrick couldn't stand to hear that guttural ha-ha and walked away.

"Wait!" Dr. Milton called out. "Brother, I'm not laughing at you. I'm laughing at the situation. A man meets his match. I was just like you at your age. And let me tell you, all you need is an audience. Ever thought about that?"

Well, not exactly. An audience would just call him crazy. Hearing moths? Hearing voices? Jumping in and out of people like changing clothes? Who would believe that?

"I may have something for you," Dr. Milton said. "Well, I'll be damned. Well, I'll be damned. C'mon on, brother."

DERRICK GETS UP AND TAKES THE PAPERS IN A HUGE STACK. He throws them in the garbage and lights the leaflets on fire just like the photos. Then he lays on his blow-up bed thinking about the family he's run from. Why did he leave? Maybe it's too much to look at his mother and sister, father and Gram and know that they will sing their own songs one day, maybe they're singing them now, showing up in random strangers' dreams, interweaving their memories like Gram's colorful afghans.

And, of course, Derrick wonders what happens when you uproot a family who is already lost. Do they get sucked so deep in the world's mayhem that life will never stop spinning? You could stick your hand right through them and feel nothing but air. Do they turn on each other, sides split like an open watermelon, pink and plentiful on the inside? Do they never recover but with each next generation get pulled deeper and deeper under, until they don't even know what over means?

Atlanta is growing colder and the leaves more sparse, the pine needles like prophets, the hungry bark heading into hibernation, and all signs pointing home, home. A moth in the corner of his room sings, *Hearts of fire creates love desire.*

TWENTY-SEVEN

She thought that all she wanted was to see her brother, her best friend, that all she wanted was to know that he was alive, breathing, being. She thought she would be happy, and though there is that part of her, the *at least I know where he is* part, the *at least his body didn't wash up the Chattahoochee* part, the largest part of her—the part that causes her blood to boil so hot that she stomps in the house, not so different from her sixteen-year-old self, and slams the leaflet down on the table—is mad as hell.

"This is your fault," she says to Mary, who is sipping coffee. Sipping coffee in the middle of the damned day, like there's nothing better to do.

"Should be happy you found him," Mary says, setting down the cup carefully, more careful than she ever was with her children. "Thanks for the text." Of course Zahra sent a text. She couldn't gather her breath enough to make a call. And say what? *We found him, but he's a bum? We found him, but he's on the street, raggedy as hell, handing out pamphlets that tell random people's stories?* Her breath catches in the same way it did on Spring Street, and she has to take a moment, gulp down her feelings to get out what she's been meaning to say for more than twenty years now.

"You're such a shitty mother." The curse word surprises even her. She's never cursed at her parents before, Gram neither. She has been a fairly good girl all her life, and now, it feels so freeing but equally sinful to say something she knows will sting.

Her mother closes her eyes as if she's been waiting for this moment. "I understand that you feel that way."

Zahra wants to scream. She wants to scream *fuck you* in her mother's face with her hot midday breath. She wants to scream so loud that it echoes throughout this whole damned city and everyone can hear how desolate she feels, and her brother will hear her the loudest, and he will come back because she needs him to, because she needs him to be better than what he's become. She doesn't scream. She levels her emotions, so they match her mother's calm.

"Derrick and I were young, still in elementary school, maybe seven and eight years old, nine and ten, something like that. He tried to tell you. He tried to tell you that he could hear, that he could maybe even see . . ."

She's not telling it right. She has to start over.

"It seems like you were always campaigning. And if not campaigning, then you were obsessing over some current event. This particular time, it was Freaknik. The Sinclair incident. Remember that?"

"Of course I do. Black man gets beat with a baton on video. 1997. You were nine, Derrick ten."

"Of course you do. That video was all you watched. It was all you talked about. You had to have said *the police* a million times that month."

"You're mad at my outrage? Knowing what you know now, you should be outraged too. It's still happening, you know. How many lives could have been saved if we stopped it then?"

"I don't know, Mary. But what I do know is that Derrick tried to tell you that he was hearing voices, seeing things, that he felt like someone was watching him, and he couldn't get a word in with you. You shooed him away. You always shooed us away. *Go play. Go read something. Go, go, go.* Well, guess what? He's gone now. We might have found him, but he isn't here, and he wasn't really there at Centennial Park today either."

"Timmie Sinclair. That was his full name. He was twenty-seven years old."

Zahra picks up a white glass plate from the table and throws it across the room. It shatters against the window frame, and she sits down, starts to cry.

Her mother doesn't flinch. "Timmie had a family. Was on his way to pick up his daughter's prescription."

Zahra is sobbing uncontrollably now.

"Five officers. Five. Could've killed that man, maybe would have had there not been witnesses. It's been done before. Over and over and over again."

Zahra finds a dirty napkin on the table and wipes her nose with it.

"Freaknik was out of control. Of course it was, things felt a little too free for us. There was a little too much joy in the air. Black people showing up and showing out, always trying to prove something. That's our biggest misconception, that we have something to prove. But the kids—those college kids—they were trying to make it right again. The bomb threats and all that mess, the feeling of unease, that wasn't us. That was white folks."

Zahra remembers very little of Freaknik other than a traffic jam and gyrating bodies on tops of cars. Gram was picking up Mary from somewhere downtown, someplace Zahra can't quite remember, and Zahra was in the back seat, and it took them forever to get there, to get back home. At first Zahra was captivated by the scene, the Black people everywhere, their skin exposed in a way that made it seem like it was for sale, but in a good way. All the latest trends, all the brightest, most distinct colors, neons and hots. Eventually the scene seemed to hypnotize her, and with no one to discuss it, Derrick at Dad's house, she fell asleep, stretched out from window to window. That had to have been an earlier Freaknik, '94 or '95. The year of the Sinclair incident, '97, was a whole 'nother story, even Zahra knows this. The turnout was much smaller that year. It was the beginning of the end.

Now Zahra realizes that Mary hasn't stopped talking, that she's going on and on about Freaknik and Black people and what's unfair, unjust, inhumane. "It wasn't about the rapes—why they stopped it. It was about Black people on white streets, on white property, about Black people everywhere." She finally pauses. "You, my child, are privileged. You've always had a roof over your head, food to eat, clothes for every occasion. I got you into a good school, started you on SAT words in fourth grade, put you in every after-school program we could afford. I gave you this." She points to her head, knowledge. "Everything you need to succeed, to fight."

Mary has done it again. Even today is not about Derrick. Even this moment is too much to give her own child, one that has been gone for days and shows up as someone else completely, barely recognizable.

"You were supposed to be there. You're supposed to mother your children. It's a verb you know. Mothering. There are actions involved." Zahra says this calmly, all out of steam. She crosses her arms, waits for the woman in front of her to speak for herself. "Well?" Zahra urges her when the response doesn't come quickly enough.

"Well, what do you want me to say? What, Zahra? What do you want from me?"

"God." Zahra sighs. "I want you to be there. For once, just be there, be here now."

Mary cocks her head to the side and pats the arms of her chair, up and down, up and down, up and down. "I was supposed to be there?" she starts, then pauses, as if this is a new question, as if it's never occurred to her how her actions might affect her children. She loses her patting rhythm, and Zahra watches her hands grip the chair tightly. "Why? Why there? Haven't you been on this earth long enough to know that you should always be in two places at once but that it's impossible?"

Zahra isn't sure what she means, but Mary goes on too quickly for her to process it.

"Do you ever wonder how Alice Walker mothered? What about Fannie Lou Hamer? Diane Nash? How about how John Lewis or Marcus Garvey or Kwame Ture fathered? I'll answer for you. No, you don't. You don't care because you subconsciously realize that it is impossible to be everything all at once. And who is to say what's important? That your life, one small life that is good, is so plump from the love of your grandmother and your dad and your uncle Richard—why is your life more important than Timmie Sinclair's or Rodney King's or Emmett Till's? Because I gave birth to you? Because you physically came out of me? How petulant and narrow-sighted of you. In order to *mother* you, I would have had to walk out of my own skin, and what good would that have done me? Have done you for that matter? Derrick is not sick because of me. Don't you see that? Derrick is sick because he sees the world around him, breathes it in too hard, and there's not a stomach in this world that can handle that. Tell him to close his eyes a little, just a little, or the world will trample him. Tell him to unsee everything he knows to be true. Oh, but you can never ask someone to be anything or anyone but who they are, so don't ask more of me, Zahra, and I won't be so disappointed in your meager understanding of the world and the people around you."

Zahra doesn't know what to say. It isn't that her mother has won this argument, but that her position is so wildly different from Zahra's understanding that Zahra cannot figure out how to address the pointed rhetorical question. *Why is your life more important?* This is not something she knows how to argue. *Because it is*, she could say and sound more childish than her mother has already made her out to be. Plus she is too caught up in the shame that comes from her mother's disappointment, the words hanging in the air. The feeling is not any more palatable because of her mother's lack of maternal instincts.

With nothing left to say, Zahra turns to leave and sees Sammie and Trey standing in the doorframe. She is embarrassed and instinctively puts her head down, shielding her face as if Sammie and Trey are the paparazzi.

"Zahra," she hears Trey say, but his voice is too soft. After Trey and Sammie make room for her to pass, she hears footsteps behind her. Inside her bedroom, she turns around to see that it's Gram, who stands still, mouth agape now that Zahra is looking at her. She has something to say, probably something in agreement with Mary; she made it very clear whose side she was on the other night, and Zahra hasn't forgotten about that. But now, Gram doesn't say anything at all but sighs and shakes her head before she leaves the room. *Well, go then*, Zahra thinks. *Everyone else has gone; what's one more?*

It's early still, not even noon yet, but Zahra goes to bed, pulls the covers over her head, where she feels safe again. She tries to shut the world out, not wanting to see or hear what anyone has to say. But it is not so easy to shut out the voices that have been there for so long. It seems like the moths have burrowed inside her eardrums. They sing Deborah Cox and Yolanda Adams and Kelly Price. They sing until their voices run hoarse, and they begin to croak out their songs instead.

At some point, she feels a warm body wrap themselves around her, and she thinks it is Trey. But no, these are Sammie's sandstone-smooth arms.

TWENTY-EIGHT

It is unusual, Sammie thinks, holding a grown woman until she falls asleep midday. Sammie watches old *Fresh Prince* reruns, and when she sees Zahra wake up and then close her eyes again, she brings her food in bed only for her to swat it away and then turn her back. It's the first time Zahra has been completely unoccupied since they've gotten here, but also, the furthest away Sammie has felt from her. She doesn't like it. Sammie still feels her own betrayal by Uncle the Asshole, but Zahra's issues seem larger; they've been with her for so long. Either way, the brightness of the day, the sun exploding into the room through nearly translucent but closed blinds, seems to mock both of them.

On the episode where Will's father cancels their road trip, and Will tries to laugh it off, only to break down to Uncle Phil, Sophia calls. Sammie tries to ignore it, but the ringing is so piercing, and Zahra is dead asleep. Sammie picks up right before it goes to voice mail.

"Zahra?" Sophia says, and Sammie recognizes the voice but not from knowing her. Sophia sounds like a specific group of white girls at her school—the type who are down for every cause, who show up to every student body meeting and are a part of every action committee but don't socialize with anyone outside of their own, thin white girls with long hair they tuck behind their ears when making a point. Sometimes Sammie feels insignificant around them, like it's an abnormal thing she's not as pompous.

"Zahra, hello? Hello?" Sophia says.

Sammie ends the call quickly. Exhales. It was stupid to answer. What does Sophia matter anyway? Sammie's not sure.

Sammie watches the day pass them by until it is pitch black again, and Uncle sticks his head in the doorway to say, "We're leaving tomorrow."

"Duh," she says, knowing how childish she sounds but not caring. He leaves without shutting the door behind him, and she slams it for effect.

||||||||||||||||||||||||||||||||||||||||||||||||||

IT'S THE MIDDLE OF THE NIGHT, AND SAMMIE HAS TO USE THE bathroom. She's been holding it, not wanting to get out of bed, but she can't squeeze it in much longer, and anyway, she can't sleep like this. The bathroom is right next to the bedroom, and she thanks God she won't have to travel far. This house is creepy. It's talkative in a way she's not used to. It's got floor-to-ceiling windows in the living room, so when she walks past the patio at night, she can't tell what she's looking at. Herself or just the backyard in the dark, a mirror of the floral couches and prints of people dancing or the trees rerooting, regrowing. The other night she thought she saw a boy; she could have sworn she saw a boy leaned up against the railing that leads to the house's basement, but Zahra assured her it was nothing, that no boy other than a young Derrick has ever lived here.

Sammie makes quick steps of it, to the bathroom, and then on the toilet peeing as fast as she can. She's washing her hands when she hears a sound. The floorboards, she thinks. Zahra says they just do that sometimes, but the sound is sharper, closer than she's comfortable with. It sounds like someone is right outside the door. She considers going to sleep in the bathtub but eventually shakes herself free of the idea. She's just being a baby. It's probably nothing. Zahra would say it's nothing. She musters the courage to open the door.

She almost screams but then clamps her hands down on her mouth hard, and the sound is absorbed. He's here. She feels the revelation all over her body. Tiny bumps along her neck, arms, legs. A boy in the shadows, a hunched silhouette that makes him appear just under six feet and melancholy. She goes back into the bathroom, slamming the door shut as quickly as she can. She locks it and takes deep breaths, looks around for an escape route, and eyes a single window above the bathtub. Beyond it, the night is coal black, and she's just as scared of leaving as she is of staying. There's a knock on the door, and she sits on the toilet lid as quiet as a mouse, drawing her knees into her chest to keep from shaking.

"Hey," the voice says, unfamiliar.

"Go away," she says, impressed by her own authority, how much stronger she sounds than she feels.

"It's Derrick. You were with my sister today, weren't you?"

Derrick? It's hard to believe that it's him—after so much talk, having him here in person feels like touching a rainbow. And how could he know her when she didn't even get out of the car?

"I saw you through the window."

Right. Windows are transparent, she reasons. She walks to the door slowly, opens it enough to peek around and see the same man she saw running across Centennial Park earlier. He's a mess, torn clothes, unkempt 'fro with the facial hair to match. She can smell him too, the wild stench of days unshowered, aluminum-free deodorant, urine, processed foods seeping through pores.

"I didn't mean to scare you," he says. "I didn't know . . ." He pauses.

She wants to speak but can't get anything out. She has a million questions to ask him but still has one hand on the doorknob and the other against the wall for leverage.

"Who are you? Have we met?" he asks.

She thought he would know. She thought he would have the answers. He doesn't. Now what? She brings her hands down softly.

"I thought you were watching me," she says. "But now, I don't think it was you at all." Like recognizing a distinct voice, Sammie can tell that Derrick's eyes aren't the ones she's been looking for.

He looks confused, like he is just about to give an alibi but then recalls something. "How old are you?"

"Eighteen. Almost."

"I had the same feeling when I was your age, that I was being watched. Only, I never found out who it was. I looked for them."

"Mmph," Sammie says, opening the door a bit wider, now exposing her whole body in the frame.

"I don't think I've ever seen you before." He stares at her intently, and suddenly Sammie is hyperaware of her skimpy pajama set; she covers her arms.

"Who are you?" he asks.

"We know Zahra, my uncle and me. We brought Zahra down here, to Atlanta, to come look for . . . well, you."

"She came all the way . . ."

"Yeah," Sammie says.

"But what about the note? I left a note."

"I don't know. Don't think anyone ever found it."

Derrick nods. "Damn, I must have really put the family through some shit."

The best she can do in sympathy is a fake smile. "Yeah," she says.

They stand looking at each other. Sammie has so many questions to ask him, but only one comes out. "You can hear the moths too, right?"

Derrick's eyes go wide. "Zahra told . . . ," he begins to say.

But Sammie points to her right ear, as if it has more power than the left. "I can hear them too," she says.

Derrick looks at her harder, the way a teacher might when she's just given the answer to a really tough question. Then he blinks the face away and it's cool and calm again.

"Well, if I may . . ." He points to the bathroom behind her.

"Oh," Sammie says. "Yeah, sure. I guess I'll just go back to bed." Then thinking about all he's put Zahra through, she adds, "So you're just back? You just show up like Luke Skywalker?"

Derrick smiles. It doesn't look like *he* even knows why he's here.

"You had your sister running after you like some crazed parent who's lost her child."

"It was stupid," Derrick offers.

"Totally," Sammie says, rolling her eyes.

She passes him in the hallway and rounds the corner to go into the bedroom, but an inch from the door, Sammie turns around to the space where Derrick was just standing. She rubs her eyes and wonders if she's hallucinating. She hears the bathroom door close and rushes into the bedroom. Suddenly, she is so cold. Suddenly, her teeth are chattering. She finds one of Zahra's old Evermount sweatshirts and throws it on. She sits on the bed, thinking.

Derrick is here, but what does it change? The moths, the tree, the feeling of being watched? Zahra has gone about her life ignoring these phenomena, and now the moths are barking mad at her, and now Sammie has been dragged into her mess and mayhem. Sammie is worried that she's not ready for this, not ready to answer whatever the world is asking of her. And if Derrick hasn't been the one watching her, well, then, who has?

She looks at Zahra, who generally doesn't sleep well but is totally out of it, like a rock, unmoving. This is what Zahra wanted, her brother back. It's good news. So then why is Sammie so reluctant to wake her up? Maybe Sammie knows that this restful peace will be short lived. Maybe she knows that the story is just starting. She shoves Zahra one, twice, three times.

"Zahra, Zahra," she says. When Zahra looks at her bleary-eyed, Sammie whispers, "Derrick's here."

TWENTY-NINE

All that looking and Derrick just washes up like creek debris. Still, the news takes Zahra's breath away, and she can only say, "What?" in disbelief.

"Here, now," Sammie says. "In the bathroom."

Zahra throws the covers off, is out of the room and into the hallway in seconds. She flings the bathroom door open. Nothing. She runs to the living room. Empty. Then there he is, in the kitchen, at the sink, coolly drinking a glass of water. She stops at the sight of him, thinner than usual—160 pounds max, in dirty clothes and with uncombed hair inches long. His beard is thick, seems to cover every inch of his face below his nose. She almost doesn't recognize him. But then he smiles, and his old dimple peeks through like the sun between clouds. And those eyes—still warm and deep brown and swimming. She rushes to him, hugs him so tight he might break.

"I could kill you," she says.

||||||||||||||||||||||||||||||||||||||||||||||

THEY ALL SEEM TO WANT ANSWERS AS THE KITCHEN GROWS thick with quiet bodies. Derrick and Mary and Gram sit at the table, while Zahra, Trey, Uncle Richard, and Dad stand around it. Everyone who kept their eyes peeled looking for Derrick rushed over to see him just alive as can be, however worn and weary. Sammie is the only one in the back of the house, still refusing to occupy the same space as her uncle. Either way, the house feels whole, like home again.

"I left a note," Derrick starts. "You didn't get the note?"

"What note?" Gram asks, leaning toward him, grabbing his hand.

"In my bedroom, in plain sight. On the bed. I explained everything. I needed a while to . . . work things out." He fidgets; he's never looked so uncomfortable in his own home. Maybe he's lying.

"Derrick," Gram says slowly. "There wasn't a note." She says it like a sad revelation, like telling him his imaginary friend doesn't exist.

"Maybe you forgot to leave it out?" Mary offers.

Derrick shakes his head silently.

"Why couldn't you text back?" Zahra asks.

"Didn't have my phone."

"And why not? It's 2019 for God's sake." Her anger comes in waves, but she remembers now, thinking he could've been dead.

"I wanted to turn everything off. Haven't you ever wanted that? For things to go silent?"

She has. She's wanted it more than anything. Peace of mind. No sense of self and communal obligation. Zahra moves to change the subject. "What have you been up to?"

Derrick shrugs. "Just working on things, I guess. And trying to figure out . . ." He clears his throat, puts his other hand on top of the one that's holding Gram's. He looks to her as if everyone else is just a part of the background.

"Have you told them?" he asks.

"Oh, Derrick, don't," she says.

"Gram," Zahra interrupts. "What haven't you told us?"

"Mom?" Mary says, reinforcing the question.

Gram gently lets go of Derrick's hands and brings her own two together. She keeps her eyes down, on the kitchen table. Mary rubs her back, willing her to explain herself.

"They're taking the house."

Zahra shoots a look of reproach at Derrick. He knew and didn't tell. The scold misses him as he's hardly made eye contact with anyone this whole time and now he studies the ceiling.

"They're taking the house?" Mary's voice is loud.

"Who?" Zahra's, the opposite.

"How? What happened?" Dad asks, an even medium.

"Money. I needed it . . ."

Mary puts her hand over her mouth as if she knows how this story ends. Zahra has rarely, if ever, seen her cry, but she holds her breath as if it can all come rushing out anytime now. Zahra has a similar feeling, knowing what this house has been to all of them, a constant, no matter how they rearranged it, how the doors swung back and forth with people coming and going.

||||||||||||||||||||||||||||||||||||||||||||

THEY MOVED IN IN 1993. THOUGH SHE WAS ONLY FIVE, ZAHRA remembers the day, a warm one, spring maybe, they wore light jackets walking up to the house in awe, excitement. More vividly, Zahra remembers what Gram said. *Been waiting for a long time for something that's mine.* Zahra watched her look around the space, the same way she used to look through her pocketbook before they went to the mall or the store or anywhere more than a short walk away. She'd make sure everything was there, everything she needed. In the house that first day, Gram took off her shoes and walked along the wooden floors.

She opened and closed the kitchen cabinets, opened the oven and practically put her whole head inside. She went down in the basement, never minding if there were spirits or not, and took a close look at the hot-water heater and the water meter and the fuse box. She went to the back of the house and turned on the bathroom taps. She flushed the toilets. She opened and closed the bedroom windows. Yes, all was here, Zahra imagined she must have thought. A whole house, ready to go, hers.

Zahra was too young to know about loans, predatory or honest, and even now, she doesn't quite understand what Gram is talking about, having never owned a house of her own, having never questioned that Gram's payments had been as high as $1,800 a month. Who could afford that? Not Gram, who worked at a department store most of her life, nor Mary, who worked half her cases pro bono and the others with legal aid. What with a house worth no more than $120,000, Zahra figured Gram was almost done paying it off. Now, Gram's face looks less fleshy than Zahra is used to, like someone has punched her and deflated her life from it.

"I didn't know what to do," Gram says, the sun rising behind her. "Seemed like a good idea to get a second mortgage. Man from the bank said I could get a new, lower interest rate, and a boatload of cash. I didn't know nothing about balloon interest rates, that it could go from six to nine in just a few years. I didn't understand negative equity, that I'd owe way more than this house is even worth. Payments been building up ever since, but at the time I thought I could use the money to buy back-to-school clothes and that desktop computer for Zahra and Derrick. Found that man at church, thought he was God fearing. Why wouldn't he be?"

Zahra remembers this man too, a Black man with a thick mustache, similar to Deacon Henry's, and a stomach that exploded from his pants, so his dress shirt came untucked and she could see its wrinkled tail. Behind the sanctuary, the outsider who looked like an insider sat in a room the church filled with round cafeteria tables to eat fried chicken and potato salad with too much relish and watery green beans on special occasions. There were free pens and water bottles on the desk, and the man had given her and Derrick one of each. They must have been around thirteen or fourteen at the time.

"Let me see that," Zahra says, referring to the paperwork Gram is holding. When she accepts the thick stack, Zahra can feel Dad and Uncle Richard peering over her shoulder.

"Uncle Richard, did you know about this?" Zahra asks, and he shakes his head slowly.

"This is my house, isn't it?" Gram asks. "How could it not be my house?" Gram has not considered that this house has always had a mind of its own, and that she hasn't been able to plant roots because there are already some in place. Dry and deserted as they are. Why should anyone get to own a place that has been around long before them and will keep on kicking long after? But Gram only wanted what the old white men have been claiming for years and years now. And what is so wrong with that? To want a piece of the pie, or more accurately, of the land?

"They can't just come and take it from you," Dad says. But of course they can. Hadn't it happened to the Jacksons up the street? And when Mrs. Ruth-Anne died, her children ran that place into the ground like quicksand. There are plenty of stories. Of people losing homes as if they are loose rings that can easily slip from your fingers. Whoops, it went down the drain. Must have dropped it somewhere. Someone else slid it off while shaking hands. And the laws are twisty and turny so that they never work out in your favor, but make such a big mess that you can't see straight out of them. Like driving through fog. Like driving through a sea of singing moths that have lost homes of their own and won't shut up about it.

"Mary?" Uncle Richard says. "Seems like you might know a thing or two?"

Mary grabs the paperwork and gets up from the table. "I'll make some calls," she says.

||||||||||||||||||||||||||||||||||||||||||||||||||||||

ALL GRAM'S TALK OF LOSING THE HOUSE MUST MAKE TREY uncomfortable. When there's enough silence to allow him to politely excuse himself from the table, he wastes no time in loading the car for their trip back to New York. Sammie watches him without lifting a finger, cross-armed on the lawn. Zahra looks at her through the kitchen window, then around, at the house being ripped from underneath her. Sammie, the exposed brick wall leading to the back rooms. Sammie, the living room where the couch is not to be sat on. Zahra was just a teenager, right around Sammie's age, when she left home and didn't look back. She deserted the house long before now, before just a handful of papers would mean Gram losing it. There's no one to be mad at but herself . . . and those damn moths that ran her away. Sammie comes inside and stands beside her, as if she knows all that's on her mind, but Sammie doesn't say anything and neither does Zahra.

A hand on her shoulder, and Derrick is at her other side. "I have to show you something," he says.

"They're getting ready to leave," Zahra says.

"Say goodbye now."

"But . . . ," Sammie begins.

"It's important," Derrick says. "The creek, the bridge."

Zahra turns to Sammie and muffles her protests in a long hug. Sammie doesn't understand yet, how the past can creep up and rip you apart, how you have to act in the moment or it'll sweep you up like a hurricane, drop you off somewhere far from where you started. When you get the chance to go back, there's no choice but to take it.

She can't look Sammie in the eye when she says goodbye but heads off quickly to find Trey.

Saying goodbye to Trey is difficult and frustrating. She feels an obligatory sense of solidarity with Sammie and so, to some degree, she is mad at him. But the larger part of her feels a small root growing in her gut. Any way she moves, she knows it's there, her feelings for Trey waiting on nothing more than water to grow. With basic air and sun, her whole body will lean in his direction, a tree at a thirty-degree angle.

"So," she says.

"So," he repeats. "We need more time, don't we?"

She nods, and he reaches for her, drawing her in, embracing her tight, the way he might squeeze his arms to climb a tree. He kisses her forehead, her cheek, her neck. She laughs in embarrassment.

"You're coming back to New York, right?" he asks her.

If she could talk, maybe she'd be a little snarky and say the obvious, that she lives there, of course. But with the lump in her throat, there's no talking without crying, so she only nods and backs away, waving.

THIRTY

When Uncle Trey gets sick, it's a good omen. He throws up just before opening the front door of his Nissan, his piecemeal breakfast—bacon, cream of wheat, a banana—all splayed on the driveway for Uncle Richard to hose off. Sammie smirks, not sure where the bridge is but determined to catch up with Zahra and Derrick. If there's one person who knows this neighborhood by foot, he's sweet on her, and she's got a bone to pick with him anyway.

Rashad's house looks nothing like Gram's ranch, but is split-level. It's one of those homes where you step inside and have to make a choice—upstairs or downstairs, the decision-making landing big enough for only three or four people. Rashad stands just inside the screen door like he's scared to let her in, but Sammie can see just as much behind him, nothing more.

Zahra says there are photos that almost every African American family has on display—prints like *Funeral Procession*, made popular by a *Cosby Show* episode, and different variations of *The Last Supper*, Jesus's hair ranging from a wooly Afro to a wavy Farrah Fawcett, skin almost always the color of wet sand. She imagines Rashad's house with both, welcoming, saying it without saying it, *Black people live here.*

She's already figured Rashad's family poor, by how he's always wearing the same outdated clothes with a lineup that she guesses is home cut, but now, in the doorway like this, there's something foregone about him and the home he's hiding, something that makes her hesitant to step inside. But really, it doesn't matter all that much since she hasn't been invited. She feels awkward standing here like this, neither of them speaking, so she looks away, to his overgrown, lush front yard, and notices the For Sale sign for the first time, nestled right into the picture book green grass that felt like walking on sponges as she crossed it just moments ago. The sign is half shaded by a dying azalea bush. Has it always been there? Couldn't have, but maybe. She knows better than to address it and turns to face Rashad again. She smiles.

"Wanna take a walk with me?"

He looks surprised by the question at first. "Where you wanna . . . ," he starts, but Sammie's nervousness takes over for him.

"Know where the bridge is?" She hadn't given much thought to how bold showing up at Rashad's front door was until now. She backs up, takes the three steps down to ground level, where her heart finally catches itself.

"Sure," Rashad says, and then steps right outside to walk with her as if he hadn't been doing anything at all just before she knocked.

"Don't you have schoolwork?" Sammie asks, then remembering it's a school day, "Don't you have school?"

"Alternative programming," he says, shrugging. "I'm smart enough to skip anyway."

"Mother Ma would murder me," Sammie says.

"Bet you're going to go to one of those big schools, huh? What do they call them?"

"The Ivy Leagues."

"Right," Rashad says. A toothpick hangs out of his mouth, and he slides it under his tongue, from left to right. It reminds Sammie of the first slumber party she went to with white girls, how they stayed up late trying to do all kinds of tricks with their tongues—unwrapping Starbursts, knotting the stems of maraschino cherries, making three-leaf clovers. It was sexual but then it wasn't. Things are plain different with white girls.

Now Sammie likes Rashad better for his tongue tricks, for the way his leisurely confidence makes her stomach flip, a kind of magic of its own. Distracted by thoughts, she loses her place in their conversation, starts over with what's been on her mind.

"Why didn't you just tell me where Derrick was?" she asks. "His family was really worried."

"I didn't know," Rashad says. "At least not for sure. I'm just observant, that's all. Couldn't have known any more than Ms. Mary or Ms. Robinson."

"But then you were wearing that shirt the other day. The one with the torch on it. . . ."

"I wear that shirt all the time," he says. "What you think? I've been leaving you signs?" He smiles, winks at her. "Well, maybe I have. But they're not about Derrick."

Sammie rolls her eyes, but even the dramatics can't hide her own cheese. She gives things a rest for now, thinking Rashad could slink his way out of just about anything. She looks around them as they head in the opposite direction of the street that leads to the corner store. They go downhill, deeper into the neighborhood, among the small houses with large, rolling green yards, the cars parked everywhere, on the street, in driveways, half spanning grass and concrete. Some cars look like nothing more than junk, old things that haven't been driven in years, an old mama's prayer for revitalization. Others don't match their shoddy circumstances, the modest houses around them a stark contrast.

"Wanna stop for Pixy Stix? That's the candy lady's house." Rashad points to a house made of brown brick. The house fits its title well, almost a toy home in its small appearance, half the size of Gram's. Sammie imagines it's all ginger bread and Twizzlers and sticky, fruity stuff inside, but she can't stomach the thought of candy at a time like this, with so much knowledge already on the tip of her tongue.

"Maybe next time," she says.

Rashad shrugs. "Never know when the next time will be your last time," he says.

It's true, but the way he says it startles her, and she smiles to cool off whatever's run hot in his head.

"It's not far from here," Rashad says. "What's at the bridge anyway?"

Sammie bites her nails, unsure of how much to tell him. She won't tell him about the feeling of being watched, how she was sure it was Derrick watching her until recently. Rashad is keeping his secrets, so she'll keep hers too.

"That's what I'm trying to figure out. Zahra's been acting *differently*, and I know she comes out here to think. I'm just checking on her."

"What's her story again?"

"Zahra's?"

Rashad nods, pulling the toothpick from his mouth and flicking it. She tries to follow it with her eyes, but it disappears, right into the sun like a dandelion seed.

"Basically she's Operation Varsity Blues but legit," Sammie says, and that's the reason she didn't really want to work with Zahra in the first place. She doesn't want to perpetuate some archaic, racist, classist system. But then she did want to go to Stanford, and she realizes the hypocrisy there. How can you want what's best for you without upholding barriers for others? She's figuring this out.

They cut through someone's backyard and walk in between a small thicket of trees.

"Why do you need her?" Rashad asks.

"Zahra?"

"Yeah."

"I don't," Sammie says quickly, almost too quickly. It's a lie. She does need Zahra. She's just not sure why yet.

"There it is," Rashad says, pointing to a bridge, a short one that it would only take three or four steps to cross. There's nothing magical or stately about it. Instead, it's ironic in its plainness. The creek looks deeper over here, and Sammie sees Zahra and Derrick standing not too far from it. Zahra is gesticulating wildly, but Sammie can only hear some of what she's saying. Something about people, and the house, and all the fucking secrets that Derrick's been keeping from her. When Derrick speaks, his voice is so low that Sammie can't hear a word, so she moves to get closer.

"I wouldn't," Rashad says, holding his arm out in front of her, a standing seat belt. She's not sure if it's a demand or a warning.

"Why not?" she asks.

"It looks personal."

Sammie is attracted to Rashad more than ever. He's insightful, careful. She cocks her head to the side and imagines running off with him. To a place where there are no moths, no eyes that stare from miles and miles away, no mothers who forget about their daughters, and certainly no colleges who establish your worth based on some carefully crafted application. They'll be TikTok stars, and people will look for them everywhere, but they'll be evasive. They'll blend in with their surroundings like chameleons. They'll hold water like cacti. They'll be here and nowhere at all, cemented only in photos, in videos, in five-second GIFs for the world to see.

"Come on," Rashad says, holding out his hand and steering Sammie away from the siblings, who've stolen her attention for weeks now. But something catches her eye, crumpled paper among the thick roots of an old oak tree. She picks it up and unfolds it.

It's a photo of Derrick but not. It's a photo of him maybe forty years from now, impossible. There are more of these flyers, scattered from the wind. Sammie picks them up like fallen coins. They are people with a twinkle in their eye, who look real and fake all at once. Rashad looks over her shoulder and laughs. He knows something. He's always known something, hasn't he?

"Why didn't you tell me where Derrick was?" she asks again.

"Had no idea," he says. "What, you think I'm a mind reader?" He smirks, and Sammie doubts her instincts. Instead, she feels the feral impulse to yell. It's like the day after Daday died and she stood on the cafeteria table, and screamed. It was before she went to P & P. She was in Ms. Franklin's sixth-grade class at PS 375. The Black kids around the way were used to yelling, to throwing their voices around like basketballs, but the height she'd gained from the table's two feet made her stand out, drawing everyone's attention. Now she wants to yell, *Who's watching us?* But then she remembers the echo of silence in the cafeteria that day some six years ago.

Instead of yelling, Sammie looks down at the flyers again. The faces remind her of what Uncle Trey said about her mother's dreams. Of Chacachacare, of faces eating away at her. Sammie wonders what one has to do with the other—Derrick and moths and faces. Then from a distance, a cheat code, the same way the smell of barbecue first comes sight unseen, is the low thrum of music. As if someone's turning the radio—rap then R & B then soul then country. If it's the moth's voices that haunt her and Zahra and Derrick, if she puts it all together, there are people, faces, singing. Alive. She looks down at her hands, arms, legs. They're as real as a photo. They're as here as a moment cemented in time.

"I have an idea," she says.

THIRTY-ONE 🦋

Derrick must be crazy. She's not sure what he wanted her to see, but there was nothing there. The creek was everything it used to be, mysterious and eerie and tempting with its lapping brown water, but that's all there is—dirty water and murky memories. Derrick kept talking about Intrenchment Creek Park, a migratory spot for animals, for humans, comparing *their* creek to something he'd read in a forest magazine. It was up to Zahra to put her foot down. The creek is just a creek is just a creek. Today, just now, that much was made clear.

She's surprised to see Trey's car in the driveway when they get back home, and even more surprised to open her bedroom door and find Sammie sitting on her knees on the floor, scattered pictures all around her. She looks like she's sorting them in some way. She's so immersed in the project that she doesn't even notice Zahra's there until she clears her throat. Sammie looks up, and Zahra thinks she's seen a ghost, or just some version of a teenage Derrick, maybe both.

"Hi," Sammie says.

"What's all this?" Zahra asks. "And weren't you all supposed to leave like an hour or two ago?"

"Uncle got sick," she says. "Serves him right."

So Sammie's still not over yesterday's news. It was a long day for both of them, but this day feels almost stranger, like moving through molasses. Time feels as thick as the air down by the creek, damp with secrets. There's something amiss about Derrick, something he's not telling her. And now Sammie's acting just as bizarre. What's she going through all of these pictures for? And "Where'd you find those?" Zahra wonders out loud.

"I asked Gram. She pulled photos from everywhere. Under the bed. In her sock drawer. On the wobbly media cabinet in the living room."

"And you're doing exactly what with them?"

"I think we should hold a séance," Sammie says, explaining it all and nothing at the same time.

"A séance?" Zahra laughs. "Sammie, look around. We're Black, and we're Christian. Séances aren't really our style."

"It's just . . ." Sammie holds up a picture. Zahra sees it's an old one of Gram's mom. It's in black and white, and bent down the middle, barely holding on. "What if your family knows something? Uncle Trey was telling me about my mom, and well, we don't talk enough to each other, do we? The generations before me, before you, maybe they have the answers we're looking for." She pauses. "Aren't there any photos older than this?"

Zahra doubts it. They're not one of those families that can trace back their ancestors to slavery, and certainly not anytime before that. A cousin did one of those ancestry tests, traced back roots to Angola, and that's pretty much the extent of Zahra's knowledge.

"Do you know if Gram has any cedar? Or I read that you can use palo santo as a substitute."

"Sammie, we're not having a séance," Zahra says.

"Do you have a pendulum?" Sammie asks, clearly not listening.

Derrick walks in. His hair's overgrown, thick beard still hiding his dimples, but he's showered and beginning to look like her brother again. "Sammie wants to hold a séance," Zahra explains.

Derrick makes a face that Zahra can't quite read. His eyebrows are up, but he doesn't seem surprised.

"Haven't you ever wondered," Sammie asks, "who your ancestors were?"

Of course Zahra's wondered, but she's also learned to fill in her curiosities with textbook templates. She imagines her ancestors were enslaved people, dark-skinned folks with thick plaited hair and an ingeniousness that allowed them to find secrets in scraps, fatback turned into mustard, turnip, and collard greens, and other meats savored just as they are, neck bones and oxtails. And before they were kidnapped, she imagines them kings and queens from the Gold Coast, communal beings living off the land. She believes they must have been storytellers, even back then, people with the gift of gab, who knew rhythm before they could talk, who hummed when they were happy and sad, thriving and struggling. Culture never really dies, does it? Not if it's anything like energy.

"It's like our family tree just stops . . . like the roots have been dug up," Derrick says.

"Like a tree that's there one day and then not?" Zahra asks.

"Or the other way around," Sammie says, as all of their eyes cast through the bedroom door. Beyond it, just outside of the house, an unchopped tree stands as proud as a cat with nine lives or someone like 50 Cent who's been shot enough times for the bullets to fill a revolver.

"Maybe Sammie is onto something," Derrick says. "All the faces—well, they probably want to be seen. And the voices—to be heard. But why would we need a séance when they've already found us? When they've already been communicating?"

Zahra bites her lip. It's implausible, but then, it's the only thing that makes any sense, that the moths and their creepy-ass voices, the resurrecting tree, the house and it's endless shouting, are trying to tell them something.

"Wait, there's more." Sammie points. It's the size of a necklace box, one where the top slides over the bottom. Anything over five by seven would be too big to fit in it. Sammie opens it with care, like she's scared to find what's inside. When she pulls the photos out, they're nothing like that old image of Gram's mom, but untarnished, as if straight from a CVS printer. Sammie passes them to Derrick, who passes them to Zahra, and they could be sharing any old images, but there's something pointedly different about these. The new photos look like they could be from a number of time periods, the eighties, the seventies, as far back as Gram's mom's time, when Black women curled their hair into tight ringlets or boasted fancy bouffant hairdos. Zahra doesn't know these people, but she recognizes them clear as day. Three of them are versions of Warren and Minnie and Natasha, from Derrick's flyers.

"Let me see them," Derrick says, holding out his hands. Then moving one under the next in a quick rotation, he draws in a deep breath, like he's swallowing everything, the air, the room, the pictures.

"Gram," Zahra calls out, almost forgetting their earlier conversation, that Gram has her own fire to put out with the house. Feelings come barreling down again—anger that they could lose the house, pity and annoyance that Gram hasn't felt she could confide in any of them, and finally, understanding that maybe Gram's recent testiness hasn't been about her at all. Zahra shakes her head.

For now, she calls louder. "Gram." If anyone knows these

people, it's her. Maybe there are other secrets she's been hiding; maybe it's not just the house.

"Those are—" Derrick starts.

"The people you've been drawing," Sammie interrupts. "Different ages, different eras maybe, but look at her eyes." Sammie leans over Derrick's shoulder, watching as he flicks through photos. "It's got to be. . . ."

"How do you know about the drawings?" Derrick asks.

"Well, I . . ."

She followed them, of course. Sammie is so nosy. She knows no boundaries lately, but Derrick doesn't seem to mind. Distracted, he swats away her excuse. "I thought they were from our time. But here, it looks like they're from the past," he says.

"How have you been drawing people you don't even know?"

"I'm not sure. They just come to me."

"It's the house," Sammie says.

And maybe she's right. If they're asking questions, then the house is answering them, with photos that seem like they've come out of thin air, a pending foreclosure, and now, the hardwood croaking so loudly that Sammie grabs Zahra's arm for security.

"What's all of this?" Gram asks, and the question is bigger than Zahra guesses Gram intended it. After all, that's what they've been trying to figure out for years now, with the moths and the voices. What is all of it?

"Show her the pictures, Derrick," Zahra says.

"Who are these people?" Derrick asks, handing Gram the thin stack.

Gram looks at them slowly, eyes squinted like there are too many memories to sort through, like she can barely see straight.

"You know where we're from, don't you?" she finally asks.

Zahra considers that word—*from*. It's not descriptive enough, could mean anything, two years ago to 1619, though she's recently heard that Africans were brought here long before that. Either way, Zahra could say she's from Decatur or Marks, Mississippi, or the Gold Coast or most correctly, a labyrinth of origins for which there are no bread crumbs other than DNA, shortsighted beyond biology.

"Africa?" she says, not knowing what Gram is looking for.

Gram laughs. "And after that, Mississippi," she says. "I figure, now, I haven't told you enough about it. Got you in this world running around with your head chopped off." Zahra brings a hand to her neck, feeling the delicate lifelines of it, the fullness of her skin.

"You know, we called my mom Mother, but I don't talk about her much because it feels like there's nothing to say."

Zahra nods.

"Tell us now," Derrick says gently.

Gram clears her throat. "They say Mother dreamed of bodies in water, faces swollen until they came up, still and silent; deadly, that Mississippi." Gram's taken on a new form, a new voice too, struggling to get it out, as if she's got rocks in her throat. "Rose, Mother's twin, heard Mother screaming throughout the night, she was so bewitched, but then Mother was never the same after Father died; none of us were. I remember looking facedown in a well, seeing my skin skip off the cool water and knowing it was far down there, a long way, and I imagined never coming up for air. That well was as stifling as the Mississippi heat, just like life then, tied like an army knot. You know they sent Uncle Richard Senior to Germany, right? Mother's older brother. He was twenty-one, and there wasn't nothing Mother could do to stop it. Praying hadn't been enough, or maybe Mother was doing it wrong.

"Senior came back and said they don't tell you what it's like to see a man's head explode and a million tiny things shoot out of it like worms wriggling to freedom, what it's like to see his neck twitch as if he's still alive, and then you feel your own neck, wondering if you're alive, because maybe you already died and this is hell. And every day after that, you check to make sure your head's still there, but maybe you lost it a long time ago, because thinking is different than it used to be and ain't no way you'll find your way home like this."

Zahra doesn't know how Gram remembers it all, where she's been storing it. Now, Gram's eyes are trained on one of the bedroom windows, and they don't move an inch as she goes on.

"They don't tell you that when you come back from the war you'll still be a nigger, and you can't run from your yellow-black skin like you ran from bombs. And their spit will feel like bullets. A million tiny things, a million bread crumbs, a million names for a nigger, but don't no one know where Senior gone. Poof, disappeared inside his own body. There but not there," Gram says, pointing to her mind, as if Senior lost it. "If Mother wasn't near her breakdown before that, it wasn't too much after. Still, she up and moved to Atlanta with little more than a nickel and a dime."

It's like the room's been sucked free of sound, no one even breathing but Gram coming up for air. There's a lot for Zahra to process, a lot of questions on her mind, like why is Gram just now telling them all of this? Zahra has only the vaguest idea of how stories can hurt, how it can be easier to forget them and act like things never happened. White people forget what they've done every day; there's no saying why the burden of remembering should be on Black folks alone.

"Maybe these people aren't Mother or Rose or Senior, but there's something about all of them, something that brings yesterday back like it was never gone to begin with."

It's enough for Zahra to drop it. She sees how tired Gram looks, eyes as heavy as a box of books, one shoulder slumped like a lopsided lampshade.

"That settles it," Zahra says, rekindling her pragmatism. They're random photos, left from way before they came to Atlanta in the 1950s. Derrick must have gotten a hold of them as children. Now he draws them from memory. Strange, but really, there's nothing unexplainable there. She's let Sammie and Derrick make her think there's something bigger going on, but it's just too far-fetched.

"It doesn't settle anything," Derrick says.

"You heard, Gram. They're not family."

"So?" Derrick says. "They need us or something."

"And Derrick's pictures are almost exact replicas. Look at her eyes. There's no mistaking them," Sammie says.

"Maybe he saw those photos when we were a kid. Someone probably left them here a long time ago." Zahra wants to close this case. There are bigger ones at hand, like the house.

"But what if we were meant to find them? What if they found us?" Sammie argues.

"It's unlikely."

"What if the voices never stop until we listen?" Derrick reasons. He's cool and calm as he says it, his arms crossed, face almost expressionless. "We should go back to the creek. That's where I hear them the strongest. And I saw someone there, too. I think she was—"

"Absolutely not," Zahra interrupts him. "It's like nine at night. Way too dark. You're both wildin'."

||||||||||||||||||||||||||||||||||||||||||||||||

TREY WOULD PROBABLY KILL HER IF HE KNEW THAT SHE WAS taking his niece out in the middle of the night, traipsing through trees, streetwalking in Decatur's dark hiding spots. It's some white-people shit, and she knows it. Trey would probably be more confused than anything. Surely, he's of a more standard variation of Black, someone who knows that you don't seek the answers but let them find you. A noise in the yard, and you close the doors. Shouting in a neighbor's house and you shut your blinds, mind your business.

Zahra checked in on Trey not too long ago, and he was still in bed asleep. Gram says it's probably just a twenty-four-hour bug, but Zahra thinks it could be more. The timing seems odd; everything does these days. Coincidences feel more impossible than the alternative—destiny, fate, divine intervention.

"Last time I went to the creek, Rashad seemed to know something. What if we invited him?" Sammie says.

"Who's Rashad?" Zahra asks.

Sammie looks at her incredulously. "Your next-door neighbor. He's my age. Or close, a couple of years younger."

Zahra's confused. No one has lived in that house for years. Growing up, the neighborhood joked that the house was haunted. Folks moved in and out every few months, returning the purchase, back to sender. But no one could tell you who owned it. Online records showed that it belonged to a Mr. Tyrell Young, but the whole block knows he lost that house in 2001, due to a bankruptcy.

"He said he knew you, Derrick," Sammie says.

When Zahra turns sharply to her brother, he only shakes his head, confused. But she wants answers. Not this half-cooked bullshit Derrick has been serving since he got home. She sees it now, the resemblance between Sammie and Derrick, not a physical thing but something more spiritual, protruding from the inside out like a broken bone, a discernible pheromone. Zahra won't let what happened to her brother happen to Sammie. She'll rip up every photo they've found, knock down every fucking cobweb that's grown in the house. She'll kill every last moth on the East Coast if she has to. She sees that there are parts of Sammie that mimic both her and Derrick, and if nothing else, she'll save Sammie from herself.

THIRTY-TWO

Zahra stomps ahead of them, a hurricane with feet. Zahra says it's all too wild to be true, a house so invested in its occupants that it's begun haunting them, a neighbor who's not really a neighbor at all. Sammie knows it's only because Zahra hasn't opened her mind to other possibilities. She must think she can will her way through the world, that her fortitude can overcome centuries of oppression. Sammie knows better. She knows that most things are bigger than her, even bigger than her understanding of them. She's still waiting for the world to show itself. "Slow down," she calls out.

Sammie has never been more comfortable in the night. Like most teenagers, she's assured in her self-righteousness, her presumed invincibility. She has no foresight to see that ghosts, spirits, ancestors can eat her from the inside out, that harm doesn't have to be wished for it to be done, that needy voices can pull you underground like quicksand or the rapidly rising levels of the Chattahoochee. She doesn't know what it's like to be here one day and gone the next, how easily life can be plucked from you, how fragile, the knee to the neck or one stray bullet through the brain, like a lamp with a string switch. One quick pull, and all goes black.

It's dark out, even with streetlights and the occasional headlights. It's quiet too, save for the sound of crickets, squirrels scampering, and every now and then, a speeding car. Some people sit outside on old lawn chairs, but even they don't seem to have much to say, just whispers and half-empty cans of Coke between them.

Of course, Sammie is only beginning to know about secrets. She has no idea that they can run as deep as an ocean with arms and legs that branch off like rivers and wetlands. They are never as straight as streams but loop around themselves and involve all subsidiaries they touch, more contagious than a cough. In all the shades of brick— cream and burgundy and burnt orange—houses they pass, secrets store in ivy-covered yards with resounding rottweilers and Dodge Chargers with leather interior, near pampas grass plumes shading signs that read NO TRESPASSING, kept out on the front porch like fresh pies, most prevalent in a community burdened by strict, impossible morality. One misstep, and the whip, judgment, jail, jobless.

Sammie is right about one thing: Secrets are like bacon grease. Stand back, and it won't stop them from popping you. They find a way to break loose no matter how much you try to squelch them, hide them like some old children's game. Years later, and there they are, screaming at you to be seen. When the people themselves are the secrets, there's no running away, only hunkering down and bracing yourself.

Sammie thinks about Rashad, with his smile like center stage, open curtains, lights up. If he doesn't live next door, then what's he been doing there, squatting? And doesn't he always seem like he's got more to say than he's letting on? Sammie gets the feeling that he's used to talking and not saying much at all.

Sammie can hear Derrick's shallow breaths beside her, and when they go off road, she can hear Zahra up ahead, clearing the path, tree branches swinging lower than Sammie remembers them on her way here with Rashad. Zahra doesn't say anything, but every now and then Derrick asks a question, "You hear the voices, don't you?" or "They want us to know something, don't you think?"

When they get to the creek, they stand in silence, and even a determined Sammie is unsure what they're doing and why they're here. But there in the trees from whence they came, she thinks she sees the familiar smile of a beautiful boy.

"Rashad?" she calls out. She catches sight of him, but he backs up, and the shadows swallow him whole. She runs to catch up.

"Rashad," she says. "Hold up."

She hears his footsteps, crunching leaves and small branches. Why is he running away from her? What is he hiding? Ordinarily, she'd be too scared to follow someone deep into the woods like this, around oaks and pines that tower above her, well into the night, but Rashad is alluring, and she trusts him, and there's a feeling of calm that passes over her. She feels free, like a little girl racing after the ice cream truck.

Before long, she realizes she's lost his steps, and she's tired. She stops, and Derrick and Zahra pull up behind her, dropping their hands to their knees as if they haven't run in years.

"Dang, I lost him," Sammie says.

She can barely see, it's so dark out, and she finally realizes how deep inside these Georgia trenches she's led them. "Shit," she says.

She looks around and sees the land for what it is—alive, resilient. She thinks about Puerto Rico, how Hurricane Maria devastated nearly almost all of its buildings, killing thousands of people, uprooting trees, sweeping through the territory like a toddler throwing a tantrum. Now, more than two years later, Puerto Rico is still rebuilding, the American relief process slow. But the rain forest replenished itself within that first year, the canopy lush and green again, the trees and flora, vegetation and vines as regal as ever. An immaculate revival. Sammie looks around, and this place is no different, green and growing. From Dr. Lawrence's fifth period on botany and zoology, she remembers that it only takes a seedling, any remnant an opportunity for regrowth. So this is not a place of ghosts at all but an altar, something connecting God and the world's inhabitants.

There's a light, just one, near a thick oak tree leaning down, the lower half of it parallel enough to the ground that you could walk along it. She looks at the tree and spots a beautiful caterpillar. Then she sees there are tens, hundreds, thousands of them along the bark, nesting, eating, lounging.

"Look," she says, and Zahra and Derrick take either side of her. "There must be a million of them."

THIRTY-THREE

Zahra watches a caterpillar metamorphose into a moth right before her eyes. And then another, two more, more, more. Their pointing is not quick enough. The moment they spot two, ten more are transitioning. Moths with bright white wings. They're everywhere, at once beautiful, now threatening.

"Let's go," Zahra says, and they walk slowly, conscious of the roots underfoot. Zahra is mesmerized by the moths in a way she has never been before.

"They're safe, right?" Sammie asks, and it seems they're all considering this same question.

Zahra's not sure, doesn't answer out loud, but she's alert of the moths' growing numbers, how they're swarming, swarming, swarming, thicker and thicker like a rainstorm.

"Run!" she screams, assessing the new threat.

They go back the way they came, their fear guiding them, arms pumping, leaves crunching.

"Faster!" Derrick screams, but Zahra is tired, no longer acquainted with this sort of cardio, and she falls behind.

She closes her eyes, the steps intuitive. Home isn't a house but a thought, a memory, a smell, a sound. She knows where she's going. Not too slow, but steady, like driving through fog.

|||||||||||||||||||||||||||||||||||||||||||||||||||||

THEY'RE ALL PANTING WHEN THEY GET BACK TO THE CREEK, Zahra the last of them. She's still catching her breath when Sammie starts laughing. Derrick looks at her for a beat but then joins in. They're both delusional.

"What's so funny?" Zahra says through breaths.

"God, grab a sense of humor," Sammie says. "We were just chased out of the woods by a swarm of moths."

"We could've been hurt," Zahra says.

"How?" Sammie laughs even harder.

Zahra drops the worry, relaxes her shoulders. It is so absurd that she almost laughs too. Amid their relief, the moths are still here, flying, looming, laying their eggs.

The transformation is a thing of improbable possibility. It gives them pause; they are as still as mannequins, as breathless as deep-sea divers. In the blink of an eye, with the quickness of the flash of an old disposable camera, the moths turn into beautiful humans, all shades of black and brown. Zahra spins around, looking for what? She's not sure. Maybe a way out. Maybe a weapon. But Derrick, slack-jawed and staring, unblinking, sits down on the grass—crisscross applesauce as if he's here to watch a movie. Sammie rubs her eyes in disbelief and follows suit. Feeling they've left her no choice, Zahra is the last of them, on the cool grass, dew seeping through her jeans.

There is a boy at the creek, throwing rocks instead of skipping them. The rocks make loud kerplunks in the water, and the boy does not seem to mind how the water bounces back at him, splashing his shirt. He is the only one singing, and it's a resounding voice, one where he tilts his whole head back on the runs. Zahra doesn't know the song, but it sounds like gospel.

To his left are a group of twentysomething-year-olds playing cards, and Zahra knows their outfits well, colorful shirts with wide lapels and checkered flare pants that match the look and style of their hair, the times, the sixties. Zahra remembers the outfits and the faces from the photo of a photo on her iPhone. Gram's siblings. Near them she spots Warren and Minnie and Natasha, Mother and Rose and Senior. What are they doing here?

Far down, behind the house where a white family used to live, Zahra spots a soul train line. People do the bump, the jerk, the twist. The cabbage patch, the Bankhead bounce. They drop it low and bring it back up again. They rub against each other like sandpaper to wood. They twerk, hands on knees. They whine, hips loose like warm Jell-O. Women throw one leg over male counterparts, one arm in the air as they gyrate. Two men kiss passionately, like long-lost lovers, while musicians beat talking drums and water drums, steel drums and bongo drums. They shake maracas and gourd seeds.

Panning to the left, on the neighbor's patio, a man strikes a woman hard across the face, and she stumbles back against the patio's railing. She's hurt, but that doesn't stop him. He begins to choke her, two big hands around one fragile neck.

"Hey!" Zahra calls out. "Hey!" She gets up without any idea of how she'll fight a man twice her size, but Derrick pulls her back down.

"You can't do anything," he says, and she searches his face for what she's missing. She wants to object because Derrick doesn't always know everything, and dead people are still worth saving, but a group of women, middle-aged, stone-faced, catch her eye before she can say anything.

The women's arms are lined with muscles that help them carry heaping piles of linens that travel toward the sky like precarious beanstalks. One woman holds a poster in protest. She sings to the others, and their loads come tumbling down like parachutes.

Zahra remembers when she was just a kid watching Mary make the bed. Shooting the sheet in the air and landing it on all four corners of the mattress like magic. Now the linens obstruct Zahra's view so she can no longer see the women's faces. As an old pair of boxers and a white cotton shirt land gently on the green grass, Zahra sees that all the women are now holding signs that reference a laundry strike. One woman in particular looks so much like Mary that if Zahra didn't know any better she would swear it was her mother's twin sister. But these women must be from the 1800s, the Atlanta washerwomen strike of 1881—they remind her of a picture she saw in one of Mary's books about Atlanta.

Farther across the stretch of a football field of private yards, Zahra spots enslaved people, an image she might find in an old history book, one woman with a baby on her back. The line of them are singing, swaying, picking; there's a rhythm to it all. She can't see what they pick and place in woven baskets.

Then there is a line of protestors. The line makes no sounds at all, though their mouths move in anguish. Zahra tries to distinguish what they intend to say, but it's impossible. They're circumnavigating the neighborhood, walking blindly, so when they've almost run into a tree or the creek or another group of people, they about-face like army soldiers and make their way in a different direction until an equally untraversable hurdle appears. When the line approaches a congregation in a circle, knees digging into dirt as they pray, the line walks right through them and a few of the prayer warriors stand up like zombies and attach themselves to the end of it.

As far back as the eye can see, there are men built like houses themselves laying brick, laughing as they go, spreading mortar like icing on a cake. There are women planting gardens, with no shortage of vegetables around them, the yards now full of peppers, tomatoes, cucumbers, and leafy greens as large as tropical palms. There are athletes warming up, doing calisthenics. Others run suicides, dribble basketballs on grass like it's nothing; they swing baseball bats and tennis rackets. Closer now, nearly right above them, Zahra, Sammie, and Derrick hear a scream and look up in the sky to find a man standing outside a floating apartment, a floating balcony. Sammie clutches Zahra's arm, and Zahra grabs Derrick's hand, but Derrick focuses on the man with a distinct mustache, with sideburns that come down his face and slice his cheeks as if they're reaching for that neat hair over his lips.

"No, don't do it," a woman screams from far away, who knows where. "We need your voice. Don't do it, Donny." But the man who Zahra presumes is Donny jumps right off the balcony and glides through the sky like a feather. Down, down, down he goes, and the woman's cries grow so loud that Sammie plugs her ears. Donny doesn't hit the ground but disappears just before it like a magic trick. Poof, gone.

People are everywhere, all the way down the backyards of the block, where there are no barriers between one person's land and the next. Now Zahra understands—Gram's house doesn't belong to her. And it sure as hell doesn't belong to the state or the bank, or some white twentysomethings trying to set a trend. But it belongs to these people here, and you can't strip them of it or ask them to go haunt somewhere else. They are in the grass and wading in the creek, on patios, roofs, hanging out of windows. Everyone needs a *home, home*. Everyone needs to be heard. So they never stopped talking. So they still have something to say.

Zahra looks at Sammie to see if she's putting it all together, that these people are here but not here. Sammie's eyes are wide, like an oyster cracked open. She looks raw, and her fingers draw slow scratches on her arms. Zahra sees the boy before Sammie; he taps her on the shoulder, and Sammie whips her head around like a feral animal.

The boy smiles at Sammie like he would a long-lost friend, one he'd been aching to see for some time now.

"Who is he?" Zahra asks.

Sammie doesn't ignore the question outright, but she's too mesmerized by the boy to answer Zahra directly. "Rashad?" she says to the boy.

"Who is he?" Zahra says louder, but what she really means is *Who is he to you?* To Zahra, the boy is familiar, older than she remembers him, but the face is not new. Something clicks, and she remembers how embarrassed she was to sit across from him at the cafeteria table in middle school, Derrick's old friend, a ballsy Black boy who didn't care what the white kids thought of him.

Now Sammie reaches out her hand to touch his face, but he backs away quickly.

"I'm sorry I couldn't tell you everything," he says.

"What are you doing here?" she asks. "Why did you run away from me?"

"I wanted to show you," he says, arms extended, circling around. All of this. He wanted to show her the moths.

"What are you?" she asks.

"Your star-crossed lover," the boy says, gleaming.

He flirts with his eyes, crinkled with long lashes. But they're also a little sad. Sunken inside of his face, hiding something. And if Zahra didn't know any better, she might say that Sammie is head over heels for this boy. The way she looks at him now is with beguilement, a longing, her whole body leaned forward like she might tip over trying to reach him.

"Well, that and you're a good listener. For the longest time, I thought I was in love with Zahra. But then I met you."

The realization pains Zahra, that he was watching as she tried to reason, relate to, make friends with those white girls. He was loving her in the most innocent way, of children who just want to find their place in the cafeteria, in the classroom, in a world that calls them too loud, ghetto, embarrassing. She has nothing to say, can't even look Rashad's ghost in the eye.

Zahra sees Sammie startle as she spots a man approaching from behind Rashad, a man whose knees knock together but hold his back up straight, proud, beaming. Sammie gets up quickly and runs to meet him. "Daday," she screams, arms wide open as if she's trying to harness the wind. "You've been watching me."

When Sammie is just a yard away from the man, and it looks like their reaching arms will connect, the people blossom into moths again, just as Daday is saying, "No, your mother is."

Then Daday is gone, a rabbit returned to its hat. Sammie turns around, and Rashad is gone too, along with the faces of protestors, fighters, friends, lovers, family. They disappear like morning dew. But the moths are still here, and their songs pierce the dark sky—old Negro spirituals and melodies composed by generations before Scott Joplin and since Ryan Leslie, remixed with funk and hip-hop, R & B and reggae. Not only do the moths tell their own stories, but they tell Zahra's and Derrick's and Sammie's too. Songs in every language, from Amharic to Yoruba, from Patois to slang from around the way. A ring shout, a call and response, from the past to the present to the future and back again.

THIRTY-FOUR 🦋

The next day, Zahra goes to Derrick's room with a question on her mind. She finds him propped up in bed reading an old copy of the *Pedagogy of the Oppressed*, looking so similar to the brother she knew as a teenager that a deep feeling of gratitude passes over her, and she acknowledges the greatness of God that Gram preaches in all occasions, abundance and devastation. When Derrick looks up at her, she knows that his presence is only fleeting and tomorrow he'll be gone. And if not tomorrow, then the day after, then one day too soon. Will he come to her in the form of a moth? What song will he sing? And this is her question about the moths they met the day before—don't some of them have their own families to haunt?

"Why us? Why here?" she asks Derrick now. "They could go anywhere, couldn't they?"

Derrick closes the book. "Remember when you first started going to Evermount, and you couldn't choose a cafeteria table? You sat with Rashad and me, then with Molly and all of those white girls, then back with us? Remember that?"

Did she? Of course she did. She nods. "Yeah. What's that got to do with dead people, Derrick?"

He shakes his head as if it's all too much for him to explain. He rubs his eyes, and for the first time since he's been back, Zahra sees how tired he is. He is like Gram on a day after the DMV, Mary after hours in court.

"Remember that first day we heard the moths? In our tree on our designated branches?"

"Yeah, sure."

"Remember the song?"

Zahra can't say that she does. She shakes her head.

"*If the sky that we look upon . . . ,*" he sings, in the way of the original, Ben E. King's version, Derrick's voice low and warbly; he could always carry a tune.

Eventually, Zahra joins him, never a harmonizer but someone who sings of her own accord.

They make it to the chorus, "*Just as long as you stand, stand by me,*" then laugh loudly at the attempt.

"Remember Ms. Richards-Price made us sing that in her music class in high school?" Zahra asks.

"We took it thinking it would be an easy A."

"Not knowing she graded by solo attempts. Of course you scored way better than me."

Derrick smiles at the memory, raises his hands in the air as a cocky explanation, *Can't help that I'm the better singer.*

Zahra swats his gesture away. "Derrick?" she says.

"Yeah?"

"Why don't you come to New York with me? We can sleep head to foot like we used to when we were kids. We'll find you a job somewhere. Maybe serving at a restaurant or working in corporate, advertising or tech. You could make a lot of money."

"Never wanted money."

"Then what?"

"Peace."

"You think you'll find that here?"

"Maybe. An old professor thinks I could teach a class, thinks I need an audience. And Atlanta is home, you know?"

"What sort of audience?"

"I don't know. Maybe I'm just here on earth to be a translator. I hear the moths. I tell their stories."

"And you'll live here with Gram?"

"Not here, here. She's losing this house, Zahra. Unless you're sitting on a huge stack of cash."

Zahra gulps down what she's been trying to deny. She looks around the room. Eyes land on the window and its dusty shelf lined with old copies of *Jet* underneath it, the ceiling she'd stare at for hours trying to answer existential questions, the closet she used to pull shut on herself during games of hide-and-seek. She listens for the house's arguments, but it is quiet tonight. Now when there are footsteps or the croak of a foundation settling, she'll think of all the people it occupies, all of the stories. A haunting and a hymn. She wonders if this is the place she'll come back to when she dies or if she'll have no scores to settle at all, having figured things out while she still could.

"All those people you wrote about, the people from the flyers, you think they lived here once? In this house?"

"I think there's a chance. Them or their family. Their lineage. Maybe before the house was even built. The land was here." He pauses. "I couldn't stand to see it get swept up from underneath us. When I found out that Gram was losing it, I had no choice but to leave. And the moths had grown so loud by then—this house an echo chamber."

"They wanted you to tell their stories."

He nods.

"I guess it's nice to know that they won't be forgotten, but what about me?" she asks Derrick, knowing life has always been so much better with him in it.

"What about you?"

"I need you, Derrick. You're my fucking brother."

"You don't need me."

"We all do. Don't you see how all the shit hits the fan when you're gone?" She looks up and sees the moths literally speckling the ceiling fan. She knows that one day Gram won't be here, and not because she's losing the house but because no one can be anywhere forever. Or maybe they can. The moths aren't going anywhere no matter who moves in.

"We've always been on opposite branches, remember?" Derricks asks, and she rolls her eyes, knowing it's true. "But if you need me, I'll ask the moths to sing to you. If you listen hard enough, you'll hear them. If you've lost your way, I'll call you back. I'll watch you."

Zahra lays her head on his shoulder. Her big brother, still cool as ever, still full of answers. "Will you bring me ice cream?" she asks.

"Butter pecan. You know it."

"Will we go on drives together?"

"Up and down Covington Highway. On loop around 285."

"And the latest hits? We'll listen to the radio nonstop, high-five when we get the chance to record our favorites?"

"No one listens to the radio anymore."

But Zahra ignores him, she's so stuck in all of her questions. "We'll look at each other and burst out laughing at nothing at all? We'll eat fat slices of Gram's pound cake and toss Mary's meat loaf in the garbage—paper plate on top so she doesn't know? We'll watch horror movies and pick honeysuckle by the creek?"

"Whatever you want," he says.

Zahra moves to the other side of the bed and tucks herself in at

Derrick's feet. He throws the book on the floor and gets under the covers himself. He wiggles like he used to, spreads his legs wide so that her portion of the bed gets smaller and smaller, and she can't hang on for long. "Derrick, I'm falling," she says.

He laughs. "Whoops, didn't see you there."

She laughs too, overwhelmed by how easily they've fallen back into place. That night, things are just as they were, and she goes to sleep smiling.

THIRTY-FIVE 🦋

October 30, 2019, on the way home, a Wednesday

Let's talk," Uncle says, and she really doesn't want to, but then, with more than thirteen hours in the car with him, she has nowhere to go.

"Fine," she says, folding her arms. They're already on the expressway, and she curses herself for thinking so much and not looking out the window as they drove out of the neighborhood. No last takes of the brick houses and the semi-deserted corner store, the brown people who look everything and nothing like New Yorkers, the Harlemites she loves.

Sammie wants to cry for Rashad. She feels stupid, going on about Spelman and being a senior now knowing that he was never given the chance to graduate or go to college. She sees him dying a million deaths in a million different ways. Slowly in a hospital bed from some rare form of cancer; then quickly, a bullet to the head, splattering the neighborhood he seems to love so much. A car accident. Drowning. Shark attack. Plane crash. Stabbed. Concussion. Then she sees Daday showing him how to use a car wrench or calling on him to help separate the trash from the recyclables, and she's jealous.

The emotions make her angrier at Uncle, madder than she was in the car the other day. It's hard to shake, that someone you trust could lie to your face like it's nothing. Always thinking he's doing what's best for her. Always thinking she won't understand. Well, of course she won't if he never gives her the chance to.

There are things that Uncle will never understand, like dreams that are prophecies and beautiful boys who can stand right in front of her and be nowhere at all. She feels like multiple lives have been ripped from her, some old scabs picked at and others fresh, bubbling with blood. She needs her mother, someone who will understand.

"I'm sorry, Sammie. Really, really sorry. Sometimes I forget how grown up you are now. A little woman. I don't have to keep hiding things from you, but I still see you as . . . I don't know . . . my little little, you know?"

Little Little. She'd forgotten the nickname, something he used to call her when he would hold his hand up for a high five knowing that she'd have to jump to reach it. She could never get high enough until he'd lower his hand, meeting her halfway.

"But I'm not that little girl anymore," Sammie says. "I'm almost a woman now. And I deserve to know about my mom."

Uncle sighs as if he's the one who's been lied to here. "You do," he relents. "You deserve to know everything."

Sammie feels like she's won something, but she's not sure what it would take for a sense of happiness to come.

"You hungry?" Uncle asks. "We could stop somewhere."

"No." Sammie wouldn't be able to stomach food right now. There's too much to think about, too many flashing faces and unanswered questions. She looks down at her phone, always in her hands,

Mother Ma says. The background photo is one she took in Trinidad, on the way to Maracas Bay, where they stopped to buy chow off a winding road in the mountains. The sky seems to go on forever, a foggy breath over the trees below. Sammie's aching to go back there. It's a little funny when she thinks about it, how Mother Ma and Daday sacrificed so much—money, friends, status—to bring her to America, but there are days when all she wants is to turn around and go back from whence she came, to fit in. She'll miss all the commodities, she knows that, but what Zahra has with Atlanta is something of a love language, and while Sammie loves New York, there are holes that poke through, and a face too, a mother across seas, so *home*, *home* feels interrupted, a pretense.

"Tell me about Mom," Sammie says.

"You should ask her."

Sammie huffs. "Asshole." She mutters it way low under her breath so she knows Uncle can't hear her, and he doesn't.

"What do you want to know?" He relents anyway.

It's a harder question than she thought. "I don't know. Her favorite color?"

"Purple, I think."

Sammie's own is green, but it doesn't matter anyway; it was a stupid question. She thinks of the probing questions Zahra asked her while working on her college essay.

"What is she passionate about?" Sammie asks.

Uncle Trey sighs. "Hmm," he says. "Good question. Well, when we were younger she was passionate about books and net ball. She had a lot of friends, and she wouldn't let you say a mean word about them." He stops to laugh, then squints his eyes hard, either in deep thought or to see the road more clearly, a traffic jam.

Finally, he goes on, "And your mother was . . . curious. I think that's the best word for her. She was always getting into something. Always investigating. When a boy in her class went missing, she was wired about it."

"What happened to him?"

"Kidnapped. Got his head chopped off. Later found out that the Lizard did it. Was a hit by the Dole Chadee kingpin. You've heard of him, right? Dole Chadee?"

Sammie shakes her head. No, she's ashamed to know so little of Trinidad's history. Of her own mother's haunts.

"Your mother was passionate about a lot of things. And she used to listen to sappy love songs. We were always behind in Trinidad, so Rochelle grew up listening to Celine Dion and Michael Bolton, until she switched over to Maxi Priest and Beres Hammond. When you were born, she was still obsessed with that song by Shaggy. What's it called?"

Sammie shrugs.

"'Angel,'" Uncle Trey coughs out, then begins to sing. "*You're my darling angel. Closer than my peeps you are to me, baby.*" He turns to her. "Know it?"

She nods, even though she's not sure. "And now? What's Mom like now?"

"And now? I don't know. Some of the same stuff maybe. I'm sure she's still asking questions and dreaming about love."

"But only romantic love?" she mumbles. Any other form of love would make her a better mother, wouldn't it? But then she thinks of Ms. Mary and how her love for the Black community as a whole has overshadowed her love for Derrick and Zahra. Like a tree high above them, maybe Ms. Mary thinks her shade is enough; she can reach so many people up there, casting a wide net from the sky. But they, or at least Zahra, wants a closer love, something she can reach up and touch, feel its leaves, beckon its prayers, her shade and her shade only. Sammie doesn't want to be so idealistic. She wants to know her mother and accept that love in whatever form it may take, but it's hard. And she's not sure how to stop being so mad. She rubs her knees, pulls them up on her seat, and wraps her arms around them. If her mother is anything like Derrick, she couldn't help herself, and it's up to Sammie to find her in the rubble.

Uncle Trey clears his throat, and she looks at him hard. He has one hand at the top of the wheel, while the other rubs his pants leg, as if his hands are sweaty. What's he so nervous about?

"What you said in the car the other day, about Zahra hearing voices . . . Is that true?" he asks.

Sammie regrets saying it. Zahra didn't deserve it, and by telling on Zahra, she was also telling on herself. Now she doesn't want to explain it to Uncle Trey, but she has to tell him something. She unfolds and refolds a gum wrapper, the words escaping her.

"Well?" Uncle Trey says.

"It's true," Sammie says, quickly adding, "But she's not crazy. The voices are . . . real."

Uncle Trey's eyebrows furrow. He reaches for his water bottle. Sammie gets to it first and unscrews the cap for him. He takes a big gulp. "How would you know? What's real and what's not?"

Sammie doesn't know how to tell him. She bites her lip, looks at her nails, two broken. "I can hear them too. But it's not like they're telling us what to do. It's not like they're satanic or anything. It's not like the movies," she pleads her case. "They sing, is all."

Uncle sighs like he just can't catch a break. "Your mother," he starts.

But Sammie cuts him off. "I know," Sammie says. "The dreams."

"It wasn't just the dreams," Uncle says.

Sammie turns to look at him. She accidentally swallows her gum. "She?" is all Sammie can get out.

Uncle Trey knows what she means. "Hears them too. The moths. Stopped listening years ago, right after she graduated from high school and decided that she wanted to be her own person and didn't want anything tugging at her. Not long after, she met your dad, and well, things turned out the way they did."

Uncle holds out his hand, and it takes Sammie a second for her to realize that he's asking for gum. She unwraps a piece for him. He chews it urgently.

"I should've known in the car that day. The moths were everywhere, just like when we were kids. I should've known, but I guess I didn't want to."

"I'm going to be fine, Uncle," Sammie tries to convince him.

"You promise?"

"I promise."

"Little Little?"

"Little Little." She nods, wondering if adulthood means choosing one path or the other.

||||||||||||||||||||||||||||||||||||||||||||||

THEY'RE BACK IN NEW YORK, AND IT'S LATE. THE SMELL OF the apartment, distinct from Gram's ever wafting pound cake, jolts Sammie into her own reality. Home, home; Mother Ma; aloo pie; cinnamon air freshener plug-ins.

She's forgiven Uncle Trey, somewhat, but is happy to be able to put some distance between them now that they're no longer trapped in the car. She's been aching to make a phone call, and she can't have Uncle eavesdropping.

She hugs Mother Ma quickly, then strides to her room, practically closing the door on Uncle Trey asking if she's hungry.

"No," she screams out at him. She goes to her closet, like she used to when she was a bold little girl and not too scared of small spaces or pitch-black rooms. Now she sits below skirts, and dresses, and her wool winter coat tickles her shoulders; she shuts herself in.

The line seems to ring for hours. It's late. Maybe she won't pick up. Then finally a click and a beat of silence, a hushed breath on the line. "Yes?"

"It's me."

"I know. It's late, Sammie. Are you OK?"

Sammie thinks it depends on her definition of *OK*, but she nods, then says out loud, "Yeah, I'm OK. How are you?"

"As always," her mother says, no explanation of what that means.

"Will you tell me about your dreams?" Sammie asks.

A sound comes out, but Sammie can't make out what it was. A sigh? A gasp? A hint of surprise? "What do you mean? Dreams?"

"Both kinds. Chacachacare and becoming a doctor."

"What did Trey tell you?"

"He says you stopped listening to the moths."

The phone goes silent as if her mother has stopped listening to her too. But then she says, "I did for a long time, but recently, I've learned to listen again." And Sammie reasons that it must have been around the same time she started feeling like she was being watched. Maybe she felt her mother's eyes. Maybe Sammie could tell her mother was paying attention again.

"We're more alike than I ever thought we were," Sammie says.

Her mother laughs a little, not mocking but happy. Maybe more warm than Sammie has ever heard her brittle voice, she says, "Where should I start?"

And Sammie learns that her mother's watchful eyes only feel like a gentle breeze on the phone; they're calming in a way, ironically similar to ocean waves. Sammie learns that people are never who you think they are. The dead ones can be more alive than those Atlanta mosquitoes, and the living can be lost and long dead but for the blood that pumps inside of them. Still, she knows it's possible to be revived at least seven times.

THIRTY-SIX 🦋

When Zahra wakes up the next morning, the bed feels big, spacious, and she kicks out her legs, stretches her arms wide and brings them up over her head. The moment of peace is broken by the most obvious revelation. She's alone. No Sammie, no coconut smell from the oil she applies to her scalp at night. Zahra gets up and heads to her old room to be sure, but when she looks in, the bed is neat, all four corners tucked tightly, and she remembers waving goodbye early the day before, while it was still dark out. Still, Derrick's got to be around here somewhere. She checks the bathrooms, the living room, the kitchen, the front yard, the patio, looks over the balcony to the backyard and finally ventures down to the basement. He's nowhere. She considers calling him but then thinks that he didn't really want to be found in the first place. A brick of understanding hits her chest, and she feels like she needs to lie down again.

When she goes back into her old bedroom, Gram is waiting for her there. Eyeing the made-up bed, she says, "You slept with Derrick?"

Zahra nods.

"Head to foot?"

Zahra nods. "You taught us well."

Gram smiles. "He's gone, isn't he?"

Zahra nods; she knows she can't talk but for crying.

"That's what men do," Gram says. "They leave." Zahra thinks about Trey packing up the car, telling Sammie to stop dragging her feet. She wonders if it's easier for men to fly.

But Gram, always reading her mind, says, "Smart of them, I guess. Can't expect everything to remain the same when you stay." She sighs, looks around the room, points to that senior portrait of Zahra that seems to captivate everyone. "You were so young then. So sure about everything. Are you sure now, Zahra?"

"Sure of what?"

"Of anything?"

It takes Zahra a while. "That you make the best pound cake in the southeast."

Gram laughs. "Just the southeast, huh?"

Zahra nods. "Your advice isn't too bad either."

Gram looks at her intently, then seems to shake away a thought. She clears her throat and says, "You'd make a good mother."

Zahra feels calmer than she's felt all week, almost as relieved as when she saw Derrick sitting at the kitchen table. Maybe a question she hasn't wanted to ask has been answered.

A single moth flits and flutters about Zahra. She eyes it intently and then listens for its song. "A House Is Not a Home." She waits for the run, *Are you gonna be, say you're gonna be, well well, well, well . . .*

Little does Zahra know how much distance the single moth can cover. Thousands of miles, from Atlanta to New York and then back again. To Zahra, then Sammie, then Derrick, connecting them like puzzle pieces, each one limb of a greater body, a deciduous tree that interlinks with its nearby siblings and disappears then reappears like history.

"It's telling you to go on," Gram says. And though Zahra has already picked up on this, having grown closer to the voices, Gram's own startles her. She's known? All along?

"I thought . . ."

"Silly of you to think that," Gram says.

THIRTY-SEVEN

Sammie likes drawing pictures of people, cakey skin and bulbous noses. Hairlines that give wigs away and gap-toothed smiles. She draws by memory mostly. Combines Zahra's wild Afro with her own dimpled cheeks and bushy brows. She puts Uncle Trey's overgrown beard just under Derrick's deep-set eyes. She draws her mother in a dress like the floral one the woman at Zahra's church wore. She sketches a hybrid of Gram and Mother Ma, the face split in half so both sides fight for your attention. She puts Rashad's smile on so many different faces, Uncle Richard's and Aunty Deanne's and Leila's and even Noah's. In her portraits, people aren't destroyed or individually created but recycled, all pieces of the past, of the people who came before them.

She likes to record short videos of herself, asking questions. *Do you believe in superheroes? What's your favorite kind of tree? Is the Black community all right? Do nonviolent crimes deserve violent punishment? Is living in a six-by-eight-feet cell and being forced to work for fifty-two cents an hour violent? To that regard, what is violence? Have you ever been to Central Park late at night and by yourself? Did you run into any ghosts? Have you ever talked to someone from inside a closet? Do you believe Wayne Williams committed the Atlanta child murders? Have you heard of the legend of Chacachacare? Is Donald Trump a real person or is it possible he's stuffed with the ashes of your white ancestors?* She puts them on TikTok or her Instagram stories, and Leila is the most frequent to answer. One day Sammie asks, *When did so many personal things become political—our bodies, our love lives?* It is Noah, alarmingly, who answers her. *Been that way since the signing of the Constitution when you consider that Black people's bodies were even more subject to political attack then,* a realist. His DM startles her, and though she is in her room alone when she sees the message, Sammie looks around as if Noah has said it right over her shoulder.

||||||||||||||||||||||||||||||||||||||||||||||||||||

THE NEXT DAY AT SCHOOL, SHE WALKS THE HALLWAYS AVOIDING him. This school has grown narrower for Sammie, having been exposed to the wide expanse of the South. She used to think this place was huge. She used to gasp every time she stepped foot on its college-like campus. She used to think that this was the most natural place in existence, more trees and less concrete than the city. But now she reckons with this school, masked by the serenity in which it lives, the trees shading designated sidewalks, the occasional brick with a donor's name, the whole community a picture-perfect Pleasantville, never mind how her classmates within it are in utter turmoil.

She sees them everywhere bopping with bookbags, carrying on like nothing is new, like the world belongs to them, and she thinks of Rashad, of how she told him that he couldn't stay in high school forever. But couldn't you? Roam these hallways like a science-statistics-sociology zombie forever? Trapped in a YouTube video where you, an almost-woman Black girl or an irresistibly handsome

Black boy or an audacious white closeted bigot, wear a Travis Scott T-shirt and rap, *Niggas think it's sweet, it's on sight, nothin' nice.*

Sammie is at her locker when someone throws a hand across her back and leans in. She can smell Listerine on his breath, and she knows it's Broderick. "Sammie, Sammie, wherefore art thou, Sammie?" he asks.

"I'm right here," she says.

"You gotta shape up on your Shakespeare," he says. "Wherefore equals why."

"Oh," Sammie says, shrugging, looking around Broderick to see if the shaggy-haired boy passing behind him is Noah. It's not. She exhales. "What's up?"

"Missed you this past weekend. James went off again, and Tiffany got so fucked up that she made out with him. Dude gets away with everything."

"Do you remember my friend Leila?" she interrupts him.

"Leila? Leila?"

Sammie nods. "Well, she has a boyfriend now, but she used to have a crush on you. She met you at the fall dance a couple of years ago, remember?"

"Hmm . . ." Broderick shakes his head. "I meet a lot of girls, Sammie."

"But she's Black. And it's like, you're always looking for Blackness but not really at all."

"Dude, I am Black," he says.

"Yeah, but wherefore art thou, Broderick?"

Broderick stands back, eyebrows scrunched together like a caterpillar. "You go down to Spelman, and now you're all Atlanta on me?" He imitates a neck-rolling, snapping Black woman. She wonders who he's gotten this routine from.

"Wow," Sammie says, throwing her locker shut. "It's not that you had to like her. It's just that, even then, it was like she was invisible to you. Sometimes I feel like I am too—invisible. Like, you don't really see me. But you can't ignore people forever. Someone, somewhere, is going to make you listen."

||||||||||||||||||||||||||||||||||||||||||||||||

THE GALL FROM HER CONVERSATION WITH BRODERICK ADDS some pep to her step, and she thinks she could say or do just about anything right now. She spots Noah down the hallway and strides toward him like a gazelle. She's got this. She's got this.

"I like you. I like you as more than a friend," Sammie blurts out, then turns around as if she herself has not said it, as if the voice is coming from behind her and she wonders who it is. But no, she grabs her throat in recognition. She's said it, just like Zahra told her to.

And now Noah, pasty, polite Noah, is looking at her as if she's grown a third eye.

"I mean, not in any serious *serious* way." She tries to fix what she's done. "And you don't have to say anything back. You can just sit there, quiet, looking at me as if . . ."

"I like you too," he says. "As way more than a friend."

She's stuck now. She has no idea what to say next. Zahra didn't go over this part. She smiles, can't help it.

"Really?" she says, looking at him in awe.

"Who wouldn't?" He blushes a bright beet red, and this relaxes Sammie.

"So . . . ," she says.

And he takes his cue. "So we should go out?"

"Really?" she says again, and he laughs.

"Yes, Sammie," he says, and she likes the way he says her name. "Are you free this weekend?"

Sammie nods, pushes her braids behind her ear, but too thick, they just fall in her face again. Noah grabs one of them, and it is nothing like when the white girls do it, but sensual. It gives him a reason to step closer. He inches in. "I guess I should just text you?"

"Or call?"

"Or call," he agrees, just before the bell rings, and they split like opposite ends of a magnet, knowing they'll both be late, two students with dreams that being tardy won't make come true.

||||||||||||||||||||||||||||||||||||||||||||||||

SAMMIE DECIDES TO TAKE NOAH TO AFRICA KINE. IT IS THE worst sort of test that she could do, taking him to the most Blackity Black spot she can think of, ordering the spiciest dishes on the Senegalese menu to see if he can stomach pepper or if his cheeks will explode, if he'll cough the food up as if he's allergic. She'll know that it's not only the food he'd be allergic to but her, her food, her roots. She has decided that she's like a tree in this way, unmoving. He'll have to build his way around her.

"Food's probably pretty good here," he says.

"Yeah?" she asks. "Why do you say that?"

"Smells good," Noah says, pointing to his nose, sniffing. "Smells like . . ."

She's on needles waiting for his response, hoping he doesn't say anything dumb, or worse, offensive.

"Smells like stew?" he says.

The simplicity of his answer mixed with relief and first-date jitters makes her bowl over with laughter. This seems to loosen him up, and he does a little dance with just his shoulders, suddenly more confident than he was just seconds ago.

"You laugh so hard," he says.

She stops dead in her tracks, serious again. "So?"

"So," Noah says, smiling. "Let's eat." He holds a hand out in front of him, an *after you* gesture, and she likes how he works her emotions in this way, from amusement to nervousness, then finally warmth.

||||||||||||||||||||||||||||||||||||||||||||||

THESE ARE THE QUESTIONS SHE ASKS NOAH: DO YOU THINK *it's sexy to watch girls kiss? If so, why? Do you use the N-word, out loud or in your head? How much money do your parents have? Does that mean you yourself are rich? What do you want to be when you grow up? Do you care more about animals than people you don't know? What's your favorite food? Do you know how to cook? Does your mom cook for your dad? Does your dad cook for your mom? Do you think a woman can be a proper mother from two thousand miles away? What music do you listen to? Do you believe in God? Do you believe in ghosts? Do you know what it's like to feel two skins at once?*

And Noah is all—*Meh. I guess anyone kissing* can *be sexy. The N-word is cringey, even in my head. My parents have a lot of money, and I'd sound ridiculous if I said none of it is meant for me. I think I want to be a filmmaker. Am I allowed to like animals and strangers? Close call between lasagna and tacos but only with corn tortillas. Don't really know how to cook, but I could learn.* Shrug, sheepish smile. *My mom cooks. All mothers are different, aren't they? What do you mean by proper? You mean driving a minivan and all? My mom doesn't drive a minivan, and she wears really revealing clothing. It's like tackling toddlers trying to shut up my friends about it. But I guess distance complicates things. I listen to a lot of pop, rap too. I like Vince Staples. Do I believe in God? Yes. Ghosts? Maybe.* Rubbing his arms up and down. *Two skins at once? I don't know. Do you?*

He reaches out a hand to touch her, but the only skin that's available is a knee poking through her ripped jeans. He rubs his hand along it, as if testing for multiple skins. His touch is electric, and Sammie stays stark still as if she's at a doctor's appointment.

"Feels like just one skin to me," Noah says, returning to his thiebou djeun, picking around bones. The way his fingers move, with speed and grace, reminds Sammie of Daday.

"It's a metaphor," she says.

"For what?"

"Having your ancestors inside of you." Sammie thinks of Rashad, how she's listened for his voice lately, and when the moths in her room rapped "Do for Love" like the anthem of a revival party, she knew it had to be him. "Well, not only your ancestors but just other people. Knowing yourself and knowing other people just as well."

"Sounds like a gift."

"Or a curse."

"Maybe a little of both," Noah says, and Sammie smiles. She likes him.

||||||||||||||||||||||||||||||||||||||||||||||||||

SAMMIE AND NOAH HAVE LESS THAN A YEAR TO FALL IN LOVE, for him to show up to the apartment with two bouquets of roses, red for Sammie and pink for Mother Ma. For Sammie to wear a silky black dress to prom that Uncle will buy at a sample sale. They have less than a year to go to second base and contemplate third. So little time to decide if they'll try to make things work or dead the relationship outright as they head in separate directions next fall. But for at least a season or two, Sammie finds love; she'll slip notes in Noah's locker, one so cryptic that he'll stop her in the hallway laughing. He'll ask, *And what about this nun at Chacachacare?*, butchering the name. Another love note will lie on Sammie's desk for days, waiting to be finished. When she'll return to it, words piercing her thoughts, the moths will be at it like scavengers, so there's only a sliver of paper with one word left, *dreams*. Sammie will gasp in realization.

For now Sammie thinks about all that has happened in the past month of her life, of meeting Zahra and hearing moths, of finding bygone brothers and resurrecting the dead. She knows that a lot can happen in a year, a million lifetimes folded together, the moths singing on and on, *What you won't do, do for love* . . .

THIRTY-EIGHT 🦋

When Zahra gets back to New York, she follows a moth to Harlem by way of the M60 and then walks down Adam Clayton. There's the usual African drum circle and stands selling sunglasses and shea butter to her right. She passes the statue of Adam Clayton Powell Jr. marching forward, as if up the stairway to heaven, and just beyond him, a gray office building that Zahra only knows for housing Upper Manhattan's rent office. She walks north. But before she reaches 141st Street, the moth swings a right down 135th and lands on a redbrick building with gold lettering and a black-and-yellow banner that celebrates the graduating class of 2019, all sorts of young brown faces smiling in uniform. Zahra pulls out her phone and takes down the name of the high school—Thurgood Marshall Academy.

|||||||||||||||||||||||||||||||||||||||||||||||||||||||

A COUPLE OF MONTHS FROM NOW, ZAHRA WILL HEAR ON HER voice mail—Sophia has gotten into Stanford, and *Thank you, thank you, thank you*, and *To what address can I mail you a surprise gift?* It's amazing that Mrs. Jacobs won't know her address, but Zahra guesses she wouldn't. By then, Zahra will be working with the high school juniors at Thurgood; she'll smile at practice essays about families immigrating from Senegal and natural hair journeys likened to religious awakenings and familial estrangements sprinkled with Spanish. She will tell Trey over mussels at their favorite Black-owned restaurant on 139th about the wild things those students say and how work has never felt so meaningful, and it won't be for weeks that she sees Derrick's face in an *Atlanta Journal-Constitution* headline, that she'll call him up and ask, *Why'd you do it?*, already knowing the answer.

|||||||||||||||||||||||||||||||||||||||||||||||||||||

A COUPLE OF WEEKS FROM NOW, ZAHRA WILL MEET SAMMIE on an uptown pier off the Hudson, upon Sammie's insistence that they be by the water. It'll be cold by then, winter peeking through the eyes of fall, and she and Sammie will be on similar accords, puffer coats, gloves. For Sammie, a beanie, which has no place over Zahra's 'fro.

Zahra's late, and finds Sammie already on a bench, two cups, one in each hand, smiling.

"Caffeine for you. Tea for me," she says.

"You didn't have to, but I'm glad you did," Zahra says, having misjudged how easily the cold nips through clothing and clings to her skin. The hot coffee is nice, but Zahra misses Atlanta, where the weather and the land are forgiving.

"So Spelman, huh?" Zahra says.

"Fingers crossed," Sammie says.

"You'll get in."

"I better."

Her confidence hasn't changed. Maybe Sammie is even more sure of herself now, knowing that there's so much outside of her realm of control and that her small decisions don't rule the world.

Zahra laughs. "That's what I've always liked about you."

"What?"

"I don't know," Zahra says, unsure of how to say it. "Your spunk."

"Spunk?" Sammie sips her tea. "Really showing your age."

"Well . . ." Zahra shrugs.

"But thanks," Sammie says. She scoots closer to Zahra, as if the world and the relatively isolated pier are listening. "Well, I thought this would be a good time for us to talk through a plan . . ."

"A plan?"

"Sure. I mean, if you're going to be dating Uncle, and you and I have this forever bond in the . . . spiritual realm, for lack of a better word, we should set aside dedicated time to check in. I mean, the moths are lonely, irritated, begrudged, insolent, but they're also us, at any moment in time, at any time of the day. We owe it to them to check in."

"Like a mental health sort of thing."

Sammie shrugs. "Sure, I guess you could say that."

"Then, my first question is . . ."

Zahra waits for Sammie's eagerness to surface.

"Well . . ."

"What's going on with Noah? Or are you still ice-cold with fear?"

Sammie rolls her eyes, but it's the hidden smile that tells Zahra everything she needs to know. She'll ask her the harder questions too, about the plight, and her mother, and schools, but checking in is as multifaceted as the people who need it. Even the moths sing love songs.

||||||||||||||||||||||||||||||||||||||||||||||||

FOR NOW, ZAHRA TREKS THE SIX BLOCKS HOME, AFRAID OF the moths; they are more powerful than she ever imagined them. To think, their ditties are demanding. To think, they really have something to say. A red convertible drives by and the woman behind the wheel, high yellow with loose brown curls, blasts music that makes everyone stop and stare, stand by, listening—the waddling toddlers playing with toys from the McDonald's across the street, and the young boys on the corner, swapping jays and laughs and loud stories dictated by wild, dramatic gestures. The older folks in their lawn chairs sipping from airplane bottles and Styrofoam cups, soaking in the last righteous and unexpectedly warm day of fall. All silent now. To them, the song is white but alright. To Zahra, it is a Black woman's song, that is until Fatboy Slim came along and made it less about the singing and more about the dance beat. No matter if it's Fatboy Slim's version playing now, Zahra hears "Take Yo' Praise," a Black woman's ballad. She wonders about that woman who sang it first. Is she lost like a grocery bag in the wind or found like a crisp dollar bill on the street? Might Zahra look in the mirror and see some semblance of her? Or might she be there like a shadow, someone photoshopped, some binocular diplopia? There but not there, here but not here. *I have to celebrate you baby. I have to praise you like I should.*

THIRTY-NINE

Derrick buys the lawn chair new, unable to find one in Gram's flooded basement. He waits for a time when Gram plans to be out for hours, and Mary has a court case, and Uncle Richard and Dad will be too tied up with Sunday football to stop by. Derrick plants the chair in the driveway like digging in roots. He steadies its gangly legs in the concrete, scratching the surface along the way. He sits down and pulls a bottle of Hennessy out of a brown paper bag. He doesn't drink it but pours some out for the homies, watches the brown liquor dribble between cracks in the driveway's concrete, watches the moths get at it quickly; there's a party going on. Derrick lights a joint and waits for the fire he set in the old kitchen to build. It's a beautiful day, and Atlanta is like a light bulb down his back, and burning the house that the bank plans to loot from Gram feels so good.

He remembers coming back from the post office or the grocery store or some other meaningless run with Gram and her telling him that Atlanta's history was new, that the old city was burned in the Civil War.

"Why?" he'd asked her, but it was Mom who answered.

"Atlanta was on the wrong side of things," she'd said. "It needed to burn."

And later, in American history class, he learned about Sherman's scorched-earth warfare, never thinking it had anything to do with him, never thinking he needed American history for anything other than a few credits and another A on his transcript, but now he eyes the wildfire in wonder, in respect. He looks down at the leaflet in his hand, a torch on the front of it, not so unlike the Tower on Capitol Avenue, and Warren's, Minnie's, Natasha's stories locked on the inside of the fold like prisoners.

He knows that the trees will always regrow, like the rain forest after a hurricane, and the moths have plenty of places to burrow in the natural landscape, but maybe this will show people, the world, that a house doesn't belong to you, and you can't just take a shit on people's lives and ask them to be quiet about it. Attracted to the fire, the light, the moths swarm him like a hive of bees, flapping their wings like crazy, going nowhere but round and round in circles, and like a choir director, Derrick leads them in song, *And I think it's time we cleared the air . . . you know I've been wanting to groove with you . . .*

866.4 miles away, there but not there, Zahra hears it too.

ACKNOWLEDGMENTS

For a long time I questioned my legitimacy as a writer—I didn't feel like a stand-out writer in school (or at least I was rarely the kid who teachers picked to read their writing for the class), I didn't get into a big-name MFA program, and I've never read the majority of the literary canon (full disclosure—I don't plan to). But I've always had something to say (sometimes too much to say), and I've always loved language, music, stories, and characters, so I wrote. Fast-forward to publishing this book, which is such an extension of who I am, this Black girl from Decatur, Georgia, who straddles the line of book smart and just-here-to-have-a-good-time, who studies song lyrics and reality TV just as much as she does Toni Morrison and Jesmyn Ward, it feels like an unthinkable feat. It is impossible to name all the people who've inspired me along the way, but I'll give it a shot. . . .

Thank you to my agent, Cora Markowitz, for truly seeing what I wanted for this novel and for helping me find the perfect publishing home for it. Thank you for finding "Paul Robeson" by Gwendolyn Brooks, kicking off this book in the best way possible. I am so honored to debut with you. Here's to many more publications, to mastering what the story wants, and believing in others' ability to love it as much as we do.

An enormous applause for Amber Oliver, my first editor, for believing in this book and writing the most insightful editorial letter I could imagine. I had these huge expectations of what it would be like to work with you, and it has been all of that and beyond. Thank you for getting it! We need more Amber Olivers in publishing!

Thank you to Maya Ziv, my current editor, for making sure this book made it to the publication date, for rooting for its success, and picking up seamlessly where Amber left off.

Thank you, Phoebe Robinson, for founding and leading the Tiny Reparations imprint. My jaw almost hit the floor seeing you in that initial Zoom meeting, and my excitement for working with you has only grown since then. You're doing so much dope work across mediums, and I'm here for it all. To the rest of the Tiny Reparations team, including Caroline Payne, Emily Canders, Jamie Knapp, and Lexy Cassola—what a time to be alive, what a family to be a part of. Thank you!!

Clink clink to first readers, who helped birth this novel through feedback and continued support—

Kimberly Faith Waid! My friend and fellow writer. Thank you for pushing me to write, for writing with me, for meeting every week to go over chapters, for helping my writing (and me) survive the pandemic, for being there.

Danielle Sheeler! You are the definition of supportive. Thank you for believing in me, for pre-ordering before I even knew that you could, for sending me a mug with your favorite quote from the book, because what author doesn't need one of those?

Olamide Odai-Alli, best friend, sister friend, since-fourth-grade-and-through-forever friend—thank you for reading this novel at the most necessary time, when I'd fallen deep into a pit of insecurities. You see me. Know that I see you, too.

Workshops can make or break writers. To all of my writing workshops, thank you for not breaking me but helping me put the pieces together—

My fellow Kimbees and everyone who works to make Kimbilio the most enriching and supportive writing community imaginable, thank you!

My Manhattanville cohorts, especially Sean Chambers—thank you for being thoughtful readers and inspiring writers!

Sanina Clark, Celine Anelle-Roche, Michelan LeMonier—thank you for making up the workshop that I can be my most authentic self with.

Yael Schick, Matthew Jellison, Madeline Ormenyi—thank you for always coming from a place of positivity, for your constant encouragement and profound insights.

To my Frans!!—Francesca, Linsey, Eboni, Xiomara, Lauren, Paige, Tracey, Nancy, Candace, Brittany, Aminata, Alfred, Jonathan, Kelauni—I know I'm missing folks, but I love y'all. Thanks for rooting for me.

To the family I found in NYC—Keith, Khai, Chris, Andrew, my cousin Lauren, and so many more—thanks for coming to my readings and for making New York feel like home.

To the friends I found at Writopia Lab, thanks for continuously checking in. Those *how's the writing going* texts and DMs aren't taken for granted, and neither are the social media likes, the fire symbols, the reposts and retweets.

To the most amazing professor and mentor, Jeff W. Bens—your voice is always in the back of my mind reminding me to write through the emotional world of my characters. Thank you for telling me that I can do it in that nonchalant way of yours. To the other professors and workshop leaders who've taught me, encouraged me, enlightened me—Joanna Clapps Herman, Fatin Abbas, Victor La-Valle, Jacinda Townsend, Janet Desaulniers, thank you for all those nuggets of wisdom, for every piece of positive feedback I clung to throughout an uncanny amount of doubt.

To the many young people who've allowed me to help you with your college essays—Kanaan, Timia, Moesae, the students from Thurgood Marshall Academy in Harlem, and many more—getting to know you has meant the world to me!

Finally, this book is not even a concept without my family. To the women who are made of meat and movement—my loving aunts, my godmother, and my dynamic, vivacious cousins, thank you for defining family in the most beautiful and bountiful senses of the word. To the men who know all the lyrics—my late grandfather, Willie Davis, my uncles, my godfathers, my cousins, my brother-in-law, thank you for being the root and the wings.

To my praying mother, Selena Davis Williams, who's got that unwavering, ever faithful head-of-the-fan-club love, who believes I should send everything I've ever written to Oprah (maybe you were onto something there, prayer hands for the book club list)—you've taught me so much about being a woman, a mentor, and a teacher, AYKT.

To my father, Fredrich Michael Williams, you are the storyteller I've always wanted to be. Thank you for loving music, for loving words, for forcing that love inside me, for being my champion, and for being a hard act to follow.

To my sister, Jaclynn Dayse, my first editor in many ways—you are an unbreakable backbone. Thank you for being my bossy big sister. Even more, thank you for being my friend, for processing life with me, for allowing me to debrief everything from the latest episode of *RHOA* to the acknowledgments I'm writing right now.

To my grandmothers, the matriarchs who've inspired me through all the familial tales you've shared, and who've unknowingly given me the space to write fiction in all you've withheld . . . Grandma Katie—thank you for always being there, for navigating life with the sort of stern grace that only comes from strength and wisdom. Grandma Barbara—I wish you were around to see me now, your manifestations come true, your stories so wrapped up in mine that they're impossible to untangle. I hear your voice—*I'll beat you up*—threatening me to be the best version of myself. I'm working on it!

To my partner, Kyle Henry, thank you for talking me up. Your talk is never cheap. If I'm even half of what you love, I'm doing it and doing it well. Gah, thank you for being a true partner, for inspiring me to create, for being a sounding board.

To the Black musicians whose songs and legacies are referenced throughout the book—we live a thousand lives through your art.

Thank you, readers! What is a story without someone to listen to it? In the wise words of Tupac, *you are appreciated*.

GONE LIKE YESTERDAY

JANELLE M. WILLIAMS

Discussion Questions

DISCUSSION QUESTIONS

1. Sammie and Zahra develop an unlikely friendship over the course of the novel. What did you make of their relationship? How did their dynamic change as they embarked on their journey together from New York City to Atlanta?

2. The moths are a mysterious, ubiquitous presence throughout the book. What did you think of them, and how did your impression change over the course of the novel? Why do you think only some people could hear them? Were you surprised by the ending?

3. "Songs in every language, from Amharic to Yoruba, from Patois to slang from around the way. A ring shout, a call and response, from the past to the present to the future and back again." The novel references countless lyrics and songs, from Zahra's and Derrick's childhood CDs to the voices of the moths. What role did music play in the book? Why do you think the moths communicated in song?

4. "[Sammie] wants to know her mother and accept that love in whatever form it may take, but it's hard." The two central mother-daughter relationships in the book are complex and fraught. Sammie's mother was physically distant, while Zahra's was emotionally

remote. How did Zahra and Sammie approach their relationships with their mothers differently? How did that distance shape their family ties? How did it shape Zahra and Sammie?

5. Between Sammie's family in Trinidad and Zahra's Atlantan roots, the moths seemed to be connected to their ancestry. How did Zahra's and Sammie's understanding of their ancestors change over the course of the novel? Zahra says that home "isn't a house but a thought, a memory, a smell, a sound." How was their ancestors' history tied to the concept of home? How did Atlanta's history continue to affect Zahra's family in present day?

6. How does Sammie's college essay contrast with Sophia's, the senior Zahra is coaching at the beginning of the novel? How does the conversation around higher education evolve throughout the novel? What do you think played into Sammie's choice to go to Spelman?

7. "When a person wants to go missing, they have every right to make like mist, don't they? And when they want to be found? Well, maybe it's not that easy to find your way back." What did you make of Derrick's disappearance? In what way was he lost, and do you believe Zahra found him? How did his approach to the moths differ from Zahra's?

8. Sammie grapples with teenage crushes that she has developed on both Noah and later, Rashad. How did Sammie's conflicting feelings over dating a white boy evolve? What did you make of Rashad and his feelings for both Zahra and Sammie?

9. Sense of place is so strong in this novel, especially the contrast between New York City and Atlanta. How did the characters experience these places differently, and what differences did you pick up on in the book's descriptions?